THE BOOK OF CROWS

# THE BOOK

SAM MEEKINGS

# OF CROWS

Polygon

First published in paperback in 2012
by Polygon, an imprint of Birlinn Ltd
West Newington House · 10 Newington Road
Edinburgh EH9 1QS

www.polygonbooks.co.uk

ISBN 978 1 84697 214 0

First published in 2011

*British Library Cataloguing-in-Publication Data*
A catalogue record for this book is available on request
from the British Library

The publisher acknowledges investment from Creative
Scotland towards the publication of this book

Designed by Dalrymple
Illustration and calligraphy by Susie Leiper
Printed and bound in Great Britain
by Clays Ltd, St Ives PLC

FOR MOLLY

# The Whorehouse of a Thousand Sighs

PART I · 80–78 BCE

My father used to tell me that if you saw a crow it meant someone was going to die. He would be drunk as usual but unable to sleep, sobering up in the shade of some lanky tree while the sun simmered the ants, and that's when he would start telling me the old stories. I never paid him too much attention – I'd usually be watching the ants to see how far they would struggle on across the burning sand before giving up. But I guess in spite of myself I must have listened to what he was saying, for those old stories are all that's left of him now. 'Always keep an eye out for crows,' he would say. 'They're nothing but tatty black messengers of death. They came the day before your mother was taken, and I don't doubt they'll come back again for me.'

I never really cared about my father. Whenever I had a little time free from lugging about the dingy, moth-bothered skins that we sold from village to village, I used to run around the scree, jumping over clumps of sandweed and dodging the snakes curled out in the sun, pretending I was a bird and could just up and soar far, far away from him. My mother, well, he used to say that she could make your heart fly clear of your body, and he often cursed the day that I split her in two. But I don't remember her at all.

In fact, it's strange how little I remember of my life before I got here. Like one of those mirages we used to hear about from desert traders, my childhood sometimes seems as if it was nothing more than an elaborate illusion, a lost possibility that no amount of longing can call back into existence.

I remember waking up and trying to turn and banging my head against one of the bars. The sun above was as bright and blinding as burning sand, and the sand below as hot and bubbling as the sun, so for the first few minutes I wasn't sure which way was up and which was down. I licked my lips. They were broken and tasted like tears. The roof of the cage was a mishmash of lashed strips of bamboo, slicing the morning sun into bright daggers of light. There was a stinking blanket beneath me, and my skin was sticky and damp from the heat after a couple of hours. The bars on the four sides were made of long sticks that must have been snapped off from some sturdy tree, the likes of which I'd never seen before. I found that I could reach my arm out to the elbow through most of the gaps between the branches, but there was no way my head could have got through. The cage wasn't small, but it wasn't big enough to stretch my body out straight either. Moving very carefully, I was able to turn over onto my stomach and then raise myself onto my knees.

When I peered out, I saw that the long bamboo pole running along the top of the cage was held by two big men, one in front and one behind. The men were dark and heavy-set, and they reminded me of raisins shrivelled in the sun. Sweat dribbled down their naked chests. For a while, I tried to pretend that I was a princess being carried to a luxurious castle and a noble prince. Before long, though, I needed to pee, and I was pretty sure that wasn't the kind of thing that happens to princesses. I called to the men to stop but they didn't respond, so I had to make do.

There were only a few cages like mine. I counted just four others, bobbing along on either side. But when I wriggled around and looked out the back, I could see lots of people walking. They seemed to be mostly mothers and children, though I could make out two or three men among them, all wearing dirty rags and bent double in the heat. They were tied together, marching in slow, tentative steps through the sand, and every one of them was panting for breath like fish suddenly snagged up from a river. More of the big men moved among them, pulling them up when they fell, or shoving them forward when they showed signs of slowing. At least I didn't have to walk. They must have thought I was pretty special.

Of course, I later learnt that I was only in the cage because they were worried about me attacking them again. One of the big men showed me his hand through the bars, so I could see the bite marks where I'd drawn blood. I didn't remember that. I didn't remember when they took my father, or how I had come to be in the cage.

There are holes in our hearts, Silk told me once, and some of our memories just trickle out when we don't want them anymore. Maybe she was right.

Every few hours the big men would dump the cages down in the sand and gather around one of the water skins hung over the mules. If they were feeling generous, they'd give me a little water too. I had to drink from their hands. Most of the time, though, they just stood about grunting in their strange language. At first I thought they were arguing with the short man on the horse, who seemed to be the boss, but after a couple of days I realised this was just the way they spoke, always shouting and waving their arms around. After the shouting they'd haul our cages back up and keep on going across the dunes.

I never wondered about where they were taking us. I know that sounds strange, but all I'd known were the little dusty villages that my father and I used to flit between. It never occurred to me that there might be something on the other side of the desert, because all the old men in the villages used to swear that it had no end – once the sand starts, they used to say, it goes on forever. They used to call it the country of death. Nobody had ever met anyone who'd been into the desert and come back out again. We'd heard about other tribes from far off, but everyone knew they went round it, not through it. The desert, the old men said, has no north or south or east or west. It just is.

At first I wondered whether I was dead, whether this was my punishment for breaking my mother all those summers before. But it seemed unlikely – what was the point of being dead if I could still feel the fleas itching and the sun frying my skin? And I realised I couldn't be dead when other people actually started dying. Sometimes when we set up camp a prisoner would fall asleep and never wake up. The other people tied to them would make a fuss when that happened, and the big men would cut the bodies loose and leave them for the crows. Sometimes, when someone was really sick, coughing up blood or their brows burning red with fever, they would also be untied. You would have thought the first thing they'd do would be to try to escape. But most of them kept walking with us just as before, following as far as they could until they had no more strength, and then they'd lie down in the sand and cry. There was no point waiting around for them to die, so we just left them to it.

At night we were set down at the bottom of the dunes while the big men struggled to make fires from the few shrubs and dry grasses they could gather. I ate like a wild hog, lapping gristly chunks of horse-meat or desert rat or still twitchy crickets from a hand pushed between the bars, but only after the big men had fed themselves. It was at these times, between the tying up of the horses and the end of evening when the big men would throw furs over our cages to keep out the cold, that I was able to talk to some of the other prisoners around me.

'Do you know where we are?' I asked the nearest cage.

A girl shuffled her big behind around for a few minutes until she finally lay on her side, facing me. Her hair was dark and ragged, and her face needed a good wash. She was a few summers older than me and might have been considered beautiful under a dim-enough light.

'We're in the bleeding desert, of course! The sand should be a clue.'

'Yes. I know that. But ... I mean ... why are we here?'

'We're on our way to the big city, I expect. When these bastards who caught us aren't robbing and raiding and murdering they probably pretend to be merchants.'

'But what do they want with us?'

'We're the merchandise.'

I didn't have a chance to ask her anything else that night, for at that moment one of the big men tossed a fur over my cage and began to shout, so I just turned over and tried to get to sleep. It's strange, out there in the desert you spend the days praying for the burning sun to ease up a bit, and the nights hugging yourself to try to keep from freezing. I listened to many of the older male prisoners arguing about which was worse, the heat of the day or the cold of the night, but it seemed to me that they were missing the point. The cold comes for your bones, but the heat comes for your flesh. It's always been like this. But in any case, I don't think those men really disagreed – they just needed something, anything, to talk about. And if there's one thing I've learnt in my life, it's that arguing is what men most enjoy doing.

The days melted into each other, and I honestly can't tell you how long I was in that cage. Since I had no idea whether we would ever reach the end of the desert, time seemed to stretch out and I couldn't be sure what day it was. All the things I'd ever known were now nothing but a dull, fuzzy blur.

I didn't ask the girl with the big bottom anything else about the city, because I wasn't sure that I would like the answer. Instead, whenever we were dropped down after another long day being lugged across the plains, I asked her about her home. She soon warmed to this, and I enjoyed listening, because I found that her old village sounded exactly like the places my father and I used to pass through. I lay back in my cage, with the moonlight dripping in between the wicker and cane, and pretended I was a little girl again. Everything she talked about was reassuring and familiar. She spoke of the same work tending the stubborn goats, the same feasts and famines coming on each other's heels, the same elders sitting round the night fires trying to summon djinns, of the same way some of the women swung their hips when they walked and the same way other women tutted when they saw them. She spoke of the snake men who hawked their slithering collections from village to village, of the music of worn drums and cicadas, and of the peace she had felt beside her husband just a few hours before the raid had begun and the big men had come and stolen her life from her.

'So why are you in a cage? Did you try to stop them too?' I asked.

'Don't be an idiot. What could I do? I'm just a woman. Anyone who fought back was stabbed, and those who surrendered are tied up in those long lines behind us. They're not worried about me hurting them. Ha! No, they're only worried about me trying to hurt myself again and leaving them with one less girl to sell.'

'I don't understand. Why would you want to hurt yourself?'

She sighed. 'You're too young to understand. When they killed my husband, I knew that was the end of my life. A woman can't survive without a man – everyone knows that.'

With that she shuffled herself into a corner and turned away from me.

I found it harder and harder to remember what the world looked like without bars interrupting the view, and I even got used to the sour, coppery taste of the water I lapped from the dark men's cupped hands. Meanwhile the sand got everywhere. I would wake up each morning to find it between my toes, in the creases of my elbows, throughout my matted hair and coating my parched tongue.

After a while my clothes really began to reek, and my back began to cramp and ache, no matter how much I squirmed about trying to get comfortable. I lay awake at night, scared of snakes slipping in under the furs, finding it impossible to block out the muffled sobs and nervous whispers of the prisoners camped down behind me. Sometimes the big men would grab one of the women from a tied-up family and drag her behind a dune, leaving her relatives to weep in shame while everyone else pretended they couldn't hear the grunts and screams as the big men took their turns. Then they would finally throw her back, bloody and dishevelled. It was at those times that I was thankful for my cage, though the girl with the big bottom told me that they wouldn't take any of the younger ones anyway.

'You lot'll be fine,' she explained. 'After all, they wouldn't want to do anything to scupper your market value.'

Just when I was getting used to the shaky journey and the sun frazzling my skin, I noticed a change in the big men. They had been grumpy and slouching for many days, yet suddenly they began to walk faster, their shoulders pulled up high and their heads darting left and right as if scanning the horizon, all the while yabbering and grunting. For once I understood what was happening. We were reaching the end of the desert.

After so long spent in the white glare of burning sunlight I couldn't properly make out the mud houses and cave dwellings till we were really close. I was so happy to see signs of life that I would have cried if I'd had any tears left. On the flat roof of one of the dwellings, a single dirty crow was preening itself. It cast a disinterested glance down at our ramshackle procession and went back to nuzzling its beak beneath one of its cocked wings, as though it had seen this kind of thing a hundred times before and was no longer shocked by anything humans did. I should have known then that things would only get worse. But instead of worrying about such an ominous sight at the time, I felt relieved. I thought it meant we had finally arrived at the end of the world: the place where you get to meet your dreams. Once again, I was wrong.

My cage was shoved onto the back of one of the many wooden carts that were waiting for us there, and after the ragged men and women behind were prodded up there too the mules were struck and we started moving again. At least now there was a bit of shade from the spindly trees surrounding the village – I could see some of the children's faces were cracked and dry from all those days in the desert, and some of the older men looked without seeing, their eyes like dull egg-whites. The sun is a terrible creature, I thought.

One of the tied-up men seemed to have an idea where we were. Every so often as we juddered down the dirt track, he would look around at the green vines with their strange fruit and say that we were definitely getting close to the city. Everyone nodded solemnly when he said that. What city? I wanted to ask, but I kept my mouth shut. Unmarried girls aren't supposed to join in adult conversations anyway, although I wasn't really sure that the normal rules of behaviour still applied.

We bounced around in the back of those carts for the next two days, stopping at villages to stock up on supplies then camping in fields while the big men kept watch. I was asleep when we finally entered the city – the one and only time I saw Gaochang, though of course I didn't know that then. Someone pushed a greasy finger into the cage to prod me awake, and when I opened my eyes I wasn't completely sure if I was still dreaming. There were people everywhere, more people than I'd ever seen before, crow-haired and flame-haired and straw-haired and tall and short and fat and thin and old and young and most of them wearing the oddest clothes I'd ever seen, long flowing robes that seemed to have stolen the colour of the sky or of dew-sparkled grass. The noise was so loud that I couldn't hear the prisoners next to me speaking. There were traders calling on the streets, holding up handfuls of raisins or pointing to barrows full of dark spices and bolts of billowing silks. Locals haggled with them in high-pitched warbles that I couldn't understand. Some of the mud-and-straw buildings reached higher than one man standing on another man's shoulders, and they leaned and tottered so precariously that I worried they might collapse upon us. There were children playing in the zigzagging alleys and men with swords being shown ornate rugs by dark-skinned men with long-flowing beards. The sound of chimes reached us from a temple in the distance, and I closed my eyes and once again gave in to my fantasy of being a princess, imagining that the bells were being struck to welcome me to the city.

The mules couldn't move more than a few steps at a time through the throng, so the big men had to jump down and push some of the traders out of the way. In the end the cart was led behind one of the tall buildings into a courtyard filled with donkeys, pigs, chickens and the straw and mess they slept in. It was then that they hauled down my cage and untied the top. One of the big men beckoned me out, but for a minute I didn't move. It might sound stupid, but for all the discomfort, I'd got used to my cage. I didn't know what was going to happen to me next, and I'm not ashamed to say I was afraid. The big man grabbed my arm and yanked me up and out. When I tried to stand up straight and take a few steps my body crumpled and I would have collapsed if he hadn't been at my side. My legs seemed to have forgotten what they were supposed to do. He barked something and pointed at the trough of water the pigs were slurping from. I didn't understand.

After a few more shouts, he grew impatient and marched me over to the trough. I didn't have the energy to struggle, but I might have put up a bit more of a fight if I'd known that he was going to dunk my head under the water. I came up coughing and spluttering, my hair slapping back across my face. It wasn't till one of the big men began to tug at my dirty clothes that I finally realised they wanted me to wash. I told them I could take care of that myself, thank you very much, but of course they couldn't understand me, and the brutes didn't even have the decency to turn their backs while I wriggled out of my foul-smelling robe. Still, I did the best I could with them leering and laughing, splashing the cold water over myself and watching puddles of sand and dust dribble out around my feet. When I was finished I was a bit disappointed to find that instead of one of those bright-coloured robes I'd seen in the marketplace I was given a sackcloth tunic that barely covered my knees. At least it was better than putting my dirty robe back on. I was already becoming good at looking on the positive side of things.

Just when I was getting used to stretching out my body again, I spotted the large cart they were rolling into the courtyard. On the top was a huge wooden cage – just like the one I'd been in, but several times bigger. There's no way on earth I'm getting into any kind of cage again, I thought to myself. However, after the big men began to whip one of the old prisoners who refused to climb up into its open door, splattering his blood over the paving stones, I hastily changed my mind. A whole horde of us was shoved inside, the door swung shut, and the big men knotted it tight. We pressed and jostled into each other's bodies as the cart wobbled round the corner back onto the city streets. Over the sound of squealing pigs and caterwauling hawkers I heard a few of the men around me begin to hurry out half-remembered prayers to ancestors under their breath.

I shoved my way closer to the bars in time to see us draw to a halt in what looked like the market square, a big open stretch of traders selling piles of pistachios, muslins, jewels, dyes, medicines and cloth. There was already a crowd gathering around us, and as the cart tipped back and the big men dragged our cage down the slope to the ground, even more people appeared, shoving their hands through the bars, pinching and tugging and stroking and groping. A middle-aged woman yanked at my hair, while a fat man prodded my stomach. I tried to slap away the more persistent hands grabbing at my breasts, but my screams and curses got lost amidst all the bustling and shouting. I did my best to hide behind some of the others in the cage, hoping the rude city people would soon get bored and leave us alone.

It was only after the first man was dragged from the cage that the crowd began to calm down, though after a few locals had approached to feel his biceps and prod his chest and gut, the shouting soon started up again. The accents were thick and most of the people around me seemed intent on spitting out each word, as if they were trying to speak with a whole jugful of water in their mouths. Then I understood: they were making bids. While one of the big men was occupied counting the coins that had been thrust into his hands for the first sale, I began to push my way to one of the sides of the cage, thinking I could prise myself between the bars.

I struggled and squirmed, and managed to push my legs out. But my father always used to say that I had a big old useless head, and now I saw that he was right. However much I twisted, I couldn't force my head to squeeze through the gap. I was too late spotting the big men coming back towards me and as I turned over and tried to move towards the other side of the cage one of them caught hold of my foot. He began to tug, and then another one grabbed my ankle. I stretched out to the other prisoners to steady myself, but they recoiled as I reached for them. The big men had pulled my whole leg out now, and I gripped onto the bars so tight I felt my hands burning. I cried and started to kick, but the man holding my ankle only grinned at me and said something to his friend, who laughed. Then they really began to pull, and I flailed and yelped as they tugged. Soon half my body had been yanked out from between the wooden bars, and once again only my head and arms remained inside with the prisoners. My hands were rubbed raw and pricked with splinters.

'Ok, ok, I've learnt my lesson. I'm sorry! Listen, I've said I'm sorry!' I screamed at the big men as they yanked harder.

They had soon lifted me from the ground completely and they turned me, letting my shoulders slide right through. It wasn't long before I felt the pressure on my head as it began to stretch the bars. I was sure that my skull was about to burst open and spill out all its juice. As I screamed they pulled a little more, and then the bars were clamped around my temples. I closed my eyes to try to stop the dizziness and pain, and at that moment I could hear the temple bells clanging deep inside my head. I was no longer screaming – I was struggling for breath. Just when I thought I was about to faint, there was a loud pop, and I was through. The big men flew backwards and tumbled to the floor with me sprawled on top of them.

The Empress, whom I had yet to meet, watched the whole stupid struggle, apparently, and she later told me it was one of the funniest things she had ever seen. 'It looked like a big wooden animal was giving birth to you,' she laughed, revealing her entire set of mouldy brown teeth. And I guess she was right in a way. That was the day my new life began.

The big men lifted me to my feet and beckoned the customers forward. A line of people approached. I gave my best smile, hoping that some kind family would take pity on me. A bearded man hooked his finger inside my mouth and pulled back my lips to look at my teeth. A short woman examined my hands and scalp. I tried not to cry when a tubby, grey-haired man grabbed my buttocks. After what felt like hours, the big man pushed them back and the sale began. People began shouting and shoving and throwing their hands up in the air. As the auction went on, most of the crowd fell quiet, until only two people were left calling out offers, a fat woman with curly brown hair and the bearded man who had inspected my teeth. As soon as one of them shouted something, the other one would holler right back. It seemed to me that they'd probably keep going until one of their throats got so dry that they couldn't shout any more, though I wasn't sure how long that would take. In the end the fat woman offered something that the bearded man couldn't beat. I wish I'd heard what she had said, but by then I was so nervous and confused I wasn't really listening to the bidding. All I noticed was a loud gasp from the crowd. Silence followed, and then the bearded man shook his head and spat. I've thought about it a lot since then, trying to work out what she paid for me. But perhaps it's better not to know how much your life is worth.

As I stared out into the crowd at the woman who had bought me, one of the big men moved behind me and slipped my hands into a knotted rope, which he then hoisted tight. I didn't even bother to struggle. What would have been the point? While the fat woman spoke with one of the big men in their language I gave her the once over. She wasn't simply fat; she was enormous. Her cheeks were great jowls that swung when she spoke, and her clothes seemed to be straining against her drooping rolls of flesh. I'd never seen anyone even half that big before, not even some of the permanently pregnant wives back in the villages. Her thighs were the size of whole roast hams, and they wobbled like the ripples in a lake as she waddled slowly towards me. It crossed my mind that she might have bought me so she could eat me, and a shudder ran over my body. There was no sign of kindness beneath her greasy brown curls, only creases and crow's feet.

'You may call me the Empress,' she said, speaking now in the familiar language of the plains. 'If you do exactly as you are told, you'll find that we'll get along well.'

It was pretty clear that, despite her haughty manner, she wasn't a real empress. In fact, I doubted that she was much better born or bred than I was. She took the free end of the length of rope that bound my hands and began to shuffle down the street with me. Her voice was as deep and scratchy as a dried-up riverbed in the middle of the desert. I just nodded nervously whenever she spoke, since my tongue was too jumpy with nerves to respond. All I kept thinking about was that this woman owned me now. My bare feet were not used to the scuffed stones and cobbles of the city, and I noticed jealously that the woman's swollen feet were stuffed into shiny red slippers.

As we veered off into a tight alley filled with families washing their vegetables in wooden buckets, she turned to me again.

'How many moons have you seen now?'

Once again I nodded nervously, then tried smiling. I hadn't seen any moon lately, and I wasn't in the habit of counting them anyway, since I was pretty certain there was only room for one up in that big tattered blanket of a sky. The fat woman's face scrunched itself into a scowl.

'Are you stupid? How old are you?'

'I've seen about fourteen summers, miss,' I said.

'Hmm. Those liars at the market assured me you were only twelve. Never mind, never mind. No one need know but us. You've got a young face, and that's the important thing. The only thing we've got to worry about is your dreadful accent, but I'm sure a few lessons should smooth that out.'

She laughed to herself a little and shook her head. That was rich, complaining about my accent. I wanted to tell her that she sounded like the boy from my home village who had his whole set of teeth knocked out by the kick of a rowdy mule, or like my father after he fell asleep drunk in the sun and a bee stung his tongue, but I thought it probably wasn't a good idea to insult her – after all, she was holding the rope that bound me – so I kept my mouth shut.

I couldn't help but peer in through the doorways of the houses as we passed: inside I caught glimpses of squat tables laden with freshly baked *naan*, children crawling over raised beds and women tending fires. The alley grew narrower and the dwellings rose up on either side of us until people had to hold back in doorways to let the Empress pass. The houses were joined together now, one long wall of dried earth, and I wondered how these people could bear to live so close to each other. Back in the villages my father and I used to travel through, there were sometimes arguments about the tiniest corner of great fields or endless plains at the edge of the desert. Some people would argue so much about a handful of land there that they'd end up in a bloody fight, and when one of them got killed the man left standing found he had to use that handful of land to bury the other anyway! So I had trouble believing people could really live so close together without killing each other. How could you keep a secret in a place like that? I was naïve. It would not be long until I found that you can fill every nook and cranny of your body with secrets and still keep your tongue silent, no matter how much it burns your mouth.

That was more than twelve summers ago now. I'm lying in bed, trying to conjure up that scared little girl being led to the outskirts of Gaochang. We travelled on up into the arid plains and valleys on the very edge of the desert, spending the next two days in a donkey cart because the Empress had begun turning red and breathing heavily from the walk.

It's hard to recall the amazement I felt when I first set eyes on this place. The Whorehouse of a Thousand Sighs. It sounds grand at first, doesn't it? Trust me, it's not that special. I haven't left this set of buildings for a single day since I arrived, and now they just look like the same old familiar piles of mud and rock to me. The banners and garlands hanging in the gateway and the courtyard are a bit raggedy now, to tell the truth, and the murals on the walls and the doorways are chipped and fading. But back then it looked like a palace. Because we're high up on the side of a hill – beyond the garish gateway most of the rooms on our level are actually caves cut into the hillside – from the entrance you can see down to the desert valley below. More importantly, as the Empress explained to me, it also means we can be easily spotted from far away. That's what all the colourful ribbons on the gate are for. A lot of merchants pass through these parts so as to trade with the middle kingdom, she said, and a lot of them get homesick.

As we approached the gateway, the Empress dismissed the donkey and his driver and pointed to a trail leading further up the hill, telling me to walk ahead of her. I was slowly getting used to her accent. We followed the trail up and came to a smaller gate, behind which I was shown a couple of badly constructed wooden huts encircling a small courtyard with a few benches, a pile of smouldering ash where a fire had been burning, a trough and a small covered room. This was where the cook lived, I was told, and this was also where we would eat, that is if we weren't invited to dine with others. The cook, she said, was her eyes and ears, and if I even thought about running away he would be sure to catch me and bring me back for the worst beating of my life. He had gone higher up the hillside to graze the camels, she told me, grinning. 'The pair of them's worth more than all you young girls put together.'

Only when we had made our way back down and had gone through the main gate did she untie the rope around my wrists. The courtyard here was much bigger, and though rough, rocky slopes jutted up around it on three sides, light still poured in from above. A long oak table stretched across the middle of the courtyard, surrounded by brightly sewn rugs and blankets. The Empress said that this was where the guests settled down to eat in the evenings if they paid enough for a party. The cushions looked as fancy as some of the strange clothes people had been wearing at the bazaar. I was impressed.

'At the end are the water troughs. One for washing, one for drinking. Try not to get them muddled up. You may not have much time for washing wherever you come from, and I know some girls just plain hate it, but it's one of the rules here that you keep yourself clean, understand? Now, you girls live on this side, and the two men live on the other side. Best to stick to your side if you don't want a good hiding.'

As we approached the girls' side, I noticed three caverns set back into the rock, their entrances covered by loose, fluttering strips of cloth. Through the gaps I could see more colourful rugs and cushions covering the floor inside. The Empress followed my glance. 'These rooms are reserved for entertaining. Unless it is your turn to clean them, you will enter them only in the presence of a guest. Understand?'

I nodded, and followed her to a heavy wooden door built into a cave at the furthest end of the courtyard. The Empress had to slide a knobbly branch from a loop at its side before she could shove it open. It took a while for my eyes to get used to the darkness. The small room was dusty and damp. There was a niche for a torch on the main wall, and on the others old rugs had been hung to cover the bare rock. On the floor were four piles of straw, each covered with a ratty old blanket.

'You'll be in here with Claws, Tiger and Silk. I'm sure they'll grace us with their presence soon enough. Everyone here has a working name. I've already thought of yours – you'll be Jade. Try and remember that. This one on the end is yours. Fresh straw and everything – no one can say I don't look after my girls.' She must have seen my worried expression. 'Cheer up, you'll soon get used to it. You might even start to like it. Some of them do. Just know that if you are a good girl, I'll take care of you. It's not a bad life here. Better than working the fields, or tending oxen, or travelling in one of those caravans in the desert. You've got it good here – don't forget that. And if you ever need reminding … well, you can always ask the other girls what happens if people get above themselves or try to make a run for it. But I'm sure they'll fill you in anyway.'

I nodded, trying to look obedient and dutiful. I wasn't going to run away. Where would I go?

'Good girl. Welcome to your new home. Get some rest today, and tomorrow we'll see about doing something with your hair and your face.'

She closed the door and I was left in the cramped, dark cavern. I sat down on my pile of straw and tried to stop the tears from pricking up in my eyes. As I sniffled I heard the branch being slid back through the loop on the door, locking me inside.

I think I must have slept that whole first day and the night too, though it's hard to be sure. I remember waking up with the feeling you get when you're not quite sure where you are, when there's still a little bit of your dreams refusing to be shaken off. There were shards of light poking through tiny holes between the rocks and a puddle of it spilling in under the door. I wanted to go home, even though I didn't know where that was anymore. What unnerved me most was the quiet; I couldn't hear a thing except my own heart thumping about in my stomach.

I'd been dreaming. Maybe even that dream – the one where I'm standing in a big open square and there are lots of people milling around, just going about their business. Sometimes I'm bartering for eggs, say, or picking up string to darn my clothes with. But at some point I always look down and that's when I start to panic and claw for breath. The eggs smash to the ground, but nobody notices. They've all turned to look at me, because my body is covered in feathers. The fluffy down ruffles in the wind, and when I raise my hand to my mouth I see that instead of a hand I have a wing. People start to shout and scream, and out of the corner of my eye I can see a couple of men running at me with a giant cage, like the kind rich people keep songbirds in. That's when I know I have to fly away, so I begin to flap as hard as I can, and the men are getting closer, so I beat my wings more and more frantically and my feet are just leaving the ground when I wake up, sweaty and cold and gasping for breath.

I must have had the same dream ten or eleven times since I arrived here. I don't know why, nor who sent it to me. Are the dead in charge of dreams? That's what Silk says, but then she's always saying things like that, and if I believed every word she said then I'd be a bigger fool than she is.

So perhaps I'd had that dream on my first night here, and that's why I was feeling so jittery. Or perhaps I first dreamt it later; it's hard to say. You can tell someone what happened one day and what happened the next, and that's why we give the days names and numbers. But dreams are harder to pin down. They always find a way of slipping free from your grasp.

I checked the door. It was no longer locked, so I pushed the heavy door open and decided to venture out. I could see three young women sitting on the bright cushions in the courtyard, and it wasn't long before one of them spotted me.

'Ah, so she's finally decided to wake up! Well, damn me if this one doesn't take as much beauty sleep as you, Silk! You need it more, of course.'

'Get lost, Claws.'

'Now, now, show some manners in front of our new colleague. You'll have to forgive Silk – she's always grumpy in the morning, though she ought to be able to take a joke. Now, are you going to come out and sit with us or do you just want to sulk all day?'

Since I didn't have anything better to do, I joined them on the cushions outside, grateful that, like the Empress, they spoke the language of the plains my father had taught me for trading and not the strange and garbled tongue of the bandits.

The one who had spoken first was clearly in charge. She looked older than the others, with lines welling up under her narrow eyes, though I could see she had tried to hide this as best she could with some kind of yellowy paste that covered most of her cheeks. She had a round face and big dimples, with her dark hair plaited behind her. I had met enough travellers in the villages beside the desert to know that she must have come from the middle kingdom. She was also the heaviest of the lot, with a big chest and big hips, both of which were wrapped in a light robe. What impressed me most were her fingernails: they were almost the same length as her fingers, and had been filed down to a sharp point at the end. I quickly sat on my hands to hide my own nails that were bitten down to the quick.

'I'm Claws,' she said, and raised her fingers in front of me. 'Yes, we've all been given these silly names. You get used to them. You're Jade, right? The Empress told us. Wow, your eyes really are green! I thought she was winding us up.'

'I knew she wasn't lying. The arrival of someone new was foretold in the formation of the clouds yesterday,' the girl to her left said. She was younger, with the milky white skin, long thin braids, big nose and high cheeks I'd heard were common among the wandering tribes in the west. I couldn't help but stare at her. She was tall and slim, and my eyes were drawn to her plump pink lips, fixed into a pout.

'Oh, you'll learn to ignore Silk soon enough,' Claws said with a nod of her head in the tall girl's direction. 'She likes to think she knows everything. You'll find the only time we get a bit of peace and quiet round here is when her mouth is full!'

Claws laughed at her own joke and Silk looked down at the floor, her cheeks turning red. I noticed the third girl, sitting off a little to the right, had not said anything. Her skin was so dark that at first I thought she had been burnt or painted. She was shorter and thinner than any of the rest of us, with straight black hair pouring down over her shoulders. Her nose was as long as winter, and her eyes were as dark as the inside of my new room. Claws caught me looking her over and smiled.

'That's Tiger. If you keep all your anger boiling up inside you'll end up the same as her. Like the rest of us, she's a long way from home now. The Empress says that's why people keep coming here: we've got everything anyone could want. We girls stick together though, so if you've got a problem you just talk to me. Tall and Homely live on the other side, and before you ask, yes, they do the same thing as us. But we don't talk to them much. Truth be told, those boys spend more time preening and making themselves pretty than the three of us put together. And you, where are you from?'

I wasn't sure what to say. 'Near the desert,' I mumbled.

'Mmm hmm. Bandits, right? Silk got here the same way, her whole tribe broken up in some dawn raid. They're bastards, aren't they? Tiger, she was part of a caravan travelling through the southern mountains when they ran out of supplies. Some merchants found her wandering near a border outpost in one of the valleys south of here and they couldn't believe their luck. She couldn't believe hers either, poor thing. It's one thing to lose your family and another to end up here.

'I'll let you in on a secret. My father was a general in the army. When I was little, we had ten servants in our house. Now look at me. The last spoils of a forgotten war.

'Those are our stories, and if you're lucky you won't ever hear them again, because let me tell you there is nothing worse than thinking of what you once were or what you could have become if things had been different. You throw away those thoughts now, sweetie, or else you'll end up broken into little pieces.' She waggled a long nail at me.

'Like Honey,' Tiger muttered.

'Watch it.' Claws gave her a sharp look. 'You trying to scare the girl? Huh? She's only just got here. Forget about Honey – that silly girl brought it on herself. Now then,' she said, turning back to me, 'The Empress told us we had to get you looking nice today, but we can't do that on an empty stomach. Let's see what the cook's made.'

Claws took me by the hand and we trundled up the path towards the smaller enclave with Tiger and Silk dragging their feet behind us. Claws fluttered her eyes at the cook – a dark, unshaven man missing most of his teeth – and he sighed and began to ladle bubbling broth out from a large clay pot set in the centre of a stack of smoking wood. A misshapen bowl was set down in front of me, and I tried to identify the grey and yellow bits floating in the murky water. Claws and Silk raised the bowls to their mouths and began to slurp noisily. From the corner of my eye I saw Tiger's nose wrinkle up as she watched the others, but when she noticed my gaze she quickly raised her own bowl and began to take small, bird-like sips. I lifted my own bowl. It was salty and as sour as a bowlful of tears, but I was hungry.

When Claws had finished she thumped the bowl down and let out a loud, rumbling belch. She smiled. 'You'll always be sure of food in your belly here, sweetie. Remember that. Much better than starving. But be careful – if you act up or give the patrons reason to complain, then the Empress will make you go hungry for a couple of days. It happened to Silk when she first arrived. Refused to do what that fat men paid extra for. She got a thrashing too, on the back of her legs. You can still see the marks.'

Once again I saw Silk blush. 'He was a bastard. I should have read it in the clouds that day. Wanted me to act like I was no better than a dog.'

'But you did it in the end, didn't you?' Claws smiled. For all her show of friendliness it wasn't hard to see that she took a certain pleasure in the younger girl's humiliation. 'Everyone gets broken in, no matter how strong you think you are. Everyone surrenders to it in the end.'

'What other choice is there?' Tiger said, her dark eyes gleaming in the light.

I didn't like the way they were talking – truth be told, it made me feel nervous, so I tried to change the subject. 'So when will I get to see the master?'

Silk cocked her head. 'The celestial master?'

'Umm, no, the master of the house. The man in charge.'

'There's no master here. Only the Empress, though as you probably noticed, her name's more of a joke than any of ours!' Claws laughed.

Silk joined in the laughter, but I was confused. If there was no man, then who looked after the money, who ordered the cook around, who made sure everything stayed right? I thought of my father, propped up under some old tree and slurring out endless orders as I cooked for him, and for a second I was glad I was here. Tiger spotted my confused expression and shook her head.

'You really don't know where you are, do you?' Her voice was quiet and gentle. 'There are men that come through every week. Or more. Our job is to please them. That's the easy part. The difficult part is to pretend that you are pleased as well, that you are happy, that you enjoy your life here. Perhaps if you act really well, then after a while you will begin to fool yourself.'

Claws snorted. 'Life's not that bad here. Some nights we have these huge dinners with drinking and music and dancing and everyone has a great time. You'll see.'

'And, none of us are here forever,' Silk joined in. 'Didn't the Empress tell you? Once we pay off our debts – you know, the money she spent buying us, plus interest, as well as for food and our rooms here and everything – we're free. She promised.'

Tiger raised her eyebrows and I saw a bitter smile play about the corner of her mouth.

'What? You don't believe it?' Claws said. 'Well then, what about Lotus and Feather? You've heard the Empress talking about them. We even had a couple of old regulars that one time who asked after Feather. Don't tell me you're turning deaf now, Tiger?'

'I've heard plenty of talk about them. But did you ever see them?'

'Of course not.' Claws snapped. 'You know that was before my time. You know very well that Silk and I arrived together only two winters before you. Feather had just left, which was why the Empress bought the both of us.'

Tiger said nothing. The cook looked at the four of us and shook his head wearily, before going back to tending the fire.

We spent the rest of the day 'doing something about my looks', as Claws put it. Silk washed my hair in a bucket of scented water, and Tiger combed and knotted it into a long braid. They took some of Honey's old robes and skirts and went about taking them in for me. Silk showed me how to make my eyes look bigger by dabbing coloured dusts around them, and Claws seemed to take a lot of pleasure in plucking out my split hairs with her long fingernails. As the three of them busied themselves transforming me, Silk kept up a monologue about the different patterns of the clouds above us, and what they each meant. She said they could tell us anything, if only we read them properly. Claws kept pulling faces as Silk spoke, but she never went as far as interrupting her. I was just glad they had stopped bickering. I liked listening to Silk. Where I saw boring lumps of fluffy white puttering across the sky, Silk saw arrows and faces and animals and bodies and coins and kings and swords and mountains and a hundred other things too. She said that the clouds were telling us that I would be happy in my new home. I smiled, but I knew she was making it up to help me feel better.

At some point in the afternoon I realised that for all their intro-ductions not a single one of them had asked me anything about myself, save for where I'd come from. That struck me as strange at first, but I soon understood. They didn't want to know about the world outside, because hearing about it would only make them feel homesick too. And I think they didn't want to upset me. But more than either of those reasons, I think they didn't have to ask me. In this line of work you learn how to read a stranger's secrets and desires pretty quickly. From a few glances at the way a man holds himself and the way he moves you can work out his whole life story. So the other girls didn't really have to ask about my father, about the villages beside the desert, about the fourteen summers of my life before I was taken here. They knew all of it the first time they saw my face.

We heard the little bell ringing from the Empress's room.

'Shit. Visitors?' Silk said.

Claws nodded. 'I reckon. The cook said he saw a caravan in the distance this morning. I'll go and see how many. You lot better get yourselves ready, and don't be messing about.'

Silk began hastily packing away her coloured dusts and then hurried to her room. Tiger stood up and put a hand on my arm. She leaned close.

'It'll hurt the first time, but don't give them the pleasure of letting them know that.'

I nodded. I didn't dare ask any more questions, because I was beginning to work out the answers for myself and I desperately did not want my suspicions confirmed. I heard the clatter of hooves and caught sight of a group of dishevelled men laughing and hollering near the gate. I ran to our shared room and closed the door behind me, my heart thumping in my stomach, trying as hard as I could to stop myself from crying and smudging the delicate colours Silk had painted on my face.

Tiger was right. That first night was the worst. I bit my lip till it bled, until I tasted my own blood in my mouth and I focused on the taste. I screwed up my eyes and wished I was back in that cage – no matter how bad it had smelt or how trapped I had been – because it was still better than this fighting in the dark. I may have been innocent, but I wasn't dumb. I knew what he wanted, what he was expecting when he took me into one of the fancy guestrooms and shoved his clammy hand under my borrowed skirts. I'd seen the village boys leading a girl down towards the stream, and the big men dragging captive women into the dunes, and I knew the rumours, and I'd listened to the gossipy housewives complaining about their hungry men, and I'd heard the speech about how the world works from one of the friendly village women who helped me out when I first got the gift of blood. So I knew. But that didn't make it any easier. The only thing I can say is it was all over pretty quickly and for that at least I was grateful.

Tiger crept across from her straw bed to mine later that night, and she helped me clean up and stroked my hair, all without saying a word. I was grateful for that too.

You know how if you work too much your hands get calluses and blisters and the skin grows so tough you really don't feel much of anything anymore, even if you hold your fingers too near the fire or grip the plough a whole twelve hours? Well, the same happens with your heart. It toughens up; it gets hard and mangled in your gut. It takes ages of course, little by little, and you don't even notice that it's happened.

Those first few moons went by in a sea of aches and nightmares and bruises and frayed nerves, and if you don't mind I won't dwell on it. In the beginning, I'd wake up every morning thinking I couldn't bear another day, and I spent all my energy trying to figure out ways to escape. The other girls left me to it, knowing that those kinds of dreams are no more than smoke – welling up in your eyes until you're blinded by tears one moment, then disappearing into the air the next. I knew from them that the Empress had contacts throughout the valley that would report back to her, and that however bad things were, if I tried to run and got caught everything would be much worse.

I was surprised to find, after only six or seven moons, though, that even if I hadn't quite got used to my new life, I could at least get through the day without crying. People are just like the lizards in the desert in that way, I reckon – whatever they lose, be it a leg or a tail or a future, they'll still keep scurrying on. I learnt how to laugh at the men's jokes, and how to disguise my yelps and cries as moans of pleasure. Claws and Silk taught me how to split myself in two, so that I was able to become someone else in the evenings without giving up the real me, the daytime me. They showed me how to fake the sweetest of smiles, how to act demure and innocent, how to serve and how to hold out for little gifts and extras from my customers without the Empress finding out. They even showed me how to clean up properly to avoid any little accidents.

During the day we played with dice and told stories about our dreams, as long as they hadn't been too scary or too realistic. We unknotted and combed and retied each other's hair, and we swapped clothes and experimented with Silk's coloured dusts. Claws even taught us how to speak the language of the middle kingdom, giving long-winded speeches and making us repeat everything she said under the pretence that we might one day be visited by travellers from her home country – but really I suspect it was because she couldn't bear to lose that last thread that kept her tied to the distant past. The days passed like this, and I even found that after a few weeks of bad weather when no one had passed our way I would begin to hope that some customers would turn up, if only so we could have some music and dancing and half-decent food and something new to gossip and joke about.

Mostly our customers were traders looking for something to do with their newly acquired goods. Although everyone knew that the Empress craved silver, we could be bartered for almost anything: buttons, reels of silk, dried fruit, liquor, jade, once even a donkey. They were mostly unkempt, unshaven men feeling homesick and sunburnt, and it didn't take much to make them happy. After all, they'd usually been in the desert for at least a whole moon before they stopped by, unloaded the camels and let their slaves set up camp outside the gate (for we had strict rules about who was allowed inside). The Whorehouse of a Thousand Sighs was a little oasis, a place to forget the heat and the loneliness. When they were done in the bedrooms they would drink and eat and laugh and tell stories about their trips and their trades, and we would serve and listen and laugh until they were ready for a second round or, even better, simply wanted to sleep.

Their little caravans made long, slow journeys between outposts in the desert, taking a couple of moons to get there and a couple of moons to return. When I was a girl back in the villages, if one little boy had something he really loved – like a shiny stone he'd found, say, or a stick shaped just like a sword – the bigger boys would tease him by stealing it then waving it in front of his face. The little boy would reach out to grab it, and then a big boy would toss it to another friend a bit further away. The little boy would run towards this boy but just before he reached him the trinket would be thrown to another boy even further away. The game would go on like this until the big boys got bored or the little boy started screaming and crying and drew the attention of a nearby adult. The way the traders worked was a bit like that. They would go to an outpost in the desert and swap their fruit, for example, for silk. Then the people they traded with would make the journey to the next town and barter that fruit for more silk or perhaps some livestock. Then those traders would travel even further east while the other traders made their way back west. There must have been thousands of little groups doing deals like this, somehow linking us to the middle kingdom in the east on one side and the great ocean in the west on the other. That's what the traders said, anyway. And it got me thinking that maybe all my days in the Empress's whorehouse were just small parts of a much greater journey, and that made things a little easier.

We didn't have any important customers until I'd been here for about two summers. I remember I was taking my afternoon nap, having already cleaned up the main courtyard after the guests of the night before had gone on their way, when the tinkling of the Empress's little bell cut through my dreams. By the time I'd shaken off the slowness of sleep and pushed through the stubborn door, the cook and the other girls, as well as Homely and Tall – who usually kept about as far away from the rest of us as they could, as if they could not bear to acknowledge the fact that we were all kept here for the same reason – were all gathered outside the Empress's room. I'd been in there many times by that point, to clean up and take orders and bring her food, and let me tell you, I've never seen a room as plush as that. More cushions and colours and silks and trinkets than you'd believe, all surrounding her huge bed. But what was truly shocking that day was that instead of anyone going into the room, the Empress was coming out.

'If you bothered listening to our guests yesterday, you will be aware of the rumours of an official of the middle kingdom's emperor travelling through the desert. Since the cook has informed me that he has seen a most regal caravan moving in this direction, I suggest we do our best to prepare ourselves.'

'And knock me over if it doesn't look longer than the bloody desert itself! Coming right this way, it is!' The cook grinned, showing his withered gums.

The Empress cleared her throat then continued. 'I would advise you all to start getting this place cleaned up. All of you wash, no excuses. I want your best dresses, your best smiles, and if I see a single yawn or frown I will line up everyone tomorrow morning and make each one of you pay. Understand?'

We understood. Within a few moments the whole place was in chaos. Even Claws – who usually went out of her way to maintain an image of unflappability – could not keep still, and was soon threatening to scratch Homely's pretty eyes out if he didn't back away from the quickly disappearing buckets of scented water the cook had heated for us. Tiger must have tugged out about a hundred of my hairs as she frantically ran the comb through the knots, and I had trouble stopping myself from cursing her.

'So what are officials?' I asked her between gritted teeth as she began to plait my hair tightly.

'My uncle was once an official in a country far from here,' she replied. 'In your language it means someone sent on a mission by a king or an emperor. Perhaps we will meet these officials. They are men who have stared into the face of a living god and survived.'

'And they really want to stop here?'

'Who knows? Maybe they're lost. Perhaps the Empress has bribed the local guides and shepherds to divert them this way. We will soon see.'

'Wait. What do you mean "in my language"? What's your language, then?'

Tiger clucked her tongue against her teeth. 'My old language is one of fire and ice. When I was brought up in my uncle's home I could speak three different languages, but there was always something special about my home tongue. It is the oldest language on earth, and one word of it spoken aloud can level mountains or cause rivers to change their course.'

'If it can do such great things, why don't you speak it now?' I asked.

'Some words are too powerful. Sometimes words show us how things really are and sometimes they disguise the world and wrap us in illusions. I do not dare speak my old language now. I no longer deserve it. Your second-hand tongue will do just fine.'

She had wound the plait along the top of my head as if it were a kind of crown. Without another word she stood up and made towards our shared room, where the four of us gathered and spent the next couple of hours painting our faces and practising our smiles and winks and knotting ourselves into the tightest robes we had. As ever, we competed to see who could do the best job of transforming themselves.

Tiger was shimmering in light silk that set off her fierce dark eyes, Silk had tied bright ribbons in her many plaits and Claws seemed to have managed to push her breasts even higher and further out than usual. Even the boys had gone all out, for when we emerged into the courtyard we saw Homely decked out in his brightest robe, while Tall had obviously stolen some of Silk's coloured dust in order to show off his sharp cheekbones and slanted sneer. I cursed them all under my breath. You see, no matter how much we all hated our work, we still wanted to be wanted. No one could bear the thought of being picked last, of having to go with the ugliest man or the lowliest of the group, of having to endure the other girls' pity or teasing the next day. Of course, the first men to pick were also always the ones in charge, the ones with more money or gifts to leave if you did well. But it went deeper than that. I know it sounds strange, but if you were picked first, above everyone else, well, that gave you a sort of power. It made you special, if only for a few seconds. Besides, no one wanted to feel that they were the last scraps, the leftovers.

Now, usually when we had a big party of men who wanted a bit of entertainment with their food, the cook sat in a corner and warbled along to his four-string hushtar. So we knew these officials were special when they brought along their own musicians. It was those two men carrying long stringed instruments who entered first, and we were all so nervous and excited we almost kowtowed to them before they started setting up in the corner of the courtyard. With them was the party's desert guide, a short mousy man who stuttered when the musicians asked him questions. I recognised him from a visit only a couple of moons before. No doubt he would be getting favours from us in the future for this brief diversion of the official, I thought to myself, and the looks that passed between him and the Empress seemed to confirm this. By the time he had settled the musicians, stationed four guards at the gate and ducked back out towards the main party, his face was puffy and slick with sweat.

The musicians began to play as the guide returned, following a few anxious paces behind a short man wearing a coat of armour made up of hundreds of tiny plates of scuffed metal that made him look, to me at least, like a giant fish with rattling scales. The official – his status was made obvious by the fact that the other three men and the guide were careful never to overtake him – had a long moustache and pointy beard, both bothered by stray sprigs of grey. On closer inspection (though we hardly dared look directly at him for more than a few seconds at a time), it was clear he was pretty old. Far older than my father had been when I last saw him. His armour struggled to contain his potbelly, and as he looked around his nose began to twitch as if he had smelt something rotten.

'It is my recollection that you assured us of a venerable palace of delights. This ragtag assemblage, however, looks better suited for slaves than one of his celestial majesty's most trusted servants. It seems we have left more persons at the foot of this hill than await us at its paltry summit.'

He spoke in the same rich language Claws had taught us, and I was happy to find that for the most part her lessons seemed to have paid off.

The guide wiped his sleeve across his damp forehead. 'Er ... well, my lord ... it's, erm, it's exclusive. But if it displeases you then, er, we could always take another route. I know of a place —'

'No. We are here now. If it were to take you as long to lead us to another reputable inn as it does for you to finish a sentence then we would not arrive till the day after the morrow!'

The three men were quick to chuckle at the official's joke – their laughs louder and more exaggerated than seemed necessary – and the guide nodded his head and cast his eyes to the floor. The old man sank down on the cushions at the head of the table and called for one of his servants to unfasten his armour. His three companions sat down beside him while the rest of us began to fetch the liquor and first dishes, since it seemed clear that they wished to fill their stomachs before they took their fill of us. For the first time, the Empress joined in, setting down steaming bowls of broth. As we trotted to and fro between the cook's fire and the long table, we were able to steal glances at our distinguished visitors. Though one of the men was at least as old as the official, with white hair and bushy eyebrows, the other two were closer to Claws' age. The guards at the gate and the front of the courtyard looked on enviously as the four men began to tear strips from the legs of mutton and pick at the sun-dried fruits. When we had finished bringing the feast, we were invited to sit beside them.

One of the younger men lifted his cup and the music quickly rushed to an improvised finish. Everyone sat silently, waiting.

'Gentlemen, might I be permitted to give the first toast? Then let us drink to our most noble benefactor, the burning celestial ruler and the very centre of the earth. To our mighty father, who has deigned to grant us a mission that we might prove ourselves. Gentlemen, to the most glorious and beneficent emperor.'

They knocked the clay cups together and downed the liquor. I wondered what the cook would think when these men finished all of the bottles he had been saving. He had told me that he had a special batch of the spirit he had fermented from the camels' milk and then buried in the earth to mature, and I was sure it was this that the gentlemen were carelessly knocking back. Nonetheless, despite not really knowing who this emperor was or why he was so important, I bowed my head when they spoke of him and clinked their cups. After a few jokes and anecdotes about their journey so far through 'these damned barbarous lands', which we all smiled and laughed at no matter how boring or hard to understand they were, the white-haired man lifted his cup, determined to follow suit.

'May I have the honour of proposing the second toast? I thank you all for humouring an old man and for giving him a chance to see the lands he had only heard about. I know well enough that this may be my last journey. So it is fitting that for my toast I should look not forward, but to the past. My brothers, let us drink to our brave predecessor, General Zhang Qian. Many autumns ago he made this same journey, so that others might follow. We are all familiar, I am sure, with his story: how the emperor charged him with exploring the wilderness of the west in order to forge alliances against the vicious Xiongnu tribes who pick like vultures at the borders of our kingdom. How he was captured and held prisoner by these same uncivilised Xiongnu for ten winters, and finally returned to his ruler with only a single one of his army of a hundred soldiers still alive. How he was sent again to bring back the wondrous horses he had seen, horses that sweat blood and that have made our kingdom invincible. How the subsequent invasions, treaties and trading alliances that have strengthened our nation were enabled by him. How we, following in his footsteps, owe him a great debt. Brothers, to Zhang Qian.'

Once again the clay cups were banged together and the liquor sloshed back. The younger men's eyes were beginning to redden along with their cheeks. It was clear from the twitching corner of the first man's forced smile that the white-haired man had outdone him. Now, I had no idea who this Zhang Qian was, but he sounded like the kind of man I would also happily drink to. Travelling far from his family and home town only to be taken prisoner by strange foreigners for many summers on end – I knew how he must have felt.

Though his words were flecked with spittle and he occasionally knocked over some of the bowls with his shaky hand, the old man was by far the liveliest of the bunch. He would often forget himself and turn to speak to us girls instead of to his superior and his companions, and the sparks of the drink danced in this eyes. He told us the stories he had heard of the neighbouring tribes and kingdoms: of jugglers and acrobats who could throw things into the air and keep them suspended motionless above the crowd, of birds whose call told of your deepest secret, of men who could throw ropes straight up and climb into the clouds, of trees on which laughing human heads grew, of medicines that could make a man live for a thousand springs and of beasts that fed on sand and rain-clouds. Eventually he broke off his long, rambling stories when the second of the young men raised his cup.

'I humbly beg you to allow me to make the last of the toasts. My brothers have spoken eloquently of our celestial master and of our noble kinsman who set out a trail that we have followed. Yet I wish to break with convention, if my most gracious master will allow it, and dedicate this toast not to a person but to the history of our motherland and the most mighty of countries. Not for us the histories commissioned by bumbling rich men who censor any mention of misdoings and pay the historian well to exaggerate their achievements and belittle those of their enemy. Not for us the histories which dwell only on a single place, or a single epoch. Not for us those histories of conjecture and guesswork. Not for us those histories that confine themselves to the past. My brother, to our quest and its assured success: to the Book.'

He grinned as his toast reached its peak and he raised his cup even higher, thinking he had outshone the others. To tell the truth, I was thinking the same. He had spoken the most eloquently and managed to put his companions down as he did so. So none of us, least of all the speaker, was expecting it when the official suddenly slapped him. The cup flew from his hands and smashed on the ground, the liquor dribbling out among the broken shards. The young man reached to his stinging face and began to stutter.

'Do you ever stop and think before your ignorant tongue gabbles out our secrets?' the official barked at him. 'Don't you remember our orders? Your tongue is so loose I'm surprised it hasn't slipped from your throat!'

'But who's going to hear us? We're alone on a mountain top at a cheap hideout with just a couple of dumb tarts for company.'

So much for being a gentleman, I thought.

'So you didn't consider that our party may have been tracked and followed, that there may be spies among our guards or hiding in places such as these? Anyway, fool, an order is an order. Remember that. Ladies, please forgive us. If you would bring some more cups and forget my foolish companion's rash words, we would be much obliged. Our mission is one of trade and trade alone, and there will be silver to help everyone remember that. Let the music start up again, and please join me in the final toast: to friends, wherever we might find them.'

I was impressed to be given a cup myself, even though the liquor was fiery and burned my throat. When I coughed and spluttered after a single tentative sip, everyone began to laugh and tease me, and the argument was soon forgotten. It all seemed pretty silly to me anyway. I mean, I wasn't ignorant, I knew what a book was – I knew some merchants and important people scratched drawings on strips of bamboo, then bound them together and took them along on their travels so they didn't forget where they were going. But these travellers were having a laugh if they really thought we'd care about a jumble of pictures on a few mouldy old bamboo slats – why would any of us want that? In any case, the four people in front of me were the only people I'd ever met who could read.

When the dishes had dwindled away to licked-clean bones and

the soggy dregs of the cook's best soup, and the musicians began to complain of blisters and sore fingers, the official nodded and held up his hand. We all knew what this meant, and the four of us girls tried not to tense up. It was time. Although the official told the white-haired man to take first pick, the old man shook his head and insisted that his superior have that honour. The official slowly rose to his feet, and we all did the same.

As his eyes studied each of the six of us in turn, I felt that familiar blush rising up from my toes to my cheeks. It was the same every time we went through this. Out of the corner of my eye I noticed Claws toying with her long plait. She must have been as anxious as I was. Being picked by the emperor's own official would give us something to boast about for ages.

'I think I shall retire with this wonderfully plump young boy,' he said, raising a hand to Homely, who grinned in return. I tried hard not to show my disappointment, to remain smiling, and I knew that the other girls would be doing the same. The second young man laughed and muttered something to the others, but the official only smiled.

'I have seven wives at home. I will relish the chance to enjoy such fine alabaster skin, a worthy dessert for such a hearty meal. I bid you goodnight, my friends, and entrust you will be ready to depart at first light in the morrow.'

As the fat young boy and the elderly statesman disappeared into a room on the other side of the courtyard, all heads turned towards the white-haired man, who was licking his lips. Though he was obviously next in rank, the idea of entertaining someone so old was one that I'm sure none of us relished. Granted, some of his stories had been pretty funny, but there is always so much extra work involved in getting old men ready before the damned thing can even get under way that I for one was hoping he wouldn't pick me almost as much as I had been hoping his master would.

'Would the fair lady from the west care to accompany me?' he said, holding his hand out towards Silk, who, of course, could not refuse it. 'Forgive me if I embarrass you, but your fine pale cheeks and great height lead me to conjecture that you are from that tribe of master horsemen the Scythians, a people of which I have heard much but have never before had the opportunity to meet.'

Silk nodded before taking his arm and leading him round the

cushions towards one of the guestrooms, while he prattled on into her ear. Although I had assumed the young man who had made the first toast would be the next to make his choice, it was instead the rude young man who had offended his master who opened his mouth to speak before the other had a chance.

'I'll take darkie here. I want to see whether the rest of her body is truly as black as her face and hands. Goodnight, all.'

He grabbed Tiger and pulled her away without noticing the look of hatred that briefly lit up her usually impassive face. Just one more man now, and I noticed Claws glance at me fiercely as she thrust out her chest and ran her tongue over her lips. On the other side of me Tall pushed his fingers through his short crop of hair and winked. This was an all-out battle, with everything at stake. I fluttered my eyelids and did my best to pout. The young man looked at the three of us nervously before stretching out his hand.

'May I have the pleasure of your company, young lady?' he said to me, and I had to work hard to stop myself from shouting out in celebration. I nodded slowly and took his hand. I had beaten them. I had been picked. My heart thumped about like a trapped bird in my chest as we made our way to the last of the guestrooms on our side of the courtyard. The last thing I saw before I slipped inside was Tall storming away and a red-faced Claws slapping one of the musicians who had obviously forgotten his place.

That was probably the day Claws turned. She had always been a little cruel in her teasing, but after that she was plain vicious. Of course, it's easy to look back now and say, oh yes, that was definitely the day everything changed. But at the time it was just another party to clean up. Sometimes I wonder if I'm telling this whole thing wrong – when I think about Tiger's story, or Silk's, I realise that I would only have the smallest of roles in them, a short description or an anecdote or two and then I'd probably just fade into the background, and that makes me question whether you can ever understand anybody's life at all. Still, you've got to try though, haven't you?

Claws was sullen and impatient with all of us for the first few weeks after the official's visit, but we hardly noticed at the time. She seemed to take pleasure tugging out the knots in our hair as carelessly as she could, and grabbed any opportunity that arose to point out our flaws – Silk's big nose, Tiger's sticky-out ears, my small breasts – and remind us of every complaint or bit of gossip she had overheard customers mention after a night with one of us – Silk lying there like a cold corpse, Tiger behaving like a man trapped in a woman's body, me so sweaty the room smelt, and so on.

We did a good job of ignoring her and shrugging off these comments, especially since we had other things to talk about. For weeks we gossiped about the rich men and how different they were from our regulars. The white-haired man's peculiar slobbering over Silk's feet, the rude young man's lazy desire for Tiger to ride him like a horse, or my young man showing himself to be so poor at handling liquor that he fell asleep halfway through the main event. Sometimes Homely would saunter over and joke about the 'exquisite girth of the official's military instrument'. Claws would hover on the edge of these conversations, veering between trying to join in and treating us with disdain, as if we were silly children. We paid her little attention and did our best not to make fun of her for being left out that night. Looking back, I think that's what riled her most. I think she would have preferred our teasing – then at least she would have known how to respond. It was our pity that she couldn't handle.

I remember one afternoon when she accused Silk of having stolen some of the powder she used to keep her hair bedtime-black. I was having a nap, so I only heard about it from Tiger. I was woken by the sound of shrieking, but by the time I made my way outside all I got to see was Silk pushing past me into our room. Tiger said that they had been fighting so loudly that the Empress herself had left her quarters and come and thrown a bucket of cold water over both of them. I saw the clump of hair that Silk had wrenched from Claws' head lying in the damp puddle, and when a tearful Silk finally emerged from our room for supper that evening the scratch marks running down her face were as fresh and pink as a summer evening. The Empress told the cook not to serve Claws for two days after that. She said it was one thing for us girls to have our petty squabbles, but quite another to damage her merchandise and run the risk of a loss of profits when the customers saw Silk's criss-cross scars.

Claws stayed tucked up under a blanket on her straw bed for

days at a time after that, and when she did come out of the room her eyes would not stop darting between us. When customers arrived she would suddenly become light-hearted, full of jokes and fluttery laughs. Yet the next morning she would return to her previous state and remain sullen and snappy. Instead of picking fights, she soon took to ignoring us all together, though she often gave the impression that she was waiting eagerly for one of us to give her an opportunity to pounce. This didn't happen until about two moons after the officials had left.

That morning Tiger, Silk and I were washing our dresses in the big wooden buckets in the courtyard. Claws was sitting a little distance away, sharpening her long nails on one of the cook's spare stubs of flint.

'Go to the Empress, girl,' Silk was saying. 'You know you have to. I've seen these things in the clouds: a struggle, something unexpected. You better get her to make something up before it's too late.'

'I'll ask her tomorrow,' Tiger said. 'It could still come.'

Even I could see she was just making excuses now. 'After eight weeks? Come on.'

'I know,' Tiger sighed. 'I hate that man. I hate him with every pore of my skin, with every single one of my pulses, with every thought stirring in my heart. But ...'

'Couldn't you talk to the Empress about it? I mean, wouldn't it be simplest just to do nothing?' I asked. The two of them stopped washing and turned to stare at me. 'What? It's not so crazy. Don't you want to, one day?'

Silk shook her head. 'The Empress would rather cut your throat than let that happen. Nine moons off work and when it's all done your breasts will sag, your stomach will droop and the customers won't want to go anywhere near you.'

'She didn't just buy our bodies: she bought our lives, our hopes, our dreams, our futures,' Tiger muttered.

'Oh, don't say that. You know I hate it when you say things like that.'

'It's the truth. Who would want a child to be born into this life? Better to never know love or beauty than to see them every day twisted into coins and aches. Better to never be born than to be born to this. I'll drink her stinking poison. I'm not afraid,' Tiger said.

From across the courtyard we heard Claws snort back a scornful laugh. Silk raised her eyebrows as Claws raised herself up and walked towards us.

'You want a family, Jade? What for – to watch them struggle through this shitty world, to suffer yourself every time they suffer? Haven't you got enough to cry over with your youth sucked dry and your body already crooked and stretched out of shape, with your pathetic hopes and soppy songs you hum while you're cleaning – that's right, we can hear you when you're doing that, and when you're moaning at night for your daddy to come and help you. Fat fucking chance.'

'That's enough,' Tiger hissed at her.

'Or do you want to be like Miss High-and-Mighty here, pretending you're not afraid of anything and that just because you used to be someone you're better than the rest of us? Or do you want to be like her over there, spending your life looking at clouds because anything is better than looking at your own face in the mirror? Huh?'

'Enough!' Tiger thrust her hand up into Claws' face.

Claws hocked and spat on the floor at our feet before turning away, muttering under her breath. Tiger shook her head and began to squeeze the water from one of her dresses, but Silk was red and on the verge of tears. When she spoke her voice shook like the spindly branches of a young tree in the wind. 'She's just bitter because she couldn't hold onto her own little boy back when she had the chance.'

As she swung back round, Claws gave out the kind of sound you might expect a wounded animal to make. Her eyes were the sharp spark of stone on flint, and in that second before she screamed again and threw herself forward her face seemed to move through such strange contortions that it looked as though she had become another person entirely. She lunged at Silk, who threw up her arms to shield herself from the furious slashes of those long jagged talons. I leapt up to pull Claws off but instead her elbow swung back and smashed into my nose, sending me tripping and stumbling into the table, blood dribbling down my chin. Both of the women were screaming and spitting at each other, and when I looked up again I saw that Silk had grabbed Claws' hair by the roots and was trying her best to wrench out whole clumps of it. I put my hand to my throbbing nose, pinching it to stop the bleeding while I pushed myself up with my free hand. It was then that I heard the most high-pitched ear-piercing glass-shattering migraine-making blood-curdlingly-terrible scream I have ever heard. I still have nightmares about it sometimes. I wake up clammy with goosebumps, remembering how Silk screamed and then staggered back, gagging and choking for air, a thin line of blood trickling down her cheek and sticking to her hair, and how Claws was also stumbling unsteadily, her face suddenly pallid, the mangled dripping egg-white ooze of what remained of Silk's left eye still impaled on her fingernail. Silk started to howl and clutch at her face. There was a curdled mess of thick blood and gunk left in the socket, and her other eye began to blink wildly in shock. Claws began to retch. It must have been then that the Empress appeared, ready to throw another bucket of cold water on the pair of them, but she quickly realised it was too late for that. I'm not sure exactly what happened after that. I sank back to the ground, feeling dizzy and nauseous as blood continued to flow from my nose. The next few hours were swallowed up with shrieking and sobbing.

I know that the Empress eventually led Silk away to one of the huts in the cook's courtyard, and I remember that Claws threw up at some point, splattering a puddle of vomit over a couple of the nicest cushions. But the order of those events is not particularly clear in my mind. Despite the horror of the situation, in many ways the whole scene felt just like a dream, and even the following morning I half thought I might see Silk walking about as usual with both of her big brown eyes staring up at the clouds. The thing that bothers me now – that bothers me precisely because I did not register the fact until I looked back at the event some days later – is that all the time the two of them were fighting and screaming, and even when they had staggered apart in the awful aftermath of that sudden malicious gouge, Tiger had stood in the same spot, expressionless and impassive, almost as if she had expected something like this to happen and was neither surprised nor particularly interested in what she saw.

The next morning I had a wonk in my nose, a restless cicada buzzing somewhere inside my head and two black eyes – though I was grateful for the pair of them. I left our room while the others were still snoring. The courtyard was silent, and if it hadn't been for the light worming through the cracks in the wall I would have thought it was still the dead of night. In the end my stomach got the better of me and I fastened my day robe and set off up the trail to the cook's courtyard. He was talking to the camels when I got there, running his blackened hands through their knotted beards as they clicked their teeth together. The fire had gone out.

'No breakfast today,' he said.

I didn't bother to ask him why. I already knew. His eyes moved from the huge hairy beasts to the closed door of the wooden hut across from him.

'How is she?'

'Not too good, if you ask me,' he said. 'But she'll live. The herbman'll be coming down later. The mistress has taken away all the glass so she can't take a peek at herself, but I'm not sure that's going to be enough. You ladies haven't got much without your looks now, have you? The mistress told her she'll buy her a beautiful leather patch to make her look as good as new, but I don't think that made her feel better.'

'Can I visit her?'

'Better not. The Empress is pretty pissed off with you lot right now. Can't say I blame her. Four girls and every single one of them a mess. This one deformed, you with a nose so bent out of shape you look closer to sixty than sixteen and the bitchy one gone half mad at what she's done. Meanwhile the other one's going be laid up for at least a whole moon recovering from the cleansing potion. Yep, she picked a good time springing that on us in the middle of all this chaos. This place is going to be seriously out of pocket for a while.'

He shook his head and moved to the side of one of the camels, running his hands through its thick fleece, checking for fleas.

'You see this beast here? Let me tell you something: it earns its keep. All the way from Persia, and the best damn trade we ever made. It doesn't eat much, a little grazing every few days perhaps, and it doesn't complain when it's hungry or tired. Sheds its hair when the frost goes and we can wind that into rope or knit it into warm clothes. Almost every day it gives us its milk for drinking or butter or for me to make into liquor for the guests. When it dies we can eat the meat and cure the skin for bags and straps. I mean, even its shit is useful – we wouldn't be able to get a fire going to cook dinner without it. And you know what? It's always calm, always quiet, never fights with the other or makes a fuss. Sure, it can get fidgety when it's horny, but apart from that it keeps itself to itself and just gets on with the day. It doesn't get into any silly squabbles. Seems to me you lot could learn a thing or two from it.'

I left him to his stinking humped horses and went back down to the courtyard. He had some cheek. I cursed him for comparing us to animals. Then my rumbling stomach cursed the Empress for punishing all of us for Claws' anger. Then my aching nose and heavy eyes cursed Claws and Silk for grinding each other down, and Tiger for getting herself into such a mess and starting the whole argument. For good measure I cursed all the men who had come through here and led me into the guestrooms, and I cursed the big men who had captured and sold me, and I cursed my father for being such a good-for-nothing and leading us into dangerous territory, and finally, when I had no one else to curse, I cursed myself.

Since Claws refused to get up, staying in our room muttering and sobbing and wailing, and with the Empress spending her time fussing over Silk, I was ordered to look after Tiger when she took the potion. As soon as I had smelt that vicious concoction brewing in the courtyard I knew it was going to be nasty. The Empress seemed to have gathered the most repulsive leaves and shrubs she could find and then stewed them down to a lumpy brown sludge. Tiger gagged and coughed as she tried to swallow all four cupfuls of the stuff, and I can't say I was surprised that the Empress left two empty buckets by the side of the little straw bed in the hut next to Silk's.

I would compose myself and try to keep a friendly face as I pushed open Tiger's door and went in, but it wasn't always easy. The room smelt of stale sweat and farts. Yet despite the stomach cramps and the bleeding, she remained much the same as ever.

'I hope it kills me as well,' she said between gritted teeth the day the syrupy blood began seeping down her thighs. It was warm and sticky and lumpy. 'I hope I keep bleeding till my whole insides come out, till I'm hollow and emptied. I hope I bleed so much this whole fucking mountain drowns in blood.'

I didn't know what to say. 'At least this will mean you won't be getting any men climbing on top of you for a while,' I said, trying to lighten the mood.

It had the desired effect – she laughed.

'I never let them go on top of me. Never. I go on top, or we lie side to side. That's one of my rules. And I hope this poison makes me so green that next time a man lies with me his prick will shrivel up and fall off afterwards. I hope it mangles me so bad that every time a man comes in he'll begin to squirm and yelp until his cock begins to burn and crackle and melt down to a scabby stump while I look down and laugh in his face.'

I thought it was probably better to let her speak, let it all come out. Just like the potion. Perhaps it was supposed to cleanse her thoughts as well as her womb, to wash everything away.

Each day I brought her bowls of broth and gave her a wash; I helped her change clothes and replaced the swabbing cloth between her legs; I cleaned out her fetid buckets, and when she was up to it I led her on little walks around the cook's courtyard. She took tiny steps, leaning on my arm, and always insisted that we stop for breaks near Silk's hut to see if we could hear anything from inside. We hadn't seen her in almost a week.

'Did you know about Claws' baby?' I whispered to her during one of our walks.

Tiger shrugged. 'Only what Silk mentioned. Remember when we drank that liquor on Silk's birthday and the two of them stayed up chatting after we went to bed? Well, Silk told me that Claws mentioned him that night, and then swore her to secrecy the next morning. 'It seems when the war finished and the soldiers took her prisoner, they had a bit of fun with her. They only sold her on to slave traders once she had grown fat and they were bored with her, so the boy's father could have been any one out of that whole platoon. The slave traders had stopped for the night in some piss-poor village when she felt the baby coming. She told Silk she snuck away from the snoring men and squatted down in a field to give birth, and then later bit the cord off with her own teeth. As you can imagine, after all of that effort she was cold and exhausted. She tiptoed off to a small house and asked the old woman there to keep the baby by the fire for the night so he could stay warm. The old woman agreed to let Claws sleep in her barn. You can guess the rest: when she woke up after a long, deep sleep she found herself in a wooden cage being carried through the desert, with the village far, far behind her.'

'And then?' I asked.

Tiger laughed. 'And then nothing. That's the end, and here we all are as proof.'

I helped her back to the hut and tucked the ragged blanket around her. As always, instead of thanking me, Tiger did her best to ignore the fact that I was there.

Trying to get to sleep that night, with Claws snuffling and murmuring in the corner, I wondered if I hadn't got my opinion of her wrong, if we'd all judged her too quickly. But as she herself had said, you have to forget the past to keep going here. I thought about her little boy, where he might be now and if he even knew whose son he was, and I have to be honest, it made me feel pretty low. I'd always imagined I'd grow up and have a family to look after. If you haven't got someone else to care for, you stop caring at all. I don't claim to know much about history and time and all those silly things the emperor's men were arguing about, but it seems to me that if you don't have a family then you don't have a history. Your history stops. You disappear.

But then what good would I be anyway? I wondered. I never knew my mother and my father was more trouble than comfort. I was just like the other three, too broken now to be much good in the world below. Claws and her bitterness, Silk and her hopeless ideas, Tiger and her buried anger. And me and my useless wishes. As I sat there stewing in self-pity, I realised for the first time that although the door to our room was never bolted from the outside anymore, I had not once thought about running away. Not seriously, anyway. The truth was, the world below scared me. The mere thought of walking down the track made me feel dizzy. At least here I knew who I was. If I hated Claws and Silk and Tiger sometimes, it was only because when I looked at each of them I saw what I might turn into. If I loved them sometimes, it was only because I had no one else to give my love to. Perhaps, as Silk says, everything that can happen will happen, and you can either struggle against its pull or drift along in its current. I'd had enough of struggling.

# A Delicate Matter of Phrasing

It was raining. Hard. Pissing it down. Raining like ... like ... like I don't know what. Li Yang would say it was raining down like a stream of shooting stars or some crap like that. Something stupid that tells you nothing. I can't play with words like Li Yang, making them mean a hundred different things at once. I hate that kind of crap. I reckon you ought to either say what you mean or keep your mouth shut. Words ought to mean something hard, something real, something you can wrap your hands around – or else nothing at all. None of this mucking about in the middle. Fuck Li Yang. Fuck the rain.

It was raining. Hard. Pissing it down. I leant back in my chair and watched it spitting against the windows. There was a stack of papers on my desk, but it wasn't worth picking through them now. Fishlips came out of his office at the end of the hall. It isn't hard to guess why we call him that. He made a show of taking out his key and locking the door behind him.

'You still here?'

'Guess so.'

'You've got to go home some time.' He laughed. 'I'd call it a day if I were you.'

I shrugged and turned back to the pens in front of me. I was trying to get them to stand up with their tips touching in a tall triangle. But I wasn't having much luck. I stole a look over at Wei Shan's desk. Where the hell was he? I hated being the last one to leave – may as well stick a sign on your forehead saying nowhere else to go. Pathetic. A crack of lightning lit up the empty room. I wouldn't want to be caught outside in that. What was he playing at? He'd said an hour, at the most. That was two hours ago. Stealing a crafty one on the sly? I wouldn't put it past him. There was no way I was going to sit here like some chump and wait for him, even if it was his turn to pay. I'd rather go home to my wife. On second thoughts, maybe I could hang around a little longer.

Once I was sure Fishlips was gone, I made my way over to Wei Shan's workstation. He had the same tatty pile of case files, project histories and blueprints as I did. A glass jar full of green tea. A photo from his wife in a cheap, tacky frame. The obligatory untouched copy of the Public Safety Office rulebook, full of statutes and decrees that no one ever bothered about. I was going to kill him. Every Thursday, we went to the Golden Dragon Seafood Palace for a few drinks and dishes. It was a grotty little place, but it was usually empty and it was always cheap. He'd better not be playing some joke on me. I wasn't in the mood.

It wasn't like he was great company either. All he ever did was complain, the boring shit. But then he'd probably say the same of me. It still beat drinking alone. My wife once asked me what we do all evening. I guess she was worried we spent all our time in some karaoke bar or in a massage parlour. I'm not sure she believed me when I told her that all we do is talk. But then sometimes nothing is harder to believe than the truth.

'So you just sit in that mangy old dump drinking cheap rice wine and chatting for two or three hours?'

'Pretty much,' I said.

'So what do you talk about for all that time?'

That was harder to answer. 'This and that.'

If I was going to be honest, I'd have to say the thing we talked about most often was how shitty life could be. Our crappy jobs. The catalogue of dim-witted things the boss said. Our nagging wives. And our prissy bits on the side – though I never mentioned Li Yang by name, and I'm not sure Wei Shan ever told me much about the young woman he was seeing on the sly, except to moan that between her and his wife he was being bled dry. I mean, a man's got to have some secrets. What else did we talk about? Hard to say. Our sarcastic children. How things used to be different. The usual. But I didn't tell my wife that. She used to interrogate me about every little thing I did as though I was some badly behaved schoolchild. Though not so much anymore.

I rifled through Wei Shan's desk drawers absentmindedly. He kept them pretty tidy. A few unopened packets of paperclips, a stapler, a couple of binders spilling their crumpled bounty. I spotted a hastily scribbled note poking out from under one of the files and I tugged it loose. His handwriting was abysmal, but I could just about make it out: Jawbone Hills, approx. 30 km west, Highway 312. Foreman = Jing Ren?? So that's where he'd gone. I checked the logbook to make sure – yep, a call had come in from Jawbone Hills just before four. I wish I'd picked up the phone instead. It always works the same way. Some nosy village busybody calling up to complain about dangerous or suspicious activity near their home. We pretend we give a shit and tell them we'll be right over to check there's no illegal activity and to make sure that everything conforms to the Public Safety Office guidelines. Then a short drive out to the countryside or the edges of town (because if there's something going on inside Lanzhou, chances are we already know about it) to see what's happening. Half the time we find some sneaky company involved in drilling, mining or building, trying to cut costs by ignoring all those pesky legalities like planning permission or permits. Invariably they are none too happy to see us, though the guy in charge is usually all smiles and handshakes, apologising for the oversight and conjuring up excuses. Then we tell them sorry, rules are rules, we're going to have to write it up and that means you're going to have to shut down business until everything has gone through the proper channels. Terribly sorry, I wish there was something I could do … and soon enough you're driving away with a fat envelope stuffed inside your jacket pocket. If the boss asks, it was all a misunderstanding. Saves on paperwork too. A half-hour drive and a bit of play-acting in exchange for more than we usually make in a month. It beats sitting at a desk all day.

So that's why he was late. Instead of a simple envelope, the manager of whatever-it-was over in Jawbone Hills had no doubt taken Wei Shan out for a fancy meal and bought him a few drinks to encourage him to turn a blind eye. Lucky bastard. It was months since I'd got one of those tip-offs. Well, there was no way I was going to wait around in an empty office while he was stuffing himself silly at some extravagant restaurant. Some friend. Fuck him. I hoped he got caught out in the rain and that it soaked through the lousy piece of second-rate tat he called a suit. If he wasn't going to bother coming back, I'd just go to the Golden Dragon on my own.

The Golden Dragon Seafood Palace was little more than a poky backroom with three or four tables topped with dirty plastic covers. The walls were bare brick and a single naked bulb swung precariously from the ceiling. The wind flapped the warped front door against its frame as I made my way inside and settled at my usual table, on the off chance that Wei Shan might still join me. Through an open door I could see the chef hunched over a dented wok, a cigarette hanging from between his lips as he furrowed his brow and poked at the dark and stringy substance he was stir-frying. The manager was sitting on a wonky stool next to a shelf of dusty bottles, picking his nose while staring up at the tiny black-and-white TV balanced on top of one of the tables. Like I said, the place is a dump.

'Bowl of pork noodles and a bottle of *baiju*.'

The manager nodded but didn't get up.

I looked at the TV. The antenna was held together with elastic bands. The manager was watching some local news programme showing the grand opening of a new primary school in some village up in the mountains. Grinning local cadres and dumpy little red-faced children waving flags. Big deal. I took out a Double Happiness and lit up. I hate the countryside. It gives me the creeps. I spent six long years driving sheep across the ragged grassland north of Hohot, and that's more than enough for this lifetime. I'd rather have a slab of concrete any day. Something steady under your feet. Something that won't get washed away every time the clouds let rip. Some folks these days are nostalgic for the old Cultural Revolution. Say it made them men. Say they have a real affinity with the peasants now. What a load of crap. No one stayed out there a day longer than they had to, especially after the old Chairman finally wheezed his last. If they found it so enriching, why are they sat at their plush desks, padding about on brand new imported carpets instead of still shovelling manure in the provinces?

Wei Shan was one of them. Give him enough glasses of the cheap stuff and he'd start getting misty-eyed about his time in Mizhi County, up near Yulin. Said he loved it, living on a farm up there, not having to think about anything but the fields and the goats. Yeah, right. Said he could lose himself in that kind of work, staring off into the unbroken horizon for hours, and that he missed the contented glow he felt when the red sun finally touched down amid the long grass. Uh huh. Said he would have stayed on too, maybe even married the daughter of the farmer he worked with, that is if his mother hadn't keeled over and he'd been called home – by the time the funeral was over, Mao had finally croaked and everyone was coming back. And so on – blah blah blah. I didn't believe him, but I nodded along nonetheless. I'm not even sure he believed himself. Things have got to be pretty shitty when you start looking back fondly on your exile and re-education. Sometimes I think that's the only reason we bother looking back – so we can pinpoint the exact moment and say, that's it, that's when I was truly happy, and everything has been downhill since then.

My bottle arrived and I filled my glass. I drained it in one go, then poured another. At least I didn't have to listen to Wei Shan droning on. Or stealing half the bottle. I helped myself to another glass. The manager set down my noodles and I checked my watch. It wasn't worth going home yet. Maybe I could call Li Yang. I started cramming the scalding noodles into my mouth as quickly as I could. I was so focused on finishing my food and getting out of there that I barely noticed the TV until the manager cranked up the volume.

I stopped chewing mid-mouthful, a few loose strands of noodle still hanging from my lips.

'... it is thought that the unstable terrain was weakened by recent storms, though the primary cause is as yet unclear. Police and local army units are already at the scene, working diligently to clear the area. A mixture of rocks, soil and other debris all but stripped the hillside bare as the avalanche gained force. Fortunately, no one has been hurt, thanks to the efforts of the local government, though the public are advised to stay away from the area surrounding Jawbone Hills until ...'

I didn't hear the rest – I was already running for the door.

The drive took forever. Time doesn't work the same way outside the city. Once the last high-rise fades out of sight in your rear-view mirror and you cross the bridge over the river, the clocks seem to slow down and stutter uncertainly through each minute. With every kilometre I drove it seemed as if I travelled back another decade until I had left the present far behind me. I'd grabbed the half-finished bottle of *baiju* as I legged it from the restaurant, and

I had it balanced between my knees as I drove. I took a swig and peered out into the darkness. Tall, tree-lined hills rose up on either side of the highway, their shapes shifting and fluctuating in the downpour like dancing shadows. The road was all but deserted, and as I sped on deeper into the valley I thought I could make out a helicopter soaring through the night far above. I listened to the hiss and haw of the creaky windscreen-wipers. Rain was trawling down off the mountain range. Trees keened against it, their branches flung out wildly in distress. A few desperate farmers with quotas to meet were braving it in the fields dotted across the slopes. Their slack waxy raincoats fluttered in the wind.

I wasn't sure why I was driving like a devil towards the scene of the accident. What was I going to do – dig through the debris till I found Wei Shan? Fat chance. I had to make sure he was all right, though I doubted he would have done the same if the shoe had been on the other foot. He'd have probably just crept back home to sleep off his groggy head. But I'd had the best part of a bottle by then, and there was no way I could skulk back to my wife and pretend to myself that I hadn't heard the news.

I spotted the exit at the last second and swerved across, following it out onto a smaller road that seemed barely finished, as if the construction workers had grown bored and downed their tools halfway through the job. I passed an abandoned tractor, a little temple of rust that had already been picked apart for scrap. The road curved around to the east and began to rise up one of the hills. Soon I could see the whirring lights of police cars on the summit high above, and it occurred to me then that the landslide had to be on the other side of the slope. My heart leapt into my mouth, and I fumbled for the last dregs of the bottle. What if more of the cliff collapsed? I found myself driving slower, wondering how much further the point was where the slope tumbled over into darkness. It wasn't long before I could make out police cars lined up in a roadblock, and before I even had time to think about what I was doing I turned off my headlights and made a sudden turn off the road and into a field. I parked beside a disused trough and opened the car door. My suit crinkled in the downpour. I squinted up the hillside. Even from here I could hear the churn of diggers pushing through the deep debris that had come tumbling down the other side. A great cloud of smog seemed to hang motionless above the peak up ahead, like the breath of some giant dragon. I tried to ruffle some of my soaking hair forward to cover the bald patches at the front, then started off through the field.

With every step I took up the slope towards the flashing lights and frantic commotion, my shoes sank deeper into the wet soil. It wasn't long before I had mud splattered all over my trousers. I thought about what I'd seen on the news. No one had been hurt – that's what they always said, regardless of how many corpses had been found. The bigger the accident, the more likely it was that nobody ever heard anything about it. There's no way the government would want to scare everyone with the truth. Get them thinking that something similar could happen to them. No way. That was another part of the Public Safety Office, ensuring the wall of silence. Of course, some big stories had to be tossed out occasionally – otherwise people might get suspicious. Most journalists know the rules.

It made sense to me. Why worry people needlessly? The world's a harsh place, and if everyone knew the kind of shit that went down on a daily basis I reckon some of them would be too scared to ever leave their homes. You've got to protect them. Especially the women and children. You wouldn't want them running round in a panic. People are like sheep: ignorant, impressionable and liable to do something stupid if you let too many of them gather together in one place. Plus the majority of them stink to high hell.

I passed close by a farmhouse, and I could see another two or three scattered across the hillside below. I bet those families were thanking whatever grubby little feudal gods they prayed to that they hadn't built their homes on the other side, where there'd probably be little left but piles of bricks and mud. Perhaps it was someone living here who had made the call that Wei Shan took. But I doubted it. I couldn't see a phone line anywhere. Probably no electricity either. They most likely didn't even know what year it was. I reached the end of the field and made my way along the border until I rejoined the road, some way above where the police were ordering everyone to turn around. I jogged further up, and I was soaked through by the time I reached the huddle of jeeps and station-wagons parked a little way off from the line of policemen.

Though the last few vehicles had been left haphazardly in odd formations, it was obvious that this little bit of cleared land had served as a car park for whatever had been going on up here before the landslide: partitions had even been marked out in white paint on the grass. A few policemen were milling about, chatting to each other and smoking cigarettes, so I kept my head down as I wandered between the cars. I soon spotted Wei Shan's old clunker and sidled over. It was mud-splattered and still dented at the back from a collision a few months back. We'd only had them a couple of years – last government department to get them, of course. As I tried the front door I overheard a couple of cops yakking about the accident.

'At least twenty metres of shit at the bottom.'

'No way we'll clear it all before morning.'

Well, I could have told them that. Especially with all those cigarette-breaks. Still, twenty metres was a lot of debris. Surely it wasn't raining that hard?

The car door was unlocked, so I slipped into the front seat before anyone had time to spot me. An old newspaper was on the passenger seat, along with a half-empty carton of cigarettes. I rooted around for something to dry my hair with, but found nothing but a few wrappers and empty bottles on the floor. Ridiculous as it sounds, I was hoping I might find Wei Shan himself, taking a kip on the back seat perhaps, or waiting for the cars behind him to clear off so that he could drive back home. No such luck. In the wing mirror I could see Fishlips talking with two men in dark suits. He'd got here pretty sharpish. Hadn't he gone back home? I didn't have time to think about that now though. It was then that I realised why I'd crept into Wei Shan's car. I was steeling myself. Trying to put off making my way to the edge and looking down. I wished I'd bought another bottle.

I stepped out and took a deep breath. As I drew closer to the line of policemen keeping the locals away from the edge, the noise of it all grew louder and more disconcerting. The echo of drills, and the revving of trucks and diggers. The competitive clamour of car horns. The chattering rain and the angry, sloshing growl of wheels caught in the mud. The frantic sobbing and shouting of a group of peasants being herded back from the edge by a gang of policemen. And beneath it all, the relentless groan of machinery booming up from somewhere far below.

Getting past the crowd wasn't as easy as I thought. Those

peasants may look scrawny, but they can be pretty vicious, even while they're blubbering. I couldn't keep track of the number of elbows that came smacking into my stomach as I attempted to shove my way between the throng of dirty, jabbering locals. Half of them were screaming to be let through so that they could get back to their homes or their families on the other side of the slope, as if they hadn't noticed that half of the hill had gone tumbling into the gloom. Didn't do much to disprove my theory that living in the countryside rots your brains.

One of the women started tugging at my arm. 'You're one of them, aren't you?' Her spit sprayed across my cheeks as she spoke.

'Yeah, he is as well. You've got some cheek, showing your face round here after what's happened!'

'Piss off. One of who?'

More of them were turning to stare. I looked around and realised I was about as conspicuous as a eunuch in a brothel. Even though my suit was stained with mud and so soaked it now clung to my skin in soggy creases, it was still a damn sight classier than the old smocks and tatty Mao jackets the rest of the crowd was dressed in. I realised a couple of policemen were even looking at me.

'... yeah, that one. Check him out, all right, Wuya?' I heard one of them say, and the stocky one nearest me stepped out of the line towards me.

'Is that right? You from the mining company?'

'Mining company? No, I'm from the Public Safety Office. My colleague was investigating.' I motioned to the expanse beyond the police tape.

The cop stole a glance back at his partner. 'Bit late for public safety. Fat lot of good you'll be now.'

'Yeah, whatever. Look, I just want to know if you've seen him round here anywhere. Maybe he talked to you lot after the accident. He's about my height, got thick-framed black glasses and —'

The cop sighed. 'I'm sorry.'

I flinched at the pity in his voice. I realised how ridiculous I sounded, but I couldn't stop myself.

'Look, comrade, please, if I could just get through and take a look —'

'No one's coming through. Best thing you can do is go back home and get yourself out of those wet clothes.'

For the few seconds the policemen had turned their attention towards me the pushing and hustling had stopped, and I had been able to squeeze to the front of the crowd. For a brief moment – before the shoving and jostling started back up and I was knocked sideways by a weeping old woman adamant that she would get through the barriers and dig through the fallen mud and brick and earth with her bare hands if she had to – I saw over the cops' shoulders and down into the murky expanse. Only a few metres behind them the whole hillside seemed to suddenly slip into darkness, as if some great chisel had come down and hacked away half the slope. I wasn't sure what I had expected, but it wasn't this. I could see jagged, crumbling edges of rock teetering on the brink, and beyond them nothing but darkness. I could only guess at the wreckage that lay far-off at the bottom, down where the rain-sodden diggers and trucks and tractors were trying to work through the debris.

Shit. I felt dizzy. I felt sick. I needed a drink. I had to get out of there.

I unlocked the door and began scrabbling on the floor at the passenger side for a plastic bag to throw over my seat, though when I squelched down I knew the water would soak through anyway. The police and the army would be there all night, digging up all the mud and brick and fallen rock and trapped corpses and all the other shit down at the bottom of the landslide. What the hell had happened there? Not for the first time in my life, I didn't have a clue what was going on.

I'd spotted Fishlips again as I wandered back between the jeeps, but as he was still nattering away with the two guys in black suits, I decided to stay out of his way and start my journey back across the field to where I'd left my car. Last thing I needed right now was his pity as well. And it wasn't as if Wei Shan ever had a good word to say about him either. I rifled through my glove compartment and managed to unearth an ancient bottle of rice wine. I downed the last of it – even though it tasted like rank old vinegar – before starting the engine.

The road wound back down the slope and soon enough I'd joined the highway heading back towards the city. It was half an hour's drive back to Lanzhou, but I hardly noticed it. I couldn't shake the image of the edge of the cliff from my mind. Could Wei Shan have survived that? Could he have been somewhere else at the time? There was no way of knowing. My tongue was fuzzy from the drink. The windscreen wipers droned on, sloshing back and forth in front of me. I spotted the skyscrapers rearing up ahead and when I crossed the bridge over the river I thanked old Steelguts Mao that I was back. It wasn't long before I was driving through familiar streets, my head lolling forward as my mind reeled. I felt dazed. The street lamps were a mess of orange light. If it hadn't been for the wet suit sticking uncomfortably to my skin, I could have fallen asleep.

Something flashed out and I swerved suddenly, my hands slower than my panic. A dog? My head thumped against the wheel as I hit the brakes and skidded onto the pavement. I pulled myself back and brought my hand to my brow, then my mouth, tasting the sour tang of blood. I was shivering, thirsty. I looked around. The rain had washed the colours from the street. There was a cigarette vendor's kiosk poking out from one of the houses. I tripped on the curb when I got out of the car, but fortunately there was no one around to see it. Everywhere was deserted. Even the dog had disappeared. I banged on the vendor's window. Nothing. I kept banging.

'Fuck off!' someone shouted from inside.

'Fuck you. Open your window, you piece of shit, or I'll send the police around to check your vending license. Then you can see firsthand how much they like being disturbed in the night.'

The window opened and a reluctant old face peered out. 'Yes?'

'Packet of Double Happiness. And a bottle of *baiju*.'

He sighed and nodded. 'Any particular brand?'

'Cheapest'll be just fine.'

I paid him and he shut the window without another word. In the car I opened the little glass bottle and dabbed some liquor on my forehead. It burned, but in a good way. I took a deep swig. Then another. My fingers toyed with the keys as I contemplated turning the engine back on. I ought to go home. My hand fell back to my lap. I would go home – but not while I still had the best part of a bottle left.

That night I dreamt of splintered timber being dragged by rushing water. Rubble, mud, rust. Broken bones. A dark mouth opening and inside nothing but jagged, broken teeth. My eyes were on fire – I could feel them burning through my eyelids. There was a storm in my skull and a terrible ache in my side. I opened my eyes, and the brown checks of the old sofa beneath me struggled to come into focus. My daughter was standing at the hob, stirring millet. Was I dribbling? I wiped my mouth and turned over, letting the broken springs pierce my back.

What time is it? I croaked. My mouth was a desert.

My daughter ignored me. Her hair was knotted back in a ponytail and she was wearing the blue and white tracksuit her school insisted on. Not eight o'clock yet, I guessed. Then I couldn't have slept for more than a few hours. I felt my shirt, my trousers. Still damp. My jacket was crumpled on the floor. Shit, I'd have to change. I stumbled to my feet and found that I was still wearing my shoes.

My daughter shook her head as I made my way to the kitchen. She was fourteen, and looked more like her mother every day. Like her mother did before she got plump and bitter, anyway; like her mother before she gave up smiling. She was going to be beautiful, once her spots cleared up and she stopped hunching her shoulders. I wasn't sure whether that was a good thing or not. Sure, it's hard to nab a decent husband and get ahead in life if you're dog-ugly. But then again I've seen the kind of looks men give beautiful women, heard the kind of things they say. Hell, I've given those kind of looks before, and I've made my fair share of dirty jokes designed to make a woman blush. I thought about asking her how school was going, how things were with her best friend – what was her name? Wei Ling? Mei Ling? Lei Ming? Oh, fuck it. She'd probably just ignore me anyway.

I looked through the cupboards and cursed myself. My wife had thrown out all the drink last month. Poured it down the sink. I'd have to make do with beer. I fought through the collection of teas. How many teas does one woman need? Oolong tea, green tea, barley tea, white tea, red tea, flower tea, lemon tea, lapsang tea, teas to help you sleep, teas to wake you up, teas to help you shit, teas to block you up. All this tea and I can't remember the last time I saw her drink a cup. The clay teapot wrapped in old newspaper at the back, saved for when guests come round. As if. Then I found them. Two bottles of beer coated in dust at the back of the cupboard. The cheapest local brand of horse piss. A woman's drink. It would have to do.

'Where's your mum?'

She raised her eyebrows and turned off the gas at the canister. After filling a single bowl with millet and washing a spoon from the pile of crap in the sink she turned to look at me.

'At work. You stink, did you know that?'

'You know, my dad never would have let any of his children talk to him like that.'

She didn't respond.

Did we have a bottle opener? I wasn't sure. I took the top off with my teeth and drank from the bottle. Shit. I'd forgotten how bubbly it was. I burped and coughed and my daughter shook her head in disgust. I finished the bottle and the storm in my skull began to dull down. The previous night slowly drifted back to me. The restaurant. The news report. The peasants and the police. The end of the world. The *baiju*.

My daughter was doing up her school bag.

'Need a lift?'

She turned and looked me up and down. Her mouth opened, as if she was about to make some sarcastic comment, but she obviously thought better of it. She shook her head. I shrugged. She left.

I'd just showered and was finishing off the second beer, when the phone rang.

'Yep?'

'It's me – Chun Xiao. Is he there?'

Wei Shan's wife. Shit. She always called me if he didn't make it back. Not that he was ever here. But whenever he stayed with his mistress he relied on me to tell his wife that he'd crashed on our sofa and couldn't get to the phone right now, but would be back home soon. He did the same for me when I stayed with Li Yang. Not that my wife ever bothered phoning around to find me anymore.

'Uh, he's not here.'

'Yeah, right. Let me guess. Puking his guts up in your toilet, is he? Too drunk to find his way back home? Tell him Cheung has got the recital tonight, so he'd better not be late.'

Cheung – his son. Shit. Double shit.

'I'm serious. He's not here. Did you see the news last night?'

'No. You think I've got time to sit round watching television while you and my husband are off drinking away his wages? I was on the night shift, you imbecile. Stop mucking about and put Wei Shan on.'

'I can't. He's really not here. I never saw him last night. Listen, around four he got a call to go out and investigate over some safety concerns at Jawbone Hills. He never came back. There was a landslide there, took the whole hillside down. I don't know if he was there at the time or —'

I stopped talking when I heard the dull drone of the dial tone. She'd hung up. Crap. What the hell was I supposed to do now? I could feel my hands shaking. That was all I needed now – to turn into a little girl. I was going to kill Wei Shan if he ever turned up.

I made my way down the five flights of stairs to find the car stretched across two spaces. It was still raining, though now it was more like a light drizzle. I'd left my sodden suit crumpled up on the double bed where my wife slept. I fished my only other good suit out of the wardrobe. It was a little tight these days, but I would rather have gone naked than wear my old blue peasant suit like the saps out in the fields. Just thinking about the countryside made me feel sick, and the events of the last twelve hours hit me with such a force that I had to lean against the car and take a deep breath. I already knew that it was going to be a day from hell.

The city was shrugging off its shadows. Dumplings were steaming on pavement stalls, and businessmen on bicycles slipped between the taxi jams. Storefronts were being unshuttered. Workers trailed muddy footprints across the bridge in yesterday's soggy overalls. A tatty flag was being raised in the town square, and a statue of old Mr Mao pointed above it all to some scrag of dishrag clouds. I went over it all in my mind. Wei Shan got the call. Who called? And why? And how did the hillside collapse? Twenty metres of shit because of a bit of rain? No way. Why did the policeman mention a mining company? I'd be damned if I knew. And the chances were I wouldn't find out now, unless Wei Shan somehow managed to crawl into work with a really good explanation. I clung to that thought, even though I knew it was absurd, because I had to believe there was a possibility that I'd turn up at the office to find him sitting at his desk with that same old scowl on his face.

I flicked through the radio channels as the traffic slowed and shunted together. Snippets of a speech by Deng Xiaoping … some half-warbled western ballad … double-talk routines from the old days … some dull news item about the opening of a school … traffic reports … weather … adverts. I turned it off. Nothing at all about the landslide. No surprise there. As if it had never happened at all.

I spent half the morning lost in my thoughts. Whenever I thought I'd got a handle on one of the blueprints I was supposed to be reviewing, I'd catch a glimpse of Wei Shan's empty desk out of the corner of my eye and after that I'd forget where I was. I wanted to call Li Yang, but it seemed a bit risky from the office phone, what with all the nosy creeps who call themselves my colleagues listening in. I needed a drink.

Fishlips came in late. One of the perks of being the boss, I guess – if any of the rest of us tried it he'd go nuts. Not that he wasn't half deranged most of the time anyway. I crept up on him while he was unlocking the door to his office.

'I saw the news last night.'

Fishlips sighed. 'Have you told anyone?'

'Not yet. Should I?'

'No. I'll talk to everyone later. Just keep it quiet for now, all right?'

'Then you think he was definitely there?'

'According to the logbook, he went to Jawbone Hills late yesterday afternoon. Poor sod. The police found his car up there. It was empty.'

'There must be something we can do. If he's still out there …'

'It's out of our hands now. Beside, they're still digging bodies out of the wreckage. It could be days before we know anything.'

'So we just sit around and wait?'

His face scrunched up into a scowl. 'What do you want me to do? Get out my bucket and spade and drive down to the site? Get a grip. Listen, I'm worried too, but there's no point getting everyone worked up till we find out exactly what's happened. He could still be all right.'

'What about the call?'

'The call?'

'Yesterday. The one that Wei Shan went to investigate.'

'Forget it. There's nothing left to investigate.'

'What about the landslide?'

'What about it? You saw the weather yesterday. Worst storm we've had in years.'

'So it had nothing to do with the mine?'

He stared at me. 'What the hell are you talking about?'

I decided to bluff. 'Wei Shan mentioned something about a mining company before he left.'

'Really? Sure you're not mistaken? Let me guess, you had a few drinks last night and everything's a little foggy? There's no mine up there. Not much of anything. I hate to say it, but it was probably just a prank call.'

'Doubt it. Why would someone do something like that?'

He shrugged. 'I haven't got time to play guessing games. We've got to try to go on as normal. I know that word isn't in your vocabulary, so just do your best to keep it together, all right? I'll let you know when I hear anything. Until then, try not to go blabbing about it to anyone.'

He shut the office door in my face. He'd let me know. Yeah, right.

He was acting like it didn't matter that he'd just lost one of his men. Sure, not one of the best. And pretty easy to replace. But still. I stood outside his office for a minute and clenched and unclenched my fists. None of it made sense. He was being even more shifty than usual. I was glad I hadn't told him I'd gone up there to take a look for myself. Though it would have been nice to see him squirm a bit more.

I made my way back to my desk, but I couldn't get much done. Apart from a few cigarette-breaks, and a trip out at lunch for a bowl of wonton and a little something to take the edge off, it passed much like any other day. The same grey sky mired above. The same clouds of dust and smog swirling up from the factories opposite the office. The same blueprints and planning applications to check through, the same notices to send, inspections to schedule, meetings to arrange. All the usual crap. And when I finally grew tired of pretending to work while I waited for the office phone to ring and bring some news, I left my desk and found the same gang of old women picking through the bins at the bottom of the building for glass or plastic to sell back to the factories, like crows picking through a carcass for the tastiest scraps.

Life likes to trick you like that. You think you're moving forward, but really you're stuck in limbo, living the same day over and over again. And so I did what I usually did, and made my way to the Golden Dragon Seafood Palace, where I sat in the same old table and ordered the same cheap brand of *baiju*, and – even though I felt like a chump when the words came out of my mouth – I even found myself ordering the same old dishes, enough for two, just in case.

It's no fun eating on your own. You're left alone with your thoughts. And the drink goes down too quick. But what else was I going to do? I only had one other real friend – Xiang, over at the newspaper office – but I didn't want to have to tell him about my day. That would only make me feel worse. All my calls to Li Yang's flat went unanswered. And I couldn't face going home and arguing with the wife. I didn't have the energy.

I soon found myself thinking about the night I met Li Yang. I was in the top floor of a restaurant, attending a big cadre's retirement party. There were skinny girls in tight silks handing out drinks. All my colleagues from the office were there with their wives. Big grins fixed on their faces as the same old jokes got trotted out again and again.

It wasn't love at first sight or anything like that. More like a feeling we'd met before, though I couldn't put my finger on when or where. We didn't talk that night. Not a single word. I was standing with my wife anyway, so what was I going to do? But our eyes met. For a second. Maybe two. Time stops. And when it stops you know you're doomed, because whatever happens, when it starts back up nothing is going to be the same. That's what it was like when I first met Li Yang. And that's what it was like when I saw the news about the landslide on TV.

The big bottle we always shared was almost finished – as if a ghost had been taking sips with me each time I raised my glass. I drained the dregs and instantly regretted it, only just managing to stumble out the front door before I spewed onto the road, narrowly missing my shoes. You get an interesting perspective on life bent double on the street. The wonky paving stones blurring and unbuckling before your eyes. The whole meal you've just forked out for replayed in reverse. And shoes. My scuffed, snub-toed work shoes looking pretty damn woeful. There was a time my wife would have polished them for me before work each morning. Or at least commented on their appearance. I had to buy some new shoes before I met up with Li Yang. Or else risk looking like some pathetic hick.

An old lady tottering down the street tutted at me, so I pulled myself up straight and told her to mind her own fucking business. Old people, they think they own the world. I wiped my mouth with the bottom of my sleeve then made my way back inside and ordered a beer to wash the rank taste of puke from my mouth. Leaning back in my chair, I let the restaurant whirr around me.

Why did I keep coming back here? There were insect stains on the walls, greasy puddles on the floor. More surprisingly, there were actually a few customers in tonight. All men, sitting hunched over their bowls as if to make sure that not a single reel of steam escaped them. Some were smoking, others staring at their hands. All of them were stealing time they didn't have, time they'd have to pay back somehow. Trust me, that's how it always works.

By the time another morning rolled to its close and I'd spent another four hours staring at Wei Shan's empty desk, I was getting fidgety. Fishlips was doing his best to stay so far away from me that anyone would have thought I reeked of raw sewage. But that could have meant anything. I couldn't stop my mind from plodding back to the landslide. Wei Shan was a drunk and a bore, but if he didn't turn up soon I worried I might end up talking to myself. Or, even worse, I might be forced to make conversation with some of the cretins and jerks here in the office. Things were getting desperate. I tried phoning Xiang, only to be told he was out on assignment. Then I tried Li Yang, but once again there was no answer. I remember Wei Shan once complaining that there wasn't much point having a mistress if you couldn't pop round and see her whenever you wanted. I knew how he felt.

So it was either spend lunchtime stewing in the Golden Dragon – on my own, again – and fritter the afternoon away until it was time to go home, or do something about this whole mess. I chose option number two – after all, if I didn't find him, who on earth was going to lie to my wife about where I was next time I met up with Li Yang?

And anyway, I refused to accept that he was dead. Not until I knew for sure. The odds were certainly against him strolling back into work without a scratch. But you can't take anything at face value these days. Take Socialism with Chinese Characteristics, for example – sounds like a con, doesn't it? Like a get-out clause. A poorly thought-out excuse for abandoning close to thirty years of ardent communist struggle and deciding to follow the capitalist road instead. But that's just what we want them to think. This is where some sap usually starts up, telling us the revolution has therefore failed. But, you see, this is just the next phase. It's low-key, sure. Low-key enough to fool the foreigners, to get the Americans pouring all their money in and setting up their factories here. But once everything improves, that will be the time when the socialist paradise springs to life. How can you expect a hundred people to share one bowl of rice? That was the first mistake. But we've learnt from it. Once we've got all the rice we need, all the engines, the re-actors, the turbines, the jets, the bullion, the rockets, the satellites, the factories, the investments and the stocks, once we've built the flats and the tower blocks and the schools and the hospitals, then we'll be able to start up the real revolution. And believe me, I can't wait. Sure, things might be a bit up in the air right now, and I'm sorry that any poor fellow can't wander into a hospital like before and see a doctor without bribes or name-dropping or special hand-shakes, but it's just for the short term. We have to put up with the mess now, but when the time comes and the means of production and all its juicy perks get shared out again, well, we're damn sure going to be the greatest nation this planet has ever seen.

As soon as the clock in the office hit twelve I was out the door. But not for long. I grabbed a little pick-me-up from the kiosk on the corner before turning around and heading right back inside. But I wasn't going to the same floor. You see, half the local government departments are stacked up in the same building. Us up on the fourth. Immigration and Traffic Control on the third. Department for Social Order and Re-education on the second. Then the police right at the bottom. I knew from experience that it wasn't worth phoning down. They either tell you to piss off or else some dopey phone operator shunts your call between different desks. I know, because we do much the same thing at the Public Safety Office when interfering busybodies try to wheedle information out of us. But hopefully if I flashed my ID around enough, it shouldn't be that hard to get taken to the police officer I'd spoken with at the top of the hill. Wuya, his partner had called him. Officer Wuya. If I was really lucky, he might even remember me from the other night.

After bullshitting the police receptionist for a few minutes with a half-arsed story about seeing Officer Wuya with regards to a new governmental initiative for interdepartmental co-operation, I followed the corridor down to the far end of the building.

There were cops everywhere. Cops jostling scruffy men in hand-cuffs. Cops spitting. Cops yakking. Cops smoking. Cops picking their noses. Cops sleeping at their desks. Cops playing with their phones. Cops playing with their balls. Cops pretending to read newspapers. Cops staring out of windows. Not sure I saw any of them actually doing any work.

Some people are pretty easy to dupe. The key is in your walk. Stalk around nervously and you'll get kicked out before you can even open your mouth. Stroll regally down the halls like you own the place, however, and no one will think to question your presence. It didn't take me long to spot Wuya – first bit of good luck in a week. He was sitting at a messy desk in his own cramped workspace halfway down the office, twirling a pair of silver worry balls in his palm. His whole appearance could be summed up in two words: fat and greasy. I cleared my throat while waiting for him to look up and spot me.

'Yeah? Do you want something?'

'I'm from the Public Safety Office upstairs. We met the other night. At Jawbone Hills.'

He sat up in his chair and set his worry balls in the little velvet box in front of him.

'And?'

'I wanted to talk to you about the investigation into the land-slide. Maybe I could see the report?'

'Huh. What makes you think you've got the authority to do that? Just because you work for the Public Safety Office? You guys are a joke. Public safety? All you lot do is examine bridges, mines, building sites. That's not public safety. It's the guys in here who guar-antee public safety. They're the ones out there solving the crimes, getting attacked by criminal gangs and venturing into the depths of the earth all for just a fraction of what you get paid for sitting in a comfy office up there and looking at blueprints. You really think you can just wander in here and demand to see the private files? Piss off.'

'Hey, I'm just doing my job. My colleague was investigating up there when the landslide happened.'

'Yeah, yeah. I remember. But what do you want me to say? I didn't get there till long after the slope had collapsed.'

'You could at least tell me what happened. Come on, if one of the guys in here got killed in the line of duty, you'd want to make sure you found out what had gone down.'

His brow furrowed and he shook his head. 'You were there. You saw what happened. Half a fucking mountain fell down. What bit of that sentence doesn't make sense to you?'

'I also saw diggers, trucks, tractors. That was almost forty-eight hours ago. And it's twenty-odd hours since the rain stopped. How much digging do you lot need to do before you find the bodies and inform the families?'

He shifted in his chair. 'As soon as we identify a body, we inform the next of kin. But it's not that simple. You do know there's a river at the bottom of that valley, don't you? It's impossible to say whether any bodies might have got carried away.'

'So you think you might never find my colleague – or any of the relatives of those people you were holding back the other night?'

'That's not what I said. And you needn't worry about those pathetic saps in the countryside – almost every one of their relatives turned up safe and sound in the end.'

I stared at him. 'Bullshit.'

'Nope. I'm deadly serious. All a lot of crying over nothing.'

'I can't believe it.'

'Suit yourself. But it's true. Maybe your colleague will turn up too. But till he does, there's nothing more I can do for you. So if you don't mind, I've got another thirteen minutes of my lunch break left before I have to hit the streets, and I'd rather not spend it having to deal with all your pedantic questions. I'm sorry, but shit happens. If you want to blame someone, blame the damn rain.'

'The rain? So the landslide had nothing whatsoever to do with the mine there?'

He sat up straight. 'There's no mine there.'

'One of the peasant women mistook me for someone who worked in a mine. You even asked me about it yourself. Don't you remember?'

'I remember those sly peasants saying any old crap they could think of to try to get past the barrier. You didn't believe anything they said, did you?'

'Fuck you. You can't fob me off that easily.'

His lips twitched into a sneer. 'Insulting a police officer. That's nice. Really professional. I'd be careful about what you say next, though, because if you look around you might notice that you're in a room full of cops who don't much like being slagged off by petty bureaucrats.'

I wanted to smack him in the jaw. The pompous prick. Lying bastard. I clenched my fists so hard my fingers began to ache. Then I turned around and marched right out of there, ignoring the sound of sniggers behind my back. I mean, what else was I going to do?

If you tell a lie long enough you begin to believe it. If you look back far enough you'll see even the shittiest times are reworked by the sickly haze of nostalgia. What I'm trying to say is that you can't trust your senses. But I couldn't ignore the fact that something wasn't right. In fact, it was seriously fucked up.

My lunch hour was almost over, but I was still slumped in a tiny noodle restaurant across the road, trying to shake off my rage. The last bubbly dregs of a nasty local beer fizzed in the cup in front of me. Either I'd now been told the same lie twice – which must mean people thought I was a gullible, simple-minded cretin – or else I really was losing it and my memory had been pickled by too much of the good stuff. In that case, another one couldn't hurt.

Could they have said something else? Did I mishear them? I pushed my little finger deep into my ear, trying to dig out some of the wax. Of course, everyone knows that people who live in the countryside and choose to work on farms must be mentally deficient in some way. Most of them are inbred too. It goes without saying that they're therefore likely to spout a loud of crap whenever they open their pinched mouths and expose their rotten brown teeth. But why would they bother to concoct a story about something that wasn't there? I finished my drink and waved for the waiter. And odder still, how could a landslide that accumulated so much debris have created so few casualties? There must have been at least thirty peasants there that evening, each one shrieking about houses or relatives on the side of the hill – did every single one of their family members really turn up unharmed? If so, where on earth had they been hiding that night? I'd seen the jagged rocks jutting out into nothingness – surely no one could have climbed back out of that?

In short, I was stumped. I looked at my watch. The afternoon shift had just begun. I leant back in my chair. Fuck it. I ordered another drink. There wasn't much point going in now. All I'd end up doing was watching the mess of files that I couldn't be bothered to check pile up higher. Or else see Fishlips bumbling about in his office, no doubt already arranging interviews to get someone to take over Wei Shan's empty desk. His desk. Shit! The little scrap of notepaper that had told me where Wei Shan was going that afternoon. What had it said? Jawbone Hills – of course. That was a no-brainer. And something about a foreman – Jing Ren? Yes, that was it. But if there wasn't a mine or a building site or a construction centre there, then why the hell would there be a foreman?

I left the restaurant and dashed across the road to a payphone at a newspaper kiosk. I knew the number to Xiang's office by heart. Luckily, he picked up.

'Lanzhou Daily newsdesk.'

'Xiang, it's me. I need a favour.'

'I'll try to sound surprised, shall I? Is there ever any other reason you call?'

'Yeah, yeah. Look, I need you to find an address. You see, I've got this complicated problem and —'

'All right, all right. I don't need the grisly details. Go on, just give me the name.'

'Jing Ren. From the nature of his job, I'd guess he'd probably be between thirty and fifty, if that narrows the search down. And odds are he lives west of the city, maybe somewhere along Highway 312.'

'Okay, I'll see what I can do.'

'I owe you one. Dinner tonight?'

'Sure. I'll meet you at that little dump you love. Silver Dinosaur Fish Castle, isn't it?'

'Very funny. I'll see you at seven-ish. By the way, can you call me back when you find the address?' I gave him the number of the payphone. 'I'll be waiting.'

'No problem.'

I paid the guy in the kiosk, giving him a little extra and telling him to wave over at me when his phone started ringing, then made my way back across the street to the restaurant. My second bottle had arrived, and, feeling pleased with myself, I ordered some boiled nuts and spicy cucumber to go with it. I'd barely had time to touch any of these, though, when I saw the man across the road waving frantically. I dashed over and listened as Xiang relayed the address.

Thank the mighty Politburo! At last, I thought, as I put down the receiver and started jogging back towards the car. At last, someone who could explain this whole sorry mess.

Even as I drove out towards Jing Ren's flat, I was feeling somehow freer, buoyed by the knowledge that soon the whole thing would be cleared up. I couldn't wait, especially since I knew that I'd continue to feel restless and uneasy until it all made sense. After all, I had to tell Wei Shan's wife something. And his son. Maybe even his mistress too. I owed him that much. Problem is, sometimes the truth is too much to ask.

It didn't take me long to find the address Xiang had given me. I was surprised that it was nowhere near as close to the outskirts as I'd assumed – in fact, Jing Ren appeared to live in a nicer area than me. On his road were a couple of restaurants, a laundry and a new fast-food place. Lucky bastard. How much were they paying him? And how did he get out to Jawbone Hills every day? That was some commute. I had so many questions to ask him that I didn't know where to begin. Once I'd parked the car and wandered into the building, some absurd impulse led me to sprint up the stairwell, two or three steps in each bound, so by the time I reached the fourth floor I was a wreck of wheezes and coughs, with my heart going crazy in my chest. I had to lean against the wall for a minute before the corridor stopped spinning. Fortunately, I'd had the foresight to stock up on Double Happiness. I lit one up and waited till the light stopped dancing in front of my eyes and the walls grew still. Then I made my way down the hall – nice, plush blue carpet with only a handful of cigarette burns and scuffs – till I found 406.

I spent a good few minutes pounding on it – if he worked in a mine, there was a good chance his hearing was pretty messed up from all the deafening drilling and digging. But no one answered. It was only then that I thought about trying the handle. It's not something I usually do. But if you're dumb enough to leave your door unlocked, then in my opinion you get what you deserve. And it turns out that Jing Ren was either pretty naïve or pretty forgetful, because his front door opened – with a gentle shove – on the first try.

As soon as I set foot inside I realised that I wasn't going to get the answers I was looking for. I was tempted to head downstairs to call Xiang and ask him what the hell he was playing at. There was no way the guy who lived here was a foreman. Near the entrance stood a two-metre-tall Ming vase decorated with beautiful paintings of concubines playing all manner of musical instruments. There was a squat, bronze Fu Lion on the counter, and a rug on the wall that looked as if it had come all the way from the deserts of Yarkand. There was a strange jade sculpture that resembled some kind of huge bird near one of the doors, and a fancy painting near the sofa. Not only was the place pristine, but it had more books than a library. There was a huge line of shelves against the far wall and a pile of books set out on the coffee table in front of the brown leather sofa. There were books stacked on the floor, and a few stray ones even piled up on the kitchen table. Now, I didn't know much about mining, but I was pretty damn sure you couldn't get much reading done deep in the bowels of the earth, even if you had one of those yellow hardhats with a torch stuck on the front.

It was pretty conceivable that there were two men with the same name in the west of the city. Xiang had obviously found the wrong one. But I was here now. I made my way over to the closest shelf to have a quick look around. I'd come all this way – it seemed a shame not to have a peek. Not that I'd heard of most of the books this guy had. Myth and Mysticism in the Age of Qin Shi Huang. Corvid Taxonomy. Comparative Linguistics and Social Semantics. The Untold Story Behind the Caves of the Thousand Buddhas in Mogao. Ornithology in the Age of the Warring States. Animism

Among the Shiwei. An Archaeological Overview of the Neolithic Sites in Manchuria. The only explanation that made sense to me was that whoever lived here was a rich insomniac who bought books purely on their potential to put him to sleep.

As I wandered along, I caught sight of a framed photo near the top of one of the shelves. It showed a thin, wiry man with thick eyebrows that met in the middle and round glasses holding up a diploma or certificate and smiling shyly at the camera. Jing Ren? There was no way that scrawny guy could have hacked it in a mine.

I made my way over to the kitchen to see if he had anything decent to drink. There was nothing in the fridge apart from a bottle of soya milk, a few wilting cabbages and a couple of eggs. A quick survey of the cupboards and cabinets yielded better results – tucked away between the rice-cooker and the packets of millet and flour was a bottle of Maotai *baiju*, still in the fancy packaging. A gift from someone who needed a favour? Or something he saved for special occasions to impress his guests? I took the bottle out and, since it was already half empty, decided there wouldn't be any harm in having a little taste. It was pretty potent – as if it had been squeezed straight from pure, fat clouds – and it left a warm, sweet tingle at the back of my throat. Not bad. But still – why bother wasting a week's wages on the posh stuff when you can get the job done for a handful of change?

I was just slipping the bottle back into its little box when I heard the door creak open behind me. Shit. I knew I should have made a run for it when I saw all the antiques. Or at least locked the door behind me. Shit. I needed a good excuse, and quick, because all this expensive crap told me that the guy who lived here could probably afford to keep a few cops or lawyers in his pocket, and he was not going to be impressed to see me rummaging through his possessions.

'Jing Ren?'

The voice was hesitant and frail. When I turned I saw an old man – and I mean seriously old, with white hair and thick bifocals and wrinkles so deep they looked as if they had been carved into his pale skin – clutching the door and peering into the apartment. I let out a sigh of relief: no one enters their own flat so tentatively. A friend? A relative? Some nosy neighbour? When he saw me, his brow furrowed into a frown.

'Jing Ren? Is that you?'

'No, kind uncle, I'm … I'm one of Jing Ren's colleagues.'

'Ah yes, of course, you're from the university. I thought I recognised you.'

'That's right. I just came to check up on Jing Ren.'

'As did I, my friend, as did I. He always seems to be out these days.'

'Yes, it seems I've missed him again. I really must be going, uncle, but please tell Jing Ren that I was looking for him.'

'Oh, everyone is always in such a hurry these days. Come, why not have a seat and wait a little with me? I'm sure Jing Ren will be happy to see us when he returns. And perhaps he will be back soon.'

Well, I couldn't exactly leave then without looking shifty. So I pulled out a chair and sat down next to the old man at the kitchen table.

'Now, tell me, are you also a member of the history faculty?'

'Yes … yes, I am.'

'Wonderful, wonderful. That's what drew Jing Ren and me together, you know. Many a night we would while away the time nattering about the past. Of course, our areas of interest did not strictly overlap. I've always been fascinated by the Tang Dynasty, you see. The age of the great poets – Li Bai, Du Fu, Bai Juyi. In a thousand years, I don't think they have ever been bettered. Maybe Jing Ren has mentioned my talent to you: I can rattle off hundreds of their poems from memory. And the great artists, the palace intrigues, the scheming eunuchs. Ha! A golden age, I do believe, and I think Jing Ren agreed, though he put up valiant arguments for the pre-eminence of his own beloved period, the age of Qin Shi Huang. But listen to me prattle on. How about you, are your interests ancient or modern?'

'Modern. I'd definitely have to say modern.'

'Ah, I see. Forgive me; I do not mean to offend, but I must admit that I am not a fan of more modern history. I find it somewhat depressing. You know, here's a curious thing: the older I become, the further back I find myself looking. I find it terribly calming, to escape into the past. But I hardly need to tell you that! We must stick together, men like you and me, for I fear we are something of a dying breed. All young people today seem to want to do is look forwards. Blinkered. Why, even my own son seems more concerned about making money and moving upwards than paying attention to the traditions and customs of our ancestors. Sad, isn't it? Between you and me, I can't help thinking that the Japanese have it right. While we desecrated our temples and burnt down many of our sacred sites during the Cultural Revolution, they safeguarded their heritage. Take a look at the traditional tea ceremony or the enduring popularity of the kimono – both originally from China, of course – and you'll see that they've protected their ancient culture while we have consigned much of ours to the scrapheap. Is there anything worse than turning your back on your history?'

I stared at him. The old man was clearly a raving loony. It was hard not to lose my temper with him. Insulting the work of the great Chinese Communist Party was one thing, but then to go and praise the Japanese too? Surely he was old enough to remember what they did up in Manchuria. If I ever get that old and stupid, I hope someone puts me out of my misery.

'No, I'm not sure there is. Listen, when did you last see Jing Ren?'

'Well, now that you mention it, I haven't seen him since Monday. But that's not unusual. He hasn't had much time for our little chats since he started his sabbatical back in September. Always out and about, at all hours of the day.'

I looked around. Something was stirring at the back of my mind. I decided to bluff.

'Hmm. You know, last time I visited, I don't remember seeing that beautiful Ming vase. Has he always had it?'

'Oh no. I've never seen it before either, to tell you the truth. In fact, the whole flat used to be pretty empty. Dusty and desolate. I used to tease him about it. Get yourself a wife, I told him – a good woman will soon make this place feel like a real home. No, he only started buying all this stuff recently. And why not? There are some fantastic pieces here. If I had the money, I'd do the same.'

'Yes … me too.' I stood up, and bowed my head. Something wasn't right, but there was only one way to make sure.

'I've had a lovely time chatting with you, uncle, but I'm afraid I have to go. I'll have to catch up with Jing Ren another day. Afternoon lectures, you see. And exams to set. You know how it is.'

'I understand. Please, don't let me keep you. If I waffle on sometimes, it's only because it is so rare for me to get the chance to converse with someone who shares my interests. I hope I will see you again?'

'I'm sure we'll bump into each other soon.'

I plastered a false smile on my face as I shook his hand and made my way out of the flat. Poor old git. Probably just wants someone to talk to. But something he said had stuck in my mind. Perhaps Xiang hadn't sent me to the wrong Jing Ren after all. But what did that mean?

I was still trying to puzzle it out when I reached the bottom of the building and emerged into the sunlight. I bought a small bottle to calm my head, gulped down a few mouthfuls and then got into my car. There was nothing for it. I was going to have to go back to the scene of the accident.

I followed the road west, out towards the highway. I couldn't stop thinking about what that old man had been saying. He must have been off his rocker. History? Give me a break. If you ask me, life is little more than a constant series of repetitions. You have a late night on the hooch, so you feel like shit when you wake up, so you start sipping again to ease the hangover. It's as simple as that. The sun rises, then sets, then rises again. As the history teacher told us at school, China was disparate, then was united, then was broken up, then united once more. Civilisations fall while others rise. War follows peace just as inevitably as peace follows war. Boom then bust, birth then death, summer then winter; we start a job, we finish the job, then we move on to the new job. History? There's no such thing.

# The Whorehouse of a Thousand Sighs

Silk's eyelids soon glued shut against the hollow socket. She had a leather patch that the Empress told her she had to wear when guests arrived, but most of the time she didn't bother with it. We soon got used to the sight of the sunken crater where her eye used to be, the dark lashes knotted across the middle like a badly stitched seam. It looked painful, and I wanted to ask her if she was still able to prise it open if she tugged on the lids, but the Empress had instructed us all not to mention it unless Silk did first.

By the time Silk first re-emerged from the wooden hut to eat with us, Tiger was already up and about, though she was still a little woozy and unsteady on her feet. Claws was eating with us too that day; as usual she and Tiger weren't talking to each other, though I could not help but notice that Claws' nails had been bitten down to the quick.

Silk sat down without a word, a forced smile fixed on her face. Claws reached across to the freshly fired *nang* and tore off a strip of hot bread. She passed it to Silk, who took it and started eating. And that was that. No apologies, no arguments, no mention of the fight; nothing. What good is sorry anyway? It doesn't make a difference to anything at all, as far as I can see. They had both spent the last couple of moons holed up thinking the whole thing over, remembering every little detail again and again, and I don't think either one had it in them to go back there.

A few weeks later, when we were collecting the camel dung for the cook's fire, Silk told us that when she had lost her eye, she had gained the ability to see images of the future. Before, you'd have expected Claws to have pulled a face or made some kind of remark, but she just nodded, as if it was the most natural thing in the world.

'If I hold my hand up over my good eye, and really focus, I can see out of the missing one. It's almost as if it's still there. And everything slowly begins to take shape – like the clouds, little clumps of light swirling into different forms and patterns.'

'Pictures?'

'Pictures, signs, omens.'

'Do you think they are messages from the spirits?' I asked.

'Maybe. I'm not sure where they come from.'

'So what have you seen?' Tiger asked.

Silk looked at her blankly.

'I mean, what is the purpose of having a gift if you don't use it? You have two legs, so you walk around instead of crawling on your hands, don't you? So if you can see the future, then what can you tell us about tomorrow?'

'Tomorrow?'

'Yes. Will we wake up and find ourselves married to princes? Will we suddenly find we look five summers younger and have new jewellery? Or will the camels puke in the washing basket again?'

Silk giggled, then covered her good eye. The sunken, empty socket on the other side stayed scrunched shut. Could she really see through that little crack between her eyelids? Or was the dead eye – wherever it might be – somehow sending its old owner reflections of everything that passed before it?

'Ok. Tomorrow. Hmm, we're going to meet something small. Maybe a bird or a dog or ... yes, that's it, a child!'

Claws looked up, her hands tightening around bunches of her robe.

'I don't think so,' Tiger snorted. 'I've had enough of that poison to make sure there's nothing left inside of me.'

I tried to make light of the situation. 'So either a baby bird is going to fall from its nest on us or a wolf cub is going to come and bother us for food, then.'

Silk smiled, but the other two just went back to scooping up the round pellets. No one wanted to talk about children. And besides, the idea was ludicrous. We'd had a few stray customers popping in from time to time, but we hadn't had a full caravan stop over for many moons. What with Tiger and Silk hidden away in the wooden huts up in the cook's courtyard, me bruised and Claws sulking, the customers hadn't been much impressed with the place. Word had gone round, and our reputation had taken a bit of a battering, although Tall and Homely could still count on their regulars. So the idea of a child appearing, or of one of us getting pregnant, was about as likely as Silk's eye growing back. But that didn't stop it happening.

The Empress had been going a bit crazy. We'd had so little trade that she hadn't been able to get much of the sweet tea or raisins she craved, and in the end she decided that if she was going to get the business back on track then she'd have to fork out for another resident. And so it happened that one morning Tall was sent to summon a donkey cart to carry her down to the bazaar. The four of us got on with our darning and took turns guessing what kind of girl she'd bring back. Claws thought she'd be looking for a really young one, while Tiger predicted she'd try to find a girl with yellow hair – even though Claws was adamant that there was no such thing. I thought she would look for one of those Xiongnu the official's companion had talked about, though I wasn't really sure what they looked like. None of us expected her to come back with a boy.

He was short and scrawny, with a greasy crop of hair and restless green eyes. Tiger said he could have been my baby brother. He can only have been ten or eleven, and the first couple of days with us he didn't say a single thing. Not a peep. With her usual delight in bestowing ridiculous names, the Empress said we would call him Boy. Since he looked too small for any heavy work she'd got him for a bargain. Though he had to stay in the boys' shared room across the courtyard with Tall and Homely, she didn't want him picking up any of their bad habits just yet so she told us to look after him for the time being. Somehow, what with the others fleeing at the first sight of our new arrival, the responsibility fell to me.

'So where are you from? No, don't want to tell me? That's all right. I reckon I can guess anyway. A little village on the edge of the desert? Am I right? Don't look so surprised – it's Silk that thinks she's a visionary, not me. Just a lucky guess. I used to live down near the desert as well, you see.

'I could introduce you to everyone down here right away, but I've got a feeling you'd rather meet our friends up the track first. It's a bit steep, so mind your step. Do you want to take my hand? There we go.'

He grudgingly placed his clammy hand in mine and I led him up the hill to the small courtyard where the cook was fanning the small dung fire with his makeshift bellows. The sick rooms, thank the spirits, had all been cleaned out and the place seemed calm. I led Boy over to the camels and showed him how to tickle behind their tiny tufty ears, how to stroke them gently and how to milk the smaller one. We took a clay cup and drank some of the watery yellow liquid, and I laughed as he screwed up his face at the sour tang. The hairy beasts ignored him as he ran his hands through their matted brown coats, and I even lifted him so he could trace the ridges of their hard hunchbacks. He seemed so taken with them that, after a few words with the cook, I hoisted him up and helped him wedge himself between the two humps of the shorter camel. For the first time, I saw his lips briefly curl upwards, before he realised what he was doing and promptly corrected his expression into a frown.

It was easy to talk to him as we walked around, his big green eyes staring up at me as I told him about my father and his schemes and all the other things I remembered from those lazy childhood villages, and I think I even started jabbering on about the stories my father used to tell about the crows. He never said a word, so I just kept on nattering. I said things I wouldn't have said to the others. I told him that he had to keep a little clump of his hometown soil deep down in his stomach, and I promised if he did that a little bud would sprout and, if he kept tending to it and never let it tangle and knot his gut, then he'd always have a piece of his home growing inside him. No matter what else happened, I said, no one could take that away from him. He didn't say a thing.

Later that night, I was tumbling through a sea of agitated dreams when I was woken by the sound of someone knocking on the door to our room. At first I thought it was one of the other girls unable to get back in, but when I saw all three of them sleeping soundly on their patches of straw I cursed my luck – it was probably a midnight customer wanting the quickest of treats. I pinned my hair up in a raggedy bun and pinched my cheeks to bring a bit of colour to them, then opened the door to see Boy standing there, his eyes staring down at his dirty feet.

'Bad dream?'

He nodded.

I reached out my hand and led him in. He snuggled down beside me on my small patch of straw, and we lay back to back as the dark settled around us.

He would keep coming to our room whenever he could after that. We get a lot of homesick men looking for comfort, but it wasn't like that. It was always the same: we never touched or even said a word to each other. Though I'm sure it couldn't have escaped the other girls' attention that we often received a visitor in the dead of night, they were kind enough to pretend not to notice. At first I told myself I let him sleep beside me because it comforted him, because it seemed to soothe away his fears. I was doing a good deed, helping a child with night terrors. But the truth was I think I needed to feel him close more than he needed me. You forget what closeness is. I don't mean touching or squeezing or any of the stuff the customers pay extra for, and I don't mean things like combing out the knots in the other girls' hair. I mean real closeness. When you forget where you are and all you feel is the warmth of the body next to you.

Out in the courtyard one afternoon – it must have been a couple of weeks after he arrived, just as the weather began to turn and we expected an upturn in business – Boy asked me why he was there. I told him. He had to find out sooner or later, and it was better coming from me than from Tall or Homely.

'It's going to hurt the first time, but don't give them the satisfaction of letting them know that,' I said.

He nodded. He'd seen it happen to some of the other boys on the trip out, after they had been rounded up and their hands had been tied and their journey into the desert had begun. He shook when he told me this, bunched his knees up so high that he could lean his head on them. But still that wasn't what he meant. He wanted to know why he was here, while all the other boys in his hometown who hadn't ventured north and got taken by bandits were still outside playing, waiting for their daddies to come home so that they could have their dinner.

'He never gave me a beating except when I stole food or said something really bad. Once I took my sister's dress and hid it up a tree – just for a joke, you know, because my brother dared me – and my father gave me such a walloping I was howling like a girl by the end of it. My legs really stung, but I knew what it was for. But what's this for? What have I done?'

I didn't know what to tell him. I didn't know what I'd done to deserve it either. Maybe I ought to have told him that he shouldn't even listen to those kind of thoughts because all they do is sink your heart in quicksand, but the surest way to make a child keep doing something is to tell him not to do so, so I had to think carefully about what I said. In the end I told him that sometimes we just have to do things we don't like, and later we'll get something back in return. I told him everything balances out in the end, even if it doesn't seem that way now. I didn't believe a word of it, but I said it anyway, and at least it stopped him asking any more questions.

He was in pretty bad shape after his first party. I stayed up all night after our guests had fallen asleep, trying to comfort him and stop his sobs from waking any of them and getting us in real trouble. We were sitting in the courtyard amidst the half-empty clay cups and the greasy mutton bones, huddled together in a pile of blankets. I was stroking Boy's hair and telling him about my first moons here and how I got through them and all the silly tantrums the girls had and anything else that came into my head to take his mind away from his ache, and I think I had just got him calm when we heard the moan. He nuzzled in closer and we waited a few minutes in the freezing darkness, wondering if we would hear it again. After a while we caught it: a long, drawn-out rasp stretching into the night.

'Don't worry, I think it's probably just a wounded dog, lost in the dark,' I whispered.

'If it's hurt, shouldn't we help it?'

I wasn't sure what to say. I had expected him to ask whether it might be dangerous, or if it might be some wolf or vengeful spirit or wild man come to tear chunks of flesh from our shivering bodies. But he was right. If this thing – whatever it was – was hurt, then we could hardly just sit around and listen to it slowly die. Neither of us could have stomached that. I got to my feet.

'Stay here,' I whispered.

'No.'

'No?'

'I can help. If it's hurt, I can help.'

I didn't bother arguing. He took my hand and we tiptoed out of the courtyard and onto the dirt track leading to the gate, the blankets still clutched about our shoulders and our bare feet scuffing through the frosty mud. The moon was pulsing down, threatening to burst and flood the sky with yellow light. A spluttered, phlegmy cough echoed out from somewhere below us, and we picked our way down the track towards it. It obviously heard us coming, because as we got closer there was a shuffling and the clatter of wood. By then I knew it wasn't any kind of wild dog, but I didn't want to scare Boy, so I said nothing. The rocks crunched and spat as whatever it was skidded further down.

We spotted him lying gasping for breath in a thin ditch between one of the weed-tacked ridges and dips. He must have been about Tiger's age, though he looked older at the time, his face flecked with dust and grime, his grubby beard slick with sweat. It was easy to see from his round cheeks and narrow eyes that he was, like Claws, from the middle kingdom. A long way from home. He wore the last tattered scales of leather armour over his mud-stained robe, and a bulky wooden box was strapped to his back. When he saw us above him he started to scramble away again, his elbows hauling the rest of his body down through the dirt. His exertions achieved little, however, and he soon gave up and collapsed into the mud. I put a hand to Boy's chest, stopping us a few paces away from the panting man. One of his calves was a mangled knot of frayed muscles and flapping skin. The dirty white of what I guessed had to be bone burned out in the moonlight and the foot beneath it twitched like a lizard's tail.

He lay there breathing heavily as we edged closer and raised a hand to the box on his back. Two of his fingers were missing and his thumb was twisted backward at the joint. His eyes met mine.

'Please,' he whimpered. I was right – he was from the middle kingdom. But then how had he ended up here on his own?

I wasn't sure what to do. We couldn't just leave him here and turn back. Could we?

'Please.'

I took a step forward and squatted down, close to his face. Dribble was slithering out over his cracked lip.

'You're hurt. Who did this to you?'

His eyes darted around and he spoke again, a jumble of frantic syllables that I had trouble following.

'We've got those two spare huts up at the top,' Boy said, and I noticed he had crouched down beside me.

'No,' I said.

'Why?'

'They're sick rooms.'

'He looks pretty sick.'

'But it's too dangerous.'

'Why?'

'Because we don't know who he is.'

'So?'

'So I said no.'

'Why?'

I was about to send him back up with a stern warning when I saw the look on his face, that little gleam of excitement and animation that only a few minutes ago had been obscured by tears.

I sighed. 'Are you going to keep on like this if we don't take him back with us?'

'Yep.'

'Then I suppose we don't have a choice.'

I bound one of the blankets round the man's bloody leg, but he pushed Boy's hand away when he tried to take the box from his back. In the end Boy and I took an arm each and hauled him up as he balanced on his good leg, then let him lean across both of us as he limped back up the track. We had to stop for him to catch his breath four or five times, and by the time we passed by the entrance gate he was almost unconscious. We tiptoed so as not to wake the snoring cook and his snoring camels and shouldered open one of the wooden huts to dump the bearded man on a reeking pile of straw and musty old blankets in the middle of the floor. The wooden box fell at his side. Pulling Boy out of the hut, I swung the door closed and bolted it from the outside. If he was carrying any secrets or dangers with him – and really, what else would an injured man making some kind of desperate journey across the hills in the middle of the night be carrying? – then I didn't want them spilling out.

The song the desert sings is a song of regret. You can hear it when the wind carries through the sand. It is a song for the seasons that pass and a song for the things that you couldn't change. Once you've heard it, the song slips into some part of your body and stays there, and you hear it again whenever you're least expecting it. Perhaps it creeps in through those holes in the heart Silk told me about. Perhaps I'm just being silly. But the things that you should have done, the things you didn't do – they stay with you. It's as though I spend half my time living in the mirror of my life, where everything turned out a little bit differently. And maybe that's why I did what Boy suggested without worrying too much about what might happen later on. I sometimes wonder if it wouldn't have been better to leave the bearded man to die out there. Better for me, better for Claws, and probably better for the man himself in the long run.

Waking the next morning, listening to the previous evening's guests saddling up and joking about money well spent, I thought perhaps I had imagined the whole thing. But what if I hadn't? I knew the other girls would do the same thing I always did after a late party – doze away until their stomachs called them up for lunch. I pulled on a warm robe and ventured out into the chilly morning.

The cook was scrubbing a pile of dirty bowls, the last of the breakfast broth going cold in his big clay urn. Apart from him, the place was deserted. I took a bowl and tried to think of a way to get into the hut to tell the bearded man to get out of here before anyone noticed.

'Those camels are looking a little famished,' I said.

'Huh?' the cook grunted.

'The camels. I was saying they look a little peckish. There's still some good grazing lower down the hill, isn't there?'

He shrugged. 'Might be.'

'Only their milk won't be good if they don't get enough to eat, will it?'

He dropped the dirty bowl he was holding into the water bucket and looked up at me. 'They can survive forty days without a single bite. That's why they live in these hellish places. Anyway, don't try and send me packing from my own home, girl – I know what you're up to. Whatever your guest is doing in that sick room, I don't want to know. But let me tell you something. You better tell him to pack his bags and crawl back off to wherever he came from before the mistress finds out you've been handing out freebies. Understand?'

I nodded, and he went back to the washing. Once I had scooped up a bowlful of broth I carried it over to the little wooden hut. The bearded man was going to need a hearty breakfast if he was to hobble out of here before the others got up. I unbolted the door and slid in, shutting it behind me as quickly as I could.

He seemed to be asleep, his eyes scrunched shut and his lips jiggering up and down as if in some silent conversation. One hand was still pressed to the wooden box that lay beside him on the straw bed. I knelt down beside him, but when I prodded him awake he spluttered something incomprehensible and struggled away from me.

'It's all right, I've brought you some breakfast.'

He looked at me suspiciously. Did he understand what I was saying? Claws had stopped giving us lessons after the incident with Silk, so perhaps my language skills were getting a bit rusty. Or maybe his brain was just completely addled. There was caked blood on the old blanket I had wrapped around his leg, and the smell of rotten meat hung about the room.

'Food.' I said as slowly and clearly as I could, rubbing my stomach to show him what I meant. 'Yum yum. You eat.'

With his good hand he reached out and took the bowl, raising it nervously to his lips. After a few cautious swigs he drained the whole thing in a couple of gulps.

'Good. Now, you go.'

He looked at me quizzically. I pointed outside.

'Go. You can go now. Bye bye.'

I tried to pull him up but he groaned in pain. 'Please.'

His good hand caught mine. He moved it under his shirt to a small purse tied round his neck. It was heavy with silver. I pulled my hand away and shook my head.

'No. I can't. She'll kill me.'

He pointed at his leg. 'Please.'

'Listen, I'm sorry, I really —'

I was interrupted by a clatter of bowls and a yelp, and I knew that the Empress was up in the courtyard. Though I briefly entertained the idea of hiding him under the sheets, I knew there was nothing to do now but own up and try to make sure she didn't find out that

Boy was involved. I got up and swung the door open just in time to see the cook clutching his head, his washing bucket upturned at his feet and the Empress's blubbery jowls glowing red above him.

'Listen, I can explain. He's not a customer, I'm not serving him. You can come in and see. I spotted him when I went out to the bushes last night. He's hurt pretty badly.'

She wobbled towards me, the loose rolls of flab on her arms jiggling as she shook her meaty fist.

'Don't you take that tone with me! I hope you haven't forgotten who is in charge here.'

I ducked back into the hut and watched her squeeze through the doorway. The bearded man tried a smile. It was the wrong tactic.

'What are you grinning about? Do you really think you can come in here and mess around with my property without paying? Who do you think you are?'

'No, mistress, please, it's not like that. He hasn't touched me. I only let him sleep here because he's hurt. Look.'

I knelt back down and unwound the blanket to show her the ripped flesh and muscle of his leg. The smell alone made both of us gag. The Empress covered her nose.

'I see, you just brought him here to stink the whole place up. Ugh! Get him out of here now, and we'll forget about the whole thing. Is that fair?'

I nodded, though I was unsure of how to get him back up on his feet again. Luckily the bearded man came to my rescue, his good hand reaching inside his robe once again to pull a coin from his hidden purse.

'Please.' He held out the coin.

'Hmm. What does he want? Can't he speak?'

The bearded man coughed, then mimed rubbing his torn leg and sleeping.

I decided to make a guess. 'I think maybe he wants a herbman to make him better. And to rest here a while.'

The Empress narrowed her eyes.

'Herbmen aren't cheap. And bed and food will need to be paid for too.'

This time the bearded man seemed to understand. He fished around for another silver coin and put it in the Empress's outstretched palm.

He put his finger to his lips.

'A secret. Who are you hiding from? Those are war clothes, aren't they? Let me guess, you're a deserter. Well, silence costs extra, I'm afraid.'

A third coin appeared, and the Empress nodded curtly, before pulling me outside the door and bolting it behind us. She warned me not to lie with him whatever he offered, because we didn't know where he was from or what kind of dirty diseases he'd picked up. Before she retired to her room, the Empress told me that she would arrange for me to meet the herbman at the gate at sunrise the following day.

I expected Claws to be at least a little excited when I told her we had a new lodger from her part of the world, but she just shrugged. She wasn't going to visit him, she said, and she didn't wish to hear any more about him. I suppose she just didn't want to be reminded of all the parts of her life she had been forced to leave behind. Ever since her fight with Silk, she had been quiet and reserved, as if all she wanted to do now was forget who she was and what she had once been. Crow's feet had pinched her eyes into permanent squints, and these days she couldn't even be bothered to knot her robe tightly to keep her breasts from drooping down over her belly. She always sat with the rest of us, but she wasn't one of the girls anymore, and instead of joining in with our bits of gossip or fantasies she would stare at Boy as he played with a spare bit of camel rope, leading it in circles as if it was attached to some invisible animal. Wherever her heart had gone, it no longer had any use for words. She was scorched earth, buckled and broken.

Silk's new power hadn't helped her foretell the soldier's arrival, but she explained that away, saying that just because she hadn't correctly identified the signs, it didn't mean she hadn't seen them. It got me wondering how he could have made it here all the way from the middle kingdom without being captured by bandits or dying of hunger. Was he running away from something or heading towards some place? His wounds were pretty recent – whatever had done that to him couldn't be that far away. I tried not to worry, but I knew that if something went wrong the Empress would be sure to blame me.

The girls and I took whispered bets on what was in his box. Silk said silver, of course, or some kind of jewellery. Tiger ventured that he probably had the head of a prince he was bringing to an enemy tribe for a reward, and that was why his room stank so much. Boy joined in and said he thought the soldier had some of the emperor's magic in there, that it was just bursting to escape and change us all into dragons. Everyone laughed at me when I suggested that maybe he had a handful of earth from his hometown to stop him getting lonely wherever he was heading to. In the end I agreed with Silk. Men will do anything for money.

It was still dark when I woke up the next morning, and the other girls were snoring. Boy was lying on his side next to me, his knees tucked up to his chest. I listened to his slow, restive breaths, drawing strength from them, until I knew I couldn't wait any longer, and I shivered my way out into the ice-sparked dark. I stood huddled in my bulky robes and blanket at the gate waiting for the herbman. He was an old, balding man with a stern, pinched face. His young, pockmarked assistant helped him down from the donkey and we started up the trail to the hut.

'The Empress sent me word that your ... cousin is sick. I have brought the necessary tools in case we have to operate. The Empress knows that my discretion is beyond doubt, yet I should tell you now that since it is quite irregular for me to work in conditions such as these, I shall require double my usual fee.'

After I had lit a torch from the last remnants of the cook's fire, I led them into the little wooden hut then held the light up above the makeshift bed and watched the herbman kneel down and shake the soldier awake. He quickly understood and began to pull away the shoddy dressing from his leg. The bone looked yellow in the dim light, the tight coils of muscle oozing a dark liquid and the last shreds of skin around it now a dull-moss green. The herbman nodded appreciatively, and poked it, producing a sickly mew from the soldier.

'I am afraid it is as I expected. Fortunately, I have come prepared. I need you to get that fire going again and boil some water, then bring it to me along with some strips of cloth. Some old clothes would do fine. And of course, let's have the payment up front, in case anything ... well, in case anything doesn't go according to plan.'

By the time I had returned with everything he had asked for, the herbman's assistant had moved the wooden box to the floor and was in the process of tying the soldier's arms behind his back. The soldier seemed to have accepted his fate.

'Now normally we don't allow ladies to be present for these procedures, but as I'm not sure you really qualify as such, and as these are pretty unusual circumstances, I would appreciate it if you gave us a little help. My apprentice is going to sit on his right leg and hold the left steady, but as you can see, he is a large, strong man, so I want you to kneel at his head, and hold him down. I've done this before, and let me tell you, even the small ones writhe and flail about, so you'll have to be vigilant. Good, put your hands on his shoulders like that – yes, there you go. Now I want you to tie that strip of cloth round his chin. That's it, nice and tight, so he's got something to bite down on. We don't want him swallowing his tongue, and I presume your mistress doesn't want him waking up the whole mountain either. Ready?'

I gave a little nod of my head, although I couldn't really claim to be anything but terrified, so I can't even imagine how the soldier must have been feeling, lying with his hands bound, his mouth gagged, his robe bunched up around his waist and a spotty boy sitting on his one good leg. Still, a man of war had to be used to things like this, didn't he? The herbman took a saw from his sack. It looked to me like the same kind village men used to cut through timber for fishing boats and bridges. After rubbing the whole clotted area with a strong-smelling liquor that I expected was even more expensive than the stuff the cook brewed, he dipped the saw in the boiling water. The assistant gripped the thigh tight and the herbman took a deep breath. I fought against the urge to close my eyes. I failed.

Despite the gag, the soldier's gurgled screams quickly filled the room and, as predicted, he began to throw his head violently from side to side, his body in twitches and spasms as he tried to pull himself free. I kept a pretty good grip as he bucked and squirmed, his face and shoulders slick with sweat. At first I thought the muffled yelps of pain were the worst thing about the whole operation, but it wasn't long before I found that the crackle and scratch of that old saw was ten times worse. The blade whistled against the bone, hissing like a snake caught by the tail. The one time I dared to look down I saw the herbman's steady hands were flecked with blood and mulch and gristle, and the assistant was dabbing hot water and liquor around the oozing cut. The smell in the cramped, sticky room soon told me that the soldier had lost control of his bowels.

'If we're lucky,' the herbman raised his voice above the walloping thumps and broken splutters of the struggling patient, 'he'll pass out soon.'

He didn't. I remembered the village men when they were setting out to break a wild colt, twisting handfuls of mane and digging in their heels as it wheeled and kicked and fought to throw them off. Then I found myself wondering what happens to all the things we lose, where they go. Silk's eye, the soldier's leg – hanging on now by only the last shard of bone and a ripped rung of trembling sinew – what happens to them? Tiger once said that everything lives on in your shadow. Perhaps that's why she gets so angry with herself (though she does her best not to show it). It must be hard to have everything you have lost fluttering behind you wherever you go.

The saw finally sliced through the last sliver of skin, and the herbman began cleaning the bloody stump. In a way I was a little disappointed. Is that all there is inside us, blood and bone and gunk? Where are all the thoughts, all the dreams, all the magic, all the secrets? The soldier's eyes had rolled back in his head, greasy whites left staring at the ceiling. When the herbman's assistant untied the gag, we found that it was specked with blood where he had bitten down into his tongue.

'Now, this bind is going to have to stay on a few days, but after that you're going to have to change the dressing every day and wash the stump as gently as you can. Though we have removed the physical manifestation, his spirit still possesses two legs, so don't be surprised if he can still feel it. Send for me if it starts to turn green again, and we'll go a bit higher. Give my regards to your mistress.'

After the swollen knee was wrapped tight and the soiled blankets changed, I followed the herbman outside and helped him mount his donkey.

'Will he be all right?'

'He'll be laid up for a while, but I believe he will live. However, his leg was crudely hacked at, and I'll warrant from the state of the rest of him that whoever did this was probably rudely interrupted before they were able to finish the job. I would be very careful if I were you.'

This was not what I wanted to hear. 'Can I ask you something sir?'

'Yes, you may.'

I pointed to the soggy wrap sticking out of his bag. 'What are you going to do with his leg?'

He stared at me as if I was an idiot. 'I'll bury it, and when the blood takes root the man's broken hopes may begin to grow again.'

My mind kept returning to the soldier's box, to the way he guarded it so closely. Men will keep anything. Trinkets, jewels, paintings, old knickknacks, animals, women. The thing is, none of those things are worth anything on their own. People pay for them and keep them and look after them and all that because of the possibilities they imagine from them. Jewels aren't worth a thing if no one is going to see you wearing them. A dog is useless if he's not going to bark and attack when robbers get close. A woman is useless if she's not going to lie down and prise open her thighs when you tell her to. All of us knew that Claws hoarded the stray coins she collected as tips from the punters, but when you think about it, they were pretty useless too since they couldn't be exchanged for anything she actually needed – like love, her child or a way home. The only things worth anything in this world are possibilities. That's why it's so hard to give up, no matter how low your life gets or how many bits of your body or your spirit you lose. As long as you can imagine a future, you keep going.

Boy asked me about the operation again and again, and seemed transfixed by the gory details.

'Where is the leg? Can I see it? Can I touch it?'

'No, it's gone.'

'Where?'

'Well, it's gone off walking on its own. It wanted to keep on with the journey and it couldn't wait for the rest of him so it hopped away down the hill as soon as the herbman had lopped it off.'

'I don't believe you.'

'You don't have to.'

'Can I go and look at where it was chopped off?'

'If he's awake, yes. But don't stay in there long, and if he gets angry you come back and tell me. And don't get too close to him. And don't touch it, or else your own leg might fall off. And don't —'

'Ok, ok!'

He ran off to look at the wound. The other girls were sewing nearby, and I saw Claws' eyes follow him towards the gate. Silk shook her head.

'You know, that just doesn't sound right. What you said about the blood and white bone and everything. I can't believe it. I mean, where were all the emotions, all the moonwaters and pulses? It was dark in there, wasn't it, even with a burning torch? So are you sure you saw everything clearly?'

'Well, actually, I tried not to look, so perhaps I could have missed something,' I said to placate her.

'I once saw a skeleton on the sand plains, picked dry by birds,' Tiger said. 'You know, once the spirit is gone, once hope is gone, there's nothing left to hold the bones together. In my homeland we return the dead to fire, and all that's left is ash. Crumbly grey flecks of ash.'

'So nothing survives?' Claws said, and we all looked round, amazed that she was joining in one of our conversations again. Her voice was deep and worn.

'The spirit survives,' Tiger said. 'It just goes somewhere else. A sheep, a man, a flower, a grain of sand, a cloud. It never stops travelling.'

'Never?'

Tiger shrugged. She was tired of us, I could tell. She didn't want to talk about her homeland, and she probably thought we wouldn't understand. Maybe she was right. And it was pretty depressing stuff she was spouting anyway. I didn't want to end up as a sheep, torn apart by wolves or desert foxes. I just wanted a good rest.

Boy came back looking disappointed. 'He's boring. He wouldn't take the bandage off and he wouldn't let me play with his box. It's not fair!'

I was getting a bit annoyed with the soldier myself. I was stuck visiting him a couple of times a day, bringing him his meals and checking the horrible fist of clumped bone where his leg ended. It was almost enough to put me off my food. I scrubbed him down with water from the bucket and tried to make conversation, but most of the time he was in too much pain to do anything but grunt and sigh.

Whenever I came in he would be curled on his side with his good arm clutched around his box, staring at it as if he could see straight through the slats of rain-buckled wood. There was no lid or catch, and the smooth joins were obviously made by a better class of craftsman than those from around here – for the life of me I couldn't see how you could get inside without taking an axe to it.

'What's in your box?' I asked one morning when I was rubbing liquor into the blistering stump.

He didn't even bother to look at me.

'Come on. I've helped you out. If it weren't for me, you'd probably be dead. The least you can do is tell me what you've got in there. You can trust me. I'm not asking you to tell me who you're running from, or who you stole it from, or where you're going to go once you're well enough to walk on crutches. I'm just interested in the box.'

He finally looked at me and shook his head.

I pointed to it, then tapped it a few time, testing the strength of the wood.

I spoke slowly, enunciating each word. 'This box. What – is – inside – it?'

He pulled it closer to his body.

'The whole world.'

'Ha! So you can speak. I knew you were just playing dumb.'

He nodded, then brought one of his remaining fingers to his lips.

'Don't tell anyone? Yep, I know, I'm good at that. We live on secrets here. Some days I don't want to talk to anybody either. Most of what people say they only say to fill the air anyway. So you've got the whole world inside your box? Great. I'm sure that'll come in handy!'

I smiled and he smiled back. He wasn't that bad-looking really, when you ignored his stump and his missing fingers. There was something intimate in his smile. And the fact that he had enough money to buy the whole world – that must be what he meant, I thought – helped him to look a little more attractive.

'I'll tell you what, I'll bring a sharp knife and some scented water and give you a shave tomorrow. Would you like that?'

I mimed drawing a knife over his throat and for a second he

looked worried. But soon we were both laughing, and I left feeling pretty good about having saved him. I didn't really care that he might be lying to me – everyone has secrets they can't turn into words, even if most of us don't haul them around with us in bloody great wooden boxes. To be honest, it was nice to be able to talk to a man who wasn't just thinking about what was under my robe. It would have been better for him, however, if he had kept pretending he couldn't say a thing. Perhaps he would even be alive today. But I don't want to dwell on that. I only want to show that I did my best to help him, and I never asked for anything in return. At least not at first.

I didn't get a chance to talk to him properly again for a few weeks. We were so busy back then, as spring slowly spread across the hill and the sun stayed longer into the nights, that if we weren't cleaning up from one party we were getting ready for the next, so I could only spare a minute or two a day to hurry in and change his bandage before rushing right back down to the main courtyard again. What with all the cleaning and primping and washing and combing and plucking and dusting and smiling and serving and giggling and fluttering and dancing and pouting, it was almost a relief to get thrown down on your back at the end of an evening. As I said, my heart had grown hard, and it took a really imaginative or degenerate request to surprise me. It wasn't so easy for Boy though. He would be fine in the mornings, mucking about at the wash trough or playing with the ribbons fluttering off the gate, but as the afternoon crept on he became quiet, tense. Sometimes he'd sit on one of the cushions and hug his own arms close for warmth. We learnt to feed him up at lunchtime, because by evening he would be almost shaking and too nervous to eat a single bite without heaving.

Boy kept coming to find me late at night, and I'd make my way outside without waking the other girls to meet him in the freezing courtyard, clean him up and hold him while he sobbed and moaned. I guess I'd given up trying to find words to comfort him by then. I knew there wasn't a single thing I could say that would make the memory of the evening disappear, that would turn back time, that would take him home. And every night without fail he'd rub the slimy trail of snot from his nose and ask me why. Well, what do you say to that? I don't know if it's worse to think there is a reason for your suffering or just to pin it down to bad luck. Either way it doesn't make anyone feel any better hearing it, so I kept my mouth shut. I just held him a little bit tighter and tried to hush him to sleep.

I remember one of those nights, in between an evening with a group of unwashed camel traders and the day a party of returning desert guides stopped by, we had a visit from a retired general and his assistant. Claws identified the symbols and insignia on his ornate robe straight away, and the Empress had to pinch herself to avoid panicking. Only the spirits know how on earth they ended up finding us, and it may have been they simply got a little lost in the hills and decided to stop at the first place they found, but it got our suspicions up nonetheless. I mean, one soldier in hiding here and another ex-military man from the middle kingdom just happens to pop by? The coincidence seemed too great.

The Empress took each of us aside while the cook took instructions from the general and his assistant for the overnight care of their mules, and warned us not to mention anything about our secret guest.

'Not a bad little place here,' the retired general said as he sat down at our table.

He was short and completely bald, and nodded his head to the tune the cook picked out on his hushtar behind us. His assistant, meanwhile, was a huge, stocky man who did not seem to take much pleasure from talking.

'And so nice to see a sister from the Han nation – if I am not much mistaken – in this wilderness. You must forgive an old man his silliness, my dear, but your face looks familiar.'

Claws blushed a little. 'I was once a daughter of the house of Yuan, sir, though that was many lifetimes ago.'

The old man nodded. 'Then I am sorry if I have brought back painful memories. At my age it is hard to keep your thoughts in your head without losing them. But wait – you are not then some relative of General Yuan Huang?'

Claws nodded, not daring to look him in the face. 'I was, sir. You knew him?'

'Alas, no. But when I was a younger man I heard of his exploits. Just like the mighty Emperor Qin Shi Huang, may his spirit burn strong, your ancestor fought hard to try to subdue the south and unite the country. Most of my life has been dedicated to smaller battles and border duties, and yet it seems to me that unity of the middle kingdom is now something that must be consigned to myth. There are more warring factions now than a man can count. But perhaps disunity is no bad thing, for how can you have such a huge kingdom without it splitting at the seams? You would need men who lived as gods to run such a thing.

'In any case, some of my father's men witnessed Yuan Huang's last stand, and they told me that they had never seen such a brave commander determined to fight to the last for his country and his people. I do believe that too, though many do not. I am afraid the official histories will condemn him as an incompetent coward, but you should know that such things are only written to explain away such humiliating losses. To admit he was a worthy general and did his best would be tantamount to admitting that the middle kingdom is not the all-powerful centre of the earth, and who knows what the people would do if they found out such a thing. I am afraid that neither historians nor soldiers have much time for the truth. But listen to me babbling on. I only wanted to say I am sorry for what has happened to your family. Let us drink to them, and enjoy some of these fine meats.'

As we raised our cups I thought I saw Claws smile, for the first time in almost eighteen moons. Perhaps the old man had spun a story about her ancestor just to gain her confidence. No, I told myself, he's just being friendly and I'm letting my mind play tricks on me. I did think it was strange that our fancy guests mentioned history so often though. I mean, who really cares about what's long past? The only history that matters is what you hear firsthand or what you see with your own eyes, and even then you're not always sure you can believe it. The past belongs to the people who had to live through it, not to jumped-up cronies in some lavish palace.

I remember that Claws, back when she was still teaching us about the language and traditions of her homeland, had told us about the emperor named Qin Shi Huang. Claws said he had not only lumped all her lot together into one big brimming, bubbling country, but that he'd also built a wall to keep out the barbarians and ordered his army to seek out and destroy all the official histories so that time could start again with him. I don't know whether that worked, but I'm pretty sure about one thing: even if you're the most powerful man in the world, no amount of orders or threats can make people forget.

'I fear this fine liquor is going to my head,' the old man exclaimed as his cup was topped up once again, his crumpled cheeks glowing in the night air. 'I have enjoyed this wonderful meal and most delightful company. And I am sorry if I have embarrassed you, young lady, with my talk of ancestors.'

'No, sir, not at all,' Claws replied.

'You humour me too much. I am afraid it is difficult at my age to show restraint once your mind takes hold of an idea. And I know something about falling from favour. Why, I would be back at home by the fire now if it wasn't for the mistakes I've made. I only accepted this ridiculous mission because he said that if I did not then my son – ah, but see, my tongue is running away from my head again! Perhaps we should retire before I say enough to get us all thrown in prison!'

We all laughed at his little joke, but it made me feel more nervous than amused. The old man reached his hand out to Claws. She hadn't been picked first for ages, not since she stopped taking care of herself and started to let everything sag. But he was old and drunk, I considered, and his eyesight probably wasn't too good.

'It's strange, when I am in distant places I yearn for home, or something that can remind me of it,' he said, smiling at Claws as she helped him to his feet. 'Yet as soon as I return I start itching to go out exploring again. Now, take your pick, Fang, but be sure to have the mule loaded by sunrise.'

I wished with all my heart that the stocky assistant would not pick Boy. I even found myself thinking I would rather he picked me, though I was certainly in no hurry to get crushed under the big brute. Luckily, he thrust a hand out towards Tiger. She nodded and marched towards one of the guestrooms, leaving him to follow in her wake. If anyone could handle him, it was Tiger.

That left the rest of us to pick at the cold dishes and finish the spittle-mixed liquor at the bottom of the two clay cups.

'Do you believe him?' I asked Silk.

She shrugged. 'Of course. Why wouldn't I?'

The echo of exaggerated moans spilled out into the courtyard.

'You don't think it's a bit strange, that an old soldier suddenly turns up here talking about missions and joking about prison and all that stuff?'

Silk grinned as she licked a bowl clean. 'No, he's just a dotty old man who can't keep his mouth shut. I don't think he's got the sense to be plotting something, nor the heart to have tortured a fellow soldier.'

'But he was a general —'

'Yeah, but you heard him, he's just doing some rich bloke a favour. If he hasn't got enough sense to pick one of us beauties over Claws, then he surely hasn't got enough of his wits about him to be trying to hunt down a fugitive. I've haven't seen anything bad on the horizon with my missing eye, so keep calm. You're just worried because you've taken a fancy to that cripple.' Silk grinned.

Boy laughed, but I shot him a look. 'I think it's probably time you went to sleep.'

'That's not fair. Why can't I stay up too?'

'You need some rest.'

'And you need some beauty sleep!'

'This isn't the time for games. Just go.'

'You're not in charge, you know. You can't tell me what to do. You don't own me!' He hissed.

Homely suppressed a snigger as Boy ran across the courtyard to their room on the other side.

The moans from the guestrooms soon faded out into the calls of owls and distant wolves. Maybe I shouldn't have been so harsh with Boy, but someone had to look out for him, to keep him in line. All I wanted was to make sure that for at least a little bit of his day he got treated like any other boy living in the desert villages or in the cities below. I bit down hard on the stone of a date until my jaw ached.

Silk and I split the last half-empty cup after the boys had retired. We shared little sips of the moonlight that swished around in the dregs of the liquor.

'I understand how you feel. I can see your heart with my special eye. But you've got to be careful. Not just with the cripple, but with Boy too.'

'I just watch out for him. Claws is worse than me – you've seen how she stares,' I replied, annoyed by her comments.

'I know. But when she looks at him she's thinking of the past. I'm worried that when you look at him you're thinking of the future.'

'So what?'

'So you're going to get burnt by your own dreams. How many of your tips and gifts have you saved up to buy yourself free from the Empress? Claws and I have been here close to five winters longer than you, and we've saved every little thing the customers have given us, and we're both still here. Do you really think by the time you're free to go that he's going to be the same little boy? You can't come here as a child and grow to be a man. Plant a tree in the dark and it will twist and contort itself to find the light, and by the time it's fully grown it doesn't look anything like a tree anymore. His troubles aren't yours. You've got to remember that. The same goes for the soldier. You take on someone else's worries as well as your own and they'll crush you. Listen to me, Jade, keep your own heart safe, and you might get free one day.'

'One day.'

She sighed. 'I'm just trying to help you. I don't need to use my special vision to see that you care about him. Just be careful, ok?'

I nodded. I wanted to tell her that despite her special vision she didn't see the way Boy relaxed back into himself when he lay beside me at night, the way he squirmed when I tickled the soft spots on the underside of his elbows and the soles of his feet, or the way his fears seemed to drift away when I whispered to him all the old stories I still remembered from before. But she'd been here too long; she wouldn't understand.

# Rain at Night

Yuan Chen,

My dearest friend, your solicitations have not fallen on barren ground. You write that

*Even the sweetest of fruits will grow rotten on the vine*
*should the farmers forget their harvest*

and there is, as ever, truth in your analogy. Perhaps I have been as one of those farmers who abandons the hard labour of the field for the altogether different labour of contemplation. Perhaps something of the hunger in me left when she did. At times I have imagined myself a man of the land, my concerns stretching only as far as the horizon, my life reaching only to where the sun wades down among the corn. And yet my old life returns to me everywhere. In the sound of the rain at night, when I catch her laughter amid the babble of the downpour playing upon the roof; in the mellow flush of twilight, when my drowsy eyes forge hopes from the shadows. What cruel masters our hearts can be.

And so it is that I decided to yield to your entreaties and return to the capital. I must admit that you shamed me with your reminders of our earliest conversations, our plans for a new poetry that would make manifest our dreams of social change. There is nothing like the memories of a young man's passion to make an older man nostalgic. Yes, I know what you would say: forty is not that old, and the most important plans take time to blossom. I was shamed too by the looks my wife gave me sometimes, by the lilt in her voice whenever the city was mentioned. Since my health has improved somewhat over the last few months, I resolved to ask my contacts at the court to petition the eunuchs on my behalf, that I might return to work somewhere in the imperial retinue. Word soon reached us that I would be welcome back, and so the decision was made.

The journey to Changan took close to a fortnight. I hope that will go some way to explaining why it has taken me so long to reply to your kindly missives. I can confirm first-hand that the emperor's scheme of rebuilding the roads has paid off handsomely. We were able to change horses every three *li*, and the majority of farmers living along these sturdy pathways were much pleased with the way the increase in trade has affected their livelihood. Of course, it is still difficult to travel far without meeting some braggard or rogue who would curse the capital and its 'endless stream of edicts'. It is difficult to reason with such fellows. Instead I did my best to listen and understand their complaints, however contradictory I sometimes found them. For how can we even consider to work for the best of the country if we do not remember the needs of the common man? The capital – as I remember you told me on one of our first meetings – is the centre of a great sea, and the laws and actions there are like stones dropped from a great height which send ripples spreading slowly out to the furthest reaches.

It felt, though I am somewhat ashamed to say it, good to be out of white clothes again. My wife tells me the ghosts are sated, and the augurs say the same, and yet … but I risk becoming a bore. You will undoubtedly chide me for indulging in my own feelings when there are bigger social ills that we all ought to be working to solve. And to show you that I have not forgotten the early promises we made, I will recount for you the events of a few days previously, when we stopped at a horse station on our journey.

After supping on leathery mallard in the dark backroom, we were approached by two tall men who requested our company. My wife retired, for it had been a hard day's travel through the marshes and sodden country abandoned since the floods, and I spoke with them for some time. The elder of the two, a stooped man wearing the fine-coloured robes of a merchant, introduced himself and his son as silk traders. Over a few cups of rice wine we talked amiably of the latest news from the capital, of the rising expenses incurred by their wives in the raising of the silkworms, and of the ever-persistent rumour that foreigners had at last discovered the secrets of sericulture. The night crept up on us, and the son soon excused himself, leaving only myself and the older man. It was then that the conversation took a more interesting turn.

He confided that, despite his hearty appearance, he feared he was close to reaching the last of his days. Yet this was not what troubled him. He had begun life as a shepherd, taking charge of his family's meagre flock when he was still a boy, after his father was killed in an altercation with a cattle herder. Though it was long, cold, bone-numbing work, there was something in the solitude that stirred him, that brought him a feeling of calm and respite that he had not known amid the bustle and arguments of the cramped family home. I could sympathise with this, and for a while we shared our common experiences of finding solace in the words of the Buddha, in the first realisation of the illusory nature of the world and, there-fore, of the self. But I shall not bore you with that, for I know you have little time for such matters these days.

The old man had been, for want of a better expression, satisfied. It was not that he had everything he needed – far from it – but that he wanted nothing more. He had no further expectations than finding a sheltered spot to sleep or of making sure that his flock did not wander away towards the eager mouths of wolves or foxes. Yet that was the time – before either you or I, dear friend, were even born – of the rebellion of An Lushan against Emperor Xuanzong. An old flicker of pride, I am somewhat embarrassed to say, led me to interject to the old man that I had written a poem about the causes of that dreadful episode, and I was delighted to find that he had in fact read my 'Song of Everlasting Sorrow'. But I digress.

The ragged band of mercenaries following An Lushan, my aged friend explained, had neither the decorum nor the ethics of the im-perial army. On the march towards Changan to rout the emperor, this vagabond army devastated every village they made camp in. The locals came to fear the soldiers staying anywhere near their homes, because there was little they could do to stop this vast swathe of men stealing their sheep and cattle to roast on their huge campfires. Plots of vegetables were pulled up, fields of cereal were hacked down. By the time the army moved on, all that would be left were licked-clean bones, ashes and freshly dug pits of excre-ment. A whole year's harvest and all of a family's livestock would disappear in a single evening.

My friend and his flock of sheep, however, were far up in the mountains when the rebel army passed through his hometown. When he returned for market day he was amazed to find that he was one of the only people in the prefecture who still had a good number of sheep to his name. At first, he told me, he feared he would be attacked by the crowd that soon thronged around him. However, he quickly realised that he was in fact in the midst of a fierce bidding competition. As the offers rose and rose he thought that it must be some kind of joke, for he was soon being offered jewels, silks and even small plots of land in exchange for his sheep. He may have been a simple shepherd, but he understood the law of the market well enough to know that he should hold out as long as he could, and see how high the offers would rise. He was not disappointed. By the end of the day he had sold every single one of his sheep, and had amassed enough money to move his family from their shoddy wooden shack to a house on a small plot of arable land all their own.

The rest of his life was a familiar story of luck and perseverance – against the prevailing wisdom of the time, instead of taking on tenants of his own or planting grain on his plot, my friend set about cultivating mulberry bushes on a vast scale and instructed the women of the household that they would now devote their time to the care of silkworms. There were some rough years, some hardships, some compromises and, as ever, an element of risk and chance. Yet since then he has become one of the richest men in the prefecture, making frequent business trips to bargain his wares in the capital and in the western desert. His small house has become a veritable mansion, his name is well respected in these parts, and his son is a hard-working young man who is soon to marry the daughter of a civil servant. He even makes frequent offerings at the temple nearby, and much of the cost of the new pagoda was covered by his sizable donations. Everything appears to be perfect.

Yet you and I both know that appearances disguise deeper truths. The old man told me that, as he grows closer to the end of his life, he finds that the riches, the arbitrary power, the fawning, the prestige – all the elements that came together to make up his life – sicken him to the very core. He had not wanted to say this in front of his son, who is keen to inherit all that is his, but sometimes, he admitted, he could not look on his beautiful house, his loving family or his expensive robes without being overcome with shame.

'All my wealth has come from the suffering of others,' he said. 'Without the famine and food shortage caused by the rebellion, I would never have got started in my business. That moment, when my whole life changed, was dependent not on luck or good karma, as I convinced myself at the time, but on the poverty of others. My sheep would never have raised such a price were it not for the sudden food shortage, if everyone else had not seen all of their possessions taken and destroyed by those soldiers. While I got rich, others lost everything. When I built my own house, others were driven from theirs. While I feasted, others starved. It only dawned on me far too late that the two were bound together.'

Although I tried to placate him, he would not listen to any of my arguments, and instead kept returning to the idea of eternal balance.

'I must atone, somehow, before it is too late.'

He had a horror of dying before he had made amends for the suffering he had profited from, for he was convinced that if he did not act soon then he would be reincarnated as a rat or a mosquito, or else forever have to dwell in one of the dark subterranean realms of which many fear to speak.

It was then, my friend, that I remembered one of our earliest conversations. It returned with such surprising lucidity that it seemed as if my mind had stored it for the very purpose of upbraiding my heart for its long sloth and indulgence. I could even recall where the discussion had taken place – in the garden of the teahouse in the south of the city, watched over by the shadow of the Big Goose Pagoda. I took the elderly merchant's hand in mine and leaned closer to him.

'You have learnt what I have always believed: that our responsibilities are to the world, not to ourselves. Since we are trapped, albeit briefly, in this physical form, we trick ourselves into believing that we are responsible chiefly to ourselves, and therefore the primal urge arises to look after one's own self above all others. In some, this urge takes over completely, and they forget everything except money and the most fleeting of pleasures. For most, this responsibility may spread to the family, and to those close around them, but not much further. It is a great irony that while we Han never skimp on the veneration of our long-dead ancestors, we often pay less attention to the needs of the living all around us.

'As is to be expected, we are often given emperors who provide a reflection of this base urge in ourselves, emperors who squander taxes on jewels, wine and concubines, emperors whose thoughts reach no further than the palace compound. However, fortunately we are also sometimes given emperors who embody the more noble sentiment that you, my friend, have shown. For we are all responsible for the world around us, and we can all work to change it.

'Ask a man if he loves his country and he will swear he does, but ask him if he loves his neighbour, and the answer may be quite different. And yet what is a country but a collection of neighbours? How can we serve our country without first looking after the people within it? The Confucians tell us that we each must look to our superior for guidance – the son to the father, the student to the teacher, the citizen to the emperor. And yet I tell you this: we must look to the men beneath us, and learn from them. If we solve the problems of the farmers, the workers, the labourers, everything else will flow from there.'

The elderly merchant nodded.

'There is wisdom in your words, friend. But how am I to go about helping these men?'

'You ask them.'

He looked at me as if I had uttered some deep heresy, as if the rice wine had utterly ruined my mind.

'Ask them?'

'Yes. You were once one of them, and you knew better than anyone what you needed: shelter from the elements, a safe pen to keep your flock in, and so on. Ask them what they need. I pride myself on being a spiritual man, but sustenance cannot come from temples alone. Instead of paying for a new pagoda, you might invest in a mill wheel, say, or pay for a small dock to be built here on the river. Give them something they can use and they will thank you more than if you had given them a whole bag of the finest silk.'

He smiled, and was still smiling the next morning when we saw them saddling up as we left the horse station. Yes, I know there is more to our responsibilities than building mills or setting up docks for fishermen. Perhaps the lesson I gave was too simple. Too easy. Yet the fundamental principle remains the same – one man, making a difference by example. If each of us changes our actions, then the whole world is transformed. That is what you told me that day in the teahouse. You talked of poetry and princes, of wilderness and the wild, of impulse and instruction. I can taste the tea – I taste the very ideas – on the tip of my tongue.

Before we carried on our journey back to the city, however, I made a brief detour. I hope you will not be too ashamed of me when I admit – in the strictest confidence, please, my friend – that I visited a shaman. During my stay in the countryside, I had heard much talk among the locals about a much-renowned fortune-teller who lived in the hills. It was said that men came from many *li* away just to consult with him, for he could read the winds and the clouds just as easily as you now read the words on this very page. When I found that my wife was overcome with fatigue and wished to postpone our travels in order to rest and recuperate at the horse station, I realised that I had been given the perfect opportunity to pay a visit to this famous medium, for I felt I had to speak to someone of the strange thoughts that have been troubling me, and I feared anyone but such a man might look upon me with either pity or derision, neither of which I would be able to bear.

It did not take long to find the solitary dwelling in the shade of one of the peaks, for the long line of people waiting outside it was visible from afar. As I drew up, I saw that it was a tiny wooden house much battered by the elements. The warped walls were laden with lichen and smattered with dry rot. You have no doubt seen many such buildings yourself, for hermits, monks and ascetics often seek to renounce the world and find greater peace in the solitude of the wilderness. Yet tell me, have you ever seen such a house surrounded by a throng of peasants?

After many hours, when my turn eventually came to enter, I found I had to duck my head under the warped beams of the splintered doorframe to make my way inside.

It was a dark and musty hovel, with a sickly smell of mildew and stewed forest fungi. The room (for, indeed, there were no other doors but the one through which I had entered) was badly lit and sparse – aside from a small grate for a fire, a pile of foul-smelling straw that must have functioned as a bed, and a candle burnt down close to the nub, the place was empty. The corpulent fellow sitting cross-legged in the centre of the floor seemed to fill more than half of the room.

'Master Zhong?'

The huge man nodded his head. He was bald, though – perhaps in compensation – he had let his beard grow so long that the ends had been tied into plaits around his chest. His jowls were ruddy and mottled with pink, his eyes tiny swirls peering out amid the folds of flesh.

'Please, sit down, my friend,' he said, beckoning me to join him on the dusty floor. 'You are very welcome here. I see from your robes that you are an official – I cannot remember the last time I talked with an educated man.'

I settled in front of him and sat motionless as he studied my face.

'I think I can guess why you are here,' he said. 'Yes, your blood-shot eyes give you away. You have not been sleeping well, am I right? You live under a storm cloud.'

I must have looked shocked, but he merely smiled.

'It is no trick, my friend – it is simply that I have met many men like you. I am sorry to say that the nature of my occupation means that I am visited most often by the desperate and the heartbroken. Please tell me what is troubling you.'

And against my better judgement I did just that, for the moment I opened my mouth the whole story came tumbling out, and it was only when I reached the end of my account of the last few months that I noticed I had been speaking for an unimaginably long time, and that the fat shaman in front of me had not said a single word. We sat in silence for some minutes, the shaman with his eyes pressed closed and I with tears stinging the corners of my own.

'What should I do?' I asked. 'Is there any way … Can you find her? What if …'

My words trailed off, and the shaman opened his eyes and smiled at me. I expected him to take out sticks with which to cast a hexagram, or study my pulse, or begin to draw up a convoluted horoscope, or attempt to speak with the spirits – I expected him to do anything except continue to sit and smile at me.

'It wouldn't help, you know,' he said.

I was confused. 'What do you mean?'

'You didn't come here to ask me to go into a trance, to speak to the dead or visit the next world. And it wouldn't help. It wouldn't make things easier. But you know that, don't you?'

I nodded, and I soon found myself smiling too, for that is just the kind of thing that you would have said. I saw then that he was right, and that I had known this myself all along, even if I had not been able to articulate it. The mood lightened, and it was not long before we were chatting away about the Great Wheel and the eightfold path, and some time later, when I stood up to leave, I felt a little lighter, a little less harried by doubts.

'Thank you for your time, Master Zhong. I see now why the locals speak so highly of you.'

'Do not mention it. I am sorry for your loss, and sorrier still that there is nothing I can do to make it better. I have enjoyed talking with you. Please, promise me this. You will not give up hope. And promise me also that you will visit again if there is ever anything I can do for you.'

I made these promises and left his dwelling, and it was only then that I understood how much it had meant to me simply to speak of all that had happened without fear of causing pain or reproach, or risking reawakening the sorrows of grief in those I love.

The rest of the journey was uneventful. The sight of the mighty junks sweeping upriver towards the capital was enough to remind us of the huge differences between the slow days in the rustic family cottage and the noise and pulse of the greatest city on earth – as was the number of beggars and lepers milling outside the city walls. I was somewhat surprised to see how vigilant security has become while we have been away; our papers, servants and clothes were checked carefully, despite the growing line behind us, before the guards admitted us through the towering gate.

I will not risk testing your patience by detailing the state of our house after the tenants had left, nor by telling you about the tedious search for new household servants. But let me ask you, do you believe that houses can retain memories? That, somehow, parts of ourselves get left behind in the places we have been? I am loath to speak of the spirit so flippantly, yet I had a sense of something so familiar the other night that it left me disquieted and threatened, briefly, to cause a relapse of my old illness.

It must have been the third night we were back when I woke to find myself in the small orchard at the back of the house. I had no idea how I had got there. It was late – the moonlight spilt between the bare branches of the peach trees and puddled silver around my feet. I bit into my hand to test whether I was still dreaming – I was not. I could hear the low whistle of the night breeze cold around my shoulders, the calling of some of the insomniac birds so popular in households these days, and, in the distance, the marching of the night guards. My wife and the servants must all have been asleep.

I was standing beside the oldest of the peach trees. The gnarled trunk splits into two outstretching branches near the base, and it was on the worn ridge where the boughs divided that she used to sit as a small child, swinging her legs while I would walk among the trees, composing verses that might make her giggle. I was not particularly surprised to find that my feet had led me in here while I was still given to dreams – it is well known that our bodies store memories as well as our minds, which is why once learnt we cannot forget, for instance, how to walk, or how to sing. Perhaps I had heard the call of one of the neighbours' birds and mistaken it for her, and this had caused me to rush down to our special spot. Our dreams do delight in that kind of bittersweet torture.

My first thought was, of course, to return to bed. And yet I found I could not move. It seemed – though I am embarrassed to write this to you, for I fear you will think me a fool – almost as if the tree was on the verge of speaking to me, as if it partook of everything that had happened amid its branches, and could share the intimacy of that knowledge with me. Writing this in the light of day, I am tempted to scratch out the last lines. But I shall not, for something in me longs to experience that moment again, that brief suppression of logic that allows a man to believe that anything is possible. The longer I leant against that old peach tree, the more I remembered, and the more difficult it became to move.

I was waiting. And that I knew I was waiting for something that would not come did not dishearten me in the slightest. I thought that I finally understood those heretics in the Sect of the Circle who deny the existence of time. For who could argue that the past sometimes returns to us, that the present is not as solid as it seems? There are those that argue that we will live our lives over, again and again, after death – but it seems to me that our memories condemn us to live them again and again in life, for there are some things from which the mind cannot shake itself free.

As I sat there, I began to think of the many different dreams the capital holds. The cottage in which I spent these last years recuperating was on the edge of a tiny village with tiny dreams. The cock's crow called everyone to their plots, and sundown sent them in for their supper. When they turned on the straw at night the whole village was as one, dreaming the tallest crops, the biggest yield, a bumper year. Even the crickets and cicadas there sang of the harvest. And it was easy to be snared by that dream, to come to think that nothing else mattered but the green shoots stubbling the fields with possibilities.

Here in Changan there are more dreams than there are people. Sitting by the window now, for instance, even though the moon rose many hours ago, I can hear revellers returning home, theatre troupes packing up their wares, all-night labourers working on the defences, the imperial guard changing shifts at the outposts and towers, messengers clattering through the street with urgent missives, priests with their jangling bells heading to and from the temple and bawdy sniggers and groans from the street-corner pleasure rooms. Each sound hints at a different dream. I have been told since my return that this incomparable metropolis now houses more than a million people! It is therefore difficult to calculate how many dreams Changan holds, though I can assure you that however many more are added it will never be full. Is there a collective noun to describe this many dreams? A rabble of dreams? A cacophony? A swarm, a flock, a flight?

Despite the chill, I stayed leaning against the old peach tree until dawn broke, and with it the spell that had kept me rapt. I have been thinking how naïve we are when we are young, how full of conceit. I once believed I had control of this body, that it was there to serve my intellect and my desire. It takes an older man to realise that we are prisoners of the body – it does with us as it wishes, and will not heed our pleas or demands. Perhaps that is why my body carried me outside. Perhaps that was also why the illness took so long to clear. Either my body is playing a kind of joke on me or it is getting its revenge for the ways in which I once took it for granted. I find myself out of breath after I have walked from my home in the south to the Sui Palace compound by the north city walls, and in winter my bones ache so much it is as if frost has somehow formed on them.

But these are insignificant gripes, and I still have not told you about the one thing I know you are anxious to hear about: my new position at court. I have left the Imperial Library behind for the Eastern Palace – it is fortunate that I am not one of those older men who come to prefer the company of books and scrolls to the messy business of interacting with people. I believe I shall relish the challenges the position of Junior Counsellor brings, though it may take a little time for me to readjust to the pace of life at the court.

I must admit that I have been amazed at how few of our circle remain in the capital. Most are gone to the provinces, to governorships or diplomatic posts in the frontiers. Only a handful – men like Hua Jinbo and Dong Jie – toil still in their relevant offices, though I must admit I have not had the nerve to seek them out.

The Eastern Palace, as you no doubt know, is now the home of the crown prince. It is a fine building, one befitting the child of heaven. I was almost taken aback by the stunning shocks of red and yellow that decorate the vaults and pillars. Whereas the Imperial Library is characterised by hushed discussions and reverent silence, the Eastern Palace is a veritable bustle of debate and argument. This is perhaps the perfect opportunity to see the blossoming of those ideas about reform and justice that you and I formed together in the bright firmament of our younger days. Though I have yet to meet the prince – the eunuchs, it seems, are never far from his side, and do not deign to speak to lowly civil servants such as myself when they can avoid it – local rumours depict him as a well-read and thoughtful young man. Good qualities, which, if properly cultivated, would make for an enlightened emperor in the future. That is, if the eunuchs have not poisoned his mind by then.

Examples of their greed and plotting are everywhere. I have been – and you must understand, as ever, that I say this in the strictest confidence – quite appalled by what I have seen in the inner reaches of the imperial government since my return. It is worse than ever before. The eunuchs have made bribery endemic in the palace, and they consolidate their powers daily. The senior eunuch is rumoured to be particularly power-hungry. Ever since our noble Emperor Xianzong – blessings be upon his glorious reign – granted them military authority in the battles to defeat the rebel provincial governors, their influence has become almost boundless. They deal out state contracts, favours and positions, and there are few who will criticise them publicly, for they are well known to harbour grudges, and their revenge is frequently fierce and spiteful.

Yet I am confident that once the crown prince learns of the extent of their corruption – once he sees what bribery, nepotism and spiralling taxation are doing to the humble peasants of our great land – he will act to ensure that we return to the golden age of his ancestors. I will not neglect my more mundane clerical duties, but

I am certain that a chance to gain his confidence will soon arise. As you once said to me, we must seek out those who have a stomach for truth, and steel them for strength.

You rightly chided me, friend, for losing sight of my optimism in my grief. You were right too, that a return to the city would help me fight free of the shadows that have been hovering beside me. My wife too is happy with the return – though she would never say as much to me, of course. I heard her humming one of the old Han lullabies under her breath when she was knotting up her hair this morning, and it was enough to keep a smile on my face until noon. I have resolved to put the sallow days behind me.

I look forward to hearing more of your adventures in the great outposts, where I have no doubt that your work will continue to conform to your high standards. Send my best wishes to your children, and keep them close to you, for nothing is so conducive to happiness as the observation of happiness in those we love. Please send me more of your poems, and when I have time I will respond in kind. I say a sutra that your health may stay strong, that your heart will stay hot.

Bai Juyi

# A Delicate Matter of Phrasing

With the old man's crazed ideas still echoing in my head, I followed the road west, out towards the highway. In no time at all I was on the outskirts, with nothing separating me from the countryside but the slow, dumb river. My car clattered over the bridge, heading out once again from the heart of the city to the far-off fields and valleys. I found myself wondering how many might have jumped last night, how many might have decided that the rushing water down there was the better option. At least they'd get a bit of peace. Fuck. That's the kind of thing Li Yang would say. I was getting soft.

Have I ever thought about it? No. I mean, of course I've thought about it. A little. But not seriously. Imagined it, maybe. What my wife's face would look like when she heard the news. Whether her cold heart might wring out a tear. Whether it would make my daughter think of me differently. What Li Yang would do, sat alone (or with another lover?) up in that sprawling expense account apartment in the middle of the city. So yes, maybe a little bit. The tug of the current. The certainty. The letting go of all the things I've spent the last few years trying to keep hidden. Sinking. The light skittering on the top of the water, the world above breaking into blur.

I pulled over and bought a pack of cigarettes and a bottle for the journey from a dumpy little roadside shack, then started off again. Back onto the highway, back towards the hills and the farms and the bits of the county no one gives a shit about. I didn't see more than five or six cars all together as I retraced the route. My head was on fire. The roads poured out of the rear-view mirror, along with the dirt tracks and the badly hacked forests and the new developments and the tiny little plots of farmland that the locals squeezed every pathetic little penny from. I kept going past the exit, since I figured there was no point ending up on the wrong side of the hill again. After all, I'd already peered over the edge once and I didn't think my stomach could hack another peep. I needed to take a look at the valley below.

If anyone had asked me exactly why I had to see it, I'm not sure I could have said. But something wasn't right. If Wei Shan was there, then why hadn't his body turned up yet? And why had both the cop and Fishlips begun acting all shifty when I mentioned the mine the peasants had been going on about? And if there was a mine, then what did it have to do with the historian whose house I'd just visited? I couldn't get my head round any of it, and for once the cheap stuff wasn't helping.

I took the next turning and followed the road around until the far side of the hill came into view. Even from far away it was clear that the whole area was a mess. No trace remained of the houses, huts, shrubs, hedgerows, crops or all the other crap that must have covered the hillside. Even the grass seemed to have been torn away in the landslide. But here and there a few trees that had somehow survived the fall flailed out almost horizontally. If I hadn't known better, I would have been prepared to wager that they were held up by some invisible thread, since for the life of me I couldn't work out why they hadn't gone crashing down the slope along with everything else. I could make out undulating heaps of rubble and mud at the very bottom. Diggers and JCBs crawled over the debris like ants on a steaming pile of shit.

Damn. Don't they ever rest? How was I going to have a look around with cops or soldiers mucking about at the bottom? They had to stop once it got dark, though. So instead of pulling a U-turn or drawing closer to the wreckage, I decided to drive on for a bit and bide my time. I still had a few hours before I had to meet Xiang for dinner. Continuing north, the road drew alongside the low-lying curve of a great trench. Or a ditch. Whatever it was, it was filled with dirt and a few small brown puddles. Surely this couldn't be the river Officer Wuya had mentioned? That muddy trickle couldn't have swept any bodies away.

I drove on in the wake of the dried-up river as it snaked round a corner and led further into the valley. Soon both the highway and the site of the accident were far behind me, though I could see little of interest up ahead apart from a thick bristle of trees at the start of yet another slope. All these hills were making me dizzy. The river

– if that's what it once was – still wasn't looking very promising. Perhaps it was filled with water further on. Or perhaps something was blocking it. Either way, I'd soon find out. And then turn back to take a look at the hillside once the guys doing the digging had clocked off.

I did my best to suppress a shudder as the road took me into the woods. I hate trees. Great twisted brutish things. All they do is take up space. And throw huge, malformed shadows over perfectly good pieces of real estate. Ugh. Not far into the forest I passed two turnings off the main track. A pair of crude signs told me that I could take the first left towards the Zhongshan Timber Company HQ or the second left to the 34th Regiment Field Centre. No thanks. Loggers or squaddies – a pretty unappealing choice. Wait. That wasn't right. I pulled over at the side of the road, hitting the brakes so quickly that the bottle of rice wine between my thighs nearly flew out to smash against the steering wheel. No infantry division out doing training and manoeuvres deep in the country would be foolish enough to publicly announce the location of its barracks. Even soldiers aren't that stupid.

I made a clumsy three-point turn and started down the turning. Surely it couldn't be. I've seen a couple on the outskirts of the city, of course. My father even visited one once – managed to get a bed thanks to an old colleague in the People's Liberation Army – though he'd left it so late by the time he finally got there nothing could be done but try to make him comfortable. It wasn't long before I saw the squat building rising up between the trees. Ha. I knew it. A little army hospital. I couldn't believe my luck. A place where those with enough connections to the military could get a private room and a doctor to themselves. The rest of us have to make do with waiting for hours on splintered chairs set between brimming bedpans and old, coughing rheumatics in the cold, crowded municipal hospitals. This was the kind of place you could only go to if you knew someone who knew someone. Or if you were an actual soldier – though everyone knew that's not how they made the bulk of their money. It was a long shot, of course, but I was gripped by the idea that this was where I might finally find Wei Shan. Besides, what else was I going to do now?

I drove off the track and down into the wood, parking deep between the trees. My car would stand out like a turd in a jewellery shop among all those camouflage jeeps and shiny black foreign cars. I drank a quick toast to the Chairman then opened the car door as quietly as I could. I felt as if I'd struck gold. I mean, what were the odds, finding this place in the middle of nowhere? Perhaps Wei Shan really was inside, and somehow I'd been drawn to him. No, that's idiotic. Instinct, that's what the guys in the office call it. Good instinct. As if. More like a handful of good luck. I took a deep breath. I knew exactly what I was looking for. But that didn't mean I wanted to find it. Get in, find the basement, get out again. I repeated it like a mantra till I was ready to go. The sun was already low in the sky. It was later than I thought. I stumbled through the mulch, my shoes half sinking in mud as I tried to find a path to the back entrance. There had to be a back entrance. There always is.

A door was propped open beside the kitchen at the rear of the building. A few dull-eyed youths were scrubbing away at the sink but no one even turned around as I walked past. I found myself in a long, empty hallway. My soggy shoes slapped against the clean, shiny floor. It didn't take me too long to find one of the locker rooms, halfway along the endless hallway, set between the admin rooms and the bogs. It was empty. Most of the time my life is dull, dull, dull. Examining structures, making sure safety procedures are followed to the letter. Boring as hell. But not today.

I hung my jacket on a spare hook and put on a white coat. I looked in the mirror set between the tiles. The face looking back was fuzzy at the edges, and couldn't seem to keep still. My eyes were bloodshot; I needed a shave. I practised smiling the way a doctor might, somewhere between reassurance and impatience. Then I moved my Double Happiness and the half-empty bottle to my new pockets. All set.

The long white corridors were practically deserted. Creepy. A few nurses wandered past, barely bothering to look up from their clipboards. Numbered doors lined each side of the hall. I put my ear to one, picking up the wheezy snores of some well-connected arsehole. No, I wasn't walking right, I realised. I should be walking like a doctor. Faster, as if I hadn't a single second to spare. As if I knew exactly where I was heading and the whole world hung on my opinion. The corridors seemed to go on forever, slipping round corners and branching off into more hallways lined with more low-hanging white lights. There must have been hundreds of people in those pristine rooms – the sick, the ill, the crippled, the terminal and, without a doubt, some who'd slipped away from life completely without anyone noticing yet. But if he was here, Wei Shan wasn't going to be in one of those. I needed to find the way downstairs. I backtracked and tried another route. The numbers on the doors began to repeat themselves. It must have taken me twenty minutes to find the stairs.

I followed them coiling down to the basement. Why is it that when a place has a secret, chances are it'll be hidden just beneath the surface? It made me think of the Cultural Revolution, when everyone was burying books in the garden or stuffing antiques and dangerous love letters under the floorboards or in the cellar. I couldn't help thinking of my father. He was a first-class cadre, and sometimes I think that was because of all the shit he kept hidden. Pushed all those secrets down into his gut, until finally his stomach took its revenge, and he ended up with a fetid little bag strapped to his side in a place like this, watching his insides pour out. If you keep holding on to all your secrets, the same thing will happen to you, my wife said. And she said it again and again and again.

My steps rang off the metal staircase. As I clanged further down my breath turned to smoke. The basement was freezing. It was the kind of cold that sticks to your skin. Stone floor. Half the lights off. Metal doors with grills. A sleepy-eyed janitor wandered through one of the doors. I told him what I was looking for and he nodded at me in deference. I followed as he held the door open. I spotted the sign on the wall and followed the arrow past storerooms, supplies cupboards, galleries of prosthetic limbs. More hallways populated only by low-swinging lights with burnt-out bulbs. Little rooms taken over by armies of filing cabinets. Then – what's this – a couple of poky, windowless classrooms with fusty blackboards. The tiny classrooms even had those funny wooden chairs with a tiny flat desk built onto the right arm, so the students could scribble their notes without the need for tables. Already I didn't like this place.

I kept going. It was the smell that got me first. Just the hint of something sour. Mould, perhaps. Mould and disinfectant. Your eyes can lie, play tricks on you. You can never trust what you hear. But if you can get a whiff of it, you're on to something. There was another metal door blocking off the rest of the corridor and another sign telling me that I'd reached my destination. A padlock hung from the metal catch. It wasn't hard to pick. I closed the door behind me and hoped that everyone down here had gone out for a long dinner. I fumbled for the bottle in my pocket and stole a quick gulp. Then I took a deep breath and tried to keep myself from falling over.

There were three rooms. The first was more filing cabinets and a deserted desk. I had a quick look around for anything that might have been of interest, but all the documents I found were filled with medical terminology that might as well have been written in a foreign language. Opposite was the examination room. A flat metal table with a huge lamp angled over it. A tray on wheels, with four closed drawers. A sink in the corner and a pair of plastic gloves poking out of the top of a bin. The room was cleaner than any other I'd been in. You could have eaten off that metal table. But there was still that smell, stronger now.

I could hear the fan purring in the third room before I'd even pushed open the door. I pulled the white coat tight over my damp shoulders as the cold air hit me. Four trolley trays, topped with four white sheets. Shit. Had I really found what I was looking for? I glanced at the clipboard on the end of one of the trolleys. Number 11. That was all it said. Nice of them to keep it brief. Well, no point waiting around. I pulled off the first sheet.

A man. Potbellied, with sunburnt neck and shoulders. Shrivelled dick curled above his wrinkled balls. Stubby toes with yellow, broken nails. There was no way this man had worked in any kind of office. He had a ratty moustache and a receding hairline. Slap-in-the-face ugly. Must have been thirty-something. Pushing forty. And what's this? The index and middle fingers missing on his right hand. Recent too. No stubs, just a mess of gunk and frayed muscle where they had been ripped off. Cuts and bruises all over both hands. The bone of his right shoulder poking up against the skin. His face was almost blue, his lips swollen. Asphyxiation. It had to be. I bent closer and smelt him. A touch of jasmine. Soap. Someone had given him one hell of a scrubbing down. I looked in his ears, up his nose. Fuck. I bet they were never this clean when he was alive.

I tucked the sheet back over his face. Poor idiot. The next two were pretty similar – a scrawny, acne-spackled teenager with a few broken ribs and a horse-faced middle-aged bugger with his arm split at the elbow where the bone had been cracked back through the skin. Both with the same bruises, the same bulging blue lips, the same broken hands covered in lacerations. As if they'd spent their last few minutes scrabbling desperately to get free. The same sickly smell of soap.

I looked at the three of them lying side by side. I wasn't ready to pull back the fourth sheet. Not yet. I tried to think rationally. Fatty, Spotty and Horseface. It would have taken more than a hundred bottles of the expensive stuff to convince me they hadn't died in the landslide. They'd clearly been buried under a huge amount of weight. I shuddered at the thought. So why the hell had Officer Wuya told me that no one had died? I asked the question out loud, but the three stooges here had obviously decided they weren't going to help me out. Their clothes would have been incinerated by now, so that was a dead end. Everything in their pockets – wallets, ID cards, black and white family photos, scribbled phone numbers or boarding house addresses – could well have gone the same way. So what had happened? The bodies had been recovered, they'd be taken here as normal procedure dictates, cleaned up, examined by a medical doctor for the death certificate and then … nothing. It was as though, at the very last moment, someone had made a conscious decision not to release the bodies to the families. I had a bad feeling that in a few hours whatever was left would likely be dissected by clumsy students or else cremated. Someone had suddenly decided that these guys weren't going anywhere. Shit. I lit up a Double Happiness and took a final look at each of their faces. Fatty, Spotty and Horseface.

I moved along to the last bed. It was like playing Russian roulette. With every body I exposed, the odds on the next one being Wei Shan increased. But I'd come this far. I rubbed my hands together to fend off the chill and yanked away the sheet.

I've got to admit, I let out a little sigh of relief, which is probably not the usual reaction when you see a corpse you recognise. But this wasn't Wei Shan. He was much too scrawny, and didn't have Wei Shan's beer-belly. Even though the face was pretty badly cut up and one eye was missing, most of the dark monobrow was still there. He'd lost his wiry glasses and the best part of his leg, but there was no mistaking the fact this was the same guy I'd seen in the photo in the posh apartment. Jing Ren.

If he had been down in Jawbone Hills too, then perhaps he was the foreman after all. But the foreman of what? Could these four have been part of a mining operation in the hillside? A bit of digging in the wrong place, or a few baldy placed explosives and they could have brought the whole thing down upon themselves. I covered him back up. Least I could do. I mean, I'd already broken into his flat and stolen a sip of his best rice wine. But as I was pulling up the sheet I noticed something near the top of his left arm. At first I thought it was a clump of mud or dirt that someone hadn't been able to scrub off. But when I looked closer it was clear that it was a tattoo. Huh. I hadn't thought he'd be the type. Didn't look like a gangster though, so how the hell had he got himself marked? Something really wasn't right here. It was a small black bird with a hooked beak and outstretched wings. A raven? A rook? A crow? I'd be lying if I said I could tell the difference.

I stamped out the cigarette and put the stub in my pocket. For a while I just stood there, until I felt my skin chill to goosebumps. But strangely enough I wasn't in any hurry to leave. There was something calming about the cold room. There's an honesty in the dead that you don't get anywhere else – a stillness that invites you to confess, that assures you your secrets will be kept.

I fingered the bottle in my pocket, though I didn't open it. The room smelt soapy and sour and I was clammy from the cold. This whole thing was a mess.

I was in the Golden Dragon Seafood Palace, a little of the good stuff left in the bottle in front of me. No time to head back to the hillside today. That would have to be tomorrow's job. After covering up the bodies, I'd legged it from the hospital and raced back to the city to meet Xiang. And wouldn't you have guessed it – the bastard was late.

I picked up my cup and tried to ease the manic pounding in my chest. I had tried calling Li Yang from the payphone in the kiosk across the street. Twice. I could imagine that ornate red telephone up in the top-floor apartment ringing and ringing, the noise filling the large rooms stuffed with expensive crap, while Li Yang was out at some posh club or fancy restaurant. Probably with some guy who had more money and status than me. I took another swig.

The owner was picking his teeth as he watched the old TV in the corner of the restaurant. Some wildlife programme about monkeys. Turns out they're just as sneaky and vindictive as us. I looked at my watch. Xiang was always late. The mad rush to get the latest copy into the printer's mitts, that's how he put it. The last-minute bulletins rushing in and screwing up the front page. The censors getting fussy and suddenly reneging on the concessions that had been agreed upon. Even though I'd never stepped inside the paper's offices, I had a pretty good idea what happened there from the way Xiang yapped on about how each tiny problem there got to his ulcer.

'Hey, it's pretty grotty in here isn't it? Maybe we ought to start meeting somewhere else.'

'Yeah, yeah, don't say it. I know, I know.'

Xiang raised his hands into the air as if to signal that a higher force was in some way conspiring to throw as many little annoyances in his path as possible. He sat opposite me and helped himself to some of the liquor.

'Oh, that's better. Hey, you look like shit. Something tells me it wasn't just another boring day at the desk. You ought to take some time off.'

'What am I going to do with time off? Spend more time with my wife?'

He laughed, and slapped his hand against the table. 'So, are we going to get any food or what? I'm starving. I've got this young trainee who can't write for shit – but of course he's the son of one of the big players in the local bureau so what can I do? – and he's handing me five pages of this long-winded bullshit about local development that I have to dig through to find a two-column story. Talk about a waste of time. Oh, hello, we'll have some sour potato, some sizzling beef, some fragrant pork and bamboo and two bowls of rice for after. Oh, and another bottle. Quick as you can, all right? Now, where was I? Oh yeah, the intern. You won't guess what happened next. He'd only got it into his head to …'

I nodded as Xiang yabbered on about his day. I smiled and commiserated, topping up his glass and mine, even though I'd stopped listening and was thinking instead about the bodies. I was thinking about all the hands that had ever touched the pale, blueish skin I'd seen. Mothers, wives, children … and then the people who'd pulled them out, who'd loaded them up and taken them to the hospital, who'd undressed them and scrubbed them down and packed them away like frozen plucked chickens. The whole thing gave me the creeps. I interrupted Xiang to see if he had any cigarettes.

'Sure thing. So, are you going to tell me what you're so worked up about or do I have to sit here guessing?'

'I don't know what you're talking about.'

'Come on. Why were you in such a hurry to find that man this afternoon? I'm happy to help, but I hate being kept in the dark.'

So I told him. We were well into the second bottle and halfway through the lukewarm dishes by the time I had finished.

'You haven't heard anything about a mine up there then? Anything at all?'

'Ha! Now you're really clutching at straws. As if journalists get told anything. You know as well as me that the moment I start digging around in things that aren't any of my or my readers' business I'm likely to get hauled off to jail. The truth is we get drip-fed most of the stories these days. It's hardly worth leaving the office – the news isn't formed out there on the streets, it's composed and configured and printed before it even happens. But I haven't been warned off printing anything about the landslide, which is interesting. If anyone high up wanted to stop a story getting out, the first thing they would do is call the editor and make sure not a single word about it appears in the press. Yet we haven't heard a thing. As far as I was aware, there hadn't been any deaths at all.'

'That's what I'd thought till I saw the bodies. You know, that's one hell of a cover-up.'

'If you ask me, you ought to leave the whole mess alone. I'm sorry about your colleague, but can't you just write it off as a careless accident? Does it really make a difference whether a mine somehow helped cause the landslide or whether it was just the rain? Either way, Wei Shan's still going to be missing. You should see some of the news we get forced to suppress – train crashes with hundreds crushed in the flaming metal, bridges collapsing and sending coach parties hurtling down gorges, floods and explosions and fires and murders that no one ever hears about. You can't let yourself get worked up about them all, you just have to let them go.'

'Accidents I can understand. But all these lies, all these bodies? It doesn't sit well in my gut. Besides, I've got to tell Wei Shan's family something.'

'Hmm. Well, if you want a bit of help, I could probably find out who this Jing Ren guy was working for. I've got a friend at the Agricultural Bank, he should be able to get hold of his account history. If you really want, I can ask him to find out if any unusual payments went into the account recently. You'll owe me one, though.'

'Not bad. I should have thought of that myself.'

'If he was working for a mining company, we ought to be able to dig up a few details.'

'Ha ha. Very funny.'

'Who knows what we might unearth?'

'Yeah, yeah. You're a real comedian.'

'Seriously, I'm happy to help – because I know how stubborn you are – but I still suggest keeping your nose out of the whole thing. Someone obviously didn't want those bodies to be found. And your boss and that police officer as good as warned you away. You keep blustering on and digging up dirt you'll end up with an ulcer like me, or a bullet in the eye. Look, you've got a good job, a respectable wife, a dutiful daughter, a nice flat, enough money and connections, a nice mistress – don't raise your eyebrows, I know you well enough to know that you have some fancy young lady you visit every so often, my friend – even a car of your own, so why do you want to go and piss it all away on something you can't do shit about? Do you really think anything you find out now is going to help bring Wei Shan back?'

'I don't know. But I can't just go back to my desk and pretend nothing has happened. Why do you think I joined the Party in the first place? I wanted to help get rid of all this cloak and dagger crap and make the country a better place for everyone.'

'Give it a rest. You joined because your father was a member, because it's the best way to rise up the ladder, because if a Party member and a non-Party member both go for a job it's always the Party man that gets it. Please don't insult me with this love-of-the-people shit.'

'Ok, I get your point. The bill. No, it must be my turn.'

I paid, and Xiang laughed to himself. I think he enjoyed the fact that for once he wasn't the one moaning about his problems. Is that why we need other people, so we can hand out some of our own misery and walk away a little lighter?

The night was fusty, full of not-quite fog. Despite the drinks and the smokes, the air shredded my lungs and I couldn't stop myself coughing. Xiang shoved his hands in his pockets and pretended to look the other way till I'd finished. He clambered into my car for a ride home, and was at least polite enough not to mention the mud-stains and the empty bottles littering the seats. Xiang lived out east, with his dumpy little wife in one of the old single-level two-room houses. No child and, rumour had it, no mistress either. He took a lot of shit for both of those, for not being a real man, but he never let it get to him. I guess that's why we got along. Neither of us had ever really given a damn about acting exactly the way you were supposed to. Which was why both of us were stuck where we were, risen about as far as we could expect to go.

Xiang was probably right. Best to just let it all go. He knew what he was talking about. When he'd been a rookie reporter, just after the Gang of Four had got arrested and everyone was saying that everything was going to change, he'd been asked to write up a piece about a guy in the local police force. This cop was a real vicious piece of work and everyone knew it. It was no secret that he made a good sideline in taking bribes from people with grudges to get their neighbours, colleagues or sons-in-law shipped off for re-education in the provinces, and Xiang was either too young or too idealistic back then to think about how the angle should be played so that no one lost face.

The truth was, that kind of thing happened all the time, and besides, everyone wanted to put the whole Cultural Revolution mess behind them by then. However, the deputy editor of the paper had seen his nephew sent away on a trumped-up charge from this guy, and, once the tide started turning against the Cultural Revolution Committee, he gave Xiang the lead, knowing that he'd be the only one naïve enough to dare to type it up. Once the story ran in the paper, well, the cop had to be made an example of, and the local unit had to make a show and dance of apology and initiate a programme to remove corruption and overhaul police procedure. At the same time, a bunch of the guy's colleagues would have to go round to Xiang's flat and beat seven shades of shit out of him. He was in hospital for four days. After that his stories had what the officials call a more measured tone. Bland, inoffensive, neutral. The same thing each week, just dressed up a little differently. No need to put anyone's nose out of line – it's only news, after all.

We smoked as we drove, watching the city wind down. Dotted lights in high tower blocks slowly blinking off, restaurants being shuttered and locked, karaoke pleasure pens showing the last few drunks the door. We shared the silence between us as I steered on past streetlamps swinging where there were once paper lanterns, and for once I drove slower than I needed to.

'Xiang.'

'Hmm. Yeah?'

'You ever heard of anyone – street gangs, businesses, religious cults, intellectual movements, party committees – going by the name of crows?'

'Are you yanking my chain? Like the birds, right?'

'Yeah, the ugly black ones. Or rooks, or ravens. Whatever.'

'Nothing worse than a warning from a crow's tongue, eh?'

'What?'

'The proverb. Don't tell me you've never heard it before?'

'Never.'

'Don't mess me around. Course you have. Like when someone says, I would invite you round to ours but my wife's cooking is worse than a warning from a crow's tongue. Meaning it's bloody awful.'

'Why do they say that?'

'That crows bring bad news, that they're unlucky? Hmm. Because of all the old stories, I guess. You know that crows were used by shamans making auguries for the emperor, right? They'd tell the future by observing what the crows were doing. You know, divination and all that. Crows feed on death, and this gives them dark knowledge. Supposedly once you eat death, you understand how everything will die. And I guess because the crows kept giving the shamans news about wars or earthquakes or other tragedies, people got pretty pissed off with them. No one wants to hear bad news. And there's another story about them, isn't there? My grandmother used to tell us these old tales when we couldn't sleep … but I can't remember half of them now. I'm sure one of them was about crows. Do you know the one I mean?'

'No, I don't think so.'

'Well, never mind ... Wait a minute, you're thinking about the tattoo on the dead guy, aren't you?'

'I don't know. It's just ... No, it's not important.'

'You sure? I could look into it. Wouldn't be too difficult ...'

'Forget it,' I said as forcefully as I could. I was beginning to think I shouldn't have told him. Not that I didn't want his help. Far from it. Getting him to find out a little information was one thing, but dragging him too deep into this sorry state of affairs was another altogether. Something wasn't right about this whole mess, and there was no point both of us putting our jobs on the line.

Xiang took the hint. He nodded and leaned back in the passenger seat. I dropped him outside his house and saw his wife peer out from behind the blinds before she opened the door – he didn't even have his own key. I drove around the block for a bit, past the new rows of scaffolding and half-finished office towers, uncertain where to go next. I could find a payphone and try Li Yang again. I could go back to work, or to the records office. But I had to go home some time.

I flicked the radio on as I drove back across town but turned it off again a few seconds later. The music bothered me. I hated the way it took my thoughts to places I didn't want them to go. Old songs, new songs, zheng and zither or guitar and synth, they're all the same. They all have that power to tug me into their current, to carry me away from myself. And when they finish I feel like I've been shown something vitally important that's been snatched away. Music unsettles me, exhausts me. And that might have been all right, if only I hadn't already had one of the strangest days of my life.

The flat was dark, and when I dropped my keys into the bowl by the door they clattered onto the floor. Someone had moved the bowl. And the little table it stood on. When had that happened? I crept across the creaky floorboards to the kitchen cupboards, only to remember when I got there that I had emptied them of drink that morning. It seemed like weeks since I'd last been home. I tiptoed past the fold-out kitchen table and opened the bedroom door.

'Don't even think about it, I can smell you from here,' my wife hissed through the darkness. 'I've had a busy day and I need some rest, all right? I left a blanket on the sofa.'

A busy day? I was tempted to tell her about my crazy boss, my missing colleague, my trip to see the police officer, my chat with some old nut in a history professor's abandoned luxury apartment or the four dead bodies I'd seen in the army hospital. But it wasn't worth the effort. I closed the door and collapsed on the sofa. I pulled the blanket up until it covered my head, until I had swapped places with Fatty, Spotty, Horseface and Jing Ren. Until the world receded and blackness swallowed the buzzing between my ears.

My mouth was full of bees, vindictive little shits stinging the crap out of me. Morning again. I knew because of the machines hammering behind my eyes, the dull aches pulsing in my sides. I knew because of my daughter making breakfast, because of the frightening growls coming from my gut. I knew because of the fur on my tongue that had sprung up in the night like dew. The world was skewed, and it didn't seem able to keep still. When I opened my eyes the whole room was circling the sofa. I managed to lift my head to see my daughter over by the stove.

Was she seriously cooking millet again? Or had I already lived this day a thousand times before?

'Sweetheart, do me a favour.'

She sighed, but she was obviously in an alright mood, because after only a few minutes she skulked towards where I was lying on the sofa.

'Dad, you smell even worse than yesterday. I mean, you really reek. You ought to take care of yourself.'

'Yeah, I know.'

'You shouldn't sleep in your suit.'

'I know. I'll shower in a minute. But I need you to run out to the stall downstairs and buy a couple of bottles of beer. Any kind'll do. The cheap stuff is fine.'

'You drink too much.'

'My own father drank *baiju* with every meal, and he made it to his sixties. And he would have beaten any of his children black and blue if we'd dared answer back to him the way you're doing now.'

'Hey, don't have a go at me! I'm just repeating what Mum said. It's not my fault you're grumpy and hung over.'

'Yeah, yeah.' I fished around in my pockets and dug out a couple of banknotes. 'Look, you can keep the change. Buy anything you want with it, I don't care. Ok?'

She sighed again. It seemed to be her chief method of communication. But she finally gave in and took the cash, then headed for the door.

'Two bottles, remember!'

I lay back and tried to stop the spinning by closing my eyes. It didn't work. There had to be a mine. That was the only explanation. And whoever the owner was, he had to be someone important. Someone who had the clout, the money and the connections to get the debris dug out and the bodies carted off to the private hospital all without anyone kicking up a fuss. Someone powerful enough to persuade Officer Wuya to lie through his teeth. But that was as far as I could get. My thoughts were toppling away from me, and my gut was squeezing itself inside out. I clutched at the blanket, at the sofa. Where was my daughter? My stomach lurched and cramped and I tried to struggle up. What was taking her so long? I rolled over and began to retch. Thick, slimy bile chugged out from my lips. Grey and brown, like pond water mixed with mucus. My stomach started to settle, and I spat and wiped my mouth.

The door creaked open so I threw the blanket down to cover the little puddle. There was no need for my daughter to see that. I could only hope she wouldn't notice the smell.

'Here.'

She chucked the beers down onto the other end of the sofa before wandering to her bedroom, taking her bowl of millet with her. I drank them both, popping them with my teeth and gulping down the rank, bubbly fizz until the room steadied and I was able to move my head without stars crashing through my senses.

My wife had already left for work by the time I stumbled out of the shower. There was a note on the table telling me not to forget our daughter's school's thirtieth anniversary celebration the following evening. And there was even a postscript scribbled at the bottom: Wei Shan's wife had called. Shit. What was I supposed to tell her? I supposed I ought to drop round after work and show the family a bit of support.

It was a bitch of a morning. Back at the office, I noticed that Wei Shan's desk had been cleared, all his files dispersed. Fishlips obviously didn't have much confidence in him turning up unscathed. A flask full of tea I couldn't face drinking sat between the folders. A notepad, pens, an old photo of an unrecognisably happy family. I shuffled through a pile of papers marked Top Priority, still thinking about the bodies I'd seen in the morgue and trying not to glance over at Wei Shan's empty desk. All of the new investigations were mundane. None of them involved more than a quick study of blueprints and putting my red stamp on plans for a few new bridges and tower blocks. I did my best to pretend I didn't give a shit. Back to normal, you could say.

No, that's not quite right. I'm giving the impression that time rolled on unobstructed, that minute flowed on to minute, hour to hour, with nothing to divert or dam the current. It didn't. Though the time before I got to my desk dragged me kicking and struggling downstream as fast as it could, once I sat down and fingered the paperclips on the pages of the first file, it almost ground to a halt. The second-hand on the clock on the wall even threatened to stop moving altogether. I spent most of the morning rifling dejectedly through brain-numbing files, slipping to the bogs to take a few swigs of booze every few hours, and contemplating phoning Li Yang.

I managed to put it off till lunch – a plate of sloppy pork and onion dumplings oozing fatty juices, eaten alone in a tiny restaurant near the office. There was a newspaper stand with a payphone outside, and if I hunched enough under the rickety shelter the rain only soaked my left side.

'Oh. Hello?'

Li Yang's voice had a hint of laughter in it. Was there someone else there?

'It's me.'

'Ah, you. I haven't heard from you for a while. I was beginning to think maybe you'd had enough of me.'

'I've been busy. Work stuff. Anyway, I tried phoning yesterday, and the day before. You never picked up …'

'Oh, I've had a run of formal dinners. I have to go, they're all friends of Daddy's. But each one was awful, just smiling and trying to look interested through a hundred boring conversations with old Party men. I spent most of the time thinking about you.'

'Are you busy tonight? Maybe we could —'

'Listen, I'm sorry, I can't. I wish I could, but I've got company. Now promise you won't be upset with me. Tomorrow I'm completely free and there'll be no one here but me. Come over. Around eight, say?'

'Well, tomorrow could be —'

'Fantastic. Don't forget how much I love you.'

'Yes, I —'

Li Yang hung up and I started wondering how I let myself get manipulated so easily. There were other people there. Who? And what were they up to? I picked up the phone again to try to distract myself from those worrying thoughts.

'Xiang? It's me. What've you got?'

'You know, you've really got to work on your telephone manner. Nothing wrong with a bit of polite chatter – How was your morning, perhaps, or It was very nice to see you last night. But no, you just leap in with your requests. You're lucky I don't start charging you for all this information.'

'All right, how was your morning?'

I could hear him laughing. 'Fine, thank you. You'll be pleased to know my contact at the bank found just what you were looking for.'

'That was quick.'

'Sure. They've got everything stored on electric brains these days. Saves a lot of time and energy.'

'So, what is it?'

'Monthly payments, starting last autumn, from the Black Light Mining Company. Pretty interesting, huh?'

'Not bad, not bad. I owe you one.'

'Forget about it. If I started counting all the favours I've done for you, we'd be here all day. So what are you going to do now?'

'What do you think? I'm going to find out what this Black Light Mining Company has been playing at.'

'Huh. Just try not to get yourself into too much trouble, all right?'

'Don't worry.'

I set the phone down, paid the guy at the kiosk and started walking towards my car. I couldn't go back to the office now. It would eat at my mind till I knew what had happened. And now I'd seen those bodies, I couldn't go back to pretending it was none of my business. I had the name of the company, so things ought to be simple from now on. I would make a quick visit to the public records office nearest Jawbone Hills then get back to work in time for the afternoon shift.

I drove over the bridge and out of the city once again. If I ever found Wei Shan, I'd give him a right kicking for getting me into this mess. I was never one of those saps who got a kick out of going somewhere new. Whenever Wei Shan used to blabber on about the sense of unbounded freedom and possibility he got from working the land I wanted to tell him to shut up. Or step up – I mean, if he liked it so much up there in the middle of nowhere, then why the hell was he in the middle of the city yapping at me? But I never said any of that out loud. Nor did I ever tell him how much I'd loathed my own experiences during that time.

I had thought the country would be a bit like home, where I wore my father's name like a shield, where I could boss people around and get my own way without anyone daring to snap back at me. I turned up thinking that I'd be giving the orders to shepherds and peasants, and that they would be in awe of my family's Party connections, of the whole pages of the Little Red Book I had memorised, of the speeches from Beijing I had heard on my father's radio and could repeat word for word. But no one gave a toss about who I was or where I came from. Not the locals, not the other young exiles either picking fights amongst themselves or chasing the local shepherds' daughters, and not the sheep I spent years mucking out and herding and sheering and slaughtering.

Did it make me a man? Did I learn anything? I learnt how to bite my tongue to stop from complaining when fed a bowl of boiled grass for the tenth time in a week, how to make time go a little quicker by retreating into my thoughts, how to regret and how to hate. My father would have been proud.

# On the Principles of Nature

PART I · SUMMER 1288 CE

Tommaso di Lovari, brother of the holy Franciscan order, former prior of the abbey of Ancona, renowned scholar of the various apocryphal apocalypses, emissary of the honourable Giovanni da Montecorvino, student of the great Bonaventure, translator, traveller, polyglot and noted cartographer, is dying.

I know this from the way his legs stir and twitch, the smell of his hair, the flaky red skin on the shaved patch at the crown. I can see it in the way his long fingers, which had once been so steadfast and unwavering when pressing a blessing to a burning brow, now clutch at shadows. I know it because this is how it also began with the others.

Since our party has recently been fully occupied with performing the most respectful rites of Christian burial, we have not moved from this dreary spot for three days. Lovari told me that we are a full week from the caves of Mogao, and, according to my calculations, it will take us at least a year before we might complete the return journey and give our report to Father Montercorvino in Sicily. We put our faith in the Lord and let him guide us. Last night, after we had said our last farewells to the young Nazario and delivered his soul unto the Lord, I gathered our party together and led them in prayer. As I proclaimed the holiest of truths to them it took all my reserves of patience to keep from losing my temper with the constant mutterings of the native guides, the incessant fidgeting of the stable-hands and the sedan-carriers, and the interminable itching of those chefs and servants from our homeland who have caught one of these foul diseases from the locals. Yet the men are weak, and they need spiritual sustenance, so I must do all I can to keep them strong while they remain so far from home.

The sun slithers up the hillside, scorching what scant tufts of grass remain among the dust and stones, and the sweat soaks our clothes. I give thanks that we are sheltered from the winds of sand that sweep across this land, winds that are enough to send a man tumbling from his horse, to blind a man or steal his speech and forever clot his calls to heaven. I cannot but remember Christ's hardships in the wilderness and the torments visited upon him, and I vow that our party shall make steady our will as He did, by taking nourishment from the blessed Psalms, the words of His Father. I give thanks too that we have adequate supplies of food as well as shelter from the elemental rages, both of which were denied to our Lord when he faced his trials.

After my morning ablutions, which are regrettably curtailed by the water ration that the master of the victuals has imposed, I take my customary stroll around the camp. It gives the men comfort seeing a man of God among them, and I feel it helps them to concentrate on their given tasks. Some of our number have been much bothered by the songs our Tartar guides sing at night to communicate with the spirits of the desert, and many more have been made fearful by the recent outbreaks of the desert sickness that has claimed three of our retinue in the same number of days. I wear out my voice telling the men that they have nothing to fear if they welcome the Holy Spirit into their lives, but nonetheless they continue to cleave to their irrational superstitions in attempts to ward off the evil humours that abound here.

I make my way from my own tent towards the circle of awnings where some of the men are tending the breakfast fires. The horses and mules are tethered not far from there, and I make a point of speaking to them first, to let our retinue know that no living thing is exempt from the Lord's plan. It was, after all, the uplifting stories of the words and deeds of Francis, the patron of our Order, that first inspired me to follow this path. I give each beast a short benediction, and check for mites, watery eyes or split hooves, to ensure that the servants are not neglecting any of their duties.

I am still somewhat sluggish as I make my rounds, since my night was interrupted by the call from Lovari's tent, and after that episode I found it difficult to sleep. Thus I make my way around the camp a little more slowly than usual, and eventually reach the supplies tent, where I hope to speak with Paul. He is somewhat typical of the locals of this strange country, being short, lithe and dark, with eyes that always seem to be in danger of becoming permanently crossed. The fine hairs of his beard resemble the frayed trails of cheap rope, hanging limply from his round cheeks, and like his fellow countrymen he seems to enjoy nothing so much as squatting down on his haunches for many hours on end. However, I make a point never to pay attention to a man's appearance. The Lord, after all, sees only our souls.

I know well enough the secret shame that stares and comments can cause, having suffered from the pox as a child back in the monastery in Assisi. I was kept in an isolated cloister for close to three months, with only the Holy Bible and an ancient, scarred monk for company. At first I greatly feared the elderly patient in the room next to mine, for not only did he seem as old as the crumbling building itself, but he had also suffered burns so terrible that his purple face looked like the bubbling, waxy mess that gathers at the stump of a candle. His face was a mask of sores and blisters; dark eyes stared out from great hooded scabs, and his nostrils and mouth were as holes carved in hardened clay. He was bedridden, and made a sound like dice rattling around in a cup when he spoke.

Yet I soon found that beneath those gruesome features he retained a keen mind, and it was he who elucidated many of the passages in the Bible that most troubled me as a child. We spent whole days in question and response, and even after the pox left me, I continued to return to the infirmary so that I might converse with my elderly friend. He seemed to understand more than anyone the worries that struck sometimes at my heart, and he saved me from loneliness by educating me about all the creatures in the Lord's kingdom, of which he had an unsurpassable knowledge. He taught me the names and unique attributes of every beast, every insect and every bird in every different country, that I might understand the wonders of creation. Though in truth I listened to the burnt man for the most part because I enjoyed his company, I have since found vital uses for the knowledge he imparted to me. I do greatly miss him, and I pray that despite his most advanced age the Lord will not deliver him to Heaven before I have returned from this mission. Though the pox left these scars and hollows dotted across my cheeks and forehead, I would gladly suffer them again for such a friend.

Already the sun is burning my toes, and I turn and scan the camp for Paul. The white sand sparks, the grey stones threaten to melt.

Paul is not, of course, our chief guide's real name. The name his parents gave him is some mess of syllables that requires laborious twisting of the tongue to pronounce. I have called him Paul on account of the fact that he is responsible for leading us out of this idolatrous land and back to the countries of true faith, although he has as yet refused my offers to baptise him. As he is integral to our mission, I have not pushed this point too much.

He has an adequate knowledge of Latin, and so, despite his inability to modify the verbs according to tense, we communicate in that grand old language. Thus he has also become the intermediary between the natives and myself, keeping me informed of the concerns of our guides and the customs of the locals while also translating the lessons I have been giving the men to help them understand the sacrifice the Son of God made for every one of us. I always ensure that the whole party sups together at dusk, so that everyone might remember that we are equal in the eyes of the Lord, though thanks to the cacophonous din made by the disparate groups in our retinue as they gorge themselves, dinner more closely resembles the chaos of a country inn than the silent unity of Christian brotherhood I remember from the monastery. The only thing that binds the locals and our own men, in fact, is their drink – since the rations of wine ran out some time ago, our servants have been forced to share the translucent spirit drunk by the locals, and many seem to have become quite fond of it. I have tried to warn them from it, since I fear it may lodge heathen ideas in their stomachs or unbalance their humours, but to no avail. I alone keep watch over our men in the evenings, for, since we left Dadu, the usually sociable Lovari has been in the habit of eating by himself in his tent, and gave the strictest of instructions that even I was not to disturb him.

Paul is standing with a stick in his hand, arguing with one of his boys. In front of them the sand has been etched with strange markings, and I take it that these are the source of their disagreement. When Paul catches sight of me his voice drops to a whisper and he sends the boy scurrying off with a scowl on his face.

'I hope you are not experiencing any difficulties with your retinue. It would be quite a shame if I had to dock your men's rations again. I assumed they would have learnt after last time, but ...' I raise my hands and give him a smile, eager to show that I am nothing if not a fair man.

'No. No trouble. He sees big dark. But I do not see.'

'Big dark? What ever do you mean? Really, Paul, how are we to talk of civilised things if you keep using such cloudy and oblique phrases?'

'Yes, yes. A cloud. A big dark cloud.'

'Oh. I see. A storm coming?'

'No storm. No trouble. He sees anything he wants. I see what really happens. Sun and wind. No cloud.'

'So there is nothing to worry about?'

Paul says nothing in response to this question, so I must assume he either did not hear me properly or did not understand what I meant.

'How is the situation with the supplies? With the water?'

'Enough water. Enough food. Insect and snake. Desert gives us more. You need more insects?'

I smile patiently.

'Paul, the question might better be phrased as "Do you require any more insects, sir?" Why don't you try it again?'

He cocks his head and lets his tongue run leisurely over his brown teeth. His skin, like the other natives, resembles well-used leather. After a moment he scratches a stubby finger through his lank black hair. I sigh.

'No, I shall not be needing any more at present. You need not trouble yourself, for I am coming to the end of my experiment. Soon I shall write up the results and so be done with these repulsive beasts. Father Montercorvino will be much impressed if we bring back a rudimentary catalogue of the unique creatures, flora and fauna found in this land. What I shall need, however, is for more water to be taken to Prior Lovari's tent. No doubt you have heard that he has been struck with the desert sickness, so we must do all we can to bring him comfort.'

'I will send it.' Paul bows curtly and then turns back to the sand.

Our customary morning interview being over, I walk back towards the other side of the camp. As I go, I notice that Paul is kicking at the sand in order to remove the markings his boy has etched there.

After finishing my breakfast, I retire to my own quarters. I wait in here so as to be available to the servants, chefs, horsemen, guides, cartographers and apprentices who may wish to pay me a private visit, since I have given each my assurance that as I am one of the few Holy men on this mission, I will happily hear their confessions and give absolution should their spirits falter during our long journey through this strange land, particularly now that their doubts and fears are being stoked by the terrible sickness that is striking down man after man in our party. Like yesterday, however, and indeed the three days that preceded it, no one comes.

I try to devote myself to a little contemplation of Athanasius's Life of Saint Anthony, but I find it difficult to concentrate given my tiredness and the persistent scuttling sound coming from the small box beneath my desk. I peer down through the air holes in the side and see two of the small creatures strutting about in their rusty-looking armour. I have whimsically named this classification sand prawns because of their bulkier bodies and paler appearance than their European counterparts, though in truth their fierce tail marks them out as quite distinct from their cousins. A third is lying curled in the corner of the box, no doubt a sad example of the creatures' violent tendencies towards one another (undoubtedly exacerbated by captivity). I must admit that I am gladdened by the knowledge that Paul will not bring me any more of these vicious beasts.

Notice soon arrives from Lovari's tent that my brother has awoken, and thus I set aside my books and boxes and make my way across the camp. I collect two bowls of pottage from the cooks on the way, and carry them both to Lovari's tent. Since the news has gone round about his sickness, many of the men seem wary to go near him for fear of ill luck, yet I have spent much of my life nursing the frail and the diseased, and have no qualms about eating with my dearest brother. At such dark times men need comfort and reassurance, and I have decided that, if he is feeling well enough, we might read the Gospel of John together.

I slip past the thick cloth and the fine netting to find Lovari lying on a pile of cushions. Despite the insufferable heat, he seems to be wrapped in at least three blankets, his brow wet with perspiration. Ever since we first met, I have thought of him as an unusually large man, filling every room he enters with his hearty laugh, his sonorous voice commanding attention from everyone. Yet now, as I kneel by his side, he seems suddenly childlike, small.

'Is that you, Rosso?' His eyes are heavy and they force themselves open only after a couple of attempts.

'Brother, I am glad you have woken. I have brought you a little food.'

'Ah, bless you, brother.'

He pushes himself clumsily up onto his elbows, this smallest of exertions drawing from him sighs and gasps at which he is clearly embarrassed. I give him the bowl.

'Do you feel any better? Were you able to rest after I left you last night?'

'The spasms are gone, and I am glad to report that the pain has lessened a little. But my legs are swollen, a fever burns in my chest and I feel as though my breath has been stolen from me.'

He looks up into my eyes. His face is far redder than it was only a few hours ago when his anguished cries summoned me to his tent, and his lips are dry and broken.

'Yes, I know what you are thinking. D'Antonio, Salvitici and then Nazario – all three suffered the same symptoms in the same order, and all three were given to the Lord before the sun had completed a single rotation around the earth. It is the desert sickness. I fear I do not have much time left.'

'That kind of talk will not aid your recovery. You must strengthen your resolve.'

He shakes his head. 'Let us be honest, brother. You saw me last night, and you see me now. You were with Nazario only yesterday morning. We both know how this illness progresses, and how it will end. I am grateful for your attempts to bring comfort to my enfeebled body, yet my spirit is still strong, and I am not afraid to face death. Indeed, I shall welcome it. The mysteries of Heaven are things of which I have spent my life dreaming.'

'The Lord may yet have other plans for you.'

'I think not, though I am not vain enough to anticipate His grand designs. But let me ask you, Rosso, are you ready?'

I shuffle my knees back a little, trying to find a more suitable pose, for in truth I am not used to staying long on such soft cushions and pillows, having spent my formative years kneeling for hours on the cold, hard stone of the chapel.

'I … I trust when the moment comes I shall not flinch from it.'

Lovari let out a hoarse laugh. 'No, brother, I don't mean death! You are still a young man, in the rudest of health. You need not worry about that yet. No, I mean taking charge of the party here. Are you ready to lead such a large group, to take charge of the retinue and finish our mission?'

I must admit I am a little piqued at such a question, for over these last three days, before he too fell ill, he has seen me administer last rites, perform funerals and calm many of the frightened men in our retinue with my well-chosen homilies and readings. However, I judge it best not to argue with such a frail man.

'I will put my faith in the Lord. He will guide me.'

'They can be a rough bunch, as bad as any heathens. And remember, they have been far from their families for close to two years now. I know you and I differ on our preferred choice of sermons, but I would advise you to take heed and follow my example by railing against the sins of the rich and the idle, and detailing the fates that await those persons after death, for the men take much pleasure in knowing that the inequalities of the world will one day be righted. Also, make sure you apply the same rules to the foreigners as to our own countrymen if you do not wish to risk sowing discord throughout the camp. You will have to harden yourself, my brother. I am sorry to place such a burden on you. I did not expect something like this to happen.'

'No one expected it. Yet perhaps you might take a little comfort that your suffering brings you closer to the Lord.'

Lovari snorts. 'The ecstasy of suffering? I confess I have never had much time for that idea.'

'Yet the knowledge of pain brings us closer to the experience of the Christ. This was one of the first things I remember learning at the seminary. Pain helps us to transcend ourselves, to empathise with the greatest sacrifice ever known.'

'That is the theology of tyrants and slave drivers. Our Lord suffered on the cross so that we might be free from suffering. The presence of the Lord is heaven, and His absence is suffering. Thus I do not suffer, I only wait.'

I say nothing. It is tempting to point out that I have read the same tracts that he has, that I have made careful studies of the documents from both Councils of Nicea, have read the Gospels in their original Greek as well as Saint Jerome's sublime Latin, have composed my own amendments and additions to Anselm's ontological argument and Aquinas's five proofs and have amassed, in only a few years, a reputation for scholarly erudition that stretches far beyond my native Assisi. However, Lovari is my elder and, for all that we disagree, I have come to respect him. I have even been entertaining the idea that the looseness with which he interprets some of the central tenets of our faith, which when we first met did little but arouse my contempt, is simply one of the ways in which the strength of my own faith is being put to the test.

'I see you do not agree, my brother. That is the beauty of grace: to some it comes as a bird, to others as a wolf. Do not worry, there are no snooping priors here to castigate us for the tiniest deviations of our beliefs.'

'Snooping priors? The very idea is ridiculous. I have never met a priest who was not honest, compassionate and benevolent.'

Lovari suddenly begins to cough, great hacking croaks that sound as though he has swallowed the whole desert and all the storms it keeps. I wait patiently for him to finish, then wipe the spittle from his cracked lips.

'Then count yourself lucky. There are some men so unscrupulous they would use faith as a mask for their ambitions. I am sure you do not need me to tell you, brother, of how lowly a creature man may sometimes be.'

'I may have spent much of my life in cloisters, but that does not mean I do not understand the world outside. I concur that man is a wretched, fallen thing.'

As I speak, I take the bowl of pottage and raise the spoon to Lovari's lips, but he shakes his head. There was a time I fed the dying abbot back in Assisi. I cannot have been more than twelve. The elderly curate was calm, contemplative and silent as he faced his final hours. I can see that this is not going to be like that.

'You must eat, brother.'

'Perhaps later. Listen, Rosso, put a cushion beneath my head. That's it, good. Now, I want to ask you something. There is no reason for us to pretend that I will be able to see our mission through to its completion. You have grown under my tutelage, and will surely go on to become a notable servant of the Cross and, dare I say it, a remarkable scholar. You are the only person here whom I can trust. This is why I ask if you will be my confessor.'

'It would be my honour, brother, to listen and absolve you of all your sins.'

Again he coughs.

'I am not sure we have time to go through all my sins. You need to know what has happened, for there may still be a chance. There are two sins you must know of … But I run ahead of myself. I must explain everything, or else you will not understand.'

Lovari takes a deep, hoarse breath. He looks up at me and smiles, the type of tender look I imagine an elder brother might give his sibling. I am mildly disconcerted; nevertheless, I once again remind myself of the Fourth Lateran Council's proposals for the confession. I bend my head, and intone the words that only the previous afternoon I had spoken over poor young Nazario.

'Most Sacred Heart of Our Lord, compassionate and true, grant us your mercy. Immaculate Maria, Holy Mother of —'

'There's no need for all of that. I seek neither absolution nor your suggestions on how I might do penance. I require you only to listen, and then you will understand what must be done.'

I grit my teeth. 'Certainly. I shall do whatever you ask.'

Lovari closes his eyes. 'You were orphaned, or at least abandoned. Am I right? Taken to the local monastery when your parents died, or left wailing outside the huge wooden gates at the top of the city. The monks, tactful as they are, probably did not tell you which. Yet instead of taking you to an orphanage, for some reason they kept you and raised you themselves. Correct me if I am wrong.'

I feel my face flush. 'You are correct. I presume you were given a detailed account of my history when you were paired with me for this mission.'

'No, the inimitable Giovanni da Montecorvino does not trouble with such trifles. It is not difficult to guess from your demeanour, from the awkward way you speak to the servants, even from the way you eat your supper. A man's personal history is inscribed in such small actions. All you have to do is pay attention.'

'I see.'

'What I mean to point out is that your earliest memories are of stone walls, of men in dark robes, some silent, some fasting, others acting as though they are unaware of the very buildings through which they walk. Your early years were filled by the ringing of bells calling the brothers to prayer, by hushed and reverent voices whispering always in that most formal of ancient languages, by evensong and mass. You lived by litany and the cane and the rote.

Of muddy scraps and bloody noses, of the gentle roughness of kin, of young girls and bawdy women, of helping your parents in the fields, of the shove and bustle of market day, of hunger and of hard-earned laughter, I would warrant you learnt nothing. This is why I must start at the beginning, that you might see how our lives have differed, and indeed, brother, how yours might have been had the monks not taken you in.

'I was born in the Kingdom of Sicily during the final years of the reign of Frederick II, Holy Roman Emperor. My father was a soldier in the Imperial Army, and died at the Battle of Parma when our side was routed from the city. I was about three years old at the time, and my sister was still in swaddling cloths. I have no memory of my father. Our family lived just outside Palermo, that great golden capital, and one of the earliest things I remember is leaving the city for a small village some days' walk away, following close behind my mother as we headed to the house of my aunt and uncle, who had agreed to take us in after my mother was widowed.

'Like all relatives, my mother's sister and her husband put on a theatre of false kindness when we saw them once a year at Michaelmas, yet soon became unbearable when there was no escape from them. They were bakers, and when my uncle was not up pressing dough or plotting with others from the guild, he was drunk and garrulous.

'I was a lonely child, more taken with daydreaming and playing with my younger sister than grinding wheat on the worn stone, and thus, for my uncle – a man who daily suffered the embarrassment and indignity of being reminded that he had sired only daughters – I was a symbol of a world that conspired to keep him down. I hated him with a fervour few can imagine. It would be tiresome to detail the petty humiliations, and the larger, terrifying brutality, he inflicted upon my sister and me.

'Though I cannot claim to have been a testament to the virtues of athletics as a young man, neither was I the frail, pathetic creature you are perhaps imagining. I wrestled with the other boys from the smallholdings behind the old mill, and more often than not my opponent was left looking far worse than I. With the same boys I crept out at night to the cockfights and dogfights in the taller barns of the village. Yet whenever I faced my uncle, my rage turned to paralysis, my well-honed strength to impotence.

'He was a man overcome by the whispering of the Devil at his ear. However, he would also lead us to the local church every Sabbath, and it was these two hours of haunting mass that provided a way out of the confines of my life. Instead of the curses and recriminations came the tremulous, righteous rage of the Latin sermon; instead of the sight of fists and sneers there was the loving stare of the Lord suspended above us on the cross; instead of my cowering mother, there was the Madonna, eternally caring and always prepared to act as intermediary for our prayers; instead of the stink of yeast and hare stew, there were scented candles and the lingering smell of the dark, mysterious wine.

'The priest was a man by the name of Sebastiano. To my mind he was an exemplary preacher, able to speak so passionately that there was not a single adult in our part of town, including my own vicious uncle, who did not fear him, and yet he was mild and honest with children like myself who pushed and shoved to be able to help out at the altar. I was amazed beyond belief to find my stuttered words taken seriously by an adult. I would have been less surprised to learn that the old, white-haired priest had wings and could fly than to find that he was happy to talk earnestly with a nine-year-old. He was a hunched, choleric man, well advanced in years, and his accent marked him out as something of a curio. It was only later that I learnt that the only way our backwoods parish would be granted such a man was because he must have been exiled for the capital in the hope of keeping him from stirring up trouble.

'Justice. Law. Sacrifice. Grace. Love. These were just vague ideas before I met Father Sebastiano, before I heard him reciting, from memory, whole pages of the Holy Book, and then translating and expostulating to anyone who would listen. He left the mysteries of the Trinity to the sacred mass – for who would dare paraphrase, interpret or summarise that profound truth when it is more fit for private contemplation? – and so, when we crowded round him after a service, he would wander between us, running his hand often through our hair as he retold the parables in a lively, humorous inflection, making each one of us feel as though it spoke directly to our own thoughts. It was then that I got that first taste of the transcendence of the Word, and was first gripped by the sense that so much more exists beyond our knowledge and comprehension.

'When I confessed to him, I found that along with absolution he gave words of comfort; along with castigation he gave me the strength of the Word. I found myself coming to the church as often as I could. He showed me sheaths of parchment he said he had saved from his last mission, and, seeing my naïve fascination, quickly invented an excuse of returning to the latest ecumenical business so that I could attempt to read them without someone standing over my shoulder. He soon began to encourage me, to explain the symbols, to let me stay for hours looking through the precious books. I felt as though I was blind Bartimaeus suddenly granted sight by our Lord, my eyes slowly being able to make out the remote horizons of a world beyond the bakery, and becoming aware of something deeper and more deeply engrained that I could not yet name.

'It was in this way that, as the years passed, I learnt the rigorous and enchanting skills of reading and writing that my parents had never known. I think perhaps this was one of Sebastiano's small acts of rebellion, of getting his own back at the powers that had banished him by unleashing the mutinous effect of a little knowledge on an unsuspecting community.

'By teaching me Latin, I felt that he gave me an amazing power over the adults around me. For now I could understand the liturgy whereas my elders could only bow their heads and submit. I think, even then, I had an idea of how the kindly priest had turned the world upside down by teaching me, and a number of others, this most sacred of things. Though many of the other young boys attended his lessons for only a number of weeks or months before suddenly disappearing and staying far from the church (events which I saw saddened the old priest greatly) I never let my resolve slip. Father Sebastiano told us that Christ would come with the Sword to vanquish the Devil who lived among us, and that we must all therefore be ready. So he set us to task. And if I learnt quicker than any of the others, repeating the conjugations of verbs under my breath as I tore the stalks from the wheat, as I sifted the grit from the flour, it was only because I believed that the fate of my undying soul depended upon it.

'It was not long before the sickness visited our village. Great scarlet pustules bubbled upon my sister's skin, and within days she sank into a fever. She was overrun with dark humours, and even the most extensive course of bloodletting could not stop her from coughing up her life-source. The coffin was cut from the cheapest of warped timber, a tiny box that could be hoisted on the shoulders of a single man.

'I turned to Sebastiano for comfort, for an explanation that would ease my grief. Yet none was forthcoming. The elderly priest spoke instead about Purgatory, where my sister's soul would flitter in torment for hundreds of years until it was purified. Prayers and tithes, the old man told me, might ease her passage. I remember running from the church, feeling abandoned and empty. I did not sleep that night, nor any other for weeks, finding that I could no longer reconcile the loving beneficence of the Lord with the true, terrible nature of my daily life.'

Lovari's pale hand emerges from the blankets to rub at his eyes, and I offer him a sip from the bowl of water beside him.

'You were young. The Lord allows for such passages of doubt in innocents,' I tell him.

'It was no short passage, brother. For, only ten days after my sister's death, I made my way to the small church, which by then I had been visiting almost every evening for five years, and I saw something terrible. A young girl, the same age as my sister had been, was walking slowly from the building. Her eyes were red, her clothes were rent and her lips bloody and swollen, though she seemed to be doing all she could to compose herself. As I drew closer I saw Sebastiano hurry from the church to approach her, to calm her perhaps with some lesson from the Gospels, though I could not hear what he was saying. He laid a hand gently upon her shoulder to comfort her. This was not unusual, for I had never met a more friendly and affectionate man. Yet he pulled the same hand away from her as quickly as he could when he saw me approaching, and that made my heart flinch. He was soon smiling and waving to me as if happy to see an old friend, but that single movement had betrayed him, and I fled from the church with anger seething through my very pores, aware at last of the reason why so many other local boys had suddenly stopped attending his lessons.

'It seemed as if in only a few weeks my entire world had been shattered, my faith and certainty torn from me. And so I grew drunk on dark humours, on melancholy and bile. I turned away from the Church and from the bitter hypocrisies I believed I had uncovered. I was barely thirteen, and thought I understood the entire world. From that day forward I would run from my uncle's house at daybreak, shirking my allotted work to drink and fight and thieve with some of the orphans and wastrels who had been exiled from the city. We played endless games of dice, and once set fire to the barn of a farmer who tried to upbraid us.'

'Come, friend, you surely exaggerate. You are making yourself sound as if you were the character of Vice in one of those market square morality plays. The truth is never so coarse, never so unadorned,' I say, though mainly in order to keep him calm and stop his fever rising, for I have no doubt that much of his past was as devilish as he admits.

He brings forth a low, rolling cough, which somehow transforms into a laugh.

'You will struggle with this confession if you continue to try to see the best in me, brother. I shall not detail the petty sins of that time, for those are ones for which I have done my penance. As I told you, it is of two larger sins that I wish to speak.

'It was barely two seasons later that I returned to my uncle's house late one evening, having evaded my household chores for the whole day, to find him red-faced and drunk in the smoky kitchen, clutching a meat knife in his good hand. I remember my first impulse was to puff out my chest to attempt to evoke a fearlessness I did not feel.

'I do not recall the words he shouted, the curses he spat as his wife and my mother cowered in the corner. I remember only the rage which stung my senses, the feeling that a storm was sparking through my veins. I spat at him. He leapt up and swung at me. The next few moments are messy, confused, though I have revisited them many times over the years. I threw myself behind one of the wooden posts supporting the low roof, then tumbled, ducked, rolled, as he leapt at me, the flailing blade glinting in the candlelight. The Devil was strong within him, and yet for once I was determined not to give in. I kicked out at him, sending him tripping over a wooden stool and crashing into the hay, from where he emerged even more red and enraged than before. He dashed towards me, and as I spun away I felt the tip of the knife slash through the top of my shoulder. You have perhaps seen the scar, Rosso. I sagged, stumbled, pressed my hand to the wound.

'His upraised hand hovered above me, and I remember his sudden laugh – a clear, bitter laugh – as he easily swatted away my pathetic attempts at defensive punches. It was then that my mother stepped forward to stop him, though she was soon knocked out of the way in the chaos. I kicked once more at my uncle's knee, knocking him off balance, before running for the door amid the sound of screams and oaths. But before I could reach it he was on top of me, his fist sending me sprawling towards the table, and as the blows rained down upon my head and chest I could only be thankful that he had lost his knife in the scuffle.

'It was only the shrill wails of my aunt which stopped him. He turned from me, then stumbled back in horror. I tried to rise on shaking feet, bruised, aching and uncomprehending – he had never before stopped a beating before I had squealed and cried and begged his forgiveness for neglecting my duties. Then I saw the mauve puddle spreading across the floor.

'My mother lay gurgling in front of us, her pale hands twitching nervously around the gash in her neck as if they were starlings come to drink from a babbling stream. Though I rushed to her side, there was little I could do to stem the flow where the knife had struck. Her lips moved, but no intelligible sound emerged. She was coughing, cawing, clawing for breath.

'You will forgive me, brother, if I do not dwell on those last hours. I do not have the strength left in me to summon her final moments. I only tell you of this terrible night because I cannot forget it, because from that day on all my actions were driven by an insatiable enmity towards the injustice I saw everywhere in the world.

'My uncle paid as little as he could for a cheap plot in the cemetery behind the church. Father Sebastiano buried my mother beside the freshly turned earth of my sister's grave. He gave candles and prayers that might help her soul in Purgatory, and that was the last time I saw the old priest before I killed him.'

I force my drowsy eyes open and look at Lovari. He is neither smiling nor scowling, lying back on his bed of cushions in the soporific desert heat.

'This is undoubtedly a metaphor, brother, and a clever one at that, for every student must in some way "kill" his teacher by surpassing him. And with your many achievements and scholarly renown you have certainly risen above your first mentor.'

'You know, Rosso, that I have no time for such laboured figures of speech.'

'Then you mean you did what any son would do for a suffering father, and helped end the life of a man in pain, just as men have no choice but to cut the throat of a dog wounded in the hunt. What you did was merciful, to save an old man the anguish and indignities of a crippling illness.'

'No. He may have been old and hunched, but he still had that same fiery energy burning inside him. I told you that there were two sins of which you have to know. The killing of Father Sebastiano is the first.'

A good confessor should ease the passing of the flesh by making steadfast the undying soul of the sinner. He should offer comfort while also urging the sinner to seek redemption before it is too late. And, before administering the final sacrament, he should do his best to ensure that the sinner is delivered into his Master's arms. As I sit beside the pale, sweating form of Brother Lovari and listen to his wild tale, however, the task at hand seems more arduous than ever.

Despite his frail body, alternating between shivering and sweating, his heavy eyes pressed closed and his breaths cracked and laboured, he seems determined that against all precedent he should lead the confession, and sees fit to admonish me when I make even the smallest of interruptions. In my only other experience of acting as confessor, young Nazario asked for absolution for the small sins of vanity and lust, while when I watched Lovari give the last rites to D'Antonio and then Salvitici, both men spoke of little but the distant homes they would now never return to. Yet I well know that Lovari is nothing like any of the other men I have ever met.

My sick friend clutches a hand to his chest, as if to calm the erratic rhythms of his heart. His eyelids flutter, and he draws in a deep, wheezing breath.

'On the very same day my mother was buried I left the village, for I knew whatever happened to me out on my own would be preferable to returning to my uncle's home. Though I had no money, and nothing upon my person save a stolen knife and an extra pair of boots for the winter months, I felt the grand confidence of youth. There was only one possible destination.

'It was easy to believe, as an unworldly thirteen-year-old, that the capital of the Kingdom of Sicily contained the whole world. It had passed through a hundred different hands, and each had left their fingerprint indelibly pressed onto it. The learning of the Greeks, the might of the Romans, the feasts and sacred mysteries of the Byzantines, the logic and mathematics of the Saracens, the law courts and new customs of the Norman kings. Strolling through the central districts of Palermo for the first time, I passed the ruins of idolatrous temples, fine stone mosques watched over by bearded imams, small synagogues, and all manner of churches, both domed and towered. I stared open-mouthed at lemons and oranges from the East set for sale alongside great husks of hardened cheese, and heard people conversing in courtly French or Arabic as well as in Latin, Greek and, of course, the natural Sicilian dialect – one that even you, my brother, with your renown as a linguist, may have trouble untangling should you one day venture to my homeland.

'In a city like Palermo, it was easy to disappear among the crowds. With my gift for languages, I found I could impersonate almost anyone. I was a prince, walking with my head held high through the markets and demanding, in a drawling city accent, foods to be added, naturally, to the bills of the most famous households. I was a light-skinned Mohammedan boy, my tongue testing out the few Arabic phrases I had picked up outside the gates, covering my head and cleaning my feet as I wandered into a mosque. I was a young monk in training, unleashing an endless torrent of Latin, giving out platitudes and loosely spun parables in return for gifts outside the great palace. Once I had gained my audience's confidence, there was nothing easier than wrangling a loan or, if that failed, slipping my hand deftly into their purses.

'Do not look at me like that, brother. I was young and hungry, and at war with the world. Whenever I felt guilty about what I was doing, I made myself recall the words of the Apostle Matthew: "Do not store up treasures for yourself, that might be consumed by rust or moths." All I was doing, I told myself, was teaching the people I met an important lesson about the transience of all human wealth. It was truly astounding how few adults questioned a well-spoken young man with a practised smile.

'I fell in with a crowd of thieves and fraudsters, who introduced me to liquor and taught me how to slip unnoticed among the tumultuous rabble in the market squares, to move unseen through the throngs surrounding rogue apothecaries hawking love potions to the unrequited, or into the background of the wrestling matches between desperate men outside the taverns. I felt invincible for a time, and like the other young men I spent my time with, I rarely thought of the gallows that might await us if we got caught.

'You will not be surprised to hear that this idyll was short-lived. It was a mere month or two before something happened that would change my life forever. I was sitting outside a cobbler's shop, chewing on some bread that had fallen from the back of a wagon, when a large shadow bore down upon me. I dropped my loaf with a start as a strong pair of hands gripped suddenly about my neck. I struggled hard against this sudden attack, and when I managed to pull away and spin around, I was amazed to find that my assailant was a priest. Not a meek old custodian of grace like Father Sebastiano, however, but a young stocky fellow full of bile. Indeed, this dark-haired priest seemed only a few years older than myself. Before I could escape, however, he shoved me to the ground, where he proceeded to place a few well-aimed kicks to my ribs. Winded and hugging my knees to my chest against the blows, I saw only that he had hitched up his ecclesiastical robe so to be able to put greater force into his kicks. I curled tighter, like an egret arched around its nestlings.

'When the brawny priest finally grew tired, he wiped the spittle from his lips and shouted at me to get up and follow him. As I did not dare move, he grabbed me by my neck and pulled me up, before pushing me forward, tumbling, tripping and dizzy, down the deserted street. We continued this way for half an hour, winding a serpentine trail through backstreets and narrow alleys, across cobblestones and squelching tracks, past mansions and hovels. When I was thoroughly disoriented, a slap across the shoulders brought me to a halt outside a tall wooden building.

'It was a grand, ramshackle complex that looked as if a Moorish palace had been fused with a rustic barn. I remember being relieved, because it was highly improbable that such a strange abode would be home to any judicial authority, though it was clear that many people dwelt within. The entrance hall was full of ill-dressed families, waiting for alms. They showed little interest in the pair of us as we ascended the narrow curl of stairs. The walls wore a few bedraggled tapestries, their interweaving patterns clearly owing a debt to the Saracen artists, yet the bleeding Christ hooked upon a knot of rough oak looming from the wall above us announced that this was no heathen abode. The priest called out a welcome in an impenetrable accent as we climbed, then stopped me outside a closed door.

'You may find it strange that, throughout the attack that had rudely interrupted my lunch, and then during the march across the city and into the peculiar house, I never once wondered why I had been singled out in this way. You see, already at that young age I felt thoroughly reconciled with fate. Just as I had never stood up to my uncle, so I did not think to ask the dark-haired priest why he had kicked me, nor why he had led me to that bewildering building.

'The door was soon hauled open and we were ushered in, though I could see little of those inside, for the room was almost pitch-black. My eyes strained through the gloom, and I naturally assumed that the place bore the sooty scars of some terrible fire. However, it soon became apparent that the darkness was simply a product of the fact that the walls, floor and ceiling had all been painted black. I felt, my brother, as though I was Jonah inside the trembling dark of the whale's gut. Indeed, although I heard voices, it took many minutes before I was able to make out the faces of the speakers.

'Two men, pointing at the ceiling, were conversing in whispers. One was tall and somewhat stooped, with tiny squinting eyes. His long habit of white serge with drooping cowl, and his domed, shaven head marked him out as a Carthusian. In truth, however, in the near darkness, he looked like nothing so much as a giant newt. His face was pasty and white, his lips long and rubbery. His companion, to my initial surprise, not only wore a long beard, but also the luscious, flowing black cassock associated with the Byzantine Church. He looked much older than the Carthusian and his impressive girth attested to the fact that the dietary requirements of his own order were nowhere near as prescriptive. Despite their differences, the two men seemed to be conversing quite amicably as they gestured above their heads. I followed their outstretched hands and saw that the ceiling was not as uniformly black as the rest of the room, and was in fact covered with tiny dabs of white paint, intended, I later realised, to represent the many constellations of the heavens.

'The Byzantine cleared his throat and turned to the dark-haired priest who had brought me to them. He spoke with a thick, heavy accent, as if his tongue had been preyed upon by a whole hive of insolent bees.

'"So, Alessio, this is the boy?"'

'My attacker grunted his affirmation.

'"And you are still convinced that he is possessed?"'

'"As I said, some of our people have spotted him outside the mosque, some at church, some in the bathhouses, and each time he was speaking a different language. I tracked him all morning and heard him speaking flawless Latin, and saying he was in training to be a priest."

'The Byzantine looked at the Carthusian and raised his wiry eyebrows. "Then they are legion. I have performed a number of exorcisms before, but never with more than one Devil inhabiting the flesh, and never with one so young."

'The Carthusian nodded gravely, but the man they called Alessio – my attacker – soon spoke up.

'"Couldn't we find a herd of swine to send the demons into? The Lord's example ought to be good enough for us, after all. There's a livestock market down near the law courts today, we could still catch it if we hurry."

'"I do not think the Good Lord had to deal with Sicilian pig-farmers, Alessio. I doubt they would think twice about setting upon us if we were to damage their livelihood in any way. No, I think trepanation may be the solution here. I have heard nothing but praise for its results."

'Alessio looked sceptical, and I began to wonder whether I would be given a chance to speak for myself at all. "What's trepanation?" he asked.

'"Well, it is truly a fascinating process." When the Carthusian finally joined the exchange, I remember being somewhat alarmed by the unnaturally high pitch of his voice. "It is quite remarkable what these men of science can do, really quite remarkable. They have endeavoured to design a metal cage that can be fixed to the afflicted man's head. Once they are thus held down, it is possible, using a sharpened gyre, to drill into the skull. This allows the demons to escape from their hiding place within the murky humours of the brain."

'"So it works?"

'"Oh yes, it seems to work marvellously. The way the afflicted man screams and writhes while the hole is being drilled is surely proof of the demons' wild excitement. Also, when the operation is finished, and the metal cage removed, the man beneath always seems calm and quiet, owing to the success of the exorcism. And it would suit our purpose, for the demons ought to be quite easy to capture as they come rushing out. However, procuring a qualified apothecary with the necessary equipment to perform the procedure on such a young man will not be cheap."

'The three holy men lapsed into silence. I must admit, I was not much encouraged by the turn of their conversation, so I decided to intervene.

'"Please excuse my interruption, sirs, but I fear there has been some mistake. I have no demons within me."

'The Byzantine raised one of his voluminous eyebrows.

'"How old are you?"

'"Fifteen."

'"You would swear that on the Holy Book?"

'"Alright, I'm one month short of fourteen years."

'"And you live on the streets, yes?"

'"For now. But only for a short time, father. I have no doubt that the Lord will soon guide me towards an occupation and a purpose."

'"Then how, if you are neither rich nor possessed, do you have such skill with languages? I warrant that you are not from one of the princely families who may pay for private tutors, and you lack both the reserve and the refined manners I would expect from a child who had spent years in a monastery."

'And so I told them of the angry home from which I had made my escape, of Father Sebastiano and the awakening of my imagination (which we all know, brother, is the beginning of hope), of my studies and ideas, and even of my rage and disappointment when my new-found faith was tested. I told them how I had worked to learn the language of the Scriptures simply because I had to, just as when a man climbing the steepest of cliffs will keep grappling upwards, for the only other option is to fall back into the depths and perish.

'Alessio muttered a distinctly unpriestly curse. "Father Teodoro will be most disappointed. This was supposed to be his experiment," he huffed.

'"Then you shall have to be most diplomatic when you tell him of your mistake, Alessio."

'The bearded man waved a long, gnarled finger at Alessio as he spoke, and with a sigh my surly attacker nodded and left the room.'

Lovari begins to cough, and I encourage him to rest his voice. He will not listen, however, and shakes his head at my suggestions that he might care to sleep a little and regain his strength. He suddenly starts to shift violently in his blankets, as though trying to shake himself free of his illness. Outside the tent, I can hear the high whirr of those despicable foreign sandflies biding their time, waiting for my exit so that they may dip down upon me and feast. My skin itches just thinking about them. The most recent red blotches are, mercifully, hidden beneath my robes – I do not want any of the men to mistake them for a punishment sent from Heaven.

I had thought Lovari's confession would take only an hour. Instead it seems as though it might take all day. Yet I must admit that there is something intriguing about his tale – if it can be trusted, that is, for I am well aware of the ways in which some diseases of this kind can cause an excess of yellow bile that may affect the memory.

When Lovari finally turns back towards me I take a cloth and clean his mouth. His spittle is flecked with blood. His eyelids, rustling like translucent moths testing their wings, slowly draw closed.

'Now, where was I, brother?'

'You were talking about a black room with stars painted on the ceiling, of two men of distinctly opposed denominations interrogating you, and of a Father Teodoro who would be disappointed by the absence of any demons,' I sigh.

'Ha. I can tell from the sound of your voice, Brother Rosso, that you are quite sceptical about my story. I do not blame you. It seems ridiculous, does it not? And yet the room itself, as I was to learn, made perfect sense. For it is rarely convenient for a large group of men to be able to crowd around a single piece of parchment, and when one ventures out at night one is more often than not distracted by cloud cover, the biting cold or the bright city torches burning upon the garrets and towers. Thus it was the ideal location for scholars to study and share their conjectures during the day.

It also provided a peaceful retreat where men of the Order could contemplate the Divine by considering the nature of the heavens. And if you think that room sounds strange, Rosso, then you would have been quite amazed when you saw some of the other rooms in that building! There was much unusual work done in those days by the Order of the Eternal Light. No doubt you have heard certain rumours in your time about us.'

I open my mouth to speak, but he cuts me off before I have the chance.

'Yes, many learned monks have at some point in their studies heard us mentioned, though few have ever come close to finding out much about us. We were for many years one of the best-kept secrets in Christendom. Father Teodoro, however, earned perhaps too much notoriety in his short life, and was sentenced to be burned at the stake for the most heinous crime of heresy some years before you were born, Brother Rosso. In fact, I remember it as if it were yesterday. There were wolf-whistles and braying cheers from many of those assembled in the city square as he was led out by the guards. These soon changed to hisses and spitting. Teodoro was by no means an old man, yet already by then he had spent many months in the gaols, and his bulging red eyes had thus come to look like the bloody skin of freshly scaled fish. His fine dark hair too was falling off in tufts. I was stuck behind a group of men who had taken their families for a day out, and had treated them to mutton legs and wine. Since that day the scent of roasted mutton has somehow mingled in my mind with the sickening smell of the flesh sizzling on the pyre, and I was not able to touch a dish of lamb, however finely prepared, for many years after.

'Father Teodoro made, as I remember, a valiant attempt not to scream when the fire was started, and it must have been close to five minutes before he began to shriek and wail. The families in front of me had thought up the most astonishing curses to taunt him with as his skin began to bubble up and blister, and thus the shouting of the crowd almost drowned out his screeches. Almost. It took far longer than I had expected, the crackling body writhing against the stake as the flames twisted higher about him, and some of the children grew restless, or else their fathers became tired of holding them aloft upon their aching shoulders, and so by the time his skin had blackened the crowd had thinned so much that I was able to push my way close to the front, and mutter my prayers over the charred remains of that great man.'

Lovari's eyes draw closed again, and he sighs. His many laborious exhalations are getting somewhat tedious, but I do not let them rankle me.

'If he suffered such a fate, he must have done something to deserve it. The sinner is the author of his own suffering, after all,' I say.

'Only the Lord knows what he truly deserved. The vengeful justice of man is not always congruent with the immutable justice of Our Father. We would all do well to remember that. Have you ever been to such a spectacle, brother?'

'I have been to a number of executions and amputations. It is the duty of all Christians to bear witness to the punishment of sinners. It strengthens one's morals, and provides a solid lesson for children.'

Lovari is breathing more heavily now. His voice has become a low rasp.

'No, no man deserves that. I could not believe it then, and I cannot believe it now. There is something rotten about a church that would resort to such punishments.'

Should I tell him that he is dribbling, or wipe his mouth a little? I decide against both courses of action, and he brings a pale hand to his brow.

'I must take a little water and attend to some more base needs. Perhaps we may continue in an hour.'

'As you wish, brother. I will return soon.'

I nod and rise, ducking beneath the nets and folds of the tent. I beckon a servant to clean up Brother Lovari, for it has become obvious that he can no longer tend to his own private ablutions.

'Rosso?'

Halfway out I turn to my brother's call.

'You must show them your heart is strong.'

As I emerge from the tent a swarm of sandflies seems to descend. They are not deterred by my raised arms, and so I find myself hurrying – regardless of my throbbing blisters – across the burning sand for cover, to the muted laughs of some of our retinue.

Bells. The low, cacophonous din that clanged out the hours. The first sharp knell that shook us up from sleep, calling us to morning prayer and somehow summoning the pink tinges of dawn from the dark. Hours later the terse peal that announced the end of our fasts, sending us in to the high tables of the hall and our steaming bowls of pottage. Bells set us to work in the gardens, bells brought us in. Bells set us to our studies, and bells signalled their cessation. There was the halting swell of the chimes before Mass, and the final, timorous ringing for vespers. There was no day they did not sound, no room their call did not reach.

That is the thing I miss the most, out here in this bedevilled wilderness. My body feels sluggish and inert without them, for it seems that with no toll to rouse me from my slumbers on some days I wake to find the servants already up and going about their duties. This is the cause of some frustration to me, yet I am at a loss as to how to rectify this situation. It is hard to know when to rest and when to pray, and I find I have to rely on my own instincts. This has yielded distinctly unsatisfactory results. I often feel hungry, tired, restless. How am I to measure out my day in the desert? I know the natives rely upon the position of the sun as it traverses the heavens, but since looking upwards even a little is liable to give me a headache, I have instead set about calculating the hour based upon the length of my own shadow. This has also yielded unsatisfactory results.

It is altogether too quiet here. I wish I were back in Assisi, sitting at the bedside of my elderly friend in the infirmary, discussing the Athanasian Creed as I change his bandages and apply holy oils to his burns. Thus do I find myself waiting out the morning sun. This is truly an ungodly place. I can hear the coarse laughter spilling in from outside, the grunts and shouts from the men as they go about their duties. It has crossed my mind that some of them may have already succumbed to the calls of the Devil out here. I must increase my vigilance.

Of course I have heard of the Order of the Eternal Light. However, I shall not tell Lovari what I know of them. I do not want him to think me biased, and besides, it is not the place of the confessor to force his own story into the confession. Yet I am certain of one thing. However trivial their deviations from orthodoxy may be, these sects are never harmless. For to question even one word of

Scripture would be akin to pulling out the foundation stone of a house, for you then risk letting the whole edifice collapse around you. They would have us blind, lost, mired in sin for eternity. It is our duty to destroy these ideas, so that they do not tempt men to stray from the righteous path.

Once again my studies are disturbed by the sound of my sand prawns scurrying about inside their box and scraping their curled tails against the sides. Though I well know that the Lord granted us complete dominion over the land and the sea, I still find it wondrous that one can exert control over a simple creature simply by denying it food for long enough. It is astounding how easy it is to manipulate these insects to anger, to inflame them until their tails begin to coil and twitch. This time, however, I am able to focus my mind and manage to get much reading done before Lovari's man summons me.

Like the three others in our party who suffered from the desert sickness before him, the ailing monk is shivering and cold. The symptoms are identical. I hurry to cover him with more blankets, and cannot help but feel a little sickened by the rank smell now emanating from his body.

'Rosso? As soon as I closed my eyes I dreamt I was burning.'

I remove my old fox fur and tuck it round him. I also manage to refrain from suggesting that his dream might be a premonitory glimpse of the afterlife.

'Perhaps it would be better for your health if we postponed the rest of your confession. Or, if you wished, we might simply hurry ahead to absolution.'

'Ah, that is the crux of it, Rosso. You fear we have little time.'

He smiles, though his eyes remain closed. His legs tremble and shake, though I am not sure he is aware of this.

'No, I will finish my story. And if you still wish to absolve me at the end, so be it. I deliver myself to the hands of the Lord, that He may do with me as He sees fit. I will continue. I must.'

I nod and make myself comfortable beside him. 'You were telling me about your meeting with the tall Carthusian and the Byzantine priest. Am I to take it that since both they and the ruffian Alessio who assaulted you in the street were working for Teodoro, that they were all in some way connected with the Order of the Eternal Light?'

'Since they are all dead now, I feel I am free to confirm that they were indeed brethren of the Order. Though on that day in the room with the ceiling of stars, bruised by my beating and bothered by talk of drilling into my brain, I understood little except that they were not ordinary men of the cloth.'

'So what did they want?'

'The Order has only ever wanted one thing. The truth.'

'The truth has been handed down to us in the blessed Scripture. There is no need to yearn for something that you already possess.'

'And yet that is our condition, is it not? We are consumed by desire, and the thirst for knowledge, for certainty, is surely the worst affliction. For there is always more just beyond our reach. I trust you are not about to tell me, Rosso, that in your many years of study you have learnt the secrets of the alchemists who would turn base metal to gold, or that you have come to work out the principle which keeps the sun spinning around the earth, or have found out the date on which the corpses shall rise from their graves for the coming of our Lord. No? Do you not wish to know the causes of our humours, the hour that the trials of Revelation will begin, what Our Lord Jesus Christ did during those many years of which the Gospels make no mention?'

'If we knew everything, there would be no need for faith, that test of the will by which we prove ourselves worthy or unworthy. We must have patience that at the final hour all will be revealed.'

'And yet you rarely miss an opportunity to quote from Aristotle, Augustine, Jerome or Aquinas. What have you been searching for in the works of these wise men if not answers, if not a finer grasp of the world around you?'

'Learning has nothing to do with faith. If I spend my days in study, it is merely to equip myself for life. You would not walk out into the desert without clothes, without a covering for your head or without a calf's bladder full of water, would you? It would surely be equally foolhardy to try to make one's way in the world without due study and preparation.'

'I agree wholeheartedly my friend, and it was the Order that provided me with just such preparation to make my way through this world. In fact, my education began that very day, for once they had sent Alessio to break the news to Father Teodoro that there was to be no exorcism that day, the two priests in the room with the ceiling of stars made me an interesting proposition. The bearded man suggested that since my skills of impersonation had led me to their attention, they ought to be utilised for the work of the Lord. When they offered me food and board in that strange building in exchange for the performance of a few simple tasks each week, I hastily agreed. I was delighted to have a roof over my head again, a new life far away from my uncle and my past. What was more, I felt that the Lord had pulled me within his reach once more, for though I did not know the theological position or motives of my hosts, they were clearly deeply religious men, and at that time I would have done anything to renew the faith I had abandoned when I ran from Sebastiano and my mother's untimely grave.

'A brief tour of the building that afternoon added to my resolve. Though many of the smaller rooms on the upper floor were locked, I was able to catch a glimpse into others to see men of all manner of dress and age sitting at desks surrounded by scrolls and bindings, or engaged in hushed debate. Among the gowns and habits of priests and monks I spotted the robes common to judges, apothecaries and physicians. There was a high table in the main room downstairs, stables and herb gardens at the rear, and a makeshift infirmary beside the kitchens, while the entrance hall was full of poor families waiting for the donations of food and alms which the Order gave out each morning.

'I shared a small room with Alessio, sleeping on piles of musty old rugs. After a few weeks I grew accustomed to my companion's surly temper, and even got used to the creaking and juddering of the stairs above us as visitors to the complex arrived and departed throughout the night. I learnt that Alessio had left the seminary in Rome only two years before, though that was the extent of my knowledge of his past, and it seemed to suit both of us not to mention the years behind us. Though his manner did not change much after our first encounter, he later apologised for attacking me, and even began to engage me in rigorous exegesis of the Gospels, long and argumentative discussions about the allegorical and eschatological dimensions of the Parables that would often go on until the cocks began to strut and call outside.

'Alessio revealed the beliefs of the Order to me, and as soon as I heard them something deep within me knew that I had found my true home. My faith had been tested by the unfairness of a world that would steal away my sister and my mother while my uncle lived, of a Church which condemned its flock to Purgatory unless they paid tithes to fill the pockets of hypocrites and pederasts like Sebastiano; but the Order showed me a new way to view the world. Yet I shall come to that later. As well as helping to guide my soul towards the one true light, Alessio also accompanied me on my first assignment. Though we have little time, I shall tell you of it, for it was the first step on a long journey that has led me to this very desert. We were to visit the Benedictine monastery a few hours to the north of the city. That was all Alessio told me as we collected our mules from the stables adjoining the ramshackle building I now called my home.

'I remember the day well. As the cobbled streets petered out into fetid marsh, the great stone bulwarks of the monastery became visible atop one of the looming hills ahead of us. Once we had passed a herd of slow oxen being driven towards the city, I turned to Alessio and enquired about what was expected of me. He informed me that, as ever, our quest was for knowledge. I was to pretend that I was a prodigal student who dreamed unsettling dreams of crows, and in this way we were to gain a certain monk's confidence and so draw out the information we sought. I knew better than to question him further, so, as our mules plodded along the winding hillside path, I set about memorising the monologue that I was to recite.

'We drew to a halt close to the top of the hill, and retrieved a couple of hard loaves from our pack, for it was close to midday and Alessio assured me that the monks would take to us much better if we did not arrive at mealtime to beg food from their table. Thus we sat out among the gorse and bracken, watching the sun send ripples through the distant city and tearing off hunks of dusty bread, though Alessio laughed away my suggestion of us sharing the carafe of wine that hung from his belt. My companion instead tested me with questions about the personas we were adopting for the day, until the time came to lead our mules up through the unkempt nettles and long grass to the monastery.

'It took some time for the huge gates of warped wood to be hauled back, admitting us into the central courtyard. Though outside the gates the hill was matted, wild and overgrown, the cobbled stones inside the compound were pristine. An elderly monk was drawing water from a well, while a vast garden was visible beside the grand chapel in front of us. The long, low stone building to my left clearly contained the chapter house and dormitories, yet I was unsure about the taller stone turret to my right. Alessio soon informed me that this was the library.

'A middle-aged man with tired, drooping eyes led us to the stables to tether our mules. Either he kept to a strict vow of silence or he had concluded that conversing with us would be as ridiculous a waste of time as talking to a mosquito biting at one's arm. The unconscious twitch of his lips suggested the latter. You know the type: cold, detached, withdrawn. You must have met many such men, Rosso, growing up in such a secluded place yourself. Is it that living in deep contemplation of the Divine these brothers forget the ways of men, and become blind to the world of dirt and blood all around? Or is it that they are irked by outsiders because strangers inevitably remind them of all that they have left behind?

'"We owe you and your brethren our deepest gratitude, brother," Alessio said. "May peace be with you. You are no doubt aware that we have come to pay our respects to Father Emiliano. He should be expecting us. You see, my charge and I have been entrusted with —"

'Before my companion could finish his well-practised speech, the monk had thrust his thumb in the direction of the cloisters and walked away from us. Alessio shrugged and pushed me towards the low stone buildings.

'Having spent your life in a monastery, Rosso, you may find it hard to appreciate the shock I felt as I looked around. You must remember that I was used to villages, to mud and grime, to two-storey shacks and back alleys bearing black rivers of piss. I was amazed at the size of the place, for it seemed as if the monks had managed to build a whole new world within those vast stone walls. Beyond the stables and the gardens we passed the kitchens and the infirmary, spotting the abbot's grand house in the distance, flanked by orchards and a small cemetery. My amazement did not cease once we had ventured inside the cloisters, for, as we searched for Father Emiliano, we came across a number of monks engaged in sorting herbs for medicinal use, the pittancer counting coins in a small office, as well as an elderly prior shouting at a number of young novices.

'For all our wandering, it was surprisingly easy to find Emiliano's rooms, and I began to think that the rehearsal for our elaborate deceit was completely unnecessary, and that perhaps I would not be required to do anything at all. Most of the monks we came across did us the courtesy of ignoring us completely. Alessio's priestly gowns elicited such unearned trust that for the briefest of moments the thought entered my mind that he might not be a priest at all, and that I too was being fooled by some elaborate ruse. Since none of the small cells had doors, it was easy enough to peer in at the inhabitants, and thus we worked our way along until we found the white-haired monk that Alessio informed me was Father Emiliano.

'He was a pinched twig of a man, the knuckles of his spine poking up against his brown habit like knots in a length of rope as he hunched over a tiny desk, his wrinkled face pressed so close to an open book that his hooked nose seemed to be brushing against the pages. Standing in the doorway, we cleared our throats and then knocked against the wall, waiting to be invited in, but it took an inordinate amount of time for the old man to notice us. Alessio finally resorted to stamping his feet upon the cold stone floor.

'"Ah! My friends, do come in. Yes, yes. Good. Do take a look – it's animal hide. Remarkable, eh? Mostly sheep, I think. Or was it goat? I forget. How many beasts do you think it took to make this copy of Ptolemy's Almagest? How many knives slicing thin slivers of their skin, how much blood? And how many months did it take the distinguished scholar to copy out the text, word by word, line by line, toiling from dawn until midnight each day? How many hours? How many oak apples did he have to pick to mix the many pots of iron gall ink he must have used? How many goose feathers for how many worn-down quills? How many candles burnt to the snub while he wrote through the long evenings? You cannot tell me, can you? This is not just a book, my friends, oh no, not just a book. You can keep your looms and your aqueducts and your wells and your telescopes. This is the pinnacle of human labour. This is an invention against Death. It is befitting that it took such work, such time, such sacrifices, and thus we should show it the reverence it deserves."

'Both Alessio and I stood awkwardly in the tiny room, unsure of how to respond to the old man's words. The coastal breeze hissed in through cracks in the stones, though it did not seem to bother our host. He moved his hands tenderly over the pages, as a child might stroke a small dog, before turning the heavy cover to set it closed. This small effort seemed to overwhelm him.

'"May peace be upon you, father. We have come on an important matter. You are much renowned in this land, and those who know you have nothing but respect for your intellect, your piety, your charity. It is said that you have read more than —"

'"You do not need to flatter me into submission," the elderly monk smiled, raising a knurled hand to halt Alessio's speech. "I do not get many visitors these days, so all friends are welcome. I see you are a man of the cloth, which heartens me. Yet I do not doubt that you are here for the same reason as all the others. You come because of your dreams."

'Alessio smiled and bowed.

'"I cannot deny it, Father. It is well known that you are the foremost expert on the interpretation of dreams on this whole island. Yet we do not wish to trouble you. You only have to say the word and we will leave you to your studies."

'"No, no, you are most welcome to stay. What is the point of acquiring knowledge if one cannot share it with others? Please be seated and I will help you as best I can."

'Alessio and I knelt down before the old monk.

'"It is because of my young charge here that we have come to you, father. He has been having most unsettling dreams."

'Emiliano nodded sagely.

'"Strange dreams are not unusual in the young. They are a natural part of the body and the mind's development. I should warn you right now that it is highly likely that I shall say the same thing to you that I say to most who come to seek my guidance. Each month I am besieged by visitors with unusual dreams, each one of them ready to quote from the Book of Job: 'For God does speak – now one way, now another – though man may not perceive it. In a dream, in a vision of the night, when deep sleep falls on men as they slumber in their beds.' And so each visitor comes to ask me, what is the meaning of my dream? What is the Lord trying to tell me? Is it a vision, a prophecy, a commandment?

'"Yet most dreams come not from the Lord, but from ourselves. Of course, that does not mean that we cannot learn something from each dream. We may learn much about the dreamer's desires, his secrets, his plans, his past. But dreams can also be false and misleading. They can be sent to tempt us, to trick us, to pull us towards sin. The Devil lives among dreams, and we must be vigilant always against him. But most of the time, however, dreams come neither from the Lord nor the Devil. As any physician will tell you, dreams can be caused by an excess of bile, by an imbalance of the humours. Nothing more."

'Alessio shook his head. "But Joseph was given dreams that foretold the future. God came to Abimelech in a dream, and Jacob was shown the eternal ladder in a dream."

'"Yes, and Noah lived 950 years, while Methuselah lived 969. The era of such prophets is over, my brother. But let me hear this young man's dream, and then perhaps I can help him."

'The two men both turned expectantly towards me. It was time for me to give my performance, and I believe I did an exemplary job.

'"I dream of barren fields. Baked red earth that blows in dusty clouds between the houses. Dried-up riverbeds and cattle so thin you can see their ribs curving out like longbows beneath their tatty, threadbare hides. And then, in the midst of all of this, I see a crow. At first it is a solitary bird, flapping its way towards me. Then I spot another, then another. Soon the sky is filled with crows, the heavens so thick with black feathers that not a trace of blue can be seen behind them. The sound of their beating wings pounds through my skull, and I clutch my bleeding ears to try to blot out the fearsome clamour. Then, just as suddenly, they are gone. I look around, but cannot see a single bird. Yet now the fields are green and full. The wheat stands tall and luscious, keening to the wind. The river pulses past and the fat cows waddle to the banks to drink their fill."

'The old man narrowed his eyes as I spoke, though I could see that he was taken in.

'"How many times have you been afflicted with such visions?" he asked.

'"Every new moon I dream the same dream, father," I lied.

'For a long time after this Father Emiliano sat in silence, his mouth pursed, his eyes staring past me, and I took this as a sign that my well-rehearsed story was having the desired effect.

'"It could not be clearer if it had come to Joseph himself. The barren fields, the dry riverbed, the emaciated cattle, these are all Biblical images that tell us that the world has grown malnourished.

It has turned away from the Lord, and so the Lord has abandoned it. The dream appears to suggest that after the crows come the world is born again. The crows must represent Christ, whose sacrifice feeds and nourishes all souls, and who gives eternal life to all who come to him. But perhaps it's not that simple," he murmured.

'"I believe it is a prophecy, father," Alessio said. 'As you say, the world has turned from the Lord. Great changes must be made to bring men back to the true path. There is surely only one way to achieve this."

'"No, no, I cannot believe it. What you say may be true, but … it is a myth, a legend."

'"But the dream, father. You said yourself that the crows must represent Christ. And I have heard that some refer to the Last Gospel as the Book of Crows. Do you not think that the dream is a message, that the time is ripe for the Last Gospel to be revealed to mankind, that his soul might be delivered from the darkness in which it now dwells?"

'Father Emiliano had turned as pallid as milk. "In all my years, I have never been asked to interpret such a dream before. The symbolism, as you say, is clear. And yet … and yet. I cannot believe it. The Book of Crows, as some of the esoteric texts do indeed call it, is nothing more than a rumour, an apocryphal heresy. The crows in the dream might as easily represent the journey of the spirit after death, or the black robes worn by myself and my Benedictine brothers. Yes, yes, that must be it. Your charge is being called to become a Benedictine monk. That is why the Lord has led you to me this day."

'Alessio stood up from the bed. "But father, if there is even the smallest chance that the dream is a message from the Lord calling us to find the Book of Crows and reveal it to the world, then it is surely our sacred duty to try to find it. What if it is not a myth? What if it is as real as the other Gospels?"

'Alessio looked up at the old monk imploringly.

'"Come, father, you are probably the most learned man on this island. I do believe there is not a single book I could name that you have not read. Help us. You must have found a reference to it somewhere, a footnote, an aside."

'Emiliano took one of his wrinkled hands in the other, and pressed them tightly together.

'"It is a fool's errand. Better men have lost their souls in search of it."

'"Then you know of some who have looked?"

'The old man shifted uncomfortably, toying with his stubby fingers.

'"I have known men destroy themselves in the desire to lose the self in the divine, and I have known men who have spent their lives digging up the earth that they might find a path to hell and so fight the Devil on their own terms. I have known men waste years at the side of the dying, desperate to see the soul as it departs from flesh, and men who have whittled away their time on constructing giant bird wings that they might ignore the wise providence of nature and soar to Heaven themselves. I have met heretics, dissenters, traitors and fools, but none is as dangerous as the man who has convinced himself that he alone can succeed where all others have failed. Forget the book."

'"But you yourself have heard the dream. Would you ignore the command of the Lord?"

'He slumped, defeated, pursing his fleshy lips.

'"Once, only once did I see the tiniest shred of evidence that it might be anything more than the most fantastical of tales fit only for the gullible and demented, though until today I have never told anyone about it. I was in a monastic library in Messina, whose exact location you need not trouble yourselves with, when I was a much younger man. I remember reading a copy of Eusebius's Ecclesiastical History, an incomparable work of the most enviable scholarship. If you are an educated man, my friend, you will undoubtedly have come across it yourself. I think it is the fifth book in which he cites the lost writings of Apollonius of Ephesus, who argued against the false prophecies of the Montanist sects in Asia Minor. Beneath this fleeting reference someone had scribbled on the page in a crude hand. I recall being much perturbed that another reader had had the audacity to deface such a work, yet my curiosity got the better of me, and I found myself reading the smudged insertion. The despoiler had written

> Apollonius was wrong, the Montanists held true
> but driven to the yellow east they go
> bearing among them the secret of the crow.

It was common in those days for brothers in the seminary to debate the ancient heresies as a test of our reasoning, and thus the fanciful tale of the Last Gospel, or so-called Book of Crows, was fresh in my mind. I thought at first it might be some childish prank, yet the Messina library offered its collection to only the most renowned scholars. Whoever wrote that note must have believed there was a link between the Montanists and the Last Gospel."

'"That is all you know?"

'Alessio seemed somewhat disappointed.

'"It is a trifle, I admit. Yet it has played on my mind many times in the years since. I am too old for riddles and conspiracies, but surely it is no coincidence that all of the writings of Apollonius of Ephesus have been destroyed. I have met no one who has heard of a single of his works surviving the centuries since his death. And thus much of what we know of the Montanists is shrouded in mystery. We know they rejected a priesthood, saw all men as equal in appreciation of the Word. We know that Montanus was taken as a prophet by his followers, yet it is unclear what he prophesied. If perhaps the sect did have access to the Last Gospel ... but no, it is too ridiculous an idea to countenance."

'"Yet you think it is possible that this mysterious sect fled east to avoid persecution, taking the book with them. That despite the fact that almost all evidence of their very existence has been destroyed, perhaps the book they stole away is hidden still, awaiting the time when mankind will be ready for its revelations."

'"No, no. It goes against everything I have ever believed."

'Alessio placed a hand upon the old man's shoulders. "Do not worry, father, all that we have spoken of shall remain between us. You have helped us unravel the message of the dreams, and for that we thank you. I know this visit has not been easy for you. Will you join us in some wine before we depart, that we might show our gratitude?"

'"A small draught, perhaps. Though I feel ashamed of myself for what I have told you. The Last Gospel does not exist. I do not know a serious scholar who does not treat the idea as anything more than a joke. You seem like such earnest young men, and I do not want you to get into any trouble on my behalf. I shall pray that your dreams do not lead you away from the righteous path."

'Alessio unstoppered his carafe and slopped a good measure of dark red wine into Emiliano's wooden cup. He then raised the bottle to his lips, and put his hand to his chest. As they drank, I looked awkwardly at my feet, embarrassed to have been excluded from this adult ritual.

'"May the Holy Spirit be with you, father. We will not interrupt your studies any longer, for the dream seems to tell us that there is much work to be done."

'The old man sighed and nodded his head as we bid him farewell. Outside the cloisters, the mute porter helped us saddle the mules and hauled the great creaking gate closed behind us. It was not until we had picked our way down the overgrown trail, through the throngs of bracken and gorse to the bottom of the valley, beyond the reach of the long flung shadow of the old stone monastery, that my companion spoke.

'"I almost feel sorry for the old fool," Alessio snorted as we turned down the dirt track back towards Palermo.

'"How so?" I asked, somewhat confused by the sudden change in his attitude.

'"Though he pretends to know everything of dreams and prophecy, he understands little. Why do you think we visited him? There are a hundred more knowledgeable men on this island. Yet most of them are selfish old misers. As it is with riches, so it is with learning. Some people crave it, and when they get it they want to hide it away so that no one else can get their hands on it. Emiliano was easy to read. He's been mocked and patronised by other scholars all his life for studying dreams. All he probably ever wanted was a little attention, a little deference and respect. At least we could grant him that, albeit at the last hour of his life."

'"How could you possibly know that?" I asked.

'Alessio merely reached down and shook the carafe of wine looped through his belt. I said nothing as I slowly realised what I had been a part of.

'He shook his head wearily. "You must know how vital it is that no one finds out what we are after. If someone else found out where it might be … it does not bear thinking of."

'Not another word passed between us on the long journey back into the city, and I recall that it was a full three days before I spoke to my roommate again. Of course, I knew that it was foolish to think that we might leave a trace of ourselves somewhere and run the risk of someone letting slip of our mission. But I was upset that he had not confided in me, that he had thought I would not have been up to the test had I known beforehand what was planned.

'Are you still there, Rosso? Are you still frowning? I imagine you are not best pleased with the direction my confession is taking. However, I am convinced that I will change your mind, as the Order changed mine. The Last Gospel is more important than anything else on this earth, and if a few men have to die to save it from the wrong hands, then that is how it must be. No, do not argue. You will come to agree, when you have heard what else I have to say.

'Now, while I still have a little strength, I wish to tell you about the night I killed Father Sebastiano.'

The late-morning wind hisses between the tents, clawing at worn cloth and threatening to uproot our entire camp. Yet Lovari is oblivious to it. He is sweaty and pale, but he knows the stages of the sickness as well as I and it seems he will not be able to rest until he has finished his laboured confession. I must admit I do not much relish the thought of listening to a man wallow in his most foul sins, yet I must steel myself, for it is my job to deliver him from the clutches of the Devil and give absolution before it is too late.

'Let me press you now, brother, to take this opportunity to ask the Lord for forgiveness. No doubt you were forced by trickery and threats to kill your old priest. I cannot even begin to imagine the guilt that must have plagued your sleep these many years, the deepest regret that must be burning in your soul.'

Though Lovari's eyes remain closed, a smile plays about his cracked lips. 'I am sorry to shock you, Brother Rosso, but it is not remorse that compels me to tell you of my past. It is not for myself that I make this confession. I am telling you what I have done, so that you will see what you must do when I am gone. Besides, I would gladly do it all again. Do you really imagine what I did was so dissimilar from what the courts do every day? Do you really believe the justice of a king or a pope is so different? A man might be set on a pyre and have his flesh charred for denying the smallest tenets of the Roman Church. Every day men have their skin flayed from their twitching muscles, every day men are broken on the rack, have their hands severed in public displays before a braying crowd, have their eyes hooked out, their tongues plucked from their gagging throats, their nails wrenched from fingers and toes, all for the tiniest of misdemeanours. I have been to public beheadings, hangings, amputations and brandings. At least I tried to be humane. Sebastiano did not suffer as the victims at those abhorrent spectacles do.'

I am appalled by the ease with which my brother has begun to utter poisonous heresies. I have never known him to speak thus before, and so I must conclude that his present malady is corrupting his mind as well as his body.

'You cannot seriously be comparing yourself to the king or His Holiness the Pope?'

'Of course not. But what is a king, what is a pope? Both derive their power from the idea that they have been chosen by the Lord, that they are His vessels, carrying out His will here on earth. Yet how can we be sure that the king and the Pope are truly carrying out the Lord's will? What if they are merely acting to protect their own interests, to store up wealth and power and to keep the world as it has ever been? You have lived in so-called Christian lands your entire life, brother. Can you really claim that they are fair and just, that they are a mirror of Heaven? No? Then you must admit that the king and the Pope do not know the Lord's will as well as they think they do.

'I do not claim to know it either, but I do know that all the Order of the Eternal Light has ever worked for is the chance to bring about the Lord's Kingdom here on earth. When every man on earth is free from the yoke of tyranny, when there is true justice, when every soul is alive to the Word, when there is no more hunger, no more war, no more plague, no more poverty; then the people of the world shall thank us for what we have done for them.

'Now, I lived in that huge complex in Palermo for close to five years before I was ordered to return to the parish from which I had fled. Scarcely a week went by when I was not asked to talk my way into a church, seminary, courthouse, mansion, or even a back-street tavern in pursuit of information. Can you imagine what it was like for me, to have grown up in fear and squalor, in the meanness and ignorance of a dirty village, and then suddenly to be presented with an opportunity to devote myself completely to the pursuit of knowledge? I awoke each morning giddy with excitement, and on the days when I was not required to slip into the private libraries of princes or notaries to steal books and documents for the Order, I was free to work my way through its own vast collection of laboriously copied books. The Carthusian happily sat with me and introduced the mathematics and logical reasoning of the Greeks, and I found myself joining many late-night discussions on the exegesis of the Gospels as my brothers and I crowded into the small refectory. The Order shared my fury at the injustice and tyranny of the world, the hypocrisy of the Roman Church, and the squalor in which many poor souls languished. The Order was a family, a school, a brotherhood. For the first time in my life I belonged. And so, when its importance was explained to me, I accepted my mission without question.

'It was the first month, and the frost was still crunching beneath my feet when I returned to the church where I had first heard the Lord calling me. The mule and cart had dropped me some hours from the village, and as I made my way across the ice-touched fields towards my old home, I recalled the words Father Teodoro had said to me only a few days earlier.

'"We live in dark times," he had said. "Do not take my word for it. Look around you. Pestilence, violence, ignorance. The church grows rich, the Pope consolidates his power and the monks grow fat while the ordinary family toils and strives. Every parish priest has the chance to deliver his community into the light. They have all failed. The Church was supposed to be a fraternity of the faithful, a brotherhood of belief. There would be no need for money, for private possessions, for servants or contracts or courts. Men might share their bread with one another, might work and study together in harmony. This has not happened. Most men cannot even read the word of Our Lord, and spend their sad lives squabbling for coins that kings and princes have dropped in the dirt. Yet there is still hope. When the world grows corrupt it must be cleansed, so that it may be remade anew. And that cleansing is the sole pursuit of the Order of the Eternal Light. The corrupt Roman Church wants to silence us. They call us heretics, traitors. Yet they know we are right. They cling to their power, their riches, and fear the day when the faithful shall rise up and prise them away."

'Those words rang through my head and steeled me for my task. A light snow began to fall, and by the time I had reached the top of the hill and saw the tiny stone church in the distance below me the leather overshoes and the sackcloth cloak I had been lent by the Order were already damp with the prickly flakes of ice drifting through the evening air.

'As I scrabbled down the slipshod trail, the rest of the village soon became visible through the hazy wash of slow-falling snow. I found myself clutching the dagger in my belt tighter to me as I made out my uncle's slanted dry earth house, sunk between shuttered-up barns and frozen fields. It took me another hour to reach the border of the cemetery. Despite the urgency of my mission, I could not help but make a detour to kneel awhile beside the graves of my mother and my sister. I wasted many minutes searching for them for they were buried without headstones or markers and the plots were now well grown over, yet I was finally able to find the twisted yew that watched over them. How long, I wondered as the snow silently fell upon the graves, till the Last Judgement is given and they might rise up from their suffering?

'I loitered there among the dead until I saw from the fading light from the church's high windows that the candles were being snuffed out. I readied myself and, with my back to the damp stone wall of the old building, sidled slowly round to the wooden door. It was kept, as ever, ajar – which is to say that it participated in the illusion that the arms of the Church were always open, though I had never known a villager visit when there was not a Mass, a feast day or a tragedy to attend to.

'A couple of worn stone saints watched with disinterest as I walked down the nave. I would have felt dishonest had I tiptoed to hide myself, and so I took comfort that the sound of my heavy overshoes slapping against the cold stone might cover the clamorous pounding of my heart. A tearful Christ of knotted wood stared down from behind the altar, and in that instant I knew He would forgive me. The shuffling coming from behind the dark curtains at the back of the church suddenly stopped. He had heard me.

'"Please be patient, my son, I shall be with you in a moment."

'Father Sebastiano's voice boomed out through the nave, and I drew to a halt in front of the altar. A pewter chalice drew light from the last of the fat candles still burning, and as I moved closer I caught the reflection of my face curved in its gleam. Upon it was a look I did not know I possessed. I thought about hiding, springing upon him as he emerged from behind the curtain. That would have been the easier path, yet it also would have been cowardly. If you are to kill a man – and I hope, Brother Rosso, that you never have to – then you must not shy from it. You must deceive neither yourself nor your victim, nor should you debase the worth of his life by turning away at the final moment. You must partake of the act with the reverence it deserves.

'The priest's white hair emerged from the darkness, followed by his hunched body. He tottered uncertainly towards me, one arm leaning on a bowed staff, the other arm stretched out in front of him.

'"I am sorry, but you must tell me who you are, my son, for my eyes do not see as they should. The world is all light and shadow now, and nothing is as clear as it once was."

'As he drew closer and steadied himself on the altar, I saw that his eyes were indeed misted over with grey, though some flicker of the deep green still danced beneath.

'"It's me – Tommaso."

'His wrinkled face broke into an uncertain smile.

'"Tommaso, my best student. I can tell from the strength of your voice and the certainty of your step that you have grown into a fine young man. You have returned to your family?"

'"No. I have come to see you, father."

'Suddenly I felt the cold beneath my damp clothes and noticed that my leg was all a-jitter.

'"Come, you jest. No one would take the pains to travel in this foul weather just to seek out a feeble old priest. I know your aunt has been most sick these days; she will be glad of help at home. But tell me, what have you been doing these last years, my son? You have been in the capital, am I right? Yes, I can tell. Your accent has changed. The same thing happened to me when I was young. Tell me, though, have you kept up your studies?"

'"I have, thanks to most learned teachers. For I have become a member of the Order."

'I had expected a shocked gasp, or a look of panic or fear. Yet Father Sebastiano merely smiled and nodded. He stared into the darkness at the end of the nave and let a thin, crumpled hand run slowly over the white stubble that dotted his pinched and crinkled jowls.

'"I have been expecting this visit for ten years, though I never imagined they would enlist one of my own pupils to carry out their foul deeds for them. That you have succumbed to their honeyed rhetoric and dark heresies pains me more than anything else. I am an old man; my life is over. But you are young, and you are gambling with your immortal soul. Recant, my son, leave them. I still have some contacts across the sea who would keep you safe."

'"You would have me live a life like yours, cowering in backwaters and villages, hiding away in the hope of being forgotten? Why would I desire such a thing? You have wasted your chance to change the world – I will not make the same mistake. It was you, Sebastiano, who taught me that Christ said he came not to bring peace, but the sword. Yet you shirked your sacred responsibility. You turned your back on the enlightened work of the Lord, for what? To mumble your high Latin over the starving and the poor. Will it feed them when harvests fail? Will it keep them warm in bitter winters such as this? Does that even trouble you anymore? I wonder whether you care about anything except groping your charges in the darkest corner of the Lord's own house."

'I thought my words might provoke him, yet all the old priest did was continue to smile that same old wide, beneficent grin, and I felt myself becoming enraged. I had been preparing myself for a showdown, yet it seemed as if he had second-guessed everything I would say – he was beyond surprise, beyond recriminations.

'"I will not argue with you, for I once burned with fury too. Doubtless you have been told how I joined the Order as a young man, how I was set alight, as you are, by the desire to right the wrongs of this dark world. I took the Oath, just as I am sure you have been pressed to, and when I realised the error of my ways, I knew there would be a reckoning. I knew about the spies, the informers, the loyal servants who would do anything to stop the secrets spilling out. I was never naïve enough to think I might escape the Order, but, yes, I tried all the same. I came here. I made a new life. Have I lived in fear? Certainly. Every day I trembled at the shadows thrown by the altar candles, every day I have jumped at the sound of unexpected footsteps. I knew this time would come. Yet it was still worth it. I have done many things I regret most deeply, but leaving the Order is not one of them."

'I stepped closer, my clammy hand tightening around the dagger.

'"You made a vow. Sworn on the most Holy of Books. You gave

your word, on pain of death. You of all people should know that there is no place a man may hide from justice."

'"When justice is done, it brings joy to the righteous but terror to the wicked. Proverbs, 21, verse 15. Think on that. Would you call yourself righteous, though you have placed the rules of a group of deluded men above the Lord's commandments?"

'"The Lord sees all," I replied as calmly as I could. "He understands the nature of sacrifice."

'"Let me tell you about justice. Justice is growing out of your youth yet having to live with your mistakes the rest of your life. I beg you Tommaso, do not let sin overcome you, as it overcame me."

'"I do not have time for this, Father. You know what must happen. Take this chance to make your peace with the Lord."

'He did not argue. I watched as he turned and, using his old staff to support him, sank to his knees before the altar. I crossed myself and asked the Lord to welcome Sebastiano into His arms and cleanse him of his sins. I slipped the dagger from the leather sheath, planning to drive it between the old preacher's huffing shoulder blades and prick the very marrow of his heart.

'I stood and waited for his prayer to be completed, for, whatever you may now think of me Brother Rosso, I would never deprive a man of his last rites. His white shock of hair bobbed up and down as he mumbled, his creased hands clasped tightly in front of him. The seconds slowed down, and I felt a breeze trawl through the nave, picking at the threads of his words and carrying them past me. I shuddered, and shrugged down deeper into my sodden cloak.

'"There, it is done. You need not fear for the state of my soul. Yet let me entreat you one last time to think on what you do, Tommaso, my child. There are other ways to work for a better world, to help the poor, to —'

'"I am sorry, father," I interrupted, and he bowed his head, sank down in supplication on the cold stone floor.

'As I stepped forward, raising the dagger high above my head, I could not tell whether the sound of heavy, laboured breathing was coming from him or me. I had not thought he would give himself over with so little struggle. Then I was behind him, standing over his bowed form, and I drove the blade down with all the ferocity I could summon.

'Yet just when I thought it would pierce through his aged flesh, he spun round and, with an agility at odds with his frail appearance, thrust his staff up to block the path of the dagger. I was taken off guard by this unexpected show of dexterity, and when the gnarled wood struck my fist the dagger was knocked from me and sent clattering across the wet stone. I gasped at the stinging pain of the blow, and made towards where the blade had fallen. But the old priest was quicker. His show of calm acceptance and resignation had been little more than a ruse – once more he swung his heavy staff, and this time caught the side of my ankle, bringing me crashing to the floor.

'By the time I had hauled myself up, dizzy and stumbling as the church spun around me, Sebastiano had reached the dagger. He turned to face me, holding it aloft, then began pacing forward. Beneath the milky fog covering his pupils, I thought I could make out the gleam of satisfaction.

'"Tommaso, did you really think it would be that easy to break the commandments in the Lord's own house? Did your precious Order not tell you of the missions I was once sent on, of the uses they put me to? It seems you are not as wise as you suppose."

'He lunged forward, and I ducked back, tumbling into the altar. Despite his bravado, his movements were clumsy and his aim ill-judged. I grabbed one of the candles from the altar and waved it through the air in front of me. Sebastiano turned his head wildly, trying to follow the light, suddenly unsure of himself. Then I threw it towards his face.

'The old priest screamed as the candle struck his cheek, the burning wax sizzling as it splattered across his wrinkled face. As he recoiled, howling and tearing at his reddened skin, I seized my chance. Taking hold of the pewter chalice on the altar, I leapt upon him.

'The first strike sent his legs buckling and he fell, clutching out at the empty air around him as though he was trying to take hold of the Holy Spirit itself. The second called up spasms from his outstretched body, and the third ended his screams. I cannot be certain of how many more times I brought the great chalice smashing down upon the back of his skull. I remember his fine white hair becoming damp and tangled with blood. I remember the crackle of the bone, the thick soft swell beneath. Only when I once again caught sight of myself in the curved reflection of that most blessed chalice did I stop.

'I let it fall beside him, that holy cup from which I had first tasted the blood of our Lord. I said a blessing that his soul might be guided through the dark fires of Purgatory, then retrieved my dagger and stumbled out into the night.

'As I limped back up the hillside towards the woodland where a covered cart awaited me, padding with great smoke-wreathed breaths through the fresh fall of snow, all I could think about was how brittle the human body is. When the Lord walked among us, what sacrifice it must have been just to be bound to flesh. The animal urges, the desperation. The blood that bubbles and boils, the bones that buck to cold weather, the skin that shrivels and burns. How strange that the imperishable soul is wrapped in such a fragile shell. A few blows and our time on earth is over. We might as well be made of glass.

'Rosso, I know I must sound callous, cruel. Yet I did what I did so that you and all our brothers in this world might have the chance for a better life. When I reach the end of my story, I hope you will feel the same. However, I will not force you. If you wish to call a halt to this confession, I will understand.'

I must admit that I feel sickened by his description of such godless violence and savagery most foul. Furthermore, though I search for a hint of remorse in his voice, instead it seems that he revels in his hellish sins, and even now seeks to explain them away. But I had suspected it might go something like this.

'I cannot pretend I am not revolted and dismayed by your past. Yet even the murderers in the gaols and the heretics the Pope has condemned to the stake are visited by a priest that they might recant and turn to Jesus Christ, blessed be his name. I stand by my most Holy duty. I will not leave you to Hell for all eternity while you might still be persuaded to ask for forgiveness.'

His dry, blistered lips curl up into the kind of curious smile of which I have learnt to be suspicious.

'Do not worry, I shall tell you everything. And I have reason to hope that, before my tale is finished, you will not only understand the necessity of these deeds, but also come to work with me, continuing the vital work of the Order once I am gone.'

As his eyes are pressed tight closed, a translucent slime gluing the pale lids together, he cannot see my affronted look. I purse my lips, and feel for my rosary. Lovari lets out a pained moan which, to spare my brother's feelings, I pretend not to hear.

'You must forgive me, brother. I can no longer feel my legs and my heart does whirligigs in my chest. The sickness is staking claim to my senses, and if I am to fight I must gather my strength. I will try to sleep, and pray I can regain a little strength to finish my story. Please, return after your midday meal and I will tell you all you must know.'

'As you wish. You must rest. I will come back soon and you can resume your confession then.'

Lovari does not respond. The restless wind is stirring through the sand. I hear my brother snoring before I have even got to my feet. He whimpers, struggles beneath his clammy blankets. And so I tuck another of the animal skins up around his neck, noticing as I do that a clump of his fine brown hair has fallen from his head. I slip it into the long sleeve of my habit and leave my companion to his fevered dreams, for some of us still have work to attend to.

# The Whorehouse of a Thousand Sighs

Spring raced straight on into autumn without a break. But regardless of the weather, I still often found myself waking up flushed and disorientated, my dreams weighing down on me like one of the rougher guests. They were always the same, ending when the tips of my feet began to lift from the ground as I beat my wings.

What Silk had said had bothered me, so instead of spending too much time with Boy in the days, I left him to Claws' hungry eyes and busied myself helping the soldier. After securing herself a few more silver coins from the soldier's rapidly diminishing collection, the Empress had called in a favour with a local carpenter and asked him to fashion a pair of wooden walking sticks, so I was soon helping the soldier hobble round the small hut. I would help him sit up and pull him up onto his good leg, letting him lean on me while he found his balance. It was slow and difficult, and more than once we toppled over together onto the floor, our bodies suddenly knotted together, giggling.

'It won't be long and you can get going again. I expect you'll be glad to see the back of this awful place,' I said as we paced slowly around the room, the walking sticks scraping against the floor.

He looked up at me briefly, but didn't reply.

'I guess you're not going to let me have a peek in that special box of yours before you go? I've always wondered what the whole world looks like.'

He smiled.

'I thought not. And you can't tell me where you're going either, I know. But tell me this, please, just to stop me worrying, because I can't help thinking that you're not going to be able to get very far, nor too quickly, hopping along on just one leg. So how do you know whoever is after you won't find you again?'

He stopped, leaning on the curved stick, and I squeezed his arm.

'I will disappear.'

'What?'

'I will disappear. I must.'

'Oh, it's that easy is it, just disappearing into thin air?'

He shrugged. 'Perhaps the birds will help me.'

'Is that some kind of joke? It's not funny.'

'No, I'm serious. They ought to help me. If it wasn't for them, I wouldn't be stuck lugging this thing through the middle of nowhere.'

'So the box has got something to do with birds?'

He didn't reply. Perhaps he had already said more than he wanted me to know. But right then I got that queasy feeling in my stomach, the one I always got when I thought about the crows in my father's stories or the feathers pricking though my skin in my wretched dreams. I used to wonder why birds couldn't just keep to the sky and leave the earth to us. But now I find myself thinking something different: why can't we keep our dreams to the present, to what we already have, instead of grasping at the future, the sky, the impossible?

He gestured to the pile of straw and I helped lower him down until he was lying on his side. Then I checked the stump again: it was a gaudy red, the hardened skin almost smothered over. When I looked up the soldier's eyes were closed and, although I couldn't be sure whether he was really asleep, I threw a rug over him and bolted the door behind me.

It seemed silly to me, caring about a box more than you care about yourself. If I'd lost my leg – or any other part of me for that matter – because of some hunk of wood, I'd probably have set fire to the thing. Silk thought it was filled with enough money to make you forget the bits that have fallen off your body, but I was becoming less sure. To leave your home and know that you may never return – well, money alone isn't going to convince you to do that. If you can't spend it on your family and your friends and other little things to show off with in front of your enemies, well, what's the point of it? And the further west you went, the harder it would be to trade with those Han coins. No, perhaps he really was protecting something more important. Perhaps it truly was the whole world in there, which would mean we were inside his box too. But wouldn't that mean it would also contain another soldier with another box with another world inside and —

'Just drink it up and it'll all be over in no time!' I heard the Empress screech, interrupting my wandering thoughts.

'No!' Claws shouted, and there was the sound of stomping feet.

I was halfway down the trail between the courtyards at that point, so I bunched up the bottom of my robe and ran down to find Tiger and Silk near the gate, holding onto Boy. In the middle of the courtyard the Empress stood with her hands on her colossal hips, her teeth clenched into a snarl. She seemed to be so angry that she couldn't move. Claws was now nowhere to be seen and everyone else had wisely got out of the range of her fury. At her feet was a spreading pool of bubbling green liquid.

'What's going on?' I whispered.

'Claws just disobeyed the Empress. I've never seen anyone do that before,' Silk said. 'I don't know which one of them is more angry.'

'Over a drink?' I asked.

Tiger raised her eyebrows. 'You remember we joked that Claws was getting fat, and laughed about how she should cut down on the *nang*, well ...'

'No! But surely she's too old,' I said.

'I guess not.'

'What are you talking about? I don't understand,' Boy whined, and the three of us turned to hush him together.

'Who do you think she got it from?'

'Could have been anyone, we were so busy once the ice melted, remember?'

'But she can't really want to —'

'It looks like she does.'

Our whispers quickly petered out when we saw Claws emerge from our room. I mean, we all knew she hoarded the gifts guests gave her under the rugs and straw in her corner, but none of us could believe how much she had balanced in her arms. It was difficult to see her face beneath all the little trinkets and glinting rings and ribbons and silks and leathers and wine skins and tiny jewels and coins and bits of cloth she was carrying. It was all that remained from night after night of carefully crafted smiles and faked groans. She dumped it in a pile on the ground in front of the Empress.

'Go on then, take it. Take it all. I only saved it for you. Take it and let me go!'

Instead of shouting back, however, the Empress seemed suddenly to grow calm. Her arms dropped to her side and she slowly shook her head, then smiled, showing her brown teeth.

'I'm afraid it's not enough.'

'What do you mean? I've given you more than ten summers, plus all of this – it's got to be worth a fortune! You could buy another girl if you traded all this stuff. Don't try to fool me.'

'For you alone, maybe it's enough. You have grown so old and fat that few of our guests want to go near you anymore. But you forget that you took my girl's eye. And for that, you owe me more.'

Claws' mouth opened but no sound came out.

'I'll leave you now, and you will put all of this mess away. Then I'll return with another cup of the medicine, and you will drink it. Do you understand?'

Claws just stood there, a tear snaking down her blotchy cheeks. The Empress turned and went back to her room. Claws didn't move from the spot, though she did begin to shake as she choked back her sobs. As soon as she noticed us looking at her, though, she let out a little cry and ran to our room, leaving all her carefully saved gifts sprawled across the floor.

'Do you think we should collect it all up and bring it to her?' I asked.

'No. Leave her. She won't want to be seen like this. She'll come and get it when she's good and ready and she's gotten rid of that crazy idea of keeping the baby,' Silk said.

'I knew it,' Tiger said quietly. 'I told you all long ago, but you did not believe me.'

'What are you talking about?' Silk asked.

'She'll never let us go. Not while we live and breathe and there's still a chance, however small, that someone will want to lie with us in the dark. I don't know what happened to Lotus and Feather, but it seems to me there's only one way you get out of here, and when that happens it doesn't matter how much silver you have.'

'No, she said it wasn't enough. She just wanted more to cover costs. She wasn't saying Claws can't leave, she was only saying Claws can't leave just yet,' Silk said.

This sounded feeble even to me, but I nodded because I wanted

Boy to believe it.

'You're only supposed to be blind in one eye, Silk.' Tiger replied. 'However much you offer, it's never going to be enough.'

Tiger walked away shaking her head, and Silk stormed off in the other direction. Boy looked up at me expectantly, and I waited for him to ask me what everyone was going on about. I tried to think fast, and I had almost worked out a particularly convoluted lie to explain away all the shouting and arguments when he spoke.

'Do you want to play?'

I smiled, then chased him out past the gate to the track between the two courtyards.

We spent the afternoon pretending to be adventurers discovering strange new lands. Boy seemed more interested in tearing up wildflowers from the slope than finding out what had happened earlier, and that suited me fine. How was I supposed to explain to him that he might be trapped here forever without even the tiniest hope of escape? Even the silly stories I made up to lull him to sleep had endings, and nine times out of ten they were of the happy kind. If you don't have an ending, a finishing line in sight that makes you push onward, then how are you supposed to make sense of the race itself? If you never see the sun go down, how are you going to be certain that it'll rise again when the cocks crow?

But he didn't ask, so I didn't have to lie. When he crept into my room later that night, once I was sure the other girls were all asleep I found myself whispering the story of the crows to him. I told him that humans and crows had lived side by side once, the birds tilling the earth with their long beaks while people sowed seeds. I explained that a group of people soon asked the crows to help them find light to guide them at night as well as in the day, so that they would be safe from the terrors of the vast darkness. The crows agreed and they flew higher than they had ever flown before and began to peck at the tattered cloth of the sky. They ripped whole chunks from the blackness and light poured through, and that's where the stars came from. But where they tore the holes in the sky, they saw through to the future, to the end of the world.

The crows returned bitter, angry, driven mad by what they had seen. From that day on they fed only on death; they became monstrous and vindictive, and enemies of humans, for they had been given the most terrible knowledge of how the world would finally come to be destroyed. I told Boy that this was why even today you cannot trust a crow, that they are unlucky and a bad omen, because they come close to us only to tell us that something bad will soon happen, to share the horrifying knowledge that they cannot bear. I told him all the things I could remember my father mumbling in the midday heat of his drunkenness, and when I heard Boy's little whistle snores I kept talking: because if you don't speak of things, sometimes they get lost so deep that when you really need them the words are buried beyond your reach.

It was a good night's sleep, untroubled by either guests or dreams, and the next morning was a lazy, jokey one, with Boy helping Silk and me to brush the camels' ragged coats. It wasn't until almost lunchtime that anyone realised that we hadn't seen Claws all morning.

Our first thought was to check with the cook, but he hadn't seen her either. The soldier was sound asleep in his hut and the other was empty. Could she really have run away, we asked each other. Where would she have gone? It was only when we got back to the courtyard that Silk spotted the thin trail of inky blood dribbling out from the first guestroom.

Silk got there first, pushing back the loose piece of cloth covering the entrance and darting inside. The rest of us just stood rooted to the spot, too scared to venture in for fear of what we might see. I expected to hear a scream, some kind of terrible sobs or wails, but nothing came. Finally I couldn't bear the silence anymore.

The smell hit me straightaway: ripe and sour, cloying, dank. The room was a mess. The beautiful cushions, the ornate rugs, all were stained the darkest red. Silk was kneeling in one of the pools of sticky blood, and as I moved closer I could hear her whispering to Claws as you might to a child just woken from a nightmare, trying to coax her best and oldest friend – who had teased her and humili-ated her and fought her and blinded her and in the end had ignored her altogether – to open her eyes, just a little, to take her hand, to do something, anything at all, to show her it was not too late.

'She's done this just to piss off the Empress,' Tiger whispered, and I turned to see she had followed me in.

I couldn't believe that. Claws was lying on a pile of cushions with her eyes pressed closed and her face clenched up into a snarl.

Her spirit might have left her, but her anger remained. Her right hand still held the curved knife she must have used to cut her stomach open. The horizontal gash just under her belly button sprawled open obscenely, the blood from the mess of broken purple coils poking out only just beginning to dry. Flies were already buzzing the wound. Not only had she drawn the knife deep across her belly, but she also seemed to have rattled it around in there before the last spasms of death took hold. There were tattered bloody ribbons, strange puffy crimson tubes, squelchy round sacs that looked like cooked aubergine, and slivers and blobs of heavenknowswhat. The whole room stank like meat left out in the sun too long. I covered my mouth with my hand to stop myself from retching and squatted down to take a closer look.

'You won't find it,' Tiger said.

'What?'

'The baby. Too small, and buried too deep. She took it with her.'

'Then at least they're together.'

'Perhaps.'

'So what do we do now?'

'Us? Nothing. It's none of our business. It's the Empress's guestroom. Let her deal with it. Claws knew what she was doing, she knew what she wanted and she finally had the nerve to do something about it. We can't begrudge her that.'

'But we can't just leave her like this. It wouldn't be right.'

Tiger raised her eyebrows. 'What's right got to do with it? We left right and wrong behind when we got carried through that gate out there. All that's here now are shitty memories and a jumble of bones. We don't need to bother ourselves with that. The real Claws disappeared a long time ago.'

Tiger shook her head and left. Was this her usual bitter anger at the world around her or something else, something closer to her heart? I wasn't sure. But I didn't feel right about just leaving Claws to the mercy of the Empress. I fetched the mop and set about getting rid of some of the blood. Silk soon joined me, getting over her sobs and sniffles to bind one of Claws' old robes around her bloody midriff until the gaping sprawl was completely covered. We thumbed her eyelids down and, when everything else was done, we decided to wash and comb and plait her long dark hair one last time. It was only then that we called the others, and Boy and the cook and Tall and Homely came in and looked at her and nodded, and then went back to their business.

The only exception was the Empress. As soon as the cook told her the news, she retired to her room and stayed in there all day, not even sounding her little bell, and so it was left to us to imagine whether it was anger, annoyance, guilt, sorrow or just plain squeamishness that kept her from venturing in to see what had become of her eldest worker.

'We should get some of her treasure for ourselves,' Boy said, nudging my arm as the four of us shared an early dinner in the cook's courtyard.

'Huh. And risk a beating from the Empress. She'll be in a foul-enough mood as it is. Even you're not that brave, Boy,' I said.

'I guess the Empress will get everything after all then,' Silk muttered.

'What's it like? Being dead?' Boy asked, and I saw Silk look at me nervously.

Tiger shrugged. 'It's like a waterfall, or a leaf.'

Boy pulled a face. He was not impressed with this answer, but he didn't seem sure how to respond. I left them to it – I wasn't in the mood to face Boy's queries or Silk's grief – and went to check on the soldier. I hadn't been in since before the scene in the courtyard the previous day, so I was sure he was getting restless. And even emptying out his brimming chamberpot had to be better than sitting round thinking about death.

The soldier – he still hadn't told me his name, though to be fair I hadn't bothered to ask, and he had never displayed even the slightest interest in finding out mine – smiled when I came in. Once I had done a little cleaning I picked up his walking sticks, letting him rest his weight on me as he pulled himself up.

'I'm sorry,' he grunted as he shifted forward onto the crutches. 'About your friend.'

I shrugged. 'Don't be. It's not your problem.'

He nodded. 'Everything is planned, you know. It is meant to be.'

'Don't be stupid. None of it was planned. She wanted to leave here and have a baby, not die.' I stopped myself, my voice beginning to quiver. 'I came in here to get away from all that, so let's just concentrate on getting you walking, shall we?'

He began walking again, slowly scraping a circle around the room, but he couldn't remain quiet for long. I began to wish for the days when he'd pretended not to be able to understand me.

'I'm sorry, but you don't understand. Everything is planned. Everything is already written. Let me give you advice: surrender to it. You cannot change it. Let it give you hope.'

I turned on him. 'Hope? How can you stand there and talk about hope? There wasn't any hope for Claws, and now we've seen that, I'm not sure the rest of us have got any hope of ever getting out of here. Every day I see hope slipping away from Boy, and one day it'll be gone and there'll be no way of him ever getting it back. And what do you hope to do – hop along a mountain range on your one leg with a stupid great box slowing you down? You'll last a day or two at most, what with the wild dogs and whoever is on your trail. I don't believe in fate, or plans, or anything like that. All people do is struggle on the best they can until their time is up.'

The soldier leant forward, his hand roughly clutching onto my neck as he pulled me closer and pressed his dry lips to mine. Now that really made my blood boil. I grabbed hold of his hand and shoved it away. For a second he tottered there, as one of the walking sticks crashed to the floor, and then he reached out – but I stepped away, leaving him to flail and collapse backwards onto the pile of straw.

Despite my anger, I began to laugh. He laughed too, lying back and shaking. Then we both stopped laughing. We looked at each other. I don't know how long it was, maybe a minute or two, or maybe just a couple of seconds, before I raised my finger to my lips and began to unknot the cord that held my robe.

Even now, looking back, I'm not sure why I did it. If he was surprised then he didn't show it, but I surprised myself. And what was even more surprising was that I actually enjoyed it. I enjoyed the hot summer air simmering my skin. I enjoyed the silence, with all the little noises held back in our throats, a stark change from the practised wails and moans I usually used to hurry men along. And most of all I enjoyed the slowness, the lack of a contract, the lack of any words between us at all.

When it was done I got up, tied up my robe and left, bolting the door behind me. Perhaps he was right. Perhaps all we can do is surrender to our fate, to find hope wherever we can. But I wished I had his certainty, his belief that everything was planned, that there was a reason for everything. Maybe he was just trying to console me. It never crossed my mind that he might actually have that kind of knowledge, that it wasn't just misplaced faith or cheap words of comfort. And it wasn't until many summers later, when I thought about that strange, sad, hopeless day again, that I realised that during the whole thing – even when he'd been nuzzling his stubbly chin against my neck, even when his lips were pressed against my ears and he let out the tiniest of sighs that only I could hear – all that time one of his hands had stayed stretched out beside him so that it was just within reach of the wooden box, as if to make sure that it would not disappear.

Claws was given to the desert. The body and the many trinkets were gone by the time we woke up the next morning, and a young man armed with a dagger now guarded our gate.

'I guess she doesn't want the rest of us getting any ideas about making a break for it,' Tiger said at breakfast.

I think Silk would have liked a proper goodbye, but we knew that all the grief in the world wouldn't have changed a thing. Most of all, I think Claws would have wanted to be forgotten. She wouldn't have wanted any part of her to be left in this dreadful place. Not her body, not her child, not her hopes, not her memories, not even the shadow she might have left hanging over the rest of us. So we did our best to try to forget. Leave the fancy ceremonies and the pompous speeches to officials and princes, and let the rest of us get on with real life: what's the point of all those words if the person they're meant for can't hear them anymore?

The Empress spent the next few weeks venting her fury by shouting and screaming and shaking her fists at anyone who disturbed her beauty sleep or spilt a little broth on a cushion or even dared to fart when she was nearby, and I'm sure she would have sent the soldier hopping off on his one leg if his silver coins hadn't convinced her to be a little more charitable. Boy stayed out of her way, his games of skipping and enacting imaginary battles giving way to long walks between the two courtyards, during which he would count as high as he could and then back down again, or else talk to himself in a whisper that no one else could quite make out. I tried to coax him into little competitions or games of make-believe, and though he would sometimes agree, he gave the sullen air of doing so only to placate me. Tiger said he was shrugging off the last protective skin of childhood, but I didn't want to believe that.

Whenever Boy skulked off in one of his moods, I went up to the soldier's hut in an effort to forget everything outside its solid locked door. He wasn't like the others – he never asked for a thing – but more importantly, when I was with him, I wasn't like I was with all the others. If Silk or Tiger guessed that I was doing a little more than necessary to aid his recovery, they were good enough not to tell the Empress, though their eyebrows might have twitched a little when they saw my hastily knotted robe or tousled hair. Each time it was the same. He would practise walking around the room for a while at first, both of us pretending that this was all that was going to happen. Then finally one of us would lean a little closer, or let a hand slip as if by accident, and then before I knew it I would be lying beside him, my face flushed as I babbled about getting back to the main courtyard and all the tasks I still had to finish before the next party arrived. Perhaps I pretended I was bringing him comfort and hope; perhaps he thought he was doing the same for me.

'So you really think everything is planned out for us?' I asked one morning as I pulled my robe back around my shoulders. 'Even this?'

His lips seemed to briefly consider a smile. 'Even this.' Then his hands reached out and patted the wooden box, as though it was in agreement with him.

I wondered how much silver he had left, how much time he would be able to buy before the Empress turfed him out and he disappeared through the cracks in memory. But in the same way that I had given up pestering him about the box or his plans, I decided not to ask. I think a part of me imagined he would stay here forever and somehow rescue me from the Empress. I should have learnt by then to have been realistic, but I think after Claws plunged that kitchen knife into her guts we had all been turning inwards, nursing our little fantasies to keep them from being crushed completely.

On my way back down that day I saw Boy standing near the gate. He was staring into the distant valley, his lips spilling out mumbles. His hair was matted and tangled, though I could have sworn I only washed it for him a couple of days before, and his hands were restless at his side. I stopped and stood beside him, putting a hand on his shoulder.

'What are you looking for?' I asked.

'Where've you been?' he replied, determined to turn the questioning around.

'I've been helping the soldier. He's still learning to walk.'

'Is he still here? He's boring. All he does is lie around. Old lazy bones. If I was a soldier I would be up by now and killing people with my sword.'

'Really?' I laughed. 'And who would you kill, my little soldier?'

'Everyone. All the bad people.'

'I think it would be much nicer to be a trader, exploring new towns and buying and selling all kinds of beautiful things, or to be a prince relaxing in a huge palace,' I said.

He shrugged, his eyes still focused on the clouds skimming the distant plains.

I wasn't sure what else to say. Maybe Tiger was right. Living here was changing him, breaking all the bits of him he couldn't protect.

'I'm scared,' he finally whispered, without moving or looking around.

I settled myself down on the dusty trail and patted the dry clump of earth beside me. 'Do you want to tell me why?'

He shrugged again, but then sat down.

'I can remember playing in a field while my mother ploughed up the soil. And I can remember a bit before then, when my father dropped me and I cried because I hurt my leg and my mother shouted at him and he shouted right back. But that's it. I can't remember any further back than that. Every day I get older, so these new memories are going to start crowding out more of the old ones. I'm scared. What if one day I can't remember my home at all?'

I risked putting my arm around him. 'Don't be scared. I can still remember when I was a little girl, and that was back before you were even born. I can remember the desert sunsets that would last for hours, turning the sand pink beneath our feet. I remember my father's silly stories and all his stupid scams, I remember the woman in the village who taught me how to count. I remember lots and lots. If you keep some things safe, then they can't go anywhere.' I said all of this as earnestly as I could, even though my own memories of the time before I arrived here grew more hazy every day.

'Like the wooden box the soldier has?'

'That's right. Keep your memories of home locked up safe in a box like that, but keep it in your heart instead of lugging it around behind you, and then you'll never forget them.'

He said nothing. We sat like that for a while, looking into the valley. Somewhere between the plains I picked out a trawl of flashy colours, the expensive red flutter of a banner being teased by the wind, the brown of a traipse of mules bearing packs, the glint of silver that can only come from swords or daggers. It wasn't difficult to guess that a party might be coming this way and, if so, that they would surely be here by nightfall. But I didn't point it out to Boy. Why scare away the child I had only just coaxed back out into the sunlight? And anyway, with all those bright colours in their retinue, the distant party looked just a bit too fancy to settle for our grubby little den. Or so I thought.

The Empress's bell rang only a few hours after lunch. The sound of that little bell had to be among the most irritating noises I had ever heard. Worse than the snorting or burping of rowdy men, worse than the guests' grunts or snores, worse even than the call of the bonebirds when they find a body to pick at somewhere in the desert. We were helping the cook shell beans when we heard it ringing, and I knew straight away that it was going to be another strange evening.

'Do you think it's more officials? That would be exciting,' Silk said as we prepared ourselves.

'No, it would be annoying. They're worse than peasants, because they think they're better and they have no shame,' Tiger replied.

We had just begun to light the lamps by the time the well-dressed men reached the gate. From the small number of people who eventually trickled through, I guessed that most of the servants and guards were camped out in various places on the hill, probably just far away enough to make sure they didn't hear their bosses having too much fun while they sat up sober and alert, guarding the bags and the sleepy mules.

Five men in lavish robes made their way to the table, followed by a single musician with an ornate hushtar. They all sported long drooping whiskers that they must have thought were fashionable, so it took me a few minutes before I realised that I had seen the man who seated himself at the head of the table before.

'I have had the pleasure of dining at this little cavern before, when I was on a mission with my illustrious uncle. I thought I would treat you all, my friends, to a little local custom. The food is, I am afraid, on the wrong side of mediocre, and the wine is somewhat sour, but both will do when you have an empty stomach. It is these feisty creatures, however, that make the trip worthwhile.'

He gestured towards us, and I saw Tiger struggle to stop her smile from slipping.

It was the same man who had come before with the older official, the young man who had upset his uncle with his loose tongue and had caused Tiger's sick spell. He was obviously in charge now. If he had so much contempt for us, I wondered, why had he come back? Surely the prospect of humiliating us wasn't enough to divert a whole caravan up a hill in the middle of nowhere?

'I see it is still the policy of this establishment to collect as many unusual specimens as possible. They even seem to have gone to the trouble to maiming one,' the leader continued, gesturing at Silk as she laid a plate of dried dates and figs on the table. Silk's cheeks turned the same shade as the skin of the rosy apples I set down beside the other dishes and I could see that she was trying hard to bite her tongue.

During the meal, only the thin, bearded man kept quiet. He barely touched the clay cup in front of him, merely toying with his food while the others took their fill. I understood how he might have felt, stuck in a place he didn't want to be, under the charge of someone he did not respect. He alone nodded graciously when we cleared the empty plates and set down the bowls of eggs, spicy stew and blood-cured beans.

'I'd give my right eye to make sure I got picked by that quiet one and not any of the others tonight,' Silk whispered as we rushed to the cook's courtyard to collect the soup.

'Those bastards are all the same,' Tiger said. 'They'll spit in your face and call you anything they can think of, but they'll still get down on their knees and beg you to keep their dirty requests a secret at the end of the evening.'

When we got back Boy was standing beside the table, holding one of the jugs of liquor. The men were well into their second toast.

'... and when those damn generals hanging round the palace like a bad smell see what we've achieved, it'll wipe the smiles off their smug faces, for sure. Let's drink to everyone who thinks we're going to fail, and to the looks we're going to see on their faces when we return to receive the thanks of the emperor!'

The fat man finished speaking and they all smacked the cups together before swigging and calling Boy forward for a refill. I could see him grimace as one of the men roughly fondled his thigh while he topped up the cup.

'My uncle too will eat his words, for we will succeed where he once gave up,' the leader said. 'But let's not waste our breath discussing those old wind-bags back in the capital. The book will be ours, and everything that goes with it. Now, let's have some entertainment. These girls may be past their best, but I'll warrant they can still dance.'

The three of us smiled graciously and moved to the empty space between the table and the musician. We raised our hands and began to sway, spinning slowly in dizzy circles as our hips called up a rhythm. I had learnt to move like this by copying the others back when I first arrived; Claws had shown me how to keep my eyes trained on the guests as I moved, but to look straight through them, to find the place where the music and my heart met and to move to it. We were not dancing for anyone – whatever the sneering men thought – but ourselves. Their laughter soon faded out, and they chewed their food and watched, all eyes upon us as we spun faster, flying far from this place and everything in it.

'Not bad. For a dump at the end of the world, I mean,' the tall man said when the song finished, and the rest of them nodded grudgingly.

They pulled us down to sit with them, and we had to fight hard to maintain our smiles and girlish laughs as they mauled at us and tried to unfasten our robes, all the while keeping up their snide jokes. At last the leader held up his cup and the others fell silent.

'As your host tonight, I reserve the right to make the final toast, though I am sorry to rob Bei of the opportunity to amuse us with his poor attempts at witticisms. As you are all aware, we have faced some hard times and privations on this mission, and I am grateful to each of you for staying the course. Yet do not think that because we are close now it will get any easier. In fact, once we find it, everything may well become even more difficult. So drink, enjoy yourselves tonight, but do not forget we still have to prove our cunning and our strength.'

After knocking back the dregs from their cups, the leader told them to hurry up and choose which of us they would take as his gift for the evening. Though they all deferred to him and claimed the first pick was an honour none of them would dare steal from their superior, the leader brushed aside their arguments and insisted. And so it was that the fat man struggled to his feet and thrust out his hand towards Tall.

'Fat and thin, eh? Together they're going to be like yin and yang!' one of them joked.

'When you are as lazy as me, gentlemen, you need a lithe one who can bend and twist any which way you want him!' the fat man retorted to the sound of much laughter.

'Your turn next,' the leader said to the tall man. 'I might recommend the dark one there; she's got a fire burning between her thighs and she won't stop till you're screaming for mercy.'

The tall man shook his head. 'No, I think I'll go for the pale one, whatever her flaws. I never much cared for the dark ones, they just look too damn dirty.'

He led Silk away as the silent man stood up and, after much cajoling from his colleagues, held out a hand to Tiger. She looked as if she was going to burst out into cries of thanks to the spirits at her good luck. The next one picked Homely and slapped his fat behind as they walked away, laughing that he needed something big to hold onto. That left the leader sitting on the plump cushions, running his eyes over Boy and me as we stood nervously in front of him.

'Hmm. Now, unlike my more adventurous companions, I usually prefer the company of a good woman. The trouble is, I'm not sure you fit that description, my dear. I seem to remember my stuck-up cousin saying he'd had a good time with you, but as with all the other choices he had made in his life, I think he was drawn to the average and unexceptional. Plus your lumpy nose has grown hideously misshapen since I was last here, no doubt as retribution from some disappointed customer. No, I think I will have to go with the boy. At least he still looks firm in all the right places.'

I saw Boy swallow anxiously as the man stood up and beckoned to him.

'No!' I yelped. I couldn't control myself.

'No?' The man's thin lips curled into a scornful smile.

'I mean, please take me. I need it, I'm longing for it. He's new and inexperienced – he can't make you feel like I will.'

'He'll learn,' the man replied. 'You are only debasing yourself, girl. Nothing puts a gentleman off more than the stink of desperation.'

'Wait. Please.' I racked my brains – I'd never had the chance to swap myself for Boy before. 'I've wanted you since you first came here with your uncle. I've thought about you every day since. I'm burning for you. I'll do anything you ask of me. Just give me the chance to spend one night in your arms.'

He turned back and looked me up and down again. As long as you're saying something good about him, a man will believe anything. A woman, meanwhile, learns to see through every compliment she ever gets.

'Anything I ask? Hmm. I had no idea I inspired as much devotion in the wilderness as I do back in the capital. Well, I do not wish to disappoint. Come on then, this better be worth my while.'

Over the next hour and a half, until we both collapsed sweaty and exhausted, I did everything I could think of to make him pant and squirm. He was clammy and rough and merciless, and I had to reach into the back of my mind for every little trick I had learnt from the others – I groaned and licked and bit and nibbled and stroked and clutched and squeezed and shook every last drop of desire from him, and though I did it all with hatred bubbling beneath my fluttering eyelids, with disgust burning on my outstretched tongue, it was worth it all if it saved Boy from one second of this man's odious company. Our flesh rubbed tender and raw; we ground each other down to dust.

My eyes shot open. I was choking and struggling. He was on top of me, his hands clamped around my throat. It was still the dead of night, silent now except for my splutters and desperate wheezing for air. I must have drifted off for a second – now I understood why we never spent the night beside the guests. His legs pinned down mine, and it seemed as if he was squeezing out everything I had inside; my eyes felt as if they were going to explode. I was clawing frantically, fighting for breath. I began to thump my fists against his tightening grip, but he only stared down at me and smiled.

'Do you really think we came all the way to this forsaken place for a couple of maimed and saggy whores? You must be even stupider than you look!' He laughed and then spat in my face, still pressing down on my airways. 'Do you think it was easy for us to return here, to pretend to enjoy your inedible dishes and pathetic attempts at entertainment, to lie with such an ugly creature and pretend it was passion? Now I'm only going to ask you this once: where is he?'

He loosened his grip and I felt dizzy as air once again rushed into my lungs. I coughed and shook, but he had only relaxed briefly. He stared into my eyes with a mix of hatred and enjoyment.

'Who, sir?' I stammered.

Once again his hands began to constrict around my throbbing neck.

'Don't even try that, whore. You cannot keep any secrets from me now. If I think you are lying, I will not hesitate to kill you. We certainly have enough silver to reimburse your mistress – hell, with the money we give her she'll be able to buy a girl twice as young and beautiful as you, which shouldn't be difficult. And don't think someone is going to come and rescue you – all your friends are probably in the same position as you by now. So talk. Where is he?'

'I don't know who you mean,' I rasped, and one of his hands broke free from the suffocating grip for a second to slap my face.

'Do you really think you can play with me like this? I was given this mission by the emperor in the expectation that I would fail, and could then be punished without the bother of my family pleading for lenience. But I will not fail. I will not! So do not test my patience any longer. Where is the soldier and where is the book? Aha – I saw that flicker in your eyes. You do know what I mean. So talk!'

He pulled his hands away from my throat to land another slap against my stinging face. Were Tiger and Silk and the boys being questioned like this too? Would one of them tell them about our soldier? If so, it seemed foolish for me to die for his secret. And yet I couldn't give him up.

'I don't know what you mean. I've never seen a book in my life.'

His hands gripped tighter around my neck.

'All right, all right. It's true, we had a soldier visit us. Back when winter was just melting into spring. He was a retired general, I

think. He was short and bald and definitely from the middle kingdom, and a stocky man travelled with him. And they had a wooden
box that never left their side. But it was just the two of them, and
they only stayed one night.'

'And where are they now?'

'I swear, I don't know. They mentioned going into the desert,
they said it was safer there,' I was rambling now, knitting lies together in the hope that the others would also mention the wrong
soldier and so get us all out of trouble.

He stopped squeezing, though his hands didn't leave my throat,
and he seemed to be considering what I had said.

'The disgraced general ... hmm, but how did he get his hands
on it? Perhaps if ... No. I don't believe you. Come on, let's have
an honest answer out of you, or I swear I'll kill everyone in this
wretched place!'

I gulped, and met his eyes. My head was still spinning, but I had
to try to convince him.

'I'm telling you the truth about the general. He was a sweet old
man, but he couldn't hold his drink, and when we asked what was
in the wooden box he said it was very special. A book, a very old
book, he said. None of us paid it much attention, though, because
none of us can read. I promise sir, that's all I know.'

His hands went slack and he lifted them to his chin. He seemed
satisfied, if a little disappointed. As I drew in long, heady lungfuls
of air he climbed off me and started to throw on his expensive
robes, tucking his dagger back into his belt. After spitting on my
face once more for good luck he marched out into the courtyard.
The sunrise had still not broken behind us.

'Come on, get out here right now!' he hollered.

Only a few minutes later, the rest of his party began to emerge
in various states of undress. The other girls, who, unlike me, had
returned to our shared room, poked their heads round the door to
watch the men gather.

'There's no time to wait. The general's got it and the chances are
he's hidden it in the desert somewhere. If any of you have gleaned
information that contradicts this, then speak now.'

The other men looked about sheepishly, as if glad they would not
need to report the paltry conclusions of their own interrogations. I
smiled to myself. No one had told them anything.

'Good. Then we leave right away. If he thinks he can outsmart us, then he is badly mistaken. Zhou, get the guards to ready the horses!'

And with that they blustered out of the yard and into the dark. After they left, we gathered to comfort each other beside the clattered debris of the night's party. Tall and Homely were whispering in their doorway, though Boy and the Empress both seemed to have miraculously slept through the whole ruckus.

'What was all that about?' Silk asked, her single eye red and watery. 'Did they turn on you too?'

I nodded, but Tiger looked confused. The quiet man had barely even touched her, she said. Silk, however, looked to have had the same treatment I received – even in the dark the purple glow of her cheeks was unmistakable.

'But why? Mine kept talking about a terrible secret. I couldn't understand anything he was saying, so he kept hitting me until I was saying anything that came into my head. I wasn't sure he was ever going to stop.' She wiped her nose, trying to stay calm. 'What the hell did they want?'

'I think they wanted the soldier,' I said, a little too loudly, since Tall and Homely cut short their conversation when they heard me. As he paced towards us, I saw that Tall's chest was criss-crossed with long cuts.

'So all that was your fault? We all were nearly killed because you fancied keeping a lover upstairs? Well, fuck you!'

He spat in my face. I was getting used to it.

'I'm so sorry. I didn't know,' I said. 'What did you tell him?'

'Piss off! I hope they come back and slit your soldier's throat. He's bad luck.'

He turned and stormed off, pulling a glaring Homely into their room and banging the door shut.

'Don't worry about him. I'm sure he didn't tell them about the soldier. It's not your fault,' Silk said.

Tiger nodded. 'Those so-called officials were just a bunch of bumbling idiots. But why did they suddenly rush off towards the desert?'

'I made up a story. It was the only way I could think of to get them out of here,' I sighed. 'They think the wooden box is hidden there.'

'So that's what they were after? There must be a whole ocean of silver in there.'

'I don't think so. The leader said it contained some kind of book.'

'Don't be silly,' Silk said. 'No one would go so crazy over a book!'

'It must be more than just a book if there are whole groups of men on missions from the middle kingdom to find it, and if our friend upstairs is willing to lose his leg over it,' Tiger said.

Silk shrugged. 'Well, whatever it is, it'll have to wait. I need some sleep. Hopefully by the time I wake up I'll have forgotten this whole bloody nightmare.

'Please don't tell the Empress about any of this, especially about the book,' I whispered to Tiger after Silk had gone.

She looked hurt. 'Jade, haven't you learnt yet how strong my silence is?'

The men who have been to the temple say that everything in the world is part of the battle between good and bad, between light and dark, and that perhaps one day one side will win. They say that there is good and there is evil, and it's as simple as that. The problem is, up here at the Whorehouse of a Thousand Sighs, I think we're somewhere in between. I mean, we're definitely not bad, but the things that go on up here don't really fall into the other category either. It's usually best, I've found, to leave men to worry about this kind of thing while us women get on with real life.

The next day, however, all I could think about was that damn book that had got us into so much trouble. My eye stung and my neck felt as though it had been twisted back to front. Curiosity finally got the better of me, so I decided to ask the soldier about it.

I was surprised at how easily we fell back into our routine of giggling and embracing, all before I'd had a chance to talk about the previous night. Everything else seemed to fade away once we collapsed in our little fits of hushed laughter and urged each other quieter. It was when we were lying together, reclaiming our breath afterwards, that I told him what had happened.

'He said they were looking for a book. That's what you've got hidden in there, isn't it? It's that book you were talking about the other day, isn't it?'

He smiled. 'It's not just a book. It's the whole world.'

'That's why you're hiding out here? That's why you're being chased? Because you've got a book that tells you something important about the world out there?'

'It tells me nothing. I haven't opened it. It's too dangerous.'

'Why's it dangerous?'

'Because it speaks of everything that has ever happened and will ever happen. The whole of history is written in here.'

'Don't mock me, I'm serious.'

'So am I.'

I thought about it. All of the past and the future written down on a few musty old strips of bamboo. It didn't seem very likely.

'And you really haven't peeked inside?' I asked.

'I wouldn't dare take that risk. If a man learns how he will die, how could he carry on? If he learns how the world will end, he will lose heart. It will make a man mad. And if the generals get it, we are all in danger.'

'Why? If the future is written down, then surely you can't do anything to change it.'

'If you know how a man will die, when he will die, then you have power over him.'

'Then why not just destroy it?'

'I can't.'

'Why?'

'I just can't. It's forbidden.'

'Who forbids it? Who gave you the box?'

'You know enough. Listen, it's too dangerous. Please, don't ask me any more.'

I sighed, but I understood. It had not taken me long to realise, living in a place like this, that the more you talked about things, the more difficult life became. Best just to pass over certain things in silence. I left the soldier alone with his box and made my way back down the track. At the gate I found Boy taking down and retying the many faded ribbons, much to the consternation of the young guard stationed there to make sure none of us tried anything stupid.

I expected him to be grateful that I had saved him from the hungry clutches of the leader the previous night. However, he hadn't even thanked me. In fact, earlier that morning he had told me that I shouldn't have bothered, that he could look after himself. Even if that one man didn't spend the night with him, he had said, there would be another in a couple of days, and another soon after that, and he would rather I just stopped fussing.

'What are you up to?' I asked, running my hands over one of the loose-fluttering ribbons.

'You've been with the soldier again,' he replied, ignoring my question. 'When is he going?'

'Soon. His stump is healing up pretty well. He wanted me to thank you for helping him that night, for bringing him up here. He owes his life to you.'

'I don't want his thanks,' Boy huffed.

'What do you want?' I said, putting a hand on his shoulder. He quickly shrugged it away.

'Nothing. I just want you all to leave me alone.'

'You don't really mean that.'

'Yes, I do. I'm sick of this place and these people and I'm sick of the stupid music and the yucky food and I'm sick of the serving and the men and I'm sick of you and your stupid excuses. I just want you all to leave me alone.'

I sensed that it would be no use trying to argue with him. He was no longer interested in my attempts to make things look better and, to be honest, I was finding it harder and harder to pretend to be cheerful around him. If the future is already planned out and this strange book says you are doomed to spend the next twenty, thirty summers spending your nights with obnoxious men, then what comfort is there? If the past is slipping through your fingers like smoke and all you have to look forward to is more of the same old feelings of shame and regret, then why even bother thinking about the future? I went back to the girls' room, and did what I always did when confronted with problems I didn't know how to solve: I tried to sleep.

But I couldn't stop thinking about the book the soldier had told me about. Was this what everything had been about, officials and tortured soldiers, retired generals and midnight attacks, all for a wad of bamboo telling people what they already know – that there will be wars and peace, love and loss, planting and harvesting, birth and death, summer and winter, remembering and forgetting? It seemed a huge waste of energy to go running about risking your whole life for what was scribbled down on a few strips of old plants.

But maybe I only felt like that because I wouldn't be able to read what it said anyway. The folks back in the desert villages talked about reading as if it were a disease, as if once you learnt to read your whole heart got jumbled up and you started spouting crazy ideas left, right and centre.

Yet the more I thought about it, the more I liked the idea of this special book. Because if it was true then it made life a whole lot easier. Think about it – if every single thing that happens is already recorded, then that must include your own life. And if your life is already mapped out, then there is nothing you can do to change it. Worrying about whether to run away or which man to marry or what to do about mysterious soldiers is just a waste of time, because the path is already laid out and there's nothing you can do to stop walking down it. It gave me a kind of comfort to know that whatever I was yet to do was already done as far as the book was concerned, that whatever life had in store for me, good and bad, it was meant to be and there was no getting out of it. You're stuck with your future just as surely as you are stuck with your past: there's no shaking it off.

It took me hours to get to sleep, and when I woke up I wished I hadn't bothered. I'd had the dream again, the one where I grow feathers. Except this time it was different. This time I managed to fly, to push myself up over the clouds. And when I flew right to the top of the sky and looked through the holes in its threadbare silk, there it was: the future. All the men yet to share my bed, all their dirtiest requests, all my sorrow, my lonely old age, and even my death, the day the hour the minute the sight the sounds the smell of it. And it was terrible.

I woke up sweaty and shaking. But the bustling of feet and the slop of water outside my door told me that new visitors had been spotted coming our way, so I pulled on my robe and packed away my thoughts and worries until they were hidden deep beneath my smile.

I think it was that day with the raisin traders, during some long and boring speech about the best way to shrivel grapes in the sun, that the plan first began to take shape in my mind. At first it was a silly fantasy, the kind of daydream I regularly indulged in when

I wanted to escape from whatever was happening around me. As I continued to nod and grin at the speaker, my thoughts fluttered away. What would it mean, I began to think, if my future – as foretold by the crows in that strange and dangerous book – was not here, but elsewhere? If it was already written, then all I had to do was call it into action.

The more I thought about it all, the more sense it made. After all, if the book told that I would escape, then all I could really do was go along with my destiny. I would just be doing what I was always meant to do. And if everything went wrong and I was caught by bandits again or starved in the desert or was found out and beaten by the Empress, then I could do little to stop that too. I just had to accept my fate. It was liberating in a way, knowing that my choices weren't really mine at all, that all I was doing was following the path laid out for me centuries before in the visions that the crows saw amid the stars. In a way it was funny that, imprisoned in a small cavern room on a poky hilltop, I found freedom inside an even smaller wooden box.

It didn't take long for my daydreams to give way to musings of a more practical nature. Whenever I was walking on the trail between the courtyards I would stop to stare down the hillside and off into the valley, calculating the best way down, trying to work out how to remain hidden and considering where I would go once I reached the bottom. After more than five summers in that place I knew who the light sleepers were (Silk and Homely); I knew who was the last to bed (Tiger) and who rose the earliest (the cook and Boy), and who would be looking for an opportunity to run straight to the Empress to give me away (Tall). I knew where the food was kept, and where the Empress hid some of the various treasures she had accumulated. But most importantly of all, from the many tales I had heard from the guests, I had learnt everything I needed to know about the tracks that wound through the desert below, about the spirits roaming the plains and the talking rocks, the hospitable and not-so-hospitable villages and outposts dotted between the dunes, and the snags and gorges around the hillside that claimed lost travellers.

One afternoon I was sitting near the gate, keeping an eye on the guard to try to work out how often he made trips into the bushes to relieve himself, when I noticed Boy up on the trail between the two courtyards. He seemed to be talking, though from that distance I couldn't hear what he was saying. When I got to my feet I saw that he was standing over one of those sneaky brown snakes that sometimes bothered the camels, the kind that pretend to be twigs just to catch you out.

'You ought to be careful with that snake,' I called out as I walked towards him. 'You can't trust him not to swing that slippery tail and spit his fangs at you!'

'I know,' Boy muttered. 'Can't trust anyone. Everyone's got fangs, everyone's got bites to give you.'

'Even me?'

He shrugged. 'I don't know.'

'We do see more fangs than smiles up here, that's true. But it isn't like that everywhere. I think there's usually at least one good person in every place you go. You've just got to keep your eyes open or you might never see them. Ugh, it's an ugly thing, isn't it?' I said, watching the snake wriggle away into the bushes.

'It's all right. I wish I could hide as well as it can. You know, it can slip past people without them even noticing.'

'You'd get bored if no one could see you. What would you do all day?'

He shrugged again. 'I'd get away from here, for a start. Maybe be a soldier or a traveller or something.'

'I see. So what were you saying to old mister slimy then, hmm? I know you were whispering something,' I joked.

'No I wasn't,' he said defensively. 'I wasn't saying anything!'

'All right, I was only playing with you.'

'I'm too old to play now. And so are you.'

He stomped off up the dusty track. I knew he wouldn't thank me for following him, so I went back to my seat near the gate. I could understand how he felt. And if he was telling his troubles or his aches to that stupid brown snake, well, at least that was better than locking them inside and letting them feast on his heart. I watched him turn out of sight behind a hunk of rock.

It wasn't long before my mind wandered from the guard I was supposed to be studying. I started thinking about Boy's words. What if he could be like the snake, and escape without anyone noticing? Maybe that was what was written in the book for his life – what if he really could do anything he wanted, like get away from here and be a soldier or a merchant or a farmer?

The idea brought a smile to my face. To know that Boy could still imagine having a different life outside, well, surely that meant it was possible. Because if you can imagine something, then it's already half real, isn't it? Once you've imagined something, all you've got to do is wait for it to take shape. And if it doesn't take shape, sometimes you need to give it a helping hand.

During my time here I've learnt a lot about how the human body works. A little from listening to some of the guests talking, but mostly just from looking and feeling. Most of it is just common sense. Even a kid knows your heart, which brews up all your thoughts and feelings, is deep in your gut. That's obvious. You can hear it rumbling sometimes, and when you've got troubles you sure as hell know it first in your belly. Dreams come from your eyes, lust starts in the bowels, and the only way evil gets in is through your nose. That's why the first thing the midwife does when she hauls out a mewing newborn is pinch the nostrils. Curses lodge in that bit between your ears, and they're the things that can set your head ringing like the temple gong. All the things you've ever done wrong stay in the blood, just beneath your skin.

Love, that comes from the skin. It spreads out slowly, like a blush that hurries down from your face until every part of you is glowing, until you can feel it warm every stretch of your body. I'm not talking about the kind of love that lessens each time you wake up next to someone and see their raggedy early-morning face or smell their stinky breath. I mean the kind of love where you would do anything to make that person's life better, even if it made your own worse. I mean the kind of love that you can get lost in, the kind of love that's so strong that it doesn't matter whether the other person loves you back or not.

After that day with the snake the only thing I thought about was my plan. And I felt calmer than I ever had before. I was happy. I knew what was going to happen, because I was suddenly certain about what was written in the book. I knew how things were going to turn out, and that faith gave me the strength and the courage to do everything I had to do. And I knew that I had no choice: I had to do it, all of it, and I knew that none of it would really be my fault:

it was already written in the book.

I'm not sure how long it was between that day and the night I put my plan into action. I know it must have been at least a few weeks, because I had to make sure I knew exactly when the guard slept and I had to sneak out on the nights we didn't have any guests to quietly dig up a couple of bottles of the camel-milk liquor the cook had buried for the winter. I spent so much time stroking those smelly camels that my hands almost grew fur. And of course I had to pack. So perhaps it was a couple of moons later. I'm not sure. Time speeds up as you race towards the future.

Everyone was groggy, drowsy from a party the night before. Our guests had just finished their breakfast and left, though by then it was well past noon. Empty bottles and dirty platters littered our courtyard, while the cook, having been well toasted for his hushtar performance, was snoozing amid a tottering heap of grubby bowls. The whole place stank of drink and piss, and there wasn't a single one of us without a dry mouth and a heavy head. It was perfect.

The three of us girls were beating out our sleeping rugs as the sun sparked copper above.

'You haven't been up to that soldier in a few days. I thought you were supposed to be encouraging him to get moving again so he can get out of our hair. What's the matter, isn't he keeping up his end of the bargain?' Silk burst into laughter at her own joke. Tiger shook her head and smiled.

'I've been busy. To be honest, with everything else going on I'd almost forgotten him. The cook's feeding him and he can hobble about quite well on his own now. But I'll go and see him tomorrow,' I replied.

'You've got to let him go, you know. He won't be able to keep paying the Empress to let him stay here forever,' Tiger said.

'I know. I know.'

It was still light later that evening when everyone turned in for an early night. Everyone except me. I lay in my bed, counting. I counted all the numbers I knew and then started again, tucking down all my fingers and curling up each one of my toes. Then I took the two bottles of liquor I'd hidden under the straw I slept on and tiptoed from the room.

The nosy moon followed me as I crept behind the dozing guard, up the trail and past the cook's room. I lit a torch from the embers of the dinner fire and, after reassuring the camels that everything was fine, I slipped into the soldier's room.

'It's late for you,' he said.

I was surprised that he was still awake, sitting up in the dark with his arms wrapped around the wooden box. His beard was long and dark, his exposed stump as pink as a skinned lamb.

'I know. I thought we could celebrate, though, with the leftovers from last night's party. It could be our last chance alone together before the Empress sends you on your way now that you're so much better.'

He said nothing, so I set the torch between two rocks in the wall and handed him one of the liquor bottles. He seemed hesitant.

'Come on. Won't you at least miss me a little?'

I took a large swig from my own bottle and he followed suit. It wasn't long before we were struggling together beneath the fuzzy blushes of tipsiness. I took his bottle from him and poured the liquor straight into my mouth before bending down to dribble it past his lips. We rushed through it, all hands and moans, rocking against each other until everything disappeared but our bodies. It was the same as the times before it, that strange sense of belonging, that feeling of overflowing into someone else's life.

'I won't forget you,' I whispered, raising the bottle to my lips.

'Please. Forget me,' he whispered back, before drinking with me.

Even afterwards, as we lay side by side and damp with sweat, he matched each of my swigs with one of his own, not knowing that where he was downing the strongest liquor we had, I was merely swallowing water, having emptied the contents of the second bottle into the young guard's tea jar while he was squatting in the bushes. I was surprised to find how easy it was to put all my feelings for the soldier aside, to do what I had to do. After all, I couldn't let my heart's little whimpers stand in the way of history.

Finally his eyes slumped to a close and his low snores stirred the air, the empty bottle rolling on the sheet beside his head. He may have been different from all the others I had known, but he was still a man, and there was no way he would have let himself be out-drunk by a woman. I untied the string across his chest and left the room as quietly as I could, his purse bunched in my fist and the wooden box containing the whole world tucked under my arm.

The camels nuzzled my neck as I unknotted one of them from its stake and led it down the trail. We stopped at a cluster of rocks a few paces above the gate. I peered over to check that the guard was still asleep – too young to hold his drink – and the silence only spurred me on.

'Did I have to stay awake all night just to play with that stinky camel?'

I jumped when I heard Boy's voice, and I turned to see him sitting on a dusty mound of dirt, just as I had instructed. He was rubbing his eyes. I smiled and beckoned him closer.

'Well, yes and no. You see, this is an extra special type of game. Did you bring the sack I left in your room?'

He nodded and pulled out the grubby hemp bag that I had stuffed with clothes and leftovers and trinkets. I put the wooden box inside, bound the top tight and slung the sack over the slobbering camel's back. I put my hands under Boy's armpits and he tried to wriggle out of my grasp.

'No. Let me go.'

'It's only a game,' I said.

'I don't want to. It smells and I'm tired. I'm going back to bed.'

'No!' I hissed. 'Get up there now!'

Something in my tone made him give in, and he let me raise him up until he could pull himself into the crease between the two humps. I placed my hands on his and showed him how to grip the tufts of straggly hair on the animal's neck, how to pull and twist and tug it in different directions. He grinned and pushed my hand away, telling me he wasn't a child, that even an idiot could ride one of these beasts.

'Now listen. Down there is the city. Don't go anywhere near it, you understand? Just keep going east – follow the sunrise, never the sunset. You want to get to the middle kingdom. You'll know when you get there because the people all have round faces and brown eyes just like Claws and the soldier. Try to join up with some merchants if you can, but watch out for bandits. You can bribe people and buy food with these coins – you'd better keep them well hidden though. If anyone asks, you're looking for your father, who is a general now stationed in the capital and will reward anyone who helps you on your journey. What you really want to do is get as close to someone important as you can and give them this box. Tell them the emperor is looking for it. You're sure to get a huge reward.'

'And then I come back?'

'No! Then you can be anything you want to be. This box is very important to the emperor there. So with all the reward money he gives you, and his blessing for bringing it to him, you could become an official or a merchant or a scholar or anything else you can think of. You can become someone else.'

He looked nervous. 'What about you? I don't want to go alone. You're my friend.'

'I know, I know. But don't worry, I'm going to get the other camel and take a different route. That way no one will get suspicious. I'll meet up with you in the capital, as soon as you've given the box back. But now you'd better be on your way before it gets light.'

He started to protest, a worried look still on his face, so I thumped the camel's rear end to get it going. After a few uncertain hobbles, the hulking beast began to lope down through the rocks and dust, driven on by its new-found freedom. I waved to Boy as they descended, until not even the moon could pick them out on the star-lit hillside. Then I made my way back up the trail.

I'd left the soldier's door unlocked. He was still asleep, his head lolling back and his lips spilling out the faintest of mumbles. I clasped my hands over my ears, knowing that if I heard even a hint of a word I understood then I might not have the courage to go through with it. The torch was still burning between the two rocks on the wall. I took it down and laid it on the floor, a few steps away from the straw bed. The rest was up to fate, I told myself. It was out of my hands. I bolted the door behind me on my way out and crept back down to our room. Silk and Tiger were still fast asleep. I stretched out on the straw and drifted off.

Everything turned out much as I had guessed it would – it was almost as if I had read the future straight from the book itself. The cook had woken first, choking on the smoke spilling into his little covered room. By the time he roused everyone with his frantic shouts, the flames from the smaller courtyard could be seen from the gate. When we spilled out of our room to see what was going on, the confused young guard was filling a bucket at the washing trough and the Empress was screaming that he might as well piss on the inferno – a single bucket wouldn't do anything; the cook was sobbing about his trapped camels (although he was obviously not moved enough to return up the trail and attempt a rescue operation); while Tall and Homely were staring at the furious oceans of black smoke spooling up towards the clouds.

'I was so stupid,' Silk said. 'Only yesterday I saw the shape of a bird in my glass eye. I should have known it was the bird of flame.'

'Has anyone been up there?' I asked, and each one of them shook their heads without turning away from the blaze.

'The cook says the fire devils are after him and there's no way he's going back up. And do you really think the Empress is going to drag herself all that way just for the sake of a couple of old camels?' Homely said.

'And the soldier,' said Tiger, quietly, looking at me.

The young guard ran past us with the bucket, heading up the trail, his eyes stung red and his feet tripping over each other. It was not long before we saw him stumbling back down, coughing and almost crying, with the bucket nowhere to be seen.

'We'll just have to wait till it burns itself out,' Tall muttered.

'Fire returns everything to its beginning. Of course we cannot fight it,' said Tiger. 'It is a god, a state in which the spirit is remoulded. Fire is so hungry that when there is nothing else left it will consume itself.'

She was right. All we could do was wait, and everything would take care of itself. Even the Empress's rage died down eventually, despite giving the cook such a brutal thrashing – despite his adamant denial that he hadn't left the kitchen fire burning that night – that we had to cook for ourselves for a week while he recovered. The nimble fingers of the autumn wind picked at the ashes of the camel, the charred splinters of four wooden doors and the dusty remains of our ruined supplies of dried fruit and kindling. The three of us girls were lumbered with the job of pulling out what was left of the soldier's blackened bones.

The box must have been destroyed in the fire, Silk said, and though everyone spent a long time searching, they were finally forced to admit that the coins too must have been claimed by the flames – or perhaps they were all in the Empress's room by now,

Tall suggested. In the chaos and commotion, no one seemed particularly concerned or upset about Boy's disappearance, and, despite my suggestion that he might have come up to play with the fire and then been swept up in it, the others all agreed with the cook that he had probably taken advantage of the general confusion to make a run back towards his desert village. After all, they pointed out, there were no traces of his body in the ashes, and though it was hard to tell from the mess of charred bones near the huts, it seemed one of the camels was missing. 'He probably started the fire himself,' Homely said, while Silk argued that it might have been the soldier himself driven to madness after the loss of his leg and the Empress taking all his money. Tall even suggested I might have had something to do with it all, but after I broke down in tears the others told him to stop being so ridiculous and insensitive.

I was still weeping when we took the soldier's burnt remains to the top of the hill. They were real tears and I meant them. I cried because he'd meant more to me than I'd realised. And I cried because he had probably known all along how it was going to end but had let it happen anyway. As we walked back down again, Silk hugged my shoulders tight. Tiger stared at me, her head tilted and her lips parting as if to say something, but she obviously thought better of it, because she closed them quickly and shook her head instead. None of us mentioned him again.

All of that was more than seven summers ago now. A lot has happened since then. Silk gave up serving men to take on the chores of the upper courtyard after the cook drank himself to death; new girls – Reed and Silver and Whisper – arrived; and a thousand merchants and desert traders have passed through. As for me, well, I suppose I'm a little fatter – but then, who isn't? I never left to meet Boy in the capital, but, actually, I had never planned to do so. Just knowing that he's somewhere far away from here is enough. And the truth is, I don't think I'd know what to do with myself if I ever left the Whorehouse of a Thousand Sighs. As hard as I try, I can't imagine being anywhere else; this place is my home.

Sometimes, even now, I think about the soldier. I still miss him a little, but I don't feel guilty. All the things that happened – to me, to Claws, to Silk and Tiger; to the Empress, Boy, the soldier – they were all written down long before we were even born. Besides, I gave up worrying about things like blame and regret ages ago. After all, history just picks you up and spins you along, like a whirlwind tearing across the sand, and there's nothing you can do to free yourself from its grip.

# Fish and Bird

SPRING 1738 CE

In the last life I remember, I was a fish, blotting the water with the curve and snag of my scales – this is not unusual, and for karma accumulated in previous lifetimes some among us have been beasts, birds, cripples or even women – and at times, sitting as a lotus with my palms cupped upon my folded legs, when the low arched beams painted deepest red and the wooden pillars and the inglenooks and the silver Bodhisattva whirling in the flickers of the candlelight and the indigo-skinned gods gambolling across the jade green of the ceiling and the smells of saffron and sun-dried red chillies and slow-boiling rice all begin to fade and I give myself over to the nothingness that is nowhere and is everywhere and is nothing and is all things, at those times I often see the world a-shimmer, loose and translucent, as though I am pulsing up, all slick fins and beating tail, towards the surface, and always just before I can throw myself up above the waves the echo of the bronze gong stirs me from my meditation and I am once again all aching sinews and weather-thickened joints, wondering how many years are left for me in this form; and it was one such morning, as I was rising from the floor of the great prayer hall, thinking of those great sages who lived a thousand years in meditation, that one of my pupils – dabbing at his dribbling nose with the sleeve of his habit, woozy with the cold that afflicts most of the boys who reach the age where their hair must be shorn in the months of frost and sleet – came and told me that it was time, and so I hurried through the gardens where, in the shadow of the ashen hills standing guard over Tashilhunpo, the novices shouted in call and response the laws of the eternal wheel, the truths of fire, until I reached the most stately rooms reserved for the Panchen Lama and, venturing inside, found the other elders gathered around the bed where the living Buddha lay, shrivelled slim and shivering; God-King most merciful slipping slowly from sense; we waited with water and cloth and the Book of the Dead, we waited for the spirit to spill from the top of the head, and, at the sixth hour and seventeenth minute after dawn, I recorded the time of death and the recital began, to guide his ghost out among the world for, though it could have left this world behind in the attainment of nirvana – immersed, consumed, changed, as a teardrop is changed when it falls into an ocean – he had chosen to return again and guide others along their journeys, and so, close to three months after the body had been cleansed, the chanting given over to silence, and work begun on his great domed tomb, it was time to begin the search; after consulting the numerous astrological charts which hung in the Gyeni Chanting Hall, I assembled a small group – consisting of another elder learned in the art of the sacred rituals, and a number of young novices who might, as well as study the process of divination and the recognition of sacred signs, assist us in placating the spirits, gods and demons that might try to assail us in this most hallowed tradition – and together we set forth through the white thunderbolt gate down the winding slope towards the city of Samdruptse, where he will return (for though the spirit may move across the universe in mere moments, it also responds to the call of its home, the pull of the earth, the memory of soil and water).

That night we saw a crow skittering across the sky, chasing the sun as it sunk into fire – the same fine red as the darker tendrils a peach reveals in the softer flesh around where the stone is plucked out – then following it down to pick upon its bones and carry them to the silver moon for nourishment, and we were much encouraged by this sign, for it is well known that Mahakala, protector of monasteries, comes among us as a crow, for those great black birds alone have sense of the movement of the spirits of the dead, and it was then that one of the novices asked about the nature of the sun, for each day it swims westwards across the sky until it slips from sight, and each morning must begin its flight again; and so – as we made camp some several leagues between the hills that give shelter to great Tashilhunpo and the town whose lanterns burned deep in the distance ahead of us – I gave him answer: that just as self is impermanent, so the light which floats above us is impermanent too, though we may look to it for a lesson: for we too are bound within a cycle which seems endless, for we may be born many times and make the same journey again and again, and only once the desires that burn upon our senses as surely as the sun burns upon our backs are extinguished may we be liberated and find unity with that which we are not; and I reminded them of the fire sermon – lust, hate, despair, delusion, grief, pain, sight, sound, smell, taste, touch, birth, death: all scald us incessantly, all are aflame within us, and thus we must grow weary, and when we are weary we shall be disenchanted, and when we are disenchanted we shall be dispassionate, and when we are dispassionate we might leave the world behind – and the novices were much gratified by my answer, though one boy (I remember well that he was one of those who find it hardest to stem the wellsprings of desire and attachment, for he had cried some forty nights unceasing after leaving his father's home in his sixth year to join us) pressed me further, saying he feared the sun would, one morning, simply cease to appear, and so I told him that the sun might indeed be extinguished by its own flames, and yet it was not for him to think upon, for neither past nor future exists, neither tomorrow nor yesterday, neither before nor after, for all are illusion, and we must remember this or risk repeating our follies for a thousand lifetimes, in a thousand bodies, as man or bird or beast, under a thousand suns.

I then told the story of a monk who lived to be a hundred and spent each day in meditation in the courtyard outside the Hall of the Guanyin, and in springtime upon finishing he would open his eyes to see the plum blossoms giddy upon the boughs and so would tend the tree with a little drink of water and by trimming off the dead stems and plucking back the weeds that stole from their soil before he went to the kitchens to attend to his communal duties, and though all who knew him said that he had given up all earthly concerns and pleasures – he ate nothing but brown rice, and spoke to no one, and said nothing, and had learnt each word of each sutra so well that he could say them all standing upon one foot – as he lay dying, a week and a day after his one hundred and first birthday, he caught sight of the same plum tree keening to the breeze, holding its buds closed tight like little fists against the winter, and he thought briefly of how he would miss the bloom that year, and so was reborn an hour later as a sapling pushing up through the brown earth and clay.

The following day we scoured the town and set about enquiring of the widows and midwives who assist at births, the herbalists and the astronomers, the gossips and the notaries, of any child born under the ribbons of clouds that scurried low across the sky some ten days before, and – after first turning up at a small house in the poorer district of the town only to find to our disappointment that a local child born around that time turned out to be female – were soon pointed towards a village three days away where it was rumoured that there had been the fortuitous event of two births within a single hour on the day of which we spoke; that evening we camped out in the gardens of a merchant who had, as a child, received his education under the late Lama at Tashilhunpo and so joined us in singing to the dead for the whole night and in the morning he ascended to the top of the hill at the south of the town and, along with many other local families, set about affixing bright rivers of fluttering prayer flags to the outpost so that their prayers might be untangled and carried aloft upon the wind in order that our quest would be met with success, and after we had given them our thanks we left the town, all before the golden light had frothed upon the valleys, and travelled on – we passed herds of slow driven yaks fat with milk and striking frail tails against flies and mites, and their wiry masters all muscle and grimace, and a few stray goats scampering across the wild dips and haunches of the rock-clotted slopes, as we wandered between the tiny scattered villages, searching for the flesh in which the spirit had settled, for he will be born again and again so that he may teach us how to slip free from our passions and longing as one might, at the end of the evening, shudder loose from the folds of the habit before lying down to sleep, all past and future lives given up and forgotten.

As we walked down among the smallholdings that clustered together like ewes in winter, I told the students of how we might learn something of ourselves from studying the small stream we spotted slipping down a mountainside; it yearns for the sea, yet bends around skews of rocks, juts, falls; leaves waver and dance upon it, and these are our dreams, briefly borne along upon its current until they sink beneath it, while new ones fall from ever-bending trees; schools of fish weave through it, and these are our hopes and desires, shimmering and swimming deep within until they are plucked out by nets and hooks; and finally, at the end of the journey, if desires are conquered and dreams cast off, the stream becomes the river and the river becomes the sea and if a man should then look for the stream among the sea he will not find it, for it is no more what it once was.

On the third day the hill cleaved itself in two and we wandered down a stony path, picking through fern and bramble as we clambered towards the houses beside the slipshod curve of a lake; as I led our procession down the treacherous slope into the valley – noticing even from that great distance the flags and banners laid out to welcome us – one of the novices came to my side and asked how we would know which child was the reborn Lama, and so I sated his curiosity by explaining the rites and signs that would establish the presence of that benevolent spirit, freshly forged in new flesh, and another took this chance to ask how many times the great Lamas would return to human form, and I answered that both the Panchen Lama and his most holy superior, the Dalai Lama, possess infinite compassion and will therefore continue to walk among us and guide us until every man has found enlightenment and so transcended this veil of illusions, and that it might take one hundred years and it might take a thousand, but I added that, considering the baseness of the petty squabbles among the locals that we were so often called to adjudicate upon, I suspected it would perhaps be closer to a million before mankind might be persuaded to turn away from its desires and so end suffering; and the first novice spoke again, enquiring excitedly whether I therefore thought there was a possibility that the rumours might be true and that there really existed an ancient book in which the first Lama had set down the details of all his future incarnations upon the earth – yet here the elderly astrologer interrupted the questioning with a curt reply that the novices should be wary of such idle prattle and should bear in mind that time is pure illusion, an elaborate web spun to ensnare us, and that they would themselves be caught within it and forced to repeat their mistakes again and again if they were not careful.

When we reached the bottom of the track, passing crowds of scrawny cloud-backed goats tearing at tufts of sun-shrivelled grass, so many of the villagers gathered round us, each offering us the comforts of their homes, meals of hot stew and yak-butter tea, each entreating us to honour their homes by accepting their hospitality, that it took more than an hour for us to make our way to the lake to refill our flasks; after we had refreshed ourselves, it was clear we could postpone our meetings no longer, and so we asked to be guided to the house where the first child was born on the day of red clouds: it was a small, musty place, one circular room set around a fire whose thick black dragon breath spilled out through a cut in the roof, and there was barely enough room for the family members themselves to all huddle on the berths beside the fire, so I bid the novices wait outside while the elderly astrologer and myself questioned the parents – a squat, sun-swollen man with bird-nest hair and a tall, scuttle-backed woman wrapped head to toe in foul-smelling shawls – about the signs that attended the birth, the pitch and tone of the first cries of the child, the celestial phenomena visible at the time and the shape conjured by the umbilical cord after it was cut; it was then time to inspect the infant lying in a crudely fashioned crib on the floor, and as soon as I saw the tiny boy – saw his almond eyes following my own, saw his plump hands thump against his side and his mouth blossom into a little laugh – I felt as though I had been struck deep in the ball of my stomach, such was the force of recognition, for this tiny child knew me, and I him, and his fat red cheeks puffed up and he gurgled to himself and I saw again in my mind that tanka of the laughing Buddha who transcended suffering with the sublime realisation that life is little more than a cosmic joke, delightfully ludicrous and in-ane; yet I knew well enough of the petty jealousies and rivalries of small communities so I kept silent, for we had to remain judicious and fair, and it would have been imprudent to pronounce upon the return of the Lama before both children had been seen and all the rites observed, and so we said nothing to the anxious parents prom-ising us sacrifices and a thousand prayers if we bestowed fame, honour and the blessings of posterity upon their family name by taking their son, but instead made our way across the village to the house where the other child was born.

We were obliged to wander around the marshes and streams – past families tending torn nets laid out upon the ground and herd-ers ignoring their beasts to bow before us with entreaties to the gods and spirits – for more than an hour before we reached our destination at the other side of the lake, a dismal abode of rotting wood speckled with damp, great blotches of lichen green spreading across the walls, and a roof which managed, quite miraculously, to keep in the cloying smoke of the pitiful fire spluttering in the centre of the room while also letting in the frost-tongued wind that turned up the corners of the lake; once again, the elderly monk and myself went in alone, and found a cluttered room whose stale air was thick with the stinging smell of yak's urine, and two women dressed in mud-stained rags, who shuffled nervously as we went through the same questions and received their worried nods and monosyllables in reply; it seemed the child's father had been killed in an accident some months before the birth, and the widow was thus left alone to care not only for the new child but also for her ailing aunt and a group of gangly yaks – the skinny young mother, her face scarred with acne and slick with sweat, told us she wished only that she might marry again, for she feared the three of them could not go on without the strength of men to carry them, and I understood her worry, for there is no comfort in a life lived only in the long shadow cast by death, yet I also knew that she would find it hard to make a new match, for few men would risk being second in affection to the son of another man, and so I felt much compassion for her situation and told her I would look upon her son; he was a tiny runt of a boy, square-headed and dark-skinned, with eyes perched too close above a lumpy potato of a nose and sickly, blistered lips which let out raspy, crackling breaths, and I had to work hard to stop a frown from settling upon my brow, for the child emitted a most foul odour, and, as soon as I stepped cautiously forward, he began to howl, his face scrunched into a purple blotch that brought to mind the pinched faces of the bats that we sometimes find folded in the dusty corners of the Hall of Contemplation.

How is the future measured out – in acts, deeds, words, in the ebb and flow of karma, of that which tips the balance and that which lives on in ripples spreading upon the surface long after the stone is sunk – in what is lost or in what remains? As I turned to face the tear-streaked faces of the two women, I could not help but think that I alone might change the current of their lives, that if I took this tiny, mewling child back to the monastery to be proclaimed the latest incarnation of the Panchen Lama, then the widow would be free to another marriage, to another life (for rebirth does not only happen after death); if not, he might become another child left at the edge of the lake for the cat-faced birds or devil-headed storms to claim, or else another mouth slowly stolen by hunger, for two ragged-boned women could not work land like this alone – and yet he was not the Lama, the other child surely was – and yet the other child might, with his looks and wits, build a life of his own; for surely it is by the strength of faith that Lamas are made, not the flicker of distant constellations in newborn eyes; and it was then that I wondered what might happen if, when the Dalai Lama came to Tashilhunpo to formally recognise the latest incarnation of his spiritual brother, I was to present this second child instead of the first as the one who would lead us from darkness, who would stay within the monastery with us and work hard upon his studies that he might rise among us and assist all in escaping the temptations of desire, the root of suffering, and unknot the bonds of dreams by which we are bound – for I wondered then if it is not faith itself that forms our future, if it is not by longing alone that each moment is called into existence; if we are made by what we give, not what we take, and it was that night that I dreamed once more that I was a fish, as I was in my last life and as perhaps I shall be in my next – and I was blotting the water with the curve and snag of my scales, pulsing up towards the surface when another, bigger fish appeared, beating its tail fast towards me, and all I saw was the deep black pit of its throat as I was swallowed, and came tumbling in; and it seemed as if I lived then as the bigger fish, consuming my former life, and trembling on through the blue for more lithe food, until an even larger fish attacked; and once more my eyes were changed and I was then the large fish who had fed on my last life, and I swam on, through streams to rivers to the coast and far out into the ocean, searching for the great whale who trawls through the ravenous deep and might open his great jaws and beckon us all in, and then perhaps there might be peace, the cavernous, endless darkness of his churning stomach, the sound of waves breaking far above, and his mournful song, rumbling out towards the edges of the universe.

# A Delicate Matter of Phrasing

It took me about twenty minutes to reach the town nearest Jawbone Hills. Along the same dull highway, halfway out towards the hills. The place was a mess, its one concession to modernity a single dingy tower block. But even that couldn't dent my sense of anticipation. I was close. I knew it. I'd been to Jing Ren's home, and I'd found out who he worked for. If I could figure everything out by the end of the day, tomorrow I'd be able to relax and enjoy my time with Li Yang. My head was swimming – I wasn't used to things going right. Perhaps that was how I knew it wouldn't last.

An old man with rancid black teeth gave me directions, and I found the dumpy little building in no time. The Public Records Office. As soon as I walked in I knew something was wrong. The uniformed woman at the front desk fidgeted nervously as I showed my ID. She didn't look up. She must have known I was coming.

'I'm sorry. I can't help you.'

Like my wife, she had plucked out all her eyebrows and had black lines tattooed on instead.

'And what is it you can't help me with?'

'You're not allowed to look at our files. I'm sorry. I've got this note for you. He said you would be coming.'

I took the piece of paper from her hand. Her handwriting was a jumble of loops and squiggles. It was a message from Mr Xu, aka Fishlips. Or, as Wei Shan used to say, the tumour that keeps on giving. Shit. How the hell had he known that I'd be coming here? Something didn't add up. He'd phoned to say that I didn't have clearance to go through their files. Oh, and he wanted to meet with me in his office as soon as I got back. So that was the end of that, was it? Great. Today was shaping up to be nearly as awful as yesterday.

I handed the paper back to her.

'I'm sorry, I have no idea who this Mr Xu is. I mean, Xu is a pretty common name these days, but there isn't a single one in the Public Safety Office.'

Her painted-on eyebrows began to rise.

'Really? But he had the right security clearance code. And he gave your name and described exactly what you would look like, and said you would probably be coming in this morning. And here you are.'

I leaned forward over her desk.

'Do you have any idea how many enemies the Public Safety Office has? Let me fill you in on something. Perhaps you're too young to remember the Great Proletariat Cultural Revolution, back when everyone was turning everyone else in. Lot of fights, lot of feuds. Lots of grudges. And some things haven't changed – there are still snitches everywhere, two-faced liars wanting to bring down this glorious country. You do know what we do, don't you? How are we supposed to keep things safe for ordinary people like you and your family if we don't have access to local information? It seems to me that you've been tricked. So I advise you to think again and give me the business registration details of the Black Light Mining Company. Then I might reconsider talking to your boss and mentioning that you tried to help dissident criminals thwart a national investigation.'

She blushed and bowed her head. My bluff had worked.

'Just the details of some local mining company?'

'That's right.'

'They'll be in the records room downstairs. I'll call down. Take a seat, it'll be a couple of minutes.'

I sat down and basked in the results of my powers of persuasion. You just keep talking till you see the tiny sharpness of the iris suddenly grow large into black, like spilt ink covering a blank page. That's when you know you've got them. Doesn't really matter what you say. You could be talking about dogs or last night's dinner or the moon. It's how you say it. It's about conviction. Certainty. It's about meaning every single word you say. And if you lie with enough assurance for long enough, you'll even be able to fool yourself.

It wasn't too hard to find what I was looking for. The Black Light Mining Company, owned by Hong Youchen, established in 1992. I thanked the uniformed woman for her time and took the tiny scrap of paper on which I'd scribbled the details out to my car. For once, the sun was beating down over the hills, the colour of a fresh, bubbly beer.

I felt pretty pleased with myself. For about ten seconds. Then I started wondering what on earth I was going to do next. So I'd found out that there definitely was a mine on Jawbone Hills. Since everyone kept denying its existence, it wasn't a great leap to posit that a) the digging or explosives or whatever they were doing down there somehow caused the accident, and that b) this Hong Youchen guy was well-connected enough to get Fishlips and Officer Wuya and possibly countless others to keep its involvement in the accident a secret. That second part also seemed to include hiding away the casualties. But that's as far as I could get. Every bit of information I managed to find only added more questions to my list. Who were Fatty, Spotty and Horseface – local peasants or miners? And why weren't the bodies being returned to their families? What was the purpose of the mine? None of the Public Safety Office files about the area suggested anything about gold, coal, iron or any other precious mineral deposits in the vicinity. Why had they employed a tattooed historian rather than an experienced site manager? And to top it all off, I still hadn't come any closer to finding out a single thing about the most important question of them all: what the hell had happened to Wei Shan?

I drove back to the city as quickly as I could. I wasn't quite sure what Fishlips wanted, but it was unlikely I was going to be offered a promotion or a raise. So far he'd lied about the mine and accurately predicted where I was going to start looking. Sneaky bugger. Then there were the dark-suited guys he'd been talking to at the scene of the accident. There was something he knew that I didn't. Things weren't looking good.

I parked my car outside the office and stopped on the steps for a quick cigarette and a good gulp or two of *baiju* before making my way inside. As soon as I walked in, I spotted Fishlips hovering by my desk. Shit. This wasn't going to be pretty. He beckoned me into his office and closed the door before slumping down in his chair without bothering to offer me a seat.

'What's been keeping you? You didn't get the message I left for you at the Records Office out near the landslide?'

'I'm sorry, what? I'm not sure I know what you're talking about. I've been out on a long working lunch, going over those blueprints for the office blocks near the river with Hu. I'm sorry it overran, but there's no need —'

'Spare me the bullshit. I know what you've been up to. I know you've been to the Public Records Office, and I know you paid a visit to a policeman the other day. You've not achieved anything except making a fool of yourself. I want you to stop this nonsense before you piss off all the wrong people.'

'Then you'd better tell me who the right people to piss off are. All I'm doing is looking for my colleague.'

'The police are looking for Wei Shan. There's nothing you can do. And please don't bother with the sanctimonious act, it really doesn't suit you.'

'You don't understand. It's not just Wei Shan anymore. I've found bodies —'

'Do I look like I give a shit? We deal in structural issues, support, balance, probabilities. Not bodies. That's not our business. If there's no safety issue, then we keep out of it.'

'How much did they have to pay you before you believed that?'

Fishlips sighed. 'I don't have the energy to get angry. Just look at yourself. Go and freshen up, then get back to your desk and do your job while you still have one.'

'What, and just forget about the corpses, forget about Wei Shan, forget about justice?'

'Don't you start lecturing me about justice or morality. Don't think I don't know what you get up to after work. You disgust me, but your father was a decent man and I owe him. That's pretty much the only reason you've still got a desk in this office. So think about that next time you're moaning about connections or corruption. And what's more, if you keep digging into this case, chances are someone's going to do a bit of digging about you – and if the truth comes out, then there's no way I'm going to stand behind you. Have a think about that. I believe you'll find that some things are better left uncovered.'

Shit-faced bastard. I didn't know what to say. I took a deep breath.

'So you want me to just pretend that nothing happened?'

'Yes. A man like you ought to be pretty good at pretending. Now go and do your job for a change, and stop acting like you know better than the rest of us. The case is none of our business. Just let it be.'

'Understood.'

I slouched out with my head down, clenching my fists so hard my nails dug deep into the skin of my palms. I let the rage burn through my pores as I strolled, as nonchalantly as I could manage, back to my desk. My teeth were grinding together and my leg was shaking up and down beneath my desk, but I made a show of opening up the file at the top of the stack and, pen in hand, scanning carefully through the application. I don't know how I managed it, but I did. I'd show him – if he wanted a robot, I'd be a robot. I made myself hold out for at least an hour, maybe a little more, until I saw Fishlips lock his office and head off to a meeting. Then I was out of there.

I went straight to the good old Golden Dragon Seafood Palace. I did think about phoning Li Yang to see if there was any chance we could meet up sooner than tomorrow night, but I didn't want to look desperate. So instead I settled at my usual table and decided, for a change, to splash out on a bottle of the expensive stuff.

When the drink came I filled my glass and raised a toast to Wei Shan. Perhaps he was still out there somewhere, after all. Why not? Life is absurd. Men have flown to the moon. A whole country uprooted its whole history over a Little Red Book. So one guy making his way out of a landslide isn't so crazy. A thousand more ridiculous things happen every minute. And anyway, I refused to believe he was dead. Not till I saw his body laid out on the slab like the others.

Not that death doesn't have its benefits. An end to all this pissing around, all this clock-watching and acting-up, all this arse-kissing and shit-stirring, all these headaches and fuck-ups. An end to the stomach-cramping, brain-mangling work of guilt and regret, and an end to the endless days of disappointments and petty humiliations. A bit of peace. I don't buy any of that other crap. Getting born again as a donkey or a flea? Superstitious nonsense, designed to stop the workers from gathering together to overthrow the tyranny of the feudal system – just you be a good little farmer for the next fifty years and maybe in your next life you'll get to be an emperor. Yeah, right. And as for all that heaven and hell stuff, well don't get me started. I can't even imagine what heaven might be like. Like being in Li Yang's arms up in the flat overlooking the river? Somehow I doubted it. Wei Shan would probably say heaven was a field in Mizhi County, out near Yulin, with a beautiful farmer's daughter and enough sun to warm you down to the toes. He could be a real bore. But listening to him still beat sitting on my own and letting my thoughts soar in relentless circles, like crows picking over the same old carcass.

I ordered another little something to keep the daydreams from conquering me and sank back in the chair, staring out of the window to see suit after suit hurrying through the cold, rushing back to their desks before their bosses noticed they'd been gone.

My mind kept coming back to what Fishlips had said. Was I ashamed? Of course. Every day I felt pretty disgusted with myself, to tell the truth. Every day I thought of what my father would have said. What he would have done. He'd probably have tried to beat it out of me with his belt. Every day I worried about what would happen if my wife found out, if my daughter knew, if it all got out. You do a thing like that and then you carry it round with you, and it poisons you from the inside out. And now my boss knew. How? Had I been followed, had someone trailed me? It wouldn't be the first time. When we're not spying on other people, we spy on each other. So now he can hold it over my head, drop in reminders whenever he needs to. The perfect way to keep everyone in line – by threatening them with their own secrets. Knowing everyone else's secrets: that's probably as good a definition of absolute power as you're going to get.

I fished in my suit pockets and dug out the note with the business registration details I'd picked up at the records office. I found myself reading the name at the top over and over again, as if it was some kind of mantra I couldn't quite fathom. Hong Youchen. Hong Youchen. It meant nothing to me. Another important businessman invisible in the well-worn camouflage of expensive suits and chauffeured cars. I picked at the damp shreds of sour potato in front of me, and realised everyone but the dozing manager had left. I looked at my watch. Almost three. It was just me and my cold dish left.

Taking my time. Letting the clear stuff tingle its way through my veins. I poured another glass. It was too late to go back to the office now without being noticed. I ought to go and see Chun Xiao. Try and explain what I thought might have happened to her husband. Not that I had a clue. But with a few drinks inside me I ought to be able to think of something suitably sombre yet vague. My sincere commiserations, and all that crap. But she wouldn't finish work before five, so there was no point rushing. I'd just have to stay here.

I toyed with my scrap of paper again. Hong Youchen. Hong Youchen. I could imagine him. A fat oaf sitting in a plush office surrounded by expensive books. Paying off hospital orderlies to make sure the bodies disappeared after the accident. I hated him already. No doubt sitting up in his penthouse imagining he had the whole city in his pocket. Phoning Officer Wuya for a little chat, just to clear things up. But how had he kept the families of the dead men quiet? Threats or bribes probably – it's always one or the other. I wanted to hunt him down and pound my fists into his stupid fat face. No, I wanted to drag him whimpering and pleading up to the top of the hill where his mine used to be, and then push him over into the great empty expanse, just to hear his bones crunch as he finally hit the bottom.

But wait. If this guy really had invested thousands into some mining operation, he wasn't going to suddenly give up. He'd probably already spent a small fortune on land leases and bribes and manpower. Sure, he'd probably keep a low profile for a while until all the fuss about the accident blew over. But then it'll be business as usual, with a new team of workers fresh from the trains.

I took a deep draught and my head began to spin. I tried to work out what to do next, but my mind wouldn't stay still. It wasn't long before I was drifting in and out of daydreams. I found myself wondering what might have happened had I been one second quicker, if I'd been passing the unmanned desk on the way back from the bogs when the phone started ringing, instead of Wei Shan, if I'd dashed over and picked it up instead of ignoring it, if I'd spoken to the irate caller – whoever it might have been – then sighed and headed off to Jawbone Hills. People think it's the big acts that change history. The grand gestures, the heroic moments of selflessness, the intractable acts of passion. But sometimes the stupidest little things can change whole lives – if Wei Shan hadn't drunk too much beer at lunch and snuck away for his third piss of the afternoon, then he wouldn't have been wandering back past that phone when it began chirping, and some other sap would be buried under twenty metres of shit while the two of us sat at our usual table in the Golden Dragon.

The walls of the restaurant seemed to be moving of their own volition, drifting off through space. The drink fizzed through to the tips of my fingers, my tongue, my spine, and I let it transform me into something fluid, slippery, set free from sense.

A couple of hours later – after I'd napped in the chair and woken suddenly to the manager switching on his crackly little TV – I swigged the dregs straight from the bottle and settled the bill. For a few seconds I thought I'd travelled back in time, because the television was still showing that boring bit of news about the new school opening up in the countryside. Some fat guy with buck teeth was being interviewed about the money he'd donated. I was sure I recognised him. I must have seen this bit before. Could the world really have been so boring that this was all the news stations had to report? Or had some suit at the top sent down an injunction ordering only good news? It wouldn't have been the first time.

When I rose, the floor began to shift, not quite as solid as it had been before, and my legs had trouble holding me up. I leaned on the window and let it lead me round to the door.

I worked my way down the street in slow motion, wondering why the pavement wouldn't stay straight. No point going into the office now. I looked at my watch, a gift from Li Yang. It was a big silver one with clockwork that you could hear buzz. From Europe. Sweden or Austria or something like that. Somewhere with a lot of snow. I'd had a hard job explaining it to my wife. I think I'd said it was a knock-off the police had confiscated and were selling on the sly. I think she even believed me that time.

Almost five. Time to take a trip to Chun Xiao. Offer up my useless condolences or tell her that I still had hope he was out there? Either way I'd be lucky not to get an earful.

The biting air was beginning to clear my head a little, so I decided to walk to Wei Shan's. He didn't live too far from the Golden Dragon. When we'd first started heading out for drinks after work I'd tried a few times to suggest we find a restaurant a bit closer to my end of town. But he wasn't having any of it. What was the point, he said. Once you've found a place that does spicy chicken or steamed tofu just the way you like it, why risk going somewhere else? Besides, he'd added, the manager was an old friend and we sure as hell weren't going to find somewhere cheaper. Well, I had to give him that. And anyway, he was stubborn as hell. Wei Shan liked change about as much as cows like abattoirs. So in the end I had to go along with him. And he was right, the spicy chicken was pretty good.

I turned the corner and nearly tumbled over some grotty old man and his poky dumpling stall. Whenever darkness starts to fall, the streets seem to fill up with idiots, as if their sole purpose in life is to make things difficult for the rest of us. I had to stop for a minute to look around. Though I'd known Wei Shan for decades, I'd only actually been to his home once or twice before. And certainly not in the last handful of years. Even the man himself stayed away from it as much as he could. I understood. Nagging wife. Contemptuous kid. Why walk directly into the line of fire when you could keep your head down in the trenches?

After taking a few wrong turns and doubling back on myself once or twice, I picked an alley that looked vaguely familiar and made my way down it till I spotted Wei Shan's building up ahead. A shabby place, full of two-room apartments where damp peeled the cheap white paint from the walls. I remembered Wei Shan telling me that his son had the bedroom and that he and his wife pulled out the sofa every night to sleep in the living room. When was it that children became more important than their parents? I mean, that's messed up. But still, I could see what they were doing. The kid probably thought he'd got it made in his own little den. Little did he realise that his parents were only looking after him so that he could get good marks in his exams, join the Party, get allocated a good job and then be in a good position to look after his poor old Ma and Pa when they reach old age. There's always a hidden catch. Even with family. No, scratch that. Especially with family.

By now I could feel sticky patches of sweat spreading across my shirt, and it was a fair bet that my face was all red and blotchy. But so what? I wasn't going to be there long anyway. Pop in, say how sorry I was. Drink a toast to him, maybe. Depending on what they had to offer. Then get out of there.

Once I reached the second floor, I took a minute to wipe my brow and try to contort my features into a suitably solemn expression. Then I banged on their door, hoping to heaven that I'd got the right flat.

A lanky teenager opened it. His black hair flopping down in a greasy fringe, his tiny eyes pressed into a glare. How old was he? Thirteen? Fourteen? Fifteen? A sudden image flashed through my mind, and all I could see in front of me was the body of the spotty kid I'd uncovered in the hospital basement. I felt giddy, nauseous, and I had to reach out for the doorframe for support.

The teenager raised an eyebrow. I wracked my brain.

'Cheung?'

'Yeah. You're the guy from dad's office, right?'

'That's me. Is your mother about?'

'Dunno.'

'You don't know?'

'That's what I said, isn't it?'

'You're seriously telling me don't know whether your own mother is in the flat?'

'I'm not her keeper. I don't keep a record of when she leaves and when she gets home from work.'

'All right, all right. Can you have a look for me?'

'Hmm. You'd better come in.'

He moved aside and I made my way inside. I felt like I should say something, but I wasn't sure what. Sorry about your dad? How you holding up? Is there anything I could do? I tried to form my mouth into any of those stock phrases, but I couldn't manage it. All of them sounded stupid. And besides, what the hell was he supposed to say to any of them? Maybe I should share some of my theories. Or would that only make things worse? By the time I'd thought of something appropriate to say, however, I turned around to find he'd already slunk away, leaving me standing alone in the empty hallway.

I took a look around. Not much had changed since the last time I had been here, four or five years back. The same gaudy statues on the hall table. The same little ceramic pot where they kept the car-keys. The same fading photos, progressing through the years as you looked from left to right, starting with the old black and white family shots – Wei Shan with his parents, Wei Shan as a

Red Guard just before he got sent up in Mizhi County during the Cultural Revolution, Chun Xiao and her old man, Wei Shan and Chun Xiao's wedding, the proud parents with a little red-faced baby, Cheung starting school and the three of them with the new car. Their whole lives summed up in seven little photos. What else is there?

The long mirror opposite the front door had been covered with a dark cloth. It seemed Chun Xiao believed in the old wives' tale that if you see the reflection of a dead body in a mirror then death will visit you soon. But there was no body. That was the whole problem. My mother used to say you had to cover all the mirrors so the spirit of a dead relative didn't catch sight of its own reflection as it started its journey into the next world. I guess the assumption was that if it glimpsed itself and recalled who it once was, it would never want to leave, and you'll be stuck with a ghost hanging round your home forever.

Silly superstitions, the lot of them. And wherever Wei Shan's spirit was, it sure as hell wasn't here. Even if he was dead, I was pretty sure he wouldn't want to hang round this shitty corner of Lanzhou watching his family mope. I mean, I sure as hell hope that the dead have better things to do than wander round all the boring old places they visited when they were alive.

I thought about my father's funeral. First thing my mother did was burn all his clothes. Except his best peasant suit, of course. He wore that in the coffin. Looked awful – he'd shrunk so thin in the weeks before his death that it billowed around him like a loose robe. But she burned all the others. Wailed for hours while she fed his old trousers and vests to the flames. She burned wads of fake banknotes too, out at the crossroads in the middle of the night, even though you weren't supposed to back then. Don't ask me why people think that you can send stuff on to ghosts in the spirit world by burning it. Load of crap, but of course you can't say that to mourners. So you have to hold your tongue.

I had a horrible thought. What if Chun Xiao had decided to burn all Wei Shan's clothes to send to him in the next life, only for him to turn up again, alive and well but maybe a little concussed? He'd be pretty pissed off. Though in all fairness most of his clothes were so crappy they deserved to be incinerated. Still, the concussion idea wasn't a bad one – perhaps he'd banged his head and lost his memory. He could be wandering about the countryside right now, trying to remember who he was and what he was doing there. At least then there was still hope. And right now anything had to be better than being stuck in this halfway state, torn between grief and uncertainty, unsure what to believe and continually clutching at the most frail and absurd possibilities.

I flicked through the post on the hall table. Bills, mostly. A few cards. And a red envelope with no writing on it. No. Tell me I was hallucinating. This wasn't good. I peeked inside. Just out of curiosity. And I was right. Stuffed full of banknotes. A dense wad of them, crisp and shiny and all but screaming out to be fondled between greasy fingers. Shit. This definitely wasn't good.

Cheung appeared back in the hall and I straightened up and smiled.

'She's not here.'

'Are you sure?'

'Of course I'm sure. Do you want to check to see she's not hiding under the bed?'

'Very funny. You even checked the bathroom?'

'I've checked. She's not here.'

'Great. That's just great.'

'She might be back soon. Might not. You can wait if you want.'

'Huh. Well ... I probably ought to get going. Lots to do.'

I knew I ought to say something else, but I wasn't sure what. Should I offer my condolences, let him know I'm here if he needs to talk to someone? Or should I tell him not to give up hope, that I had a feeling his father might still turn up? I couldn't decide.

'So ... how's the erhu going?'

'It's the pipa. I play the pipa.'

'Of course, of course. How was the big recital?'

He shrugged. 'So so.'

'Well, I hear you're pretty good.'

'Whatever.'

'You keep practising, I'm sure you'll make everyone proud.'

'Yeah.'

'Well, I probably ought to get going.'

'You said that already.'

'I know, I know. Tell your mum I stopped by, okay?'

'Sure.'

He closed the front door behind me and I reached for my pack of Double Happiness. Stupid kid. Teenagers all seem to share this uncanny knack for making you feel dumb. I took a drag. I had to cut him some slack. But now I was confused. Did I need to come back, to make a proper condolence call? Or would that do? I'd showed my concern, hadn't I? And anyway, I couldn't sit round there waiting for Chun Xiao to come home from work all evening. I'd suffocate.

Well, that was a waste of time. I was reminded of something Wei Shan himself used to say. Life never moves in a straight line. He said it every time he'd had a few too many, which was probably most days. You think you're always moving forward, but that's a joke. He used to say that life was more like the drive from hell. You keep making wrong turnings and finding yourself in dead ends, and once you get going its almost impossible to turn around or reverse out without hitting something. You get stuck on roundabouts and ring-roads that lead you round in endless circles. And then there are the other drivers. Once you got him started, Wei Shan could rant away for hours. But I knew what he meant. My life was filled with wasted journeys. Today more than ever.

I made my way back outside and threw my stub to the curb. Maybe I should have said something a bit more optimistic to Cheung. Told him I'd do whatever it takes, that I wouldn't rest until I'd hunted down the bastards responsible for the landslide and made them pay. That wasn't the kind of thing I could say without getting laughed at. But what the hell. I would find out what happened there that night. I owed Wei Shan and his family that much. And besides, I'd come this far. I'd found bodies, a mine, and I had Hong Youchen's name. And now I'd seen the anonymous envelope full of cash in Wei Shan's home. I was close. I had to be.

So there was only one thing for it. I had to get to the bottom of this whole mess once and for all. I had to take a look for myself.

⊂⊐

Forty-five minutes later I'd left the highway behind and was back on the dirt road leading to the top of the track, though this time there were no police cars in sight. Even the little makeshift car park marked out on the drenched grass was deserted. I parked and stepped out. The whole hill was ominously silent now the diggers and tractors and army trucks had gone, and it also seemed horribly still, as if it were waiting stoically for the next calamity. It reminded me of some wretched creature that had endured its skin being flayed from its back, knowing all the while that worse was yet to come.

I'd brought a decent torch and tied plastic bags around my shoes to protect them. I made my way over to the edge and crouched at the top for a while, listening for voices, footsteps, anything. Nothing but my breath, ripped and ragged in the cool night air.

Despite the dark, I could just about make out a track leading along the ridge where countless shoes had scuffed the grass and mud. I followed it across the peak until it veered suddenly over the edge and into nothingness. I got down on my hands and knees and peered over. I could see crags of rock and what looked like rivers of mud trickling slowly down into the black. How far to the bottom? It was impossible to tell, and I was pretty sure I didn't want to find out. Here and there amid the streaks of crumbling earth rubble had accumulated against bumps and ledges. But at least there appeared to be a few solid footholds – lodged rocks, clumps of roots, even a few surviving tree-stumps. Far below I thought I could see the glint of something metallic, a tin roof from a peasant's shack, perhaps, that had been dragged down with the rest of the hillside. Sharp knuckles of stone, clumps of gravel, and ... there! Two splintered juts of timber rising up in parallel from the slope. A doorway? Had to be worth a look.

I lowered myself down, feet first, my toes straining to find one of the first footholds I'd spotted below. But before I knew it my feet had slipped on the wet earth and I soon found myself slipping and skidding through the mud and gravel, gaining speed so quickly that I had to throw myself forward into the dirt to stop from tripping down into the abyss below. I reached out and grabbed hold of a clump of roots and weeds embedded in the earth, holding on as tight as I could while half the hillside seemed to tumble down past me in a mad and ceaseless rush. I was choking on dust and grime, my eyes stinging. I'm not sure how long I lay like that, waiting for the slope to settle and my heart to stop hammering like an alarm clock in my gut. When I pulled myself to my knees, my eyes were stinging, and the taste of blood and ash was deep in the pit of my throat. And I'd only managed to get down two or three metres. Shit.

I crawled over on my hands and knees, getting scratched and muddy as I made painfully slow movements towards the juts of timber rising up a little to my left. It felt like hours by the time I made it to what must have once been the entrance to the mine. A great pile of dirt and stone had gathered between the exposed wooden beams that had marked the doorway, and I had to dig for a few minutes to clear enough space to push myself through.

I was going back into a mine, after countless people had died inside because of a landslide. I stopped to wonder if this was the stupidest thing I'd ever thought of doing. Well, it was definitely up there on the list. But it wasn't as if I had anything better to do, and I'd only beat myself up about it later if I turned back now. So I dug my torch out of my pocket, flicked it on and ventured in.

Inside it was darker than a crow's eye. I half slipped on the squelch beneath my feet. Streams pulsed through the dirt and rock; I reached my free hand out to steady myself on the low ceiling. The wet walls crumbled wherever I gripped. It was like walking blind into the gut of some strange creature. I knew from looking over enough official regulations that all miners were supposed to wear hard-hats with fitted lights, but chances were that unless they had some important visitor to impress, the workers here had probably only had a cigarette lighter between them. If that.

The light from the torch trailed off into the darkness. So far the roof seemed surprisingly sturdy. I guess much of the landslide had just poured straight over the top. I was guessing it wasn't going to be the same story further down. I mean, all those miners must have come in along this path on Monday. But none of them made it back up. I tried to work out what the odds were of the whole thing collapsing on me. Did the recent landslide mean it was more or less likely? I wasn't sure.

The passage swung to the left and my torch picked out the start of a handrail set into the stone. I took hold as I turned, rust rubbing against my skin. I took a few more steps before my feet tripped against a pile of mud and rubble. With each step it seemed as though I was sinking further into a muddy sludge that had filled the passageway. How far down did this thing go? I ran the light up into the distance, letting it linger on the larger rocks and the giant broken splinters hanging almost horizontal where the wooden supports had given way. I leant one hand against the crumbly wall to steady myself, every stumble and curse echoing into the darkness ahead, far beyond the reach of the straining torch.

The tunnel turned again, and I grasped for the handrail. The ground was higher now, lumpier, and fallen rock and earth littered the path. I passed under the remains of a broken archway. Huge hulks of splintered wood had been pressed hurriedly back against the walls. So I wasn't the only one who had been down here since the accident. Is this what all the police and soldiers had been doing – propping up supports and digging the fallen rocks and earth out of this tunnel in order to pull out the bodies trapped deeper inside? A few sharp rungs of moonlight pushed through from holes somewhere above. A shiver ran its way down the knots of my back, as cold as icy water. What was to stop this part of the tunnel from crashing down again? What was to stop me getting trapped without any other way out, just like those other poor buggers, with bones broken by the rocks raining down and left to fight and thrash and struggle and scream against the avalanche until the air ran out?

The yellow light stuttered over gravel and stone, and the tunnel soon dipped and began descending at a more rapid rate. I had to hunch to stop my head from banging on the low-hanging fangs of rock overhead, and I felt the cold, damp air spreading goosebumps across my skin. I imagined the dust-dressed men stomping in each morning, leaving the day behind as they wound down further under. I imagined men of few words losing even the slightest impulse to speak – after all, how could language compete with such darkness? I imagined their eyes drawing in for it, learning it, their ears alert to the sound of each stubbed toe, the thwack of each pick, the creek of each cart, each phlegmy cough, each grunt and each fart sounding out deep under the earth.

No, that couldn't be right. I'm not ashamed to admit that what I know about mining could be written on the back of a cigarette packet, but even I could see that something didn't quite add up. There were no tracks for carts, no evidence of anything being dragged back up. So what the hell had they been doing down here?

When I was a Red Guard, back in early '67 our group had gone to the old temple behind the market. There were seven of us, each fizzing with energy, that tightly coiled fervour which springs your muscles into action and won't let you keep still. Caps on heads, Little Red Books in jacket pockets, fire in our stomachs and on our tongues. Every inch of our bodies given over to that singular passion that comes when you know that you are right, possessed by a brightness that burns through you. By the time we got there we were about ready to tear the whole fucking feudal relic down. There'd been centuries of monks fleecing good honest people with their myths and rules, of binding noble workers in chains of fear and belief, and we had come to settle the score.

At least that's what we told each other as we tore the place up, pulling down shelves of scrolls and using them to feed the bonfire we started in the main courtyard. We smashed tables and altars, burnt rugs and wall hangings, pissed in begging bowls and wine cups, confiscated the last tiny golden buddhas, and ripped up pages of verses, scriptures, proverbs, histories, commentaries and all the rest of that crap. We even found a wrinkled old monk hiding out the back, near the bell tower. The others had fled weeks before, but I guess he had nowhere else to go. We tugged off his saffron robe to add to the fire, leaving him naked and shivering as we spat on him and cursed him and hit with one of the torn-down shelves, just for good measure. He shat himself in the end, and none of us could much be bothered to carry on after that.

But I'm getting sidetracked. Memory has a way of doing that, setting you on paths you have no interest in heading back down. What I thought about standing in the mine was one of the tankas I saw there, in the temple. It was pretty much the last thing we tore down. It had been hanging in the cramped back room where the ugly old monk had been sleeping. It was one of those pictures of a thousand buddhas, like they have in those caves not far from here in Mogao. It was a ratty old thing, faded and a bit mouldy at the edges, run-of-the-mill, in fact – big fat boss Buddha floating on a giant lotus in the centre, doing that funny thing with his fingers pressed together, and all his half-naked helpers floating around him. Buzzing around his head were little angel buddhas, taking it easy in heaven, dancing on clouds or sitting by luscious green trees sprouting from stars. And then underneath big Buddha was the underworld: the demons with gnashing teeth and freaky grins, buried deep beneath the earth. They seemed so energetic, so raucous, so free – so much more alive than the ones lazing about on the clouds up in heaven.

At the time I had just thought it was a stupid painting, a hangover from a world of superstition and slavery. Yet as I slowly wandered deeper under the earth, it all made a macabre kind of sense. Those above are complacent, lobotomised by calm and comfort. You do nothing too long and you forget who you are. There was something about this darkness, this depth, that sharpened my mind. It brought the shadows into focus.

Time had thickened and slowed as I had descended, the way your limbs move slower when you wade through water. It was like being in a giant rabbit warren – every few metres the tunnel branched off in different directions, and I would follow one only to find that it suddenly stopped, and then I'd have to retrace my steps before exploring another turning. Whatever they were hunting for, they must have had trouble finding it. Occasionally I wandered over damp, rotting planks thrown across holes that stretched even deeper down. Nothingness. It's denser than you imagine.

I felt like I had been walking for hours; yet without my slow, cautious hunt for the tiniest of clues, and without all the wrong turns and doubling back, the miners could probably have covered the same stretch in only a few minutes.

Finally the tunnel opened out, the narrowing walls and low-dipping ceiling spreading into a wide cavern. It was a mess. And it stank. Large rocks strewn across the uneven ground, a dirty jacket soaking up a puddle, and the furthest wall half demolished amid a pile of rubble. I could see moonlight pouring in fits and starts through the great broken crag above. So this is where the ceiling had fallen in. I ran the torch along the ground by my feet, and could make out tracks where large rocks (or bodies?) had been dragged through the muck. Whoever had got down here after the landslide had done a pretty good job of cleaning everything up. It must have taken twenty, thirty men to move all the debris and unearth whatever – or whoever – was buried below. And they wouldn't have been able to do anything without diggers, pulleys and all the rest of that crap. That must have been some operation.

However they'd managed it, they'd done a pretty impressive job. There was nothing left but great stacks of rocks and rubble pushed against the furthest walls. And that awful stink. I hated to think about what it might be. I felt my pockets, hoping I'd remembered my smokes. I hadn't. No bottle either. Shit.

I spotted something glinting and made my way over to one of the piles of rubble near the closest wall. Amid all the rocks and earth I spotted the shiny remains of picks and hammers and a few smashed hard-hats. It was only when I started making my way over the wreckage towards the far end of the cavern that I realised what the smell wafting off the fallen rocks was. That thick, charred smell that gunpowder leaves. So they had been blowing something up. Why bother with safe, careful hand-grafted labour when you can knock down whole walls in seconds with a cheap mix of salt-petre and cracker paper?

I could picture it. One charge too many, then a sudden after-shock, a rumbling of rocks and the hissing of water, and before they knew it they were running for their lives. Some might have been able to make a dash back up the tunnel, only to find the supports collapsing and earth and water pounding towards them. But Wei Shan wouldn't have come this far. He'd only come to talk to the manager. They'd probably been near the entrance, jabbering away about all kinds of crap when the ground they were standing on was suddenly snatched away from beneath their feet.

But even though I knew – knew in the very pit of my gut – that I wouldn't find him here, I kept going. I couldn't stop myself: I called out. Just once. 'Wei Shan?' My voice rolled off the rocks and returned to me. 'Wei Shan? Wei Shan?' With each echo I felt more ridiculous. If Wei Shan's ghost was loitering anywhere nearby, then right now it was probably laughing at me.

Or else it would be asking what the hell I thought I was doing, poking about deep beneath the ground when I could have been downing a glass of shudders back at the Golden Dragon. Truth be told, I wasn't really sure anymore. I should have turned back ages ago, but the further I ventured, the more I felt the tug of something unknown pulling me deeper into the darkness.

I swept my torch between the rubble. There had to be something. Anything. The acrid stink of gunpowder was making me gag. Why use dynamite? I doubted cutting costs had anything to do with it. Whoever Hong Youchen was, he obviously had enough to bribe police and local officials to keep this whole pile of shit hushed up. No, this was about speed. I could see it all clearly. Someone was in a hurry. The mad rush to get the new mine up and running. Bribing officials for permits and paying off the inspectors. Roping in that old college professor with the dodgy tattoo. Probably recruiting the first men to turn up in the morning without worrying about prior experience or skills. Hacking the earth away to dead ends in every direction until they found what they were looking for. Erecting the clumsiest of feeble supports without thinking of the potential for disaster. Then blowing away whole chunks of the hill as quickly as they could. It was a miracle that something hadn't gone wrong sooner.

I'd just about clambered over the last ridge of fallen rock to complete my circuit around the cavern when I spotted the passageway. A small hole at the foot of the wall, opposite the tunnel that led back out. I walked over, bent down and stuck my head in. Even with the torch, I couldn't make out how far it stretched. Was this the last place they'd been digging? Could be. I might as well check it out. I was about to start down the craggy passageway when something pulled me back. I was stuck in the dark, somewhere in the rotten bowels of the Jawbone Hills, while my wife and daughter bitched about me at home, while Li Yang was probably giggling at another man's jokes, and all for what? Fishlips and Xiang had both warned me off, each in their different ways, but I had still bothered to waste my evening in this cold and damp tomb of a place. And the more I thought about it, the more ridiculous it all seemed. I had somehow convinced myself that if I understood what the hell was going on down here, then I'd have found a little slither of justice for Wei Shan, not to mention Jing Ren, Fatty, Spotty, Horseface, and all the others whose bodies had been carted off. But that's not how things work. You can't bring justice to the dead. They don't care. They're dead. It doesn't matter to their rotting corpses if the truth comes out, or if it stays hidden forever. Justice only matters when you've either got something to prove or something to lose. Wei Shan probably didn't have either anymore. Why do we think we need to understand everything, to make sense of the things that touch our lives? I don't know how my car works, I don't give a shit, in fact, but I'm still happy to get in the old heap of junk every day. Why should this be any different? But somehow it was.

There was nothing left to do but crawl in. After all, my suit was already a mess. And all the restaurants would be shut by now anyway. My knees scratched against the rocks, and I pushed forward on one hand, the other aiming the torch into the distance. They must have been working at it one at a time from here, with picks and trowels. My palm scraped and cut on something sharp. I didn't need to shine the torch on it to know that it was bleeding. Part of my trousers snagged and ripped. The now-torn plastic bags over my shoes rustled and hissed as I dragged myself forward. This is the kind of stupid thing that happens when I don't have enough to drink, I thought. Perhaps there was still a half-empty bottle rolling under the passenger seat. Or buried under the useless business cards in the glove compartment.

I kept crawling. And the darkness kept going, squeezing tighter into black. I kept going because it was better than torturing myself about whether or not I had a bottle left somewhere in the car. My wife was wrong when she said that I drank because I hated that I'd turned into someone I didn't want to be. I didn't drink because I was pissed off, nor because the world had screwed me. I drank because there was nothing else to do. And anyway, only a little. Not half as much as most of the people I know. Or used to know. My father used to drink till he'd be shouting at the walls. Lips spitting, fists flailing. I wasn't like that. I just wanted something to blur the edges, that's all.

The tunnel corkscrewed in, closing around me. I sunk down onto my elbows, shuffling awkwardly through the shifting ridges of dirt and flint. The whole mountain heaved above me. Each breath more dust than air. My tongue must have been as black as a nightmare. My nose was thick with grime, and my senses were slowly dropping away: smell, taste, sight. My hands were starting to go numb from the cold and the scrapes. A dull ache rang through my body, and my ears were on overload, turning every tiny scuffle and echo into the portent of a landslide.

I stopped to catch my breath. Out here in the villages, some of the families still bury their dead in the earth, despite official regulations. What if you woke up and found yourself lying deep beneath the ground, with nothing but the worms and your last thoughts for company? It's not the idea of being buried alive that's scary, it's more the thought of surviving. Of lying there, unable to move, and waiting for a death that doesn't come. I pushed up onto my elbows and started again.

Then I saw it. My eyes were so messed up and fuzzy from the darkness that I wasn't sure at first. I shone the torch up and down, left and right, round and round, back and forth. Then just to check I shuffled forward, the last few metres. This was it. I even reached out my frozen hand to touch it. I'd reached another dead end. A wall of rock. As far as they'd bothered to dig. And I'd found nothing. I set down the torch and rested my head on my outstretched arms. Where were they trying to get to? Between the sound of my panting breaths, I could hear something dripping, some stretch of ice water trickling down. It was then that I realised I couldn't turn around. The only way out was to crawl backwards.

It must have been close to a quarter of an hour later than I emerged, arse first, from the tunnel. What remained of my suit was clinging and soggy, and scrapes and scratches crisscrossed my arms and legs. I spat. Once, twice. Mouthfuls of thick, sooty phlegm. I'd have had a better night if I'd just thrown myself off the bridge.

The pursuit of knowledge is supposed, in some way, to be quantifiable. You ought to be able to know you're getting somewhere. But with every step I took I understood everything a little bit less. How was I going to find out what happened now? Locate Hong Youchen and turn up on his doorstep demanding to know what was going on down there? Somehow it didn't seem very likely.

I wiped the grit out of my eyes. Something was sticking to my knee. I shone the torch over it. Half a piece of crumpled paper had attached itself to my trouser leg, probably while I'd been crawling through that stupid tunnel. I reached down and tore it off.

The faded grey print was all but illegible. Smudged beyond recognition and torn right where the words began. All I could make out was a mess of intersecting lines. Some kind of map? Well, maybe. Perhaps if it hadn't been soaked right through and turned into a sodden blur, I could have made a more educated guess. But what else are you going do with a funny-looking squiggle of interlinking lines? If I squinted, it looked like the kind of thing my daughter used to draw when she was small. I flipped it over. Either the ink had run in a really peculiar way to create the biggest coincidence I'd ever come across, or I was holding a scrap of paper with a picture of a little black bird. Just the same as the one I'd seen tattooed on Jing Ren.

A crow. Damn. Maybe I should have let Xiang do some research into the tattoo after all. But at least I had a clue now. Some solid bit of evidence. And I was pretty sure that somehow it bound this whole mess together. But how?

This was getting too complicated. All I'd got in return for the last few hours of risking my life in this grubby little hell-hole was a cryptic image and a shitload of extra questions to answer. 'Wei Shan,' I called out once again. 'Wei Shan, if you're not already dead, I'm going to kill you.'

Then I shoved the paper into my pocket and started to make my way back up.

When I finally got back to my car some forty minutes later, I searched under the seat, in the glove compartment, in the back, and even cranked open the boot for the first time in about a year to hunt down any unfinished bottles. I struck gold beneath a mouldy raincoat next to the spare tyre. Just a couple of sips left. Sour, past its best. But still good. A shiver in a bottle. A tingle sent down to the tips of my fingers.

Disappointment? You get used to it. I was amazed at how light it was outside, despite the thick blanket of grey cloud, despite the hard rind of dull moon, and I couldn't stop blinking as I drove. The lights on the highway were unbearable, heavy stars scalding my retina, and it wasn't long before the burning pain of it forced me to take the first turn off and wind home slowly through the villages. Places of power-cuts and bonfires, of five-to-a-bed and cooking on home-stoked fires, of myths and rumours. Places of darkness – and right now that was all I could cope with. What must it have been like for the workers, down there all day and emerging to the painful unfamiliarity of sight each evening? I squeezed my eyes shut, then forced them open again.

The car juddered down shoddy dirt roads. My eyes slowly got used to the lights spilling from paper-covered windows, the bare bulbs in village stores where muddy carrots and potatoes were strewn across the floor, waiting to be bartered for. I slowed down when I spotted a crowd outside a grotty dumpling café beside the track. Village people are always up to something. I strained my neck to see – they were crowded around a small black and white TV. Thirty, forty people huddled together in front of the tiny screen. An old extension cord snaking through the mud. I pulled up and got out. The café was still open, so I bought a little bottle of the cheap stuff and a snack. When the greasy-haired woman running the place spotted my car over at the edge of the track she upped the price. I guess that's economics for you.

I stood next to a tall man with a face that appeared to have been whittled from oak.

'Got a light?'

'Sure ... Got a spare?'

'Sure.'

I joined the small group, lazily gathered before the glare. The stains on my torn suit, the dust matting my hair, the plastic bags still knotted around my ankles – none of that was out of place there. The dingy, the dirty and the dispossessed. The smell of sweat, of stale smoke. I studied the tops of the heads in front of me. Greasy, wild, lank, dirty or balding, none of them could have seen a bath or a barber for at least a month.

'What's on?'

'Something from Hong Kong. Can't understand a word. But the fighting's good. The blood looks almost real, you know?'

I nodded and peered a little closer. I'd seen this one before. Bruce Lee dancing circles round men with nunchucks. But I was happy to stand and watch, gulping from my fresh bottle. It helped the rest of the day get washed away, submerged by the tide of high kicks and lightning punches. Bruce was pummelling the crap out of some yellow-haired American. It was just like the old days. The whole group of us were united in our hatred, united in our satisfaction at the noble honesty of the humble working man pounding the corrupt imperialist into the concrete. United by ideas, bound by blood. But whereas the Red Guards were bound together by allegiance to a dream of a bright new future, our unity was severed as soon as the credits started to roll and the men began to stomp off one by one to their cramped homes and grumbling wives.

I was tempted to sleep on the back seat. Hell, it'd be more comfortable than the old sofa again. But I'd only get another earful about letting my daughter down. So I drove back with the best part of my brain still stuck down that mine somewhere, and somehow I even managed a quick wash in the sink before I sunk down into a bottomless sleep, hoping beyond hope that anything but another day would meet me at the other end.

# Rain at Night

PART 2 · MAY 815 CE

Yuan Chen,

My dearest friend, I have been delighted to hear of your many successes. I am glad that your family remains in rude health – it is a fine thing to have such a virtuous young man waiting to inherit the mantle of his family's name, the flame of their pride. I have no doubt that he shall make you proud in the future, so do not be too harsh on him for his small failings. And I am heartened to learn of your daughter's progress on the guqin, for nothing so marks out a young lady of fine birth as the ability to bring harmony to a household – remember the wisdom of Confucius, who taught that music binds hearts together, bringing balance and order into even the most chaotic of lives.

Please accept my deepest gratitude for the poems you sent. Your work continues to inspire, and reading your carefully wrought words has sent me more than once to fetch water with which to mix the last of my ink sticks. I see that you have not wavered from our shared aim, of creating work that balances the natural language of the common man with an appreciation of those profound moments when everything is suddenly made unfamiliar. I too have been working to strip away all ornate and archaic language from my poems, in the hope that they will be able to touch not only the well-educated scholar but also the labourer sweating in the fields. To read, after all, is to experience the world again, to see with new eyes.

I believe I am at last beginning to gain the confidence of the crown prince. Since I last wrote to you, I have progressed from the more menial duties of cataloguing the tradesmen's accounts and expenses to judging pleas for pardons sent directly to the prince. These are, admittedly, few – for the young man's position ensures that he serves more as a symbol for leniency than as an actual arbitrator of justice – yet they make for stimulating appraisal. The work has the entirely expected side effect of upsetting the eunuchs – who feel that they are better qualified to judge on matters of mercy than a lowly mandarin – and consequently I fear my name is hot on their tongues. As ever, I do my best to pretend that I do not notice their pinched faces always peering over my shoulders.

Last month, however, I was presented with a wonderful opportunity. The prince's history teacher – a senior Confucian with much renown in the city – was suddenly taken ill. The Confucian had recently been teaching the prince about how the present troubles with the rebelling provincial governors began. They had, understandably, been discussing the reign of the prince's illustrious ancestor, the noble Emperor Xuanzong, whose long rule is still much spoken of even though it ended some sixty years ago. It so happens that in one lesson the Confucian had mentioned my poem about the emperor's tragic romance with the concubine Yang Guifei. Indeed, it seems that wherever I go these days, people ask me if I am the same Bai Juyi who composed 'The Song of Everlasting Sorrow', and I have recently taken to denying it completely.

Thus when I heard that I had been summoned to take over teaching the period to the crown prince while the Confucian remained in his sickbed, all on the basis of that single poem, I was naturally a little nervous. It certainly occurred to me that it might be some trick by the eunuchs to encourage me to loosen my tongue, in the hope that my exposition of the poem might include some slander of the former emperor – which would therefore provide the eunuchs grounds on which to banish me and give the prince a 'lesson' about the loyalty of mandarins. Yet it seemed more natural to assume that the Confucian himself had suggested me as he knew I would not make an attempt to usurp his position (as many of the senior scholars are keen to do), and because a discussion of poetry would provide something of a diversion for the young man. However, these thoughts did not do much to calm my nerves, and I spent many hours rehearsing what I would say before my appointment.

As I was led through the inner chambers of the Eastern Palace, my mind was so busy going over all the things I wished to say to the prince that I paid little attention to the legendary silver statues, the ancient scrolls and the murals of yellow dragons that shimmered across the walls. My escort left me at the door of the prince's study, where I stood for ten minutes waiting to be admitted. If this is one of the tricks the mighty employ to enhance the sense of awe and power, then it works. By the time I was called in, both my palms and my brow were damp.

The crown prince was dressed in the long-flowing yellow robes of the imperial family, and greeted me from behind an ornate wooden table. He was tall – almost my own height – and had sharp, interrogative eyes unusual in one so pampered.

'You must be our illustrious poet. Please, be seated,' he said as soon as I entered.

'I am most honoured to be granted an audience with your imperial majesty. Please let me say how proud I am to be given this opportunity.'

He nodded – used, I am sure, to such deference. Then he sat across from me, and folded his arms down on the table.

'Your poem intrigues me.'

Like his noble father, the crown prince had evidently learnt that it is of the utmost importance for a ruler to speak as concisely and directly as possible, using no more words than is absolutely necessary. It seemed clear that he planned to lead the discussion, meaning I had wasted my time preparing a lecture about the period.

'You do not strike me as a particularly romantic-looking fellow, and yet your verse is full of hyperbole and exaggeration.'

I must admit that I was not expecting such criticism from someone so much younger than myself, but I tried to remain composed.

'Sometimes it is necessary for a poet to exaggerate in order to create the desired effect.'

'Hmm. You write that "Though there are three thousand beauties in the palace / his heart sees only one." Can Emperor Xuanzong really have had three thousand concubines?'

'That is what people say. Though you see, majesty, the high number here serves only to show that it is all the more remarkable that the emperor paid attention to one woman and one woman alone. The number need not be taken literally – it is used figuratively to show the incomparable beauty of Yang Guifei, and so helps to explain how your ancestor's love for her blinded him to the other things going on around him.'

'So your calculation is based on hearsay, conjecture and the desire to make a point? I see. A little later you say that the emperor showered so many gifts on Yang Guifei's family – giving her siblings important titles and influential court positions – that mothers and fathers across the country began to wish they had borne girls instead of boys. This assertion is patently ridiculous. All families want boys, to carry on the name of the line and, in the country, to work on their farms. Yes, poet, you see I know something of the situation of the land that I may one day be responsible for. Furthermore, how can you claim to know the feelings of the general populace at that time when only the emperor can truly know the heart of his people?'

'Again, I must apologise. Of course I cannot presume to know the will of the people – as your majesty so rightly points out, only one with the Mandate of Heaven can do that. I only wished to show how much the emperor cared for Yang Guifei – many people grow weary of flowery language that talks of love and furtive glances, yet everyone can understand the bestowing of titles and honour. They are the official representations of the private passion. I also wanted to suggest that people became envious of the favours shown to Yang's family, since the fame of the love affair surely helped spark the concerns that led to the rebellion.'

The young man nodded and I thought I saw – for a mere fraction of a second – a flicker of a smile. Was he toying with me? I was not sure. His retainers remained motionless behind us, their faces kept curiously blank, as if they were untroubled by the material world.

'Let me ask you, poet, do you believe it?'

'Forgive me, majesty, but believe what? That the events happened exactly as outlined in my poem? I would not dare suggest —'

'No. I am asking you whether you believe that love is strong enough to consume a man in this way, whether you believe that love really could change history.'

'That is a question each man must answer for himself. Yet if we are to judge a man, sometimes we must ignore his words and look instead to his actions, for these are the true measure of one's convictions. Your great ancestor Emperor Xuanzong ruled for close to forty years, and presided over a flourishing empire. The first twenty years of his rule saw him defeat competing claims to the throne, put down border rebellions and re-establish the ancient trade routes with the west. It was the golden age of art and poetry – of Li Bai and Du Fu among others. It was not until around thirty years into his reign that the emperor became infatuated with this beguiling young lady. He was no longer a young man, and certainly not naïve about the ways of women or the ways of state. Perhaps the number of wives and concubines waiting on him did not actually reach the thousands as I stated in my poem, but it certainly numbered many hundred. He was a proud father, a benevolent ruler. We can therefore only imagine the inner conflict he was faced with when he found himself falling in love with the young wife of his eldest son.

'That is what led me to conjecture that her beauty must have been incomparable. For one woman to stand out amid a whole palace of the most attractive women in the whole empire, she must have been remarkable. Though it should be noted that men always find themselves wanting the things that are just beyond their reach – history has a way of toying with us like that. Your ancestor was not the type of man to give up once he had his heart set upon something. He was, like all of your family, both resolute and blessed with a remarkable intelligence. He was able to persuade the young woman of the virtues of the Taoist vision of the universe, of the necessity of deep contemplation.'

'You mean, he sent her to a convent.'

There was that flicker of a smile again. I tried not to smile myself, for I was still acutely aware of the company I was in.

'In a manner of speaking, yes. She became a Taoist nun, and as such could later be invited into the court as Spiritual Advisor.'

'I suppose there are no records of how the prince felt about his father sending his wife away and then taking her as his own lover?'

'Alas, no. We must assume that either he did not care about her in the same way ...'

'Even though she was clearly the most beguiling woman around.'

'... or else he put the emperor's needs before his own. Whatever the case, before long she was given the title of Guifei, marking her out as the favourite in the palace.'

'Yes. In your poem they "spend burning nights beneath the lotus nets / and cannot be roused for the morning court". Do you really imagine the emperor neglecting his sacred duties just to spend more time with a mere woman?'

'I am afraid it is corroborated by the records of attendance for the last years of his reign. Of course, I am not suggesting that this love affair was the only thing that prompted the sudden problems in the dynasty – rather that it is a symbol of the changes that can affect the whole life of a man when he begins to see the world in a different way. As we get older, we tend to re-examine our lives, our feelings – this is what I imagine happening to Emperor Xuanzong.'

'Then love is what the ancient sorcerers would call a particularly potent spell, that ensnares the senses.'

'Forgive me, but your majesty makes it sound as if it were a disease, something to be avoided at all costs.'

'Perhaps the story of my ancestor's life is proof that it should be. Love is best left to the common man who has nothing better to worry about. I am grateful that my own bride has recently provided me with sons, and for that I thank her, but I would never break off affairs of state simply to visit her. No, love clearly muddies the mind – why else would the emperor appoint his lover's cousin as prime minister, despite his obvious inabilities?'

'Sometimes it takes the greatest foresight to consider the smallest details. The emperor probably thought that Yang Guozhong was likely to be loyal to him, since he was related to Yang Guifei. In much the same way, he probably thought he was building support by decentralising power and giving licence to regional governors. Perhaps it is that love diminishes our foresight, for it encourages us to live only in the present.'

I was becoming aware that the scope of the lesson – though perhaps discussion would be a better term – was gradually shifting. Where I had sought to discuss the prisms through which we seek to understand the past, the crown prince seemed more interested in examining the effects of love.

'Yes, your poem sees the emperor and his concubine spending all their time performing scenes from opera together – it is well known that through singing and dancing some priests seek to forget the world. Perhaps they were doing the same. But it did not work, did it, poet? I enjoyed the image you use in your poem, of the sound of erhus and zithers slowly being drowned out by the sound of war drums gradually drawing closer.'

'The An Lushan rebellion, yes. An Lushan was a regional commander of a huge area in the north. As Yang Guozhong became ever more corrupt and the court descended into petty squabbles and money grabbing, the populace began to grow disenchanted. There had been floods, famines and bad harvests for a number of years, and yet at the same time taxes were being increased to fund the lascivious lifestyle of Yang Guozhong and his circle, while the infatuated emperor appeared to ignore everything except his beautiful concubine. It wasn't difficult for a power-hungry man like An Lushan to drum up popular support under the pretence of ridding the court of corruption. Of course, I am certain a historian could give a far more comprehensive analysis of the causes of the rebellion. If I did not offer many details in my poem, that is only because there seemed to be no need to waste words describing something with which everyone is already familiar.'

'I understand. New petty tyrants from distant outposts seem to appear every month these days. That is the true legacy of the love of which we speak. Love is fodder for tragedy. In your poem, you build upon descriptions of long, lazy nights where the emperor and Yang Guifei could not be separated from each other's arms, only to suddenly turn to the violent end of the romance.'

'It is a classical juxtaposition, intended to make the climax more dramatic.'

'Indeed. The death scene is my favourite part of your poem. The details of this period are not new to me – everyone knows the story of my ancestor fleeing the capital with his concubine, of the imperial guard refusing to go any further without the emperor ridding himself of Yang Guozhong and Yang Guifei. How quickly the story of my ancestor's anguish has been turned into popular legend! It seems that everyone can now recount how the emperor had no choice but to consent to the guards strangling his concubine, and there are many lurid stories that focus on her death throes, her broken body or her snapping bones.

'Yet your poem is different:

> The emperor's army makes its stand,
> refusing to march until she twists and cries.
> Her jade bracelets, her gold earrings
> fall into the mud and dust. No one moves
> save the emperor, who raises his wrinkled hands
> to cover his eyes.

You do not show us the blood. You do not show us the moment of death. And yet we feel it, we are somehow a part of it. How do you do that, poet?'

'I must confess, majesty, that I am not sure I can answer that question. Sometimes I am unsure of the source of the poems I write, where the feelings and impulses arise from.'

'Hmm. I have heard many stories of love. And yet your poem is the first that presents emotions as so insistent that they overcome all else. Is there no room for sense, for morality, for duty? You present my ancestor not as an aged ruler making a single political mistake, but as a competent man ensnared by his feelings. You seem to be suggesting that it could happen to any of us – like catching the plague or being sent a curse. You depict a man who had single-handedly brought about a golden age in our great nation and ruled in an exemplary fashion for three decades suddenly being taken by surprise by a love that destroys every aspect of his former life, leaving him broken, crushed. I must confess, poet, that the idea frightens me. And you can be assured that I am not a man who is easily frightened. When the first wave of the An Lushan rebellion was subdued, and it was safe for the emperor to return to the capital, you show him defeated —

> *He sees nothing of the palace though they pass the gate.*
> *The lotus flowers stirring the lake*
> *are not lotus flowers – they are her half-smiling face;*
> *the curve of the fallen willow leaves*
> *are the curve of her eyes as they close. He sees*
> *through tears: the buds begin to bloom,*
> *the autumn rain, her shadow in their room.*

Even now that she is dead he cannot move without seeing her. What kind of a spell is this? I would expect him to be bitter, to swear and curse and plot – after all, because of this woman he has been forced to abdicate in favour of his son! What further indignity could befall him? I want to ask your opinion, poet – is there no cure for this, no palliative? A soldier might wear a suit of armour to protect from his foe, yet how might he shield himself from this?'

I must admit, dear friend, that I was at a loss for words. I cleared my throat, and looked around at the impassive faces of the guards. They were not going to be of any help. Whatever the prince was trying to steel himself towards, I was not sure I could help. Though he was himself married (despite his young age – such is the prerogative of the imperial family) and, it was rumoured, had a fair number of concubines, he clearly knew little of the emotion of which I had written. I cleared my throat again.

'As you said, majesty, your noble ancestor could not move without seeing his dead love. That is the truth of it: that love exists deep in the stomach, in the heart, in the senses. Some are immune, some are struck again and again, and some can never shake themselves free.'

I could tell that the prince was not satisfied with this answer from the way in which his eyebrows twitched, yet he was evidently well practised – unlike many of the people I have met – in keeping his feelings carefully hidden.

'Emperor Xuanzong died only a few years after the rebellion. And yet you would have us believe that even his death is not the end of their story! You close your poem by writing "Though even heaven and earth will one day be extinguished / this sorrow has no end." I am familiar with the concept of unending sorrow. The Buddhists tell us that suffering is the one constant in life, while the Taoists assert that it is fruitless trying to stop the natural way of all things. Yet I must admit that I have not come across the idea that heaven and earth shall end. Surely they are immutable, endless – otherwise the emperor's Mandate of Heaven would be fallible.'

'Of course, and yet nothing is ever certain except for sorrow. Houses collapse, cities are razed and even dynasties change. The astronomers tell us that sometimes stars are born and die in the same night. Suffering is the only constant.'

'Then it is another metaphor?'

I nodded, though it should have been clear that it was not. Nothing is infinite, save nothingness itself. Heaven shall perish, as shall earth. All that will remain will be the ghosts of our anguish. Yet I had more sense than to risk angering the prince.

'Good. I was worried you might try to espouse some dangerous philosophy, like those heretics who deny the existence of time. We had one hauled to the palace last week – the fool told us that time did not exist, that progress was an illusion. He said that we die each day, that we live forever in each minute. Heretical rubbish – everyone knows that the emperor stands at the centre of time, directing its unfolding. Yet there are many who would have us question the whole universe. There are even some who would question the emperor's claim to understand its most complex workings. But you and I know that some truths are beyond the common man, and must be left for those who have the knowledge of heaven, do we not?'

There was something fierce in his eyes, as if he was challenging me. I hoped to see it turn into a smile. It did not.

'Of course, majesty.'

Why had I said that? It was a sentiment with which I did not agree – the common man should have as much right to examine and question the world around him as the royal family. I felt as if I had betrayed myself and my ideals, friend, simply to keep out of trouble. I understand, now, how easy it is to make a sycophant of a humble man, how easy it is to be coerced by the weakness of one's heart. It was then that the young man – who it is said has already decided that he will take the name of Emperor Muzong when his reign begins – leaned closer and whispered something that profoundly shocked me.

'You are a man who puts much stock in words, poet, to show us the truth about ourselves. Tell me, what do you know about the sacred book of my ancestors, the one which records the history of all future dynasties?'

I gulped. 'Majesty, I have heard such myths, but there is an old saying that the man who thinks only of the past and the man who thinks only of the future both lose sight of today.'

He did not appear much interested in my reply. 'Who is to say what is myth and what is fact? As we have agreed, some truths are beyond the understanding of the common man.' He continued to whisper, and I realised that perhaps he was making sure the eunuchs listening in did not catch this part of his speech. 'I would give anything to find this sacred history, and with it restore this kingdom to its former glories, for it shall tell of the outcome of every war, the state of each harvest, the plots of each would-be usurper and rebel. I have started a search across the very length and breadth of our nation. But listen, poet, your verse marks you out as an expert in the history of this great nation. So please give me an honest answer – where should I look for this book? Is there hope? How might we find it and unpick its secrets?'

The crown prince rose to his feet before I could reply. 'You need not answer now. Think it over and marshal your learning, for much depends upon it. We shall speak again. I have been satisfied with our meeting. Your work intrigues me, however much I may disagree with some of its assertions about my noble ancestor. Love, history, suffering ... there are many further questions I would put to you. Thus you will return at the beginning of the next lunar cycle, and we will discuss "Rain at Night".'

I got up to kowtow, but before my palms had a chance to slap the cold stone floor the prince was gone from the room, accompanied by all but one of the guards. I was escorted from the inner chambers hurriedly, making it clear that my presence was no longer required. For a while I stood in the garden of the Eastern Palace, watching the bustle of eunuchs and guards as they marched past the gingkoes, preoccupied with the papers in their hands and the plans in their heads.

My friend, I hope you will not be too ashamed of me. I should have argued my beliefs instead of holding my tongue – I should have made it clear that love is a blessing, not a curse; that history is always unkind to those rulers who forget about the common people; that even heaven must admit its fallibility for us to learn from our mistakes. I should have argued for the common man, instead of acquiescing to keep myself in good favour. I have tried to convince myself that I spoke as I did so as to gain the confidence of the young man – his paranoia must surely have something to do with the influence of the eunuchs – and therefore put myself in a better position to influence him at a later date (when I will raise the idea of the well-needed reforms of which you and I often speak). Yet I fear that there is some deeper instinct guiding my cowardly actions, some part of me – however much I desire change and an end to corruption in the government – that craves only peace and quiet, that no longer has the heart for struggle. You must think me a fool.

How I found my way home is a mystery to me, for I do not remember taking a single step, my head was swirling so with thoughts. I was pondering how it is that people can bend the words of any poem to find the meaning they wish to see, regardless of what is written. I was thinking too that a man's words might easily be taken and twisted and used against him. The prince seemed to see nothing but dangers – were these the natural fears of a young man trying to deal with the immense responsibilities that faced him, or the beginnings of something more dangerous? When I arrived home, I collapsed into my bed and closed my eyes, trying to drown out the shrill cries of the goatherds driving their wares to the market, and slowly let sleep creep up on me.

As you can see, things are not as easy for me as they once were. Even the slightest worry is enough to threaten to break the dams and bring my illness rushing back. I slept the rest of the afternoon and, after supping with my wife, retired once again and was abed the entire next day. Do not worry – that was days ago now, and I have quite recovered. I am presently steeling myself for my second meeting with the prince, which will take place after the new temple has been dedicated – though I hear the roof has not yet been finished, even at this late date! I intend to let my convictions guide me this time, though I have not yet decided what to say about this mythical book of his ancestors he has asked me about. I shall dedicate myself to finding out more, and then I will answer from my heart. I will not give you reason to doubt my determination again.

There, the ink stick is almost rubbed down to dust, so I must finish. To answer your question: no, although the trees are now in blossom, I have not lingered in the orchard since the incident I wrote of in the previous letter, and to tell you the truth, I think it does me good to avoid revisiting too many memories. I may yet regain something of my former life. My nights are often restless, yet I console myself with the sounds of the city, the knowledge that hope lives apart from us, and may be found in even the strangest of places.

Please tell me more of your adventures – I have no doubt that your plans will soon result in further success. Send my best wishes to your children, and remember not to bind them with too many strict rules, for nothing is as important as the testing of one's own limitations. If you can bear my brief and clumsy criticism, please send more of your verse. I say a sutra that your shoes stay strong, that your palms stay open.

Bai Juyi

# On the Principles of Nature

PART 2 · SUMMER 1288 CE

Most of the men in our company have chosen to eat alone in their quarters – with three deaths from the desert sickness in as many days, and now with Brother Lovari struck down by the same symptoms, all are fearful of falling prey to this foul plague, and no one is sure who might be afflicted next. Therefore I too retire to my tent to take my midday meal. After eating I rest for an hour untroubled by dreams – unlike Brother Lovari, who I am sure is suffering not only the spasms and pains of his wasting sickness, but also the torments that must surely afflict a conscience as guilty as his. I wake to the familiar sound of our heathen guides shouting indecipherable orders between themselves in the midday heat. I worry that this journey is softening me. Back in the monastery, I would have retired to bed after an early supper, to be up again after dark for the Nocturns that make up Matins. Then another rest and up for Lauds, welcoming the dawn light as it is drawn in red swirls across the sky. Every day spent standing or kneeling for no less than sixteen hours. Here all I seem to do is rest and wait.

The interminable heat, rising off the scalding stretches of white sand, hits me once again with a sudden ferocity as I venture from my tent, and I soon see Paul hurrying towards me.

'Good afternoon, Paul. May the Lord's blessings be upon you. I trust that —'

'Must go.'

I try not to let my polite smile slip, knowing full well that these heathens know nothing of etiquette or civility.

'Surely you are not thinking of leaving us? You know I value your stewardship, and I do believe you and your men have been well compensated for taking on this assignment.'

'No. Not I. All. All must go. Now.'

His leathery face scrunches into a frown, his eyes disappearing beneath the dark slips of sun-wizened skin. Is he frightened? I silently admonish myself for devoting too much time to Lovari. I should have led everyone in prayer this morning and reminded them that the Lord is always among us. I fear that while I attend my sickly brother the men may let themselves be overcome by fear and superstition. I must lead by example, that they might see how their betters act and so be shamed into mending such foolish ways.

'Come, there is no need to hurry. The men are anxious enough as it is. Besides, we have enough supplies, do we not? And the camels and donkeys will be glad of another day's rest. Until we have shaken this cursed sickness or else committed the last sufferer to the earth, we must stay where we are, for you know as well as I that it is impossible to administer adequate care and provide spiritual succour while we are travelling.'

Paul's lips twitch open, and his brown teeth push through.

'No. Must go. Now. The winds will steal our skin.'

'Paul, you are trying my patience. Only this morning you told me you were certain that we would not be troubled by storms. Now you tell me that we must leave before the desert winds besiege us. What will you say tomorrow? No, we are all getting used to the night winds, as bothersome as they may be. Besides, we cannot move Brother Lovari at the present moment. Any sudden exertion – even his litter being moved – might kill him. I cannot risk that. We must wait.'

'We ride two days to Thousand Buddhas. There are many wise men there. Many herbs. They can make him strong again. But we cannot stay. Please, the winds —'

I placed my hand up in front of me.

'Paul, that is enough. I am in charge here, and I know what is best for all of us. You would do well to remember your place. Let me tell you again, we will not be going to Mogao. Now, I have other duties to attend to. Get one of your charges to bring some more water to my tent. And do not go spreading these foolish ideas about wind storms among the men, understand?'

Paul gives a curt bow before hurrying off towards where the tethered donkeys are nosing indolently in the sand. I shake my head and decide to make a tour of the camp to raise the men's morale.

I do not much care for this idea of leaving Lovari at the mercy of strange apothecaries. In my days as a novice at the monastery, I did not shirk from my weekly duties helping the infirmarian care for my burnt friend – that most learned elderly monk I used to spend hours conversing with, and whom I must admit I often find myself missing terribly – as well as the other sick and elderly among our brethren, and I believe I picked up much knowledge of the workings and balance of the sanguine, the choleric, the phlegmatic and the melancholic humours, as well as learning how to perform a simple bloodletting. Furthermore, I stayed close by D'Antonio, Salvitici and Nazario when they were afflicted by this same sickness, so I know well the stages in which it lays waste to the body. These foreigners, however, seem to have no understanding of such things. I worry they might start some unholy witchcraft – I have noticed that some of my own countrymen in our party have, in imitation of the natives, started to boil their drinking water with strange, dark leaves which emit the most beguiling of smells. They even deign to drink this peculiar concoction, no doubt believing in the magic these potions contain. I make a vow to put an end to such dangerous and vile practices.

The men seem most pleased that I have come to supervise their work. I soon strike up conversation with two of the stable-hands who have been attending to our beasts. They seem disheartened to have been taken so far from their families only to spend each day with flea-flecked donkeys, so I recount the story of Our Lord's triumphant ride into Jerusalem upon the back of a noble ass for their education, and am just about to follow this with a brief discussion of the most Holy life of Saint Francis when they remember an urgent piece of work the steward had set them earlier. I then speak with the men manning the fires, attempting to calm their worries about the recent outbreaks of the desert sickness, before correcting some of the hasty assumptions of the cartographers sketching in their tents; I have a short debate with the pittancer about our finances, and check for myself that the tallies made by the clerk in the supplies tent correspond with our provisions.

The heat rises from the blinding sand and settles stickily in the folds of my habit. I scratch my blisters and bites, unable to concentrate while my brother's story remains unfinished. The box in which my strange creatures dwell is left unopened, for they are no doubt drained by the morning's experiments and thus deserving of rest. Soon one of Lovari's servants comes to summon me and I make my way across to where his stricken body lies.

'I hope you have passed a better few hours than I, brother.' Thus does Lovari greet me as I sit down beside him. His eyes are scrunched shut. He is swaddled inside his many blankets, which emit a most unholy stench. His face is swollen, and he continues to shiver, while every few moments the pile of dank furs at his feet stirs and twists as his legs twitch. 'I dreamed that I was alone upon a mountaintop, with only crows to keep me company. Furthermore, when I awoke from my nap I found the pains in my side grown even worse.'

'Consider the crows, Jesus said to his disciples, for they neither plant nor harvest. The Lord alone feeds them.' I quote Scripture to try to reassure him, though in truth his dream has made me think of something quite different – namely the darkness the crows must surely represent, the same darkness that may soon welcome Lovari into its depths.

I lift his sweaty head in my hands and rearrange the cushions so that he might settle back in comfort.

'I am glad you have returned. I was worried that this morning's revelations might have scared you off.'

'I shall not abandon anyone under my care, no matter how odious I may find their actions. I have come to urge you once again to recant.'

Though I speak with all seriousness, Lovari smiles at my words.

'I think you fear we are running out of time. I still have the strength to finish my story. Yes, Sebastiano's death was odious. I would not have killed him had there been another option. Yet we are men who have devoted much of our lives to the contemplation of the nature of sacrifice. The one for the many. That is how I saw it then, and it is how I continue to see it now. The sacrifice is a lesson we must not forget.

'I returned to my brethren in the Order of Eternal Light back in Palermo after that night, and never again set foot in my uncle's village. The next three years brought more rich experiences than I have time to recount to you now. Suffice to say that over these years I learnt more of the Last Gospel. We were certain, in those days, that its discovery was imminent, and there was a palpable sense of excitement running through the great house, each room filled with men poring over ancient maps and forgotten tomes.

'They were giddy, blissful times. I was drunk on books and drunk on faith and drunk on secrets, and, as every drinker believes when intoxicated, I thought that we were invincible. Though Alessio and I continued on secret missions under the auspices of Father Teodoro – stealing into mosques, talking ourselves into the stately abodes of princes, bribing guards to let us slip into the fetid subterranean dungeons beneath the city to meet with men whom the world had abandoned, all in pursuit of keys to that great puzzle – I was never again asked to take a life. We lived as a great brotherhood ought to, holding everything in common and breaking our bread not only with the usual flood of exotic visitors but also with the destitute and ragged poor who each day milled about our doors. It was therefore one of the darkest days of my life when I set about razing the grand old building to the ground.

'It was before dawn on a dull autumnal day during my twenty-first year when I was roused by the clatter of hurried feet outside our room. I opened my eyes to the sound of worried shouts, and already I knew that something was terribly awry, for before that day I had never heard even a raised voice inside the walls of our complex. It was still dark, though from the light of a single candle I saw that Alessio was fully dressed and sitting at our shared desk, studying an old map so attentively that I wondered whether he had heard the sounds of panic and alarm spreading throughout the building. Since members of the Order were often sent upon twilight assignations, I did not think to question the fact that his bed did not appear to have been slept in.

'"What's happening?" I stuttered.

'Alessio's nonchalant shrug worried me almost as much as the frenzy I could hear all around us. I leapt out of bed and threw on a dirty shirt before opening the door. Streams of people were rushing through the hall. Most of the men were, like me, in a state of undress, wearing looks of shock and confusion on their unshaven faces. Despite the agitated flapping and the shrill cries of disbelief from many among us, it did not take long to ascertain what had happened.

'A little earlier that night, Father Teodoro had been seized on his way to a clandestine meeting by the royal guard and charged with the most heinous crime of treason. One of the Order had been on the way to the same meeting when he had witnessed Teodoro being marched towards the gaols. The rumours on the street told that Father Teodoro was accused of conspiring to overthrow the king and plotting to make an attempt on the life of the Supreme Pontiff. By the evening the inquisitors in His Majesty's dungeons would have used their skills to force a false confession of the same from our leader.

'"But ... but what on earth will happen to us?" a bearded Greek priest beside me began to stammer when the news was imparted.

'I am ashamed to say that most of our thoughts similarly turned quickly to the question of our own safety. We had all heard stories about men working for Frederick II or the Pope attending many of the guilds and churches in search of seditious plotting, yet we had thought ourselves immune. It seemed, though, that we had not kept our secret as well as we should have. And if Father Teodoro had been found out, then how long before the royal guard came for us?

'All that could be seen for the next hour was the sight of my brethren hurrying about their rooms and flinging open cupboards, desks, shelves and drawers, and bundling anything they could into bags improvised from table cloths and old robes. By the time dawn broke through the windows, the building was almost deserted. After trying to find out all I could from the other monks, I had returned to our shared cell, where I sat speechless and scared, trying to work out what I might do. My friend, however, had already shoved his quill, his ink and his second shirt into a small leather bag and was hovering about the door.

'"Come on, get up and get out of here. I won't say it again. You should count yourself lucky that you haven't got much to lug away with you. Come on! What do you think you're waiting for?" Alessio shouted at me, jolting me from my thoughts.

'It was then that I realised where I had to go.

'Since the stables had been vacated, there was nothing to do but run, retracing the route from memory, for I had been there once many years before. It took me close to an hour, running barefoot through the backstreets, over the hunched stone bridges and cutting across the private herb gardens of Palermo to reach the site of our secret library. The stone house was just within my sights when I felt a hand grab my arm and haul me suddenly back into the fetid alley behind me. I stumbled backwards, and would have fallen into a stream of caliginous brown water had it not been for the steadying grip of the hooded figure who stood before me. I pulled away and raised my hand to fend him off when I suddenly caught a glimpse of the pasty white chin and rubbery lips protruding from beneath the fall of his cowl.

'"We must be quiet, my friend. You should not have come here," the Carthusian hissed.

'It was a shock to hear his high voice so far from our sanctuary, and for a moment I did not know what to think.

'"I have to do something, brother," I whispered.

'He nodded, his eyes darting distractedly around us. He led me further down the alley and pulled me into the doorway of a down-trodden carpenter's workshop.

'"It is not safe. The royal guards are watching this area carefully. They must have followed Father Teodoro from here. They are probably waiting to see whether anyone comes to claim the books. I have been waiting here to make sure that none of our brethren get caught in this trap."

'"But what about all our writing, the maps, the correspondence? They will find our secrets."

'The Carthusian shook his head.

'"No. Knowing what you already know, Tommaso, you cannot seriously believe that any of us left anything that could be used against us. The old books will have no meaning for them if they do not know what they are looking for, and the private documents are all written in a code that it will be impossible for the royal guards to decipher. Father Teodoro was well aware that this might happen one day. It is a minor setback, nothing more. Are the others gone from the great home?"

'"Yes, they fled as soon as they heard the news," I replied bitterly.

'"Do not think badly of them. They were only doing as instructed. We must lie low, Tommaso, we must let them believe they have won. We shall scatter ourselves across the continent, and gather again once the danger has passed. You must not give up the search. We will find it, be certain of that. I know of a place you may go – but first, you must do something for me."

'And so it was that, only a few hours later, I stood holding a flaming torch aloft outside the great complex where I had come to understand my calling. I had checked the stables, the kitchens, the hall, the studies, the library and even the black room with the ceiling of stars. All I found was a clutter of parchment and worn rags, books warped with damp and scrolls whose fine lettering had faded and bled beyond comprehension. Yet the Carthusian was right: we often hid our most important parchments in secret places in case of an unexpected visit from the royal guards, and in their haste my fleeing brethren may have forgotten to remove them. They could have been stashed in any spider-webbed nook, amid the straw padding of any of the beds, behind any shelf or cupboard. And unlike the missives collected in the Order's private library, few of them were in code. A single one of those hastily scribbled notes might implicate any number of us. The risk was too great. The building had to be destroyed.

'I had just lit the torch from the embers of the kitchen fire and was moving round to the back of the complex – so that the blaze would not be seen from the neighbouring houses until it was too strong to be stopped – when I caught sight of something moving inside. Fearing that it was one of the local beggars come for the daily distribution of alms, I ran back in. My calls produced no response, and it dawned on me that it might be one of the royal guards hunting for conspirators. I sprinted through the dining hall, weaving between the long benches where we had once shared our supper and our hopes. I held the burning torch aloft as I darted from room to room. It was only as I passed the staircase that I heard the sound of a warped floorboard moaning beneath someone's step. I spun around and saw him. He was standing at the top, his stocky shadow thrown onto the bleeding Christ outstretched upon the landing wall.

'"You're persistent, I'll give you that. But you ought to know better. Why don't you put out that torch and get out of here?"

'He pushed a hand through his greasy hair. He was sweating, despite the mild weather.

'"Alessio, come on. We don't have much time before the royal guards and the Pope's spies start rooting through for evidence."

'He laughed and, as he fingered his belt, I noticed that he was wearing a dagger.

'"The Pope's spies, as you call them, already know everything about this place. And now that I have finally unearthed the hidden maps those foolish monks left behind in their panic, the entire brethren are going to face the wrath of our most Holy Father. And to think, all I needed was a few hours alone here! We should have done this much sooner! Now, I was going to let you go, runt, but you're beginning to give me serious doubts. Go on, get out of here and I might still find a way to forget your name when His Eminence asks."

'I felt dizzy, my grip on the torch slipping.

'"What kind of a game is this?" I stuttered.

'But even as I spoke, I understood. I understood the nervous energy with which he had gone about every task, I understood his guarded manner with the other monks and priests there, I understood why he had always appeared to be suppressing a sneer when he talked of Father Teodoro, and I understood why he had given the poisoned wine to the old monk, Emiliano. And I understood why he had been up and dressed and so calm when the terrible news had come through that morning.

'"All this time?" I asked, my voice close to breaking.

'"All my life!" he bellowed. "I made a most Holy vow to ensure that no man ever finds that book. I would rather die that let it be looked upon by mortal eyes!"

'There were things I could have said. Explanations I could have sought, recriminations I could have shouted. A calmer man might have found a way to engage him and dig out the details of how he had betrayed us, of how much they knew. But all I could think of was the years we had spent in the same room, our thoughts and fears stripped down and exposed before each other, and I felt a rage stirring my senses – the same feeling that must have stung the mighty Samson when he was betrayed.

'It was one of the only times in my life when my emotions have overcome me. You know, Rosso, I sometimes wonder whether what we speak of as possession isn't really something quite else. Could it be that some men just become so overwhelmed by rage, by bile, by anger, that they can no longer hear the voice of the Lord guiding them, and so are easy prey to the whirlwinds of their emotions? Was it really demons that Our Lord cast out from that afflicted man and into the herd of swine, or was it simply that he freed the man from the chains of his rage? I know only that, as I swiped the torch at the nearest tapestry, I felt as if everything was happening to someone else and I was merely an observer. Yet there was no Devil guiding my hand – it was spite and malice alone that drove my actions.

'I was amazed at how quickly the ratty old tapestry caught, for the greedy yellow flames were suddenly chewing their way up the walls. Alessio let out a shout and began to charge down the stairs towards me. I swung the torch down, pressing it to the lowest of the wooden steps, hoping the dry tinder would crackle up before my roommate made it to the bottom. I heard him free his blade from the leather sheath and I straightened back up to see that he was almost upon me, the red at the heart of the fire dancing between us reflected in his eyes. I had seen him fight before, and knew I could provide no match to his wiry strength. Perhaps I should have turned my back and fled, but my feet would not bear me away, and so instead I braced my left arm in front of my face and waved the flame blindly ahead, a beacon of hope held out against the inevitable.

'Was it my faith that saved me? It would be comforting to think so, Rosso, but I am afraid I cannot say that it was. I am no more devout than others who die in earthquakes, in shipwrecks, in needless wars. Why should I be saved and not them? Though I would like to think that it was fate that led me from the blazing building without even a single mark upon my flesh, it would be more prudent to say that I was lucky. Who can explain the strange mathematics of chance? I heard a sudden thump and pulled back my arm to see that Alessio had tripped on one of the steps. His leg buckled beneath him and, as he tumbled forward, his arms flailing hopelessly at the fiery tapestries, I caught his eye. His look spoke only of hatred, of the black bitterness that gnaws at hearts.

'I flung myself aside as he crashed to the floor beside me. His arm was twisted beneath his body, and I had to fight hard to suppress the urge to kneel beside down and help him up. A faint murmur from his lips was the only sign that he was still conscious, though his closed eyes told that this state was far from certain. By then the smoke was beginning to peel tears from my eyes, to cloy upon my tongue. I had to leave. Before I fled back I bent once more and set the torch down on the floor – then left my former home forever.

'By the time the rafters yielded to the fire and the building came crumbling down upon itself in a cloud of vicious black smoke, I was halfway across the city. The Carthusian had given me enough money to pay for board in the backroom of an inn for a few days.

I stayed for Teodoro's public execution, but by that very evening I had left Palermo, and was on my way to meet a craggy boatman who would ferry me to Messina. That was the beginning of a year-long journey, conducted for the greater part under the cloak of night and winding through the most desolate and pestilential regions, that would finally take me to the abbey in Ancona where – first as a novice and brother and then, thanks to my exemplary education at the sanctuary, a sacrist, obedientiary and finally prior – I was to spend the next twenty-five years of my life.'

I am about to interject when a terrible scream reaches us from outside. Lovari's eyes are still screwed closed, but his head turns wildly on the pillow, seeking out the direction from which the noise came. There is silence for a moment and then jeering.

'Rosso, what is happening? Rosso?' Lovari rasps as I rush out from his tent.

It takes my eyes some time to focus through the shimmering golds, the burning yellows, the amber swells of the desert, and so for a minute it seems as if I am running blindly through pure light. It is not difficult to follow the sound of catcalls and bawdy shouts. When my eyes finally begin to pick out form and shape I see them: the mass of servants, translators, cartographers and guides huddled in a circle outside the supplies tent. I have to clear my throat several times before the group reluctantly moves aside to let me through.

'Would someone kindly tell me what all this commotion is about?'

I am unimpressed to hear a giggle coming from behind me. A stable-hand points a grubby finger towards something sprawled in the sand. It is one of the Tartars. I say a quick prayer under my breath. Not another one. I approach the inert figure, though I have difficulty identifying him, as most of our native helpers look identical. The man's mouth is agog, and only the whites of his eyes are visible.

'Surely you men have not forgotten your Christian charity? Who will help me lift this poor fellow up?'

As I speak our men take a step backwards, with much crossing of themselves. Before I can lay a hand upon him, however, I notice Paul at my side.

'Steward, what ails your man so?'

Paul's face is scrunched into a scowl, and he raises a hand to prevent me kneeling.

'Evil. Do not touch. It has him now.'

Paul will not look me in the eye.

I push past Paul and bend down beside the fallen Tartar. I press at his legs and ankles, count the beat of his heart, listen to the fall and rise of his breath. Then I let out a sigh of relief.

'The desert sickness!' A Genoan voice rises from the crowd.

'That's number five!' Another man calls out. 'None of us is safe. We've been delivered into the valley of the beast!'

'Silence!' I shout, rising to my feet. 'I will not tolerate such behaviour! Yes, he is clearly ill – the effects of this country's remorseless sun are hard for any man to endure. But he has none of the symptoms shared by our brothers D'Antonio, Salvitici, Nazario or Prior Lovari. This poor man needs water and rest, that is all.'

Paul finally stares up at me.

'No, no. He screamed. He twitched. Look.'

I stare down at the man. His face is a little red, yet any fool knows that to stay in the heat too long is a challenge to the flesh – even Our Lord managed only forty blistering days wandering the infested wilds. I myself have seen the whole horizon waver in the midday heat, have felt the hot air squeeze upon my temples until the whole world begins to move as a ship might, tottering giddily through frothing waves. These are Hellish tricks, but I have had the mettle to resist them. It is of no surprise that the natives are lacking in spiritual strength.

I feel Paul touching my shoulder, and flinch at the indiscretion before carefully brushing his hand away.

'We must go. The Thousand Buddhas will wash him clean. Spirit voices call us from our path. The call is too strong.'

He nods gravely, and I begin to feel more than a little aggrieved that he is trespassing so upon my authority. Yet before I have the chance to put forth my case for staying and tending to this poor Tartar's heat sickness, our own men begin to murmur in fervoured agreement.

'I've heard them. Ever since this plague came upon us. Strange whispers, carried by the wind —'

'And me! Hissing voices around the tent in the dead of night —'

'Demons. I've had my best knife go missing and the last of my wine and —'

It suddenly seems as though almost every man among them is crossing himself, and I realise I must restore faith and order among them before the whole rabble lose all sense of propriety. After ordering Paul to let some water trickle upon the unconscious man's lip and so cause him to be revived, I raise my hand high above my head and, with the most sonorous voice I can summon, call for calm.

'My friends, fellow Christians and fellow countrymen, there is no need to give in to fear. The beloved of the Lord shall dwell in safety by him; and the Lord shall cover him all day long. Think on that and muster your courage. Together, with our faith, we will drive this cursed sickness from our camp! To your knees before the Lord, and pray for the state of your souls, for Prior Lovari, and for our young companion, for the Lord loves all men as they are brothers. Let us pray.'

And so I lead the men in the Lord's prayer, checking carefully as I recite those well-loved lines that every eye is screwed shut and every pate bowed towards the earth, while Paul and the other natives look on awkwardly. And lo, our petitions to the most loving Lord bear fruit, for what should happen but the Tartar boy begins to stir. I touch my hand to his brow and murmur a hurried blessing.

The crowd lets out a gasp and pushes forward as the Tartar slowly, giddily, pushes himself up to a sitting position, shielding his eyes from the light. He mumbles a few indecipherable grunts in Paul's direction, and my steward nods in response. Satisfied with my work, I make my way back towards Lovari. This will give them all a lesson – not that one, of course, should be needed – about the incomparable strength that faith begets.

However, by the time I push back the fibrous netting overlapping as windbreaks at the entrance to the tent, I find that Lovari is fast asleep once again. Shrill wheezes rise from his sweaty form, while his pale cheeks puff and swell with the heavy breaths. I say a brief benediction, then retire to my own tent, for I would not wake him when he is in such need of rest. As I stride back across the sand I cast a glance towards the rabble of servants, scouts and stable-hands – the godly men from our home are grinning and giving thanks for the little miracle, while the recovered Tartar stands with Paul and the other natives, huddled together in a gloomy sea of scowls.

✛✛✛

In my own tent I feed my sand prawns and then decide to devote an hour of the afternoon to the works of Saint Augustine. Yet I cannot concentrate on my studies, and instead my mind turns to the first time I heard the name of Prior Tommaso di Lovari. It was five years ago, when I was summoned to the presence of the great Giovanni da Montecorvino – a man who was already then famed throughout Christendom, for Pope Nicholas IV himself had commissioned him to spread the glorious Word of God to the infidels, heretics and unbelievers beyond the realm of the Byzantines. It was a mission which I and the other brothers at the Franciscan monastery in Assisi had followed with much anticipation, for what could be more important than building a ministry of faith that could reach to the furthest corners of the world? We oft discussed and debated the progress and tribulations of this noble scheme in our dining hall, whenever news reached us from the outside world.

The envoy had recently returned from his mission in Persia, and a messenger arrived at the monastery one morning announcing that before his return to the Papal States, Montecorvino would stop over for a number of days in Assisi, in pilgrimage to the tomb of the founder of our order, and that during that time the great man himself wished to see me. I thought there must be some mistake, for how could my name be known to such an illustrious man? I had only two score years behind me, and though my modesty must admit that I had achieved a modicum of renown among my brethren thanks to my prodigious skills at translation, composition and oratory, I marvelled at the fact that I had been heard of outside the monastery walls.

Father Montercorvino was residing as a guest of the local duke in a fine palace a day's ride from the monastery, and thus it was with a mixture of youthful nerves and giddy anticipation that I set forth the following morning. Past the tawny fields of swaying wheat, through the tiny village set around the crumbling stone mill, and right up until I was admitted through the iron gate into the courtyards of the ancient castle, I could not rid myself of the terrible suspicion that I would be scoffed at and turned away, a victim of some malicious prank. Thankfully, I was spared such a humiliation. A tall man in fine livery escorted me through the warren of hallways until we reached the splendid decoration of the guest quarters, where I was bid enter by the honourable Montecorvino himself.

'You must be the young man I have been hearing so much about. Stop fidgeting and sit down, will you? Good. Now, set to work on translating these four parchments. You may use that quill and ink, but try and make your finished work readable. My eyes always tire when trying to make out monkish handwriting, and I have a headache already. Go on, boy, you may begin.'

It was not quite the introduction I had anticipated. I sat myself down at the desk he had gestured towards and, after stealing a glimpse at the cropped brown beard, hooked nose, fierce sorrel eyes and turret-jutted chin of the great man, I set about the task he had outlined. I laboured for little over an hour as he paced the room behind me, and the thought of his presence only a few feet away was so overpowering that I did not dare let my eyes rise higher than the parchment, ink-pot and slow curve of the fresh-feathered quill with which I furiously scribbled. Only once I had finished my task did I risk straightening my back.

'So?'

The great missionary took the pages from my hands and, after the most cursory of glances over my work, leant forward to stare straight at me. I did not know where to look, and it seemed some minutes before I could call up the courage to meet his gaze. His look spoke of authority, of restlessness and resolution. I fear mine spoke only of timidity.

'What can you tell me of them?'

I forced myself to swallow and take a deep breath, lest my tongue should babble forth before I got a chance to compose myself.

'Well, the first was an early Latin hagiography of Saint Anthony and his trials in the desert, the second was a letter in the Greek that is now spoken by our Orthodox brothers in the east, the third was the apocryphal book of Ruth written in the ancient Greek of the sophists and Platonists, while the fourth was the language in which the Moors composed their heretic prayers to the black stone, though I must admit I struggled with that, having only had access to some half dozen Arab texts.'

His mouth bristled into the beginnings of a smile. He straightened himself up and began to pace towards the high oak bookshelf at the back of the room.

'You will forgive my little test, but you will understand that each man in my service must prove his worth. Your friend at the monastery has spoken most highly of you. No doubt you know well of whom I speak. An extraordinary linguistic ability coupled with a most untainted devotion, I think those were his words. Come, do not blush boy, these are gifts you were given by Our Lord, so do Him justice and be proud of them.'

He stopped speaking and began to move some of the heavy tomes aside. Since I did not know how to respond to his speech, I decided to say nothing at all, but instead worked on cultivating a percipient and sagacious look with which to impress him. He finally retrieved what he had been furrowing for, and returned to the desk bearing a long roll of cloud-grey scroll, which he began to unfurl before me.

'This is a map of the earth. As you will see, the Pope resides in the very centre, and the whole of Christendom spreads out from him. You will notice that our cartographers have not scrimped upon detail. Our knowledge extends now to three points of the compass, to the furthest reaches of the islands of the Britons in the west, to the Viking lands of the north, and to the dark jungles of the Africas in the south. Only parts of the east remain unaccounted for, namely those beyond Jerusalem and Arabia. As you may know, I have recently ventured as far as Persia, just here. The proceedings of that expedition need not concern you. However, while I was there an idea came upon me. Tell me, brother, what do you know of the vast plains of Cathay?'

I stared down at the scroll and gulped. Beyond the mighty twin rivers of Persia there was little save empty space, a great expanse of the map that the cartographers had left blank.

'I know that our ancestors knew the populace of that strange land as Seres, the people of silk, for they alone hold the secrets of that miraculous cloth. It is said that the men of Cathay breath only through their noses and that while we trade in gold they swap slithers of paper, and where we write with quills they prefer the thick brushes of painters. It is also well reported that bordering Cathay is a country whose populace are preserved in some eternal youth, and any traveller who enters shall not age a single day though he stays there many years, though I put no more faith in this rumour than in any of the stories of phantoms and two-headed beasts the local farmers tell on feast day to scare one another.'

Montecorvino nodded, and ran a hand through his closely cropped beard.

'I see you have as good a memory for gossip as for facts. Yet many of those rumours appear to be correct. Indeed, they were gathered some twenty years ago in a report by one of our Franciscan brethren, Friar William of Rubruck, who travelled to the Mongol capital of Karakorum – up in the north here – on a mission for His Royal Highness Louis IX of France. However, he never made it as far as Cathay itself, and so his testimony is based on hearsay alone.

'Yet I have reason to believe that the great Khan who rules over the vast continent could be a useful ally to us. Together we might be able to cleanse Christendom of the vast evil of the Moorish infidels. The minds of those natives have not been troubled or warped by the lies and heresies of the Jews or Moors. And think also, my brother, on all the lost souls in that distant land who might be saved if we were to bring the Word in all its glory to their shores. I have a mind to build a great cathedral there that we might show them the righteous path of the Lord. Yet we must proceed cautiously. I cannot make public my aim, nor even bring this matter up formally with the Papal authorities, until I can be certain of success. Thus I am in need of a small delegation to prostrate themselves before this Khan and find out whether he may be persuaded to be friendly to us. If so, I will then make the journey myself.'

He must have noticed my mouth gape ignobly as I realised what he was suggesting, and that same small smile twisted upon his lips.

'Come, it shall not be difficult. There are already a number of Italians in Cathay, lured by the promise of trade in rich silks, jewels and fruits, and it is reported that the Khan is most tolerant of foreigners. You will travel with a group of merchants who well know the route across the plains of Persia, around the black-hearted mountains, and down through the eastern desert. You will be provided with a full livery of servants, scouts, cartographers, chefs and stable-hands, though it is imperative that you must mention the purpose of your mission to no one save the Khan himself. I shall arrange for a ship to deliver you to Antioch in forty days, where you shall meet with your guides. No, do not protest – I have faith that you will not let me down.'

He rolled the scroll back up and knotted the ribbon tight around it. Then he moved behind my chair and set his hand upon my shoulder in a manner which I imagine was supposed to confer a paternal assurance, though it instead had the opposite effect of making me shudder with worry.

'You will be assisting Prior Tommaso di Lovari of the abbey of Ancona. He has written a much-admired apology for the apocryphal apostles and has worked under my auspices as an emissary once before. Though he is your elder, I believe you will find that the two of you have much in common – aside from scholarly notoriety, you are both renowned for your unfailing devotion to your vows as initiates of the order of our own most Holy Saint Francis. No doubt this will be the beginning of a great partnership.'

He moved in front of me and looked me in the eyes, and I saw once more the purpose that kindled them.

'You will not let me down.'

I shook my head hurriedly, though it was clear that this was not a question. I rose to my feet and gave an awkward bow – it was obvious that I was being dismissed. He did not require my assent, for he must have known that few men would have the courage or lunacy to refuse him. He pressed the wound scroll into my hands, and also a curled length of parchment – containing writing in a cryptic code that, once deciphered, gave details of the journey I was to make – before bidding me good day. Yet just as I was at the door, his voice rang out once more.

'I recall that you and Prior Lovari also have something else in common. Think on it, for more instructions shall surely follow.'

With that the hardy wooden door was hauled closed, and a servant was once again at my arm, escorting me back to my horse.

I had been chosen. The Lord had answered my calls. As I rode back through the villages to the monastery, I was buoyed by a great elation that was tempered only by the fear of failure – and the dreadful repercussions that might accompany it – which such responsibility invites.

✠✠✠

My thoughts are disturbed by the great slurring of the sandflies outside my tent, a cloud of tiny succubae waiting to feast on my lifeblood in a terrible mockery of the Holy Eucharist. I call a servant to enquire whether Brother Lovari is yet awakened. The reply soon returns that he is still given to his slumber, and so I take the opportunity to recline on my bed of lumpy cushions and moth-eaten rugs and return to my reminiscence.

The ship set sail six weeks after my encounter with Giovanni da Montecorvino, and I remember standing nervously at the bow, beneath the great wing-like web of sails, watching my homeland slowly obscured by the grey clouds skimming up from the waves. I spent much of the journey confined to my berth, for the tumbling and jutting motion of the ship much disturbed my constitution, and I admit that more than once I awoke from fevered dreams in which I had imagined myself Jonah trapped in the juddering belly of that great sea beast. Two servants from the monastery accompanied me and did a passable job of preparing meals under such difficult circumstances. I was thus greatly relieved when the high domed towers and grand stone fortresses of the port of Antioch came into sight on the morning of the eleventh day.

My first glimpse of Prior Tommaso di Lovari was granted me when I stumbled down the gangplank, grateful for the solid, motionless earth beneath my feet once more. Just as I was saying a prayer thanking Saint Barbara for helping deliver me safely from the trials of the ocean, I noticed a bulky shadow looming over me.

'By my soul, I don't think I've ever seen a fellow so green about the gills!' he boomed.

I looked up to find myself confronted with Lovari's broad grin. I had thought for a moment, thanks to his great height and strong shoulders – as well as the stark rudeness of his remark – that he was a shiphand or idle workman, and was about to chastise him for his ill-judged comments when I realised with a start that he was wearing the hooded grey robe and rope belt of the Franciscan brotherhood. He had deep-set eyes the colour of moss after a storm. The dark umbra dotted across his cheeks told that he had not bothered to shave that morning.

'Father Lovari?'

'Call me brother, for on this mission we are equals, my friend. Ah, I see your name is apt! I might advise keeping your hood up through some of the areas we will be travelling through, since in some of these lands red hair is considered the mark of evil.' He grinned as he spoke.

I was somewhat affronted by his words. I was, and indeed remain, a firm proponent of the proposition that monks ought to remain austere and sober, so that the common man might see how devoted they are to that most solemn of truths. Laughter is the work of the Devil, and shows only that a man does not understand the severity of his earthly situation.

In short, I was unimpressed with Prior Lovari's deportment. I remember offering him only a curt reply and quickly suggesting that since we were all assembled we might now start our journey without further ado.

Despite our shared purpose, and the wealth of similarities that the honourable Giovanni had spoken of, our initial relationship was somewhat strained. As we journeyed through the first plains of the Persian land, it became clear that Lovari preferred the company of the merchants who were guiding us, and often stayed out long after I had retired to my tent, discussing all manner of useless trivia – about the men's families, their hometowns, the nature and economics of their trade – with them. I even once caught him making jokes with the servants, a sight which perturbed me greatly. I felt that he was not paying proper attention to the observation of the rites and vows of our faith, yet he laughed off my admonishments and even had the audacity to tell me to try to let my spirit be open to the new experiences so that I might learn a little myself.

We sailed the Persian drifts (where we had journeyed for one whole year) for the lands of men whose faces are as though blotted with ink, and whose hearts, it is rumoured, are no less dark; taking with us victuals for twenty months, along with a mass of servants, donkeys, tents, steeds, chefs and lackeys; we had good weather for the most, though the sun brought a sickness that buried the two servants from my own monastery and caused some other men to propose that we turn back. Lovari, however, had a fine gift for persuading each to stay.

It was not until one early summer evening long into our journey, when we had made camp in a winding valley in the dark man's land of singing crows and wild spices, that Lovari and I began to become close. We had been travelling fourteen long months, and though I had at first been content to retire early at night to my prayers and spend the long days' walks or rides in silent contemplation of the wonders of the Lord's creation passing in front of our eyes, I was by then beginning to long for a little lively debate of the type that the monks would engage in back at the monastery. I will readily admit that I was perhaps a touch envious of Lovari's easy manner with the other men, since my own attempts to strike up conversations with the merchants about the esoteric nature of the Trinity or the deeper reasons for the Greek and Roman schism had not produced the animated discussions I had anticipated.

As the sticky, stewing heat had not dissipated with the sinking of the sun that evening, I had taken the opportunity to sit out and take solace in the comfort of the great canopy of stars lit across the dark. I was much amazed to see the moon looming closer than it ever had in Assisi, so that it seemed to fill almost a quarter of the sky, and I overheard some of the servants whispering that if the dark planet was truly tumbling down from the heavens then we were surely entering the end of times spoken of in the Book of Revelation. It was then that I heard Lovari's booming voice ringing out to chide them for their ignorance.

'I am afraid this is not the beginning of the Second Coming, my friends, for the Holy Bible says nothing of the lunar sphere crashing down upon us. No, what you are witnessing is simply a change of position. Just as the length of your shadow appears longer or shorter depending on the rotation of the sun across the sky above us, so the size of the moon appears to differ depending on its position as it roams across the heavens. Think on it, my friends, for the good Lord gave you heads that you might contemplate his work. Now go and tend to the night fires, for your companions are well in need of help.'

His argument was impressive – he had clearly studied the ancient logicians and come to conclusions similar to my own.

'May I join you, brother?' he asked.

I nodded my assent and he approached, gathering up the loose folds of his habit before he settled beside me upon the dry grass.

'I am not usually one to devote my time to idle wonder-mongering, but the sight of the moon calls something within me to sit and look on. It is most calming, for it reveals to us how small our trivial problems are compared to the scale of the Lord's grand design,' he said.

'I think we find it calming because it is a constant,' I replied. 'We see the same moon here in the dark mountains of the heathen land as we see back in our homes in Christendom. Just as Jesus Christ is with us wherever we go, so the light of the moon will not fail to guide us in even the most remote corner of the earth.'

Lovari turned to me and smiled. 'I think you may be right. The natural world is full of signs and messages that the philosophers attempt to unravel. Yet all of them bring us back to the Lord, from the smallest creature whose physiology has been designed so painstakingly through to that great grey orb above us. We are truly blessed.'

'Amen.'

We sat a while, staring upwards, and I found I was pleased by his company. It seemed that I had judged him too soon, and I silently chastised myself for my sin. Emboldened by his speech, I ventured to draw the older monk into further discussion.

'Brother Lovari, may I ask you what your learned opinion is of the philosophers who would have it that the moon is populated, just as the earth is, with cities and animals and men such as ourselves?'

'I fear it is an absurd notion, for it defies logic. It has long been established that plants need heat and light from the sun to grow, and that animals need these plants to eat in order to survive. Thus all forms of life are connected, and indeed depend on one another. Yet any farmer will tell you that if the weather is too hot, the crops will begin to shrivel and die, and the earth will harden to dust. Well, since it is obvious that the moon is closer to the sun than the earth is, since they both float high above us in their arcs, it is a logical supposition that the moon must be much hotter than the earth. No plants would grow under such unyielding heat, and thus there would be nothing for man or beast to feed upon.'

I nodded vigorously. 'Why, I am of exactly the same opinion. I believe a man should strive to learn of the world around him before he begins making suppositions about the heavens.'

Lovari stretched backwards, reclining upon his elbows. 'And yet the astrologers have done much work which truly stimulates the mind. Did you know that they have calculated that the sun is twice the moon's distance from the earth – as even the amateur might attest when comparing their relative sizes as they appear to us. This must mean that the sun travels at double the moon's speed, for both take exactly one day to complete their trajectory around the earth. It is truly fascinating.'

'I am impressed at your most erudite knowledge, brother. If I may trouble you further, might you then tell me your own theory of the purpose of that great grey orb?' I asked.

'Certainly. I believe the moon functions in a similar way to a looking glass. Yet instead of showing us our reflection, it shows us that which we fear. It is a dark, oppressive place, oft bathed in the most impenetrable of shadows. We see a place that has not been visited by the Lord, and so must remain forever shrouded in the darkness that ignorance begets. It is a symbol of Purgatory, of the darkness of life without Grace, and as such would teach us much about our fallen state.'

We talked on for an hour or so, our conversation meandering across the strange bodies that fill the heavens, comparing theories and debating syllogisms, and I soon felt completely at ease in his company. For the first time in over a year I was filled with the warmth that good conversation brings, and I found I was able to think of the monastery back in Assisi with far less longing and homesickness.

Even after we had both exhausted our voices and had nothing further to say, we continued to sit side by side, staring up at the great moon above us. And as I stared it seemed for a while that I could discern great mountains, ruinous valleys, terrible dark rivers and huge desert plains chiselled across its surface. Yet all that seems now as nothing, for I have come to believe that there are no greater mysteries than the mysteries between men.

My eyelids feel fleshy, cumbrous, and I have to pinch my forearm to ensure that I do not drift into a light sleep. This would not have happened in the monastery – I worry that waiting in this accursed desert is affecting me as badly as it is the other men. I know I ought to rise and give victuals and prayers to the Tartar to speed his recovery, as well as check that the servants are not gambling away their rations, yet I cannot seem to rouse myself in this heat.

Many philosophers have remarked upon the strange hold that our memories have upon our person. What I find strange, as I lie here thinking on my relationship with poor, sickly Lovari, is how arbitrarily it picks what to keep and what to discard. It took another nine months from the time we entered the Khan's vast continent to the day when the great stone walls of his capital came into view, and yet it now seems that even some of the strangest wonders of that trip are beginning to fade, to gather dust amid the restless clutter of my memory's storeroom.

We navigated snowy passes and rested in cities conjured from mud and clay; we passed impenetrable walls and fortresses as well as ruins that the merchants told us had been sprawling towns only years before; we met with men who ate fire and others who fed only upon the lowliest weeds and muddy grubs they dug from the ground. We witnessed men born without bones who could thus twist their bodies into strange serpentine shapes, men who talked to stones and men who never left their steeds, even sleeping upon their saddles. We averted our eyes from women who carried their kin in wicker baskets set upon their backs and leather-skinned women who knew no shame and so paraded their wanton nakedness for all to see. We crossed ourselves when we passed red temples where men struck bronze bells and fell to pray to idols of war and gold, and stood agape when we saw whole cities drifting away down rivers, or sinking so deeply into their reflection that we could hardly tell which was real and which ghost. We drifted through storms of dust and storms of hail, passing men with red eyes, black eyes, amber eyes, copper eyes, and, most pitifully of all, a tribe of men who let themselves be ruled by women. We wept most bitterly for them.

Despite these most strange sights, it must be said that most of the travelling was dull. We stopped in cities and villages once every few weeks, and then only to replenish our supplies. Most of the days were spent in barren deserts, on rocky trails, or trudging across overgrown wilds. We lost some twenty-two men in total, including servants, from stomach sickness, heat fatigue, fever, boils, snake bites, bubbling blood and an excess of melancholy humours. The journey was both physically and spiritually gruelling, and Lovari and I soon had our hands full either giving the last rites or listening patiently to increasingly fraught confessions.

Yet our relationship improved, and we were soon spending much of each day in conversation. We had grand discussions about how we might bring the heathens we encountered into God's grace, about the sacred mysteries expounded by the Gospels, and about how we might keep our flock of merchants, workers and servants from falling prey to the many sins that tempted them in these barbarous lands.

Lovari also proved to be a keen botanist, and would often point out the many wondrous examples of the Lord's design on our travels, from the tall green spray of gingko to the ancient bending cypresses and red birches, the hornbeam and the giant redbud, and all the other manifestations of God's love for us, the branches and the leaves reaching out in rapture to their creator, and soon the days passed more quickly.

'It should not be long before we reach the great capital of Dadu,' Lovari told me one morning when we were taking a rest upon a low hill in the dusty fields of northern Cathay.

'But if you are hoping to learn much of the history of these people, Rosso, I am afraid you will be greatly disappointed. From what the merchants have told me, the city is almost entirely new. The ancient dynasties had their capital at Changan, far south of here. The Mongols were naturally keen to make their capital in the north, yet had burnt the great city of Yanjing to the ground during their invasion. From its ashes, they built Dadu. As you can see, it is a city of many names, and the Mongols themselves call it Khanbaliq, the city of the Khan. Be wary, my friend, for cities with many names often have many different faces and, like men, they rarely show their true visage to strangers.'

I had nodded pensively, rather irritated that he had managed to glean more information about our destination than I had.

'Look yonder! Where the great river tempers down to the east. Can you see? Can you see?' the chief scout called out.

Lovari and I were soon at his side, staring down into the hazy distance.

I was initially too embarrassed to admit that I could see nothing save for the blur of the river as it tripped into the horizon. And so I nodded along with Lovari as he exclaimed with joy that we must have finally reached our destination. It was hard not to let some of his excitement infect me. We returned to our horses and, for the first time in many months, we began to move at a vigorous pace, buoyed by the possibility of ending our epic journey before nightfall.

As we began our descent, however, I slowly began to make out the high stone walls of the great city ahead of us. When we drew nearer, the incomparable scale of the city became clear. We joined a wide road and found ourselves milling slowly among traders, messengers, diplomats, soldiers and noble families borne upon great litters, all queuing to enter through the towering city gates.

'It seems you need not worry about your fiery hair being stared at, Rosso,' Lovari said as we joined the long line. 'Look around you – the place will be full of foreigners and strange-looking fellows.'

Though I did not appreciate the joke at my expense, I saw that my companion was right. I could see men of all colours, from all corners of the earth. There were the blackened grub-eaters from the land behind the mountains, Persians with their cropped beards and their covered women, hordes of beggars so scarred from pox or plague that their features were barely distinguishable beneath scabby, sunken flesh, and of course the Tartars themselves, babbling away in their strange, birdlike language. The city, it was told, drew people from across the world: dancers, doctors, drifters, dreamers, painters, poets, musicians, merchants, missionaries, apothecaries and architects, each one desiring something different of it. The great noise that rose from the bustling crowd brought to mind the ceaseless clamour of languages that must have been heard in the tower of Babel.

'It might be said that the Khan himself is a foreigner in this vast country,' Lovari continued, his voice lowered. 'His grandfather was born in the northern plains across the border – he was by all accounts a most fearsome man, leading his band of warriors on horseback through every city in Cathay until each one either surrendered or was razed so completely that nothing of it now remains. He thus created this whole vast empire in only a matter of decades. And so the Khan has inherited the largest kingdom in the world.'

'And now look at all the men waiting to honour him. He is accumulating the whole world's knowledge, and all without having to venture beyond his palace,' I replied.

'As the Book of Proverbs tells us, "A wise man hath great power, and a man of knowledge increases his strength."' Lovari said.

We cut short our exchange there, for we had finally reached the yawning mouth of the city, and the guards – their chests buffed in great scales of leather armour – set about checking our documents and seals.

Never in my life has my mouth been so agog as when I entered that city and stared around in amazement. The streets were divided into narrow lanes, many of which themselves split into alleys and courtyards, and my senses were so assailed that I imagined at first that we had been led into a gargantuan labyrinth. It was truly the most crowded place I have ever ventured into. There were people everywhere: market traders unfurling rugs and exotic fruits upon the street; the natives going about their daily business dressed in the most gaudy cloaks; rust-skinned children skipping naked through dirty puddles; the Mongol guards, with their long manes of knotted hair and thick brown beards, parading around on horses, as is their wont; and many thin, barefoot men swathed in saffron robes, with heads so cleanly shaven that they seemed to glint like polished bronze in the sunlight.

A man with a drooping grey moustache sidled up to me and began shouting 'Hsschshii chiir! Hsschier chiir!'

I leapt back, tumbling into Lovari, for the man was brandishing a pair of squirming adders. As I stood up, I crossed myself and said a quick prayer that Saint Christopher might protect me from these diabolical creatures.

'What manner of place is this?' I stuttered as we pushed and elbowed our way through the narrow, crowded streets. I kept my hand upon the flanks of the pack mule in front of me, lest I should be prised from our party by another madman adamant on practising his witchcraft on a true believer.

We turned a corner and I was amazed to see, rising above the single-storey houses and taverns, a great tower rising in the distance. From somewhere within its confines there burst forth the sound of a mighty drum, sending out deep, trembling notes that rippled through the streets and seemed to linger upon the air far longer than one might countenance.

Lovari shouted above the din that swelled about my ears. 'The drum tower is said to stand at the centre of the city, and it sounds each hour to let the populace know the time.'

'How on earth do they contrive to measure time so exactly when the sun burns upon them without respite from dawn till dusk?' I shouted back.

'It is said to be some trick with water, though that may just be another of the fantastical rumours going around. But look how straight this road it, my brother. The whole city is set out upon the fundamentals of mathematical logic, with streets and precincts arranged almost like a chessboard. It is a wondrous act of design, truly wondrous.'

I could not share his enthusiasm, for I had heard that the people of Cathay put much faith in geomancers, and it made my flesh shiver to think that the city had been arranged using the principles of such black magic, with some heathen magician divining the direction of streets and the most prescient sites for building upon the whim and call of demons and malicious spirits. However, I did not wish to dampen Lovari's high spirits, so I said nothing.

Like the rest of our party, I was soon pushing myself up on my toes and craning my neck in an attempt to view the top tiers of another huge building soaring up through the centre of the packed city. This time I could not hide my amazement. The walls of the great palace – for what else could it possibly be? – were gold and silver, and even from a distance the shapes of the dragons, firebirds and great beasts adorning it were clearly visible. Each successive level was narrower than the one below, and the roof was decorated with vermillion and yellow and blue and many other unnameable hues, so that the place seemed to be aglow in the afternoon light. At the edge of the roofs were great swelling grooves, like curling lips rising up in the beginnings of a sneer. The tiles had been varnished to such a lustrous sheen that the sun seemed to dance upon them.

'The Khan's palace,' Lovari said. 'If we are lucky, we may get to see the great hall, though most of the complex is reserved for the great leader and his concubines, and no other man may enter upon pain of death.'

'What of his advisors?' I asked.

'I am informed that the government is held in a number of stately halls in the outer courtyards. It is rumoured that instead of knights and gentleman from the great families advising the emperor, the men of the Khan's government are chosen by examination alone.'

'I would not trust such foolish gossip,' I replied. 'I cannot imagine a leader would heed the advice of the son of, say, a fish-seller, no matter how well he had learnt to write!'

The guide leading us called out and we turned a corner, taking us onto a wide, open street, lined with wiry trees the likes of which I had never seen before. I looked to some of the buildings, and noticed the signs outside. I was transfixed, and could not but stop and stare. I had encountered the strange, indecipherable language of the Cathaians before, but seeing it so large and so close – the great brush-strokes of bold black ink smeared in dabs and crosses above shop fronts and inn doors – reminded me how far we were from Godly men. Their language is one of smears and smudges, of shadow and swirl. One of the words seemed to depict the ravages of a storm, while in another I thought I could discern the outline of some hellish black beast.

I upped my pace, and returned to Lovari's side.

'I have never seen such a strange and diabolical city so filled with pagan magic,' I said.

My companion gave me one of his infuriating grins. 'It is the rule of travel that men compare the new places they visit with the memory of their homes. Some see only similarities, some only differences.'

I was not much impressed by this response. However, as we turned into yet another small alley, I found I could not keep my peace. 'I see that we are heading in a new direction. Why do we not go straight to the palace? Remember that Father Montercorvino did entreat us to make haste,' I said to my companion.

'It will take a number of days, perhaps weeks, to obtain permission to enter the palace. We must move through the proper channels and observe their rituals with respect, brother, no matter how strange we might find these people, for we cannot risk offending our hosts. Remember that the fate of millions of souls depends upon us.'

We walked on, our noses assailed by countless queer smells as we passed many a tavern. Men sat at crowded tables or perched upon their haunches on the street, feeding on steaming balls of dough or bowls of what looked like lengths of thin grey string. They drank from tiny white cups, fashioned, it seemed, from strange bright shells unknown in our country. It was no wonder they were a race of such insubstantial height if they did not take wine and meat at every meal.

'Then, pray tell me, what is our destination?' I asked.

'Our men have been travelling for close to two years, far from the comforts of home. They are weak creatures of flesh, brother, but they have helped us no end and our journey would have been impossible without them, and so I fear we must turn a blind eye to their celebrations. The merchants have promised them a trip to a street of a certain repute, and so we shall be lodging near there.'

'I am afraid your meaning is unclear to me, brother. Yet I would be glad of a comfortable bed and a hearty meal, if one may be found in this place.'

However, the meaning of his words soon became painfully clear. The street the merchants led us to seemed populated with sinful women – tiny young things who looked barely out of swaddling and old crones missing most of their teeth; thin creatures whose ribs bulged through the fabric of their robes as well as the most lascivious of wobble-fleshed wenches. Many called out to us as we made our way to the inn where we were to lodge, and so I crossed myself and did my best to keep my eyes focused upon the cobbles in front of me.

I had half a mind to quote Scripture at Lovari, yet he was still my elder, and I realised that this was simply another test that the good Lord was putting me through. I am pleased to say that I passed admirably, though on many evenings my rest was interrupted by the cacophony of grunts and moans that spilled from the lines of cheap backrooms surrounding the inn. And so it was that our party had finally arrived in the great city of Dadu, walking straight into the open arms of Sin herself.

# A Delicate Matter of Phrasing

### PART 4 · 26 FEBRUARY 1993 CE

I drew the dull blade against the grain, hunched forward over the bathroom mirror. After finishing another long and boring day in the office – feigning nonchalance in front of Fishlips, trying to stop myself from staring over at Wei Shan's empty desk and thinking about the dead bodies, the mine, the crow – I'd rushed back home for a shave. I couldn't go to meet Li Yang looking like a wreck. Flecks of stubble were collecting in the sink. Even in the weak light of the bare bulb I could see the scuffs on the tiles. A heating box and a loose-swinging showerhead hung to my left, and to my right was a Western toilet – one of those unhygienic things where you sit on a fold-down plastic seat whose warmth tells you someone else was sitting in exactly the same space only minutes before – that my wife had insisted on.

Someone started banging on the bathroom door. I ignored it. My head was beginning to throb, and I couldn't stop thinking about the landslide, the bodies in the hospital. Why couldn't I let it go? Why did I let it enrage me and twist my gut into knots? After all, similar things happen every day. Trains crashing, bridges collapsing, mines falling to pieces, factories going up in flames, all because of some greedy businessmen with good connections cutting corners to bump up the profit margins. But not for long, I thought. The Party knows what it's doing. Once we've built up the economy, once we're level with the Americans, then we'll be ready. This is just the groundwork for the next stage of the revolution, the greatest stage, when we'll pull the rugs out from under all of their feet. But what if … no, that just wasn't worth thinking about. It must happen. Soon. Otherwise what was the point of all of this?

Someone started banging on the door again. My hand slipped and I nicked my chin. Damn. I dabbed at the blood with a shred of toilet paper. The banging grew louder.

'Give me a fucking second, all right? I'll be out in a moment.'

The banging stopped. Footsteps stomped away. I splashed water over my stinging face and reached for a damp towel. Then I grabbed one of my wife's brushes and tried to push my hair around to try and cover up the receding patches at the front. It didn't work. I gave up. Li Yang wouldn't mind. I hoped.

The footsteps were stomping back.

'Dad! Hurry up! What are you doing in there? Mum says you need to come out now so that I can get ready.'

I unlocked the door to find my red-faced daughter standing with her hands on her hips, still wearing her blue and white school tracksuit. Her nose creased up in an expression of distaste that was an exact facsimile of the one her mother always pulls just before she launches into a tirade – like a hawk drawing back its beak, its whole body tensing up as it prepares to swoop towards its prey.

'Dad, you reek of *baiju*. What are people going to think?'

I opened my mouth, but wasn't sure how to reply. I was missing some vital link in this conversation.

'At least you shaved. Now can you let me get ready, please?'

I stepped out of the way and she barged past, locking the bathroom door behind her. I can't remember when we got the lock fitted. I remember in the early days of my marriage I used to wander in and brush my teeth while my wife would be combing her long dark hair, a single blue towel wrapped around her body.

Down the hall I found the bedroom door ajar. My wife was back. My initial instinct was of course to turn around and tiptoe away as quickly as possible, but I needed to at least change my shirt before I met Li Yang, to put on something that didn't have the tang of sweat and nerves and stale smoke. I took a deep breath and walked in.

'Oh, it's you.'

She was buttoning up a high-necked brown blouse, and I wondered for a minute who else she thought it could have been coming into our bedroom. She had a wonderful way of making me feel that I wasn't welcome in my own home.

'Close the door, would you?'

I pushed it shut, and stood awkwardly in the corner as my wife finished dressing. She then began rifling through a small jewellery box embossed with little grey baubles that once looked like pearls.

'Now, about the school celebration this evening.'

That was what my daughter had been talking about. Shit. I fumbled for words.

'Yes. I've been looking forward to it. Only —'

'It's important to Peipei. Her teachers decide what marks she gets, which determines where she can study later, and what kind of job she'll be allocated. So we need to make the best impression we can.'

'Of course. It's important to me too. It's just I've —'

'I can see you've at least made the effort to shave this time. So I'm really sorry to say this, but I think it would best if I took her. Alone. I know half the teachers from meetings at the education board anyway, so I think they're more likely to warm to me. Don't make a scene, all right? Just tell Peipei that something important has come up at work.'

I didn't know whether to laugh or feel offended. I decided I ought to at least make a show of acting as though I cared that she thought I was too embarrassing to take to our daughter's school. I was a Party member working for the local Public Safety Office. If anyone could give a good impression to a bunch of lazy teachers, it was me.

'Shit. You know I care about her too. I'm the one who works every day to pay for her books and her uniforms and all that crap, you know.'

'Don't do this. You remember what happened last time we went down to the school together. And you stink of drink. What do you think her teachers, and her friends, and her friends' parents, are going to think? And if people see us like this ... well, they won't believe we're good citizens. Everyone knows that children inherit their parents' faults, and whatever we do or say tonight is going to reflect on her.'

'Give me a break. My best friend's just fucking died, all right.'

'I know that, and I'm sorry. But someone has to think about our daughter.'

'I think about her all the time!'

'Then prove you care about her by doing something decent for a change. Stop coming home drunk or spending all hours out with other women – don't give me that look, I'm not so dumb that I don't know what it means when you come home smelling of perfume – while I'm here helping with her homework and cooking her meals. Your only discernable social talent seems to be for pissing people off, and your snide little comments aren't going to help to-night, all right?'

She hooked a pair of light blue plastic earrings through her lobes, one after the other. Her ears hadn't been pierced when we got married. Had they? I wasn't sure, and it suddenly seemed important. She stood up and smoothed down her blouse, her dark trousers. Her hair was a rigid bun, and as far as I knew it hadn't been unknotted or left to hang loose for the best part of five years. She looked at me and sighed.

'Just stay here, all right? We can talk about it properly when I get back.'

She twanged an elastic band around a pile of business cards and put them into her handbag. Since when did teachers need parents' business cards? I moved aside to let her march from the room. She always gives off a sense of having a clear purpose. I guess that's what riles me so much.

I sat on the bed and flicked through the jewellery box. Earrings, a few faded bracelets, a necklace I had bought for one of our early anniversaries and a couple of seashells amid the other trinkets. The low purr of voices reached me from the sitting room. I held the shells up to the light, examining the familiar dents and scratches. They still had that smell of salt and brine, as though they'd only left the shore a moment ago. The voices had stopped. I replaced the shells and grabbed a clean jacket from the wardrobe. Time for a quick drink before I went to Li Yang's.

My wife and daughter were just leaving through the front door when I got to the sitting room. My daughter spun around when she heard my footsteps, and I stopped on the spot, halfway to the kitchen. Her eyebrows knotted together, and her lips parted. Both of us were waiting to see what she would say. Was she disappointed I wasn't coming, or relieved? I realised I didn't have a clue. My wife reached out and put her hand on her shoulder, and led them both out. The front door closed behind them. I went to see if there was any beer in the fridge.

It was almost seven. An hour left. I switched on the TV and sat down. The news again, showing a flood in one of the southeastern provinces. Despite my wife's whingeing, I wasn't in any hurry to get one of those new colour television sets. I like black and white. It gives everything a kind of legitimacy. Take these grubby peasants using pots and pans to clear the river out from their bedrooms. In black and white they look like they've just stepped out of history, like the continuance of a long line of honest Chinese peasants, unchanged since the first emperor some two thousand years ago. They remind you that we're all tied to the past, no matter how bitterly we struggle to break free. In colour they would just look like the same unwashed mugs loitering outside the stations and the mines round here, the ones you do your best not to get too close to on account of the smell. You put people in black and white and suddenly they seem to matter.

I finished my drink and turned off the TV. I picked up the beer bottle. We'd had none left the other day. So who'd bought it? There are gaps and holes and fuzzy bits in my memory, but between creeping around a morgue and being buried beneath the earth I was pretty sure I hadn't stopped at the shops for a couple of bottles of horse piss. My daughter? No way. My wife then? Had to be. I stared at the green glass, wondering why. She hated the taste of it, and she hadn't had any of her friends round to our place for months. What had happened to our old friends, the other young couples we used to go out with? Perhaps she'd bought it to soften my reaction to being barred from the school anniversary celebration, or just to make sure I didn't drink anything stronger.

I gave up trying to figure it out and headed down to the car. The streetlights seemed to gain in intensity the closer I got to Li Yang's flat. As I drove I kept one eye on the digital clock flashing its urgent green message in the middle of the dashboard. I didn't want to get there early and look too eager. But neither did I want to be late, and make it look as if I didn't really care. Because I did care, no matter how much I tried to stop myself, no matter how much I tried to pretend otherwise, no matter how sickened and revolted I felt with myself for acting like this. I was a married man. With a good job, a half-decent flat, a beautiful daughter. I was a man with a respectable family and Party membership for fuck's sake. But I couldn't turn back now.

As I approached my destination the buildings grew higher, more imposing. This was the most exclusive, most expensive part of town. Brand new restaurants flanked by marble Fu Lions. Green parks with padlocked gates. Shimmering glass tower blocks everywhere you turned, and yellow cranes swinging through the sky above the riverside flats, hauling bricks up to heaven. It wasn't just Li Yang who lived round here, there was also my boss, the local cadres, the men who'd bought out all the failing factories, and probably a couple of rich, myth-chasing mine-owners too.

It was about a month after I first saw Li Yang at the cadre's retirement party that we bumped into each other unexpectedly in the lobby of a hotel where some big Party bureaucrats were about to be honoured. Even though we had never even spoken, somehow it felt as if we already knew each other intimately, as if we were old friends with so much between us that we didn't need to talk about the past. We crept away after the ceremony, and that was it. I mean, I'd cheated on my wife before. More times than I can remember. But never when I'd been sober. It would only happen after a few too many drinks, when I couldn't bear the thought of going home. And immediately afterwards I'd feel ashamed and revolted and I'd drive back to the house as fast as I could, and, for the next couple of days at least, I'd try my hardest to be the perfect husband, the perfect father. It never lasted, though. A few weeks later I'd find myself doing the same thing, wandering through the seedy alleys on the other side of the river, drink and desire suppressing my shame.

Until I met Li Yang. And then everything was a thousand times worse. I couldn't lie to myself anymore; I couldn't blame the booze or the boredom or my father or my frustration or anything else. It was me. That was who I was. Some people would say it's a bourgeois urge, a failure of that internal class struggle which we all must keep alive in our hearts if we are to retain our moral compass. But I think it's worse than that. Sometimes your heart gets stuck somewhere, and if it's in too deep then no amount of Mao Zedong Thought can wrestle it free.

I left the car behind a flashy new seafood restaurant. I parked in a different place each time. Never too close to Li Yang's building. I passed men in expensive-looking Western suits walking along the river with women in fur collars, and I suddenly felt worried that everyone who glanced at me would somehow be able to guess my dirty secret.

The doorman waved me through without looking up from his paper. I got into a lift that hummed noisily as it juddered upwards to the eleventh floor. I felt my pockets for cigarettes and found that I still had the screwed-up map from the mines in there. It's funny what stays with you. Guilt, anger, shame: they're about as easy to escape from as your own shadow. It's often the things I've tried my hardest to forget – my father, those long years in the grasslands of Inner Mongolia, the faces of the dead – that are the most persistent. As if memory is always playing a trick on you, letting you know that you're not really in control. You're its slave, and you must bend to its will, however much you try to resist.

I knocked on the door. I didn't have a key. I didn't want one. My wife was always rummaging through my stuff, and there was no way I could explain a chunky, ornate brass key like the ones they used in this building. I smoothed down my jacket, and felt a smile making war with my frown for the first time in days as the door slowly opened.

'Hello, you. I wondered when you'd finally make it. Well, don't stay out there, come in.'

Li Yang was wearing a long silk dressing gown, and clutching a lit cigarette. I shut the door behind me and wandered into the huge living room. Despite the number of times I had been there before, I was still amazed at the look of the place. The long, black leather sofas that swallowed you when you sat down. The antique table and chairs somehow saved from destruction in the Cultural Revolution. The huge windows overlooking the flow and turns of the river. The air-conditioning box, hissing out cool air. The silk sheets in the bedroom. The bronze statue of some long-forgotten deity – the Money God, perhaps, or the God of Things That Might Have Been.

'Don't I even get a kiss? You've no idea how bored I've been with all the banquets I've had to attend this week. Entertaining my father's friends, laughing at their jokes, making sure their glasses stay topped up. It's absolutely exhausting, it really is. Pasting on the same rigid smile for Mr Three Factories and his wife Mrs Foreign Facelift, pretending to be interested while Mr Politburo rattles on about his youngest-ever-PLA-general son, and trying to stay polite while Mr I Marched With Mao asks me why I haven't got married and started a family yet. Absolutely frightful. So come on, what are you waiting for?'

I moved closer. Our arms met, then our mouths. The last four days melted away as we kissed. I let my hands graze the softness of the silk gown, the warm arched curve of back beneath. His stubble brushed against my face, his tongue pushed insistently into my mouth. I pulled him closer, breathed him in. Our teeth bashed together.

He pulled away, his lips knit into a smile.

'There's no hurry, you know. We've got all night.'

He pulled himself away and sat down on the sofa. I didn't want him to look desperate, so I stayed standing, running my eyes over the books on his bookshelf. He had a pile of musty hand-bound volumes that I hadn't seen before. They looked as if they'd been picked up at the flea-market. A handful of the classics – *A Dream of Red Mansions*, *Journey to the West*, *The Collected Poems of Bai Juyi*, *All Men Are Brothers* – and a few old books I'd never heard of.

'I didn't have you down as a scholar,' I joked.

'Oh, you'd be surprised,' he said. 'There's some good stuff in there. Everyone knows the ancients were way more liberal than all the stuffed old shirts around today.'

'What are you talking about?'

'Come on, surely even you've heard of people like Qu Yuan?'

'He was a poet during the Warring States period, right? A minister in the Chu government, and a patriotic supporter of the Chu King.'

'Ha! You think verses like "The Longing For Beauty" are about his patriotic feelings? Give me a break. All right, then: what about all the emperors of the Western Han Dynasty? They had some distinctly tall and muscular concubines, if you know what I mean.'

'That's probably why the dynasty fell. No wonder we needed a revolution. The ancients were barbarians.'

'Oh, you're a silly little thing, aren't you? I've got a whole shelf full of classical works about male love. Some could even teach you a thing or two.'

'I don't believe you. All that stuff got destroyed in the Cultural Revolution.'

'Something always survives – you just have to know where to find it. And there is some truly filthy stuff in those books. I've got the diaries of gigolos during the Ming Dynasty, accounts of the life of Long Yang, and all manner of epic verses depicting in detail the art of love. Some of them are quite cheeky, let me tell you.'

'Quite cheeky? That kind of stuff isn't a joke. The Party defines homosexuality as a major psychiatric disorder, you know? You shouldn't have any of that stuff. It's degenerate and dangerous.'

'Of course I know! You think I haven't seen people carted off to prisons, sent to labour camps, just because of their feelings? I've seen men beaten so badly they have to suck their food through a straw, so don't you tell me about the Party and its morality.'

'All right. Don't have a fit.'

He sighed. 'Let's start again. Let me get you a drink.'

He wandered off to the kitchen, his silk robe trailing out behind him. I settled myself on the sofa and waited. When he returned he was carrying a dark bottle and two tall glasses.

'Wine. A gift from one of the ambassadors my father knows. I thought we could share it.'

He pulled a strange metal contraption from his pocket. There was a round gyre with a sharp tip that he pushed into the top of the dark bottle; as he turned the handle of his odd machine, thin silver wings set on either side of the gyre began to rise up towards his hand. I decided to pretend I had seen that sort of thing a thousand times before.

He poured the thick red liquid into the tall glasses. They looked needlessly fiddly, like tiny goldfish bowls balanced upon the thinnest of necks. Most of the men I knew were happy to drink their *baiju* from a rice bowl, a cracked mug or even straight from the bottle if necessary. I took the glass from him and held it at arm's length. The smell was overpowering and slightly sickening. Li Yang clinked his glass against mine. He was grinning.

'In some countries people drink this and pretend it's the blood of a god they murdered.'

I shook my head. 'Piss off. I may not go to all the fancy Western parties you go to, but I'm not stupid. You won't get me that easily.'

He tipped the glass back and sipped. I did the same. Li Yang was watching for my reaction, so I tried my best not to cough or splutter. It wasn't easy. The stuff was thick and sweet and disgusting. I felt sorry for all the people stuck in those poor countries who only had this rancid stuff to drink.

'So, did you miss me?'

'Of course.'

'Oh, I'm not sure I believe you. I think you've been visiting all those burly men down at the police station, and you haven't had time to think of me sitting up here, enduring all these frightful soirées and waiting for you to call.'

He was still grinning. How did he know I'd been to the police station? Sure, it was only a few floors below mine. But still. He reclined back on the sofa, raising his legs and resting them on my lap. I was never sure when to take him seriously.

'It's been a shitty week,' I said, trying to change the subject. 'All I've been thinking about is seeing you.'

'Seeing me? Is that all? Surely you want to do a little more than that, don't you?'

Li Yang downed the rest of his wine and then reached for my glass. We sat in silence for a few minutes, his legs sprawled across me. There were so many things I'd imagined saying once we were together, and all of them had disappeared now I was here.

Li Yang was always saying we ought to go to some of the new restaurants, to the cinema that had just appeared on the other side of the river, or to the skating rink in the Great Dragon Hotel. But I could never see the point. We'd spend half the evening worrying about being seen, and where was the fun in that? All I wanted was to feel him close to me. I could spend an hour just listening to him breathing. I'd never felt like that with anyone else.

Before I'd met Li Yang, all my other encounters had been rushed, urgent. Ten sweaty, shameful minutes, silent apart from the panting and the grunting, and then off in different directions hoping no one had seen us. No names. Never give your name. Never the same man twice. But with Li Yang it was different. There was no urgency. Since we knew we would end up under his silk sheets eventually, we could put it off, delay the moment and savour the anticipation, the frisson in the air between us. I could fool myself into thinking, if only for a little while, that I was at home there, and that I would never go back to my wife, my job, my life.

'Oh, I've got this fantastic machine from Japan. I have to show you. I guarantee you'll love it.'

Li Yang leapt up and ran to the other room. Every time I saw him he had some new toy, some strange piece of foreign junk that was the latest or the most expensive or the most talked about. I certainly had no interest in seeing anything from Japan – it was common knowledge that they were just cosying up to America until they were strong enough to try to invade China once again. Everyone knew they would never give up their ambitions to enslave us. But I couldn't say that to Li Yang. I didn't want to risk sending him off into one of his tantrums.

He came back carrying a circular box with a fat lens at one end. It looked like some kind of futuristic weapon. He pulled one of the chairs out from under the dining table and balanced the machine on it. Then he left the room again.

I thought of some of the other odd contraptions he'd got excited about in the past. Like this cube painted with different coloured squares that you were supposed to twist around until the colours matched up. Or – one of his more enduring obsessions – gum. Short flat sticks that looked like torn-off strips of cardboard. You put one in your mouth and it went soft. Sometimes it tasted of mint so fierce it made your mouth numb, and sometimes it tasted of strawberry. I couldn't decide which was more disgusting. And the worst thing was that you couldn't swallow it. Ever. It made my jaw ache just chewing the damn thing. What was the use of a piece of food you couldn't eat? I'd had to take mine out after a few minutes and hide it in my pocket so as not to offend him. I'd only remembered it when I got back home. By then it was binding the inside of my trousers together like some kind of ultra-strong glue. It had taken hours to wash it out.

Li Yang wandered back in with a shoebox, which he set down next to the chair.

'You're going to love this. I just know it.'

He knelt down on the floor beside the circular machine and his robe billowed across the floor like a shimmering puddle of light. While he tried to get it to work I went to the kitchen to look for something decent to drink. It took me a few minutes to find a bottle of *baiju* hidden behind the Scottish whisky and Russian vodka and a whole horde of other bottles with indecipherable labels. He had dozens of unopened bottles, relics of banquets and bribes, left to fester at the back of cupboards. I poured out a glass and took a sip. It was good. For a minute or two I pretended I was someone else.

By the time I had settled back on the sofa Li Yang had finished with the shoebox and had plugged the circular machine in. It made a sound like an old fridge. He rushed over to the windows and closed the curtains.

'Does it have to be so dark? I'm really not in the mood for these silly games.'

'Don't be such a spoilsport. Now, just keep looking at the wall in front of you.'

I did as he said. I heard him fiddling about, and then a dull light spread a face across the wall. The white teeth blurred first larger, then smaller, before finally coming into focus. It was a huge snapshot of Li Yang, smiling out from what looked to be the lobby of a plush hotel. His head was at least four times bigger than in real life, his eyes huge tawny swirls.

'It's like having a cinema in your own home. Isn't it fantastic? All I had to do was get my pictures reprinted on these little slides, and the light shoots them up onto the wall. Who wants to squint at faded photos when you can recreate the whole experience right in front of you? I've only got about twenty made so far, but don't worry, I'm going to get hundreds more.'

He stood behind the sofa and clicked through the photos, talking me through each picture the machine whirred into focus before me. There was Li Yang at a local cadre's inauguration, Li Yang with his father at a banquet for someone's birthday, Li Yang toasting the happy couple at a wedding, Li Yang with his family at Spring Festival, Li Yang receiving an award from the local college. I sipped my drink and nodded along.

His words soon began to wash over me, and the images merged slowly together. I could guess what he was trying to do. He had worked his life into a neat story, one that I was supposed to collude in. I had no doubt that he believed the narrative he provided along with the photos was true – but it was a truth only he would have recognised. He wasn't showing me the facts of his life. He was showing me the person he wanted me to see. With all the background details of his past, all the parts of his life he didn't like, shifted out of focus or else left out entirely.

'Where are your older pictures? Those were all the last two or three years. Pretty much just the time I've known you. What are you trying to hide?'

He tugged the plug from the wall and let out another little giggle, though I was pretty sure this one was of a different timbre.

'I'd have to dig through another box to find all the older ones. And some of them haven't kept too well. But they'll be top of the pile when I get round to making some more. I just thought you'd like to see the ones you're in.'

'I wasn't in any of them.'

'Oh, but you were. You were in the glint of my eyes in most of them, in the thoughts behind my smile. You were in there somewhere.'

He threw open the curtains. I finished my drink.

'But now I think about it,' I continued, 'you've never shown me a single picture of when you were young. You must have some round here somewhere. Why is that, Li Yang? Were you a fat child, a spotty teenager? Are those photos just too repulsive to be seen?'

'You can be a real bitch, you know? No, I wasn't fat or ugly. Maybe I just didn't enjoy that time as much. Did you think about that?'

He slumped down beside me.

'Now you've put me in a bad mood. I thought you'd like the slides. You might think I have it easy up here, with everything paid for by my father and all these dinners and connections, but it's not like that. When I was a child, everyone told me how great my dad was. They didn't need to add that I'd never measure up, because I could see it in their eyes. I've been called different, strange, odd, conceited, precocious, spoilt … you name it. Always behind my back though, of course. For as long as I can remember I've endured people being nice to me because of my family, even though they make it obvious that they think I'm a bad son, a bad citizen, a bad Chinese.'

'Come on, don't do this. I was only winding you up.'

'I know, I know. But I've always had my father's shadow towering over me. Even back during the Cultural Revolution – thanks to his influence, I did six months or so as a barefoot doctor near the end, but that was it. And, you know, I didn't mind the teasing, all the crap you get from the bitter peasants in their shitty little villages. They thought everyone from the city was a bit odd, so to them I was just the same as all the others passing through. I kind of liked being somewhere where I wasn't judged against my father and found wanting.'

'I know the feeling.'

Li Yang looked at me and tilted his head. Then he smiled and leapt up again. He took my empty glass and darted off towards the kitchen, bringing it back close to overflowing. He knelt down and pressed it into my hand.

'If you could wipe away all of the past and start again, would you do it?'

I shrugged. 'If I could escape my own family, my time in Inner Mongolia, my marriage, some of the crappy bits of my work ... well, I wouldn't be me. I might be happier. I'd certainly be less messed up. But I'd be someone else. And if I was given someone else's life, who's to say I wouldn't fuck that one up too?'

'What if you could escape me?'

'I've tried. I can't.'

'But if you could?'

His eyes flicked up into mine and, though his lips twitched towards a smile, I wasn't sure whether he was teasing me or not.

'I wouldn't dare. I'd suddenly find gang members following me down dark alleys or squad cars pulling me over wherever I went. What with all your contacts, it wouldn't be safe for me in Lanzhou anymore.'

Li Yang pulled me down to him and we kissed. He was urgent, insistent, and I tasted blood when he bit down on my bottom lip. Soon our hands were grasping, stroking, gripping, and it wasn't long before we were stumbling towards the bedroom. Li Yang dropped his robe to the floor and grinned. I watched the slow heave of his shoulders as he breathed, the firmness of his belly, the proud curve of his cock. I pulled off my shirt and yanked down my trousers before moving to him, shoving him down across the bed. He yelped and shrieked in delight. Soon I was on top of him, pushing my weight down and crushing him and spreading him and squeezing him. I searched and found him, the tight knot of muscle gulping me in. The heat, the tug. I closed my eyes and began to move, drawing moans from the flailing body beneath me.

I'm not sure how long it lasted. Time stops save for the thumping of your heart, the duration of your gasping breaths. Afterwards we lay tangled in the clammy silk. I reached for my trousers and dug out the half-finished packet of Double Happiness. For once they seemed strangely apt. I made my way back to the living room to find my lighter, leaving Li Yang sprawled on the bed, as proud of his naked skin as if he had won it in some dubious bet.

The last slide was still glowing on the wall, and as I passed my jaw almost hit the floor. It was a picture of some lavish dinner – everyone was holding up their glasses for the first toast. There was a fat man, sitting right next to Li Yang, holding his glass up and grinning a buck-toothed grin for the camera. I was certain I'd seen him before. Who the hell was he?

'Hey, come here a minute,' I called to Li Yang.

'Why don't you come back in here? Don't think I'm finished with you yet!'

'I'm serious. Come here.'

Li Yang wandered into the living room. 'You called? How may I serve you, master?'

'Very funny. This picture, where was it taken?'

'Some nice restaurant on the riverbank. Three-storey place. I can't remember the name. Why, have you worked up an appetite?'

'No, it's just I recognise this man, but I can't work out why.'

'My business partner? You've probably seen him in the paper or at some important function. His father is the Party representative for the whole damn province. Even my father kowtows to him. Most of my father's colleagues are lining up to offer him their daughters for marriage. You should see them around him – simpering as if they're eunuchs in an imperial palace. His dad spends so much time up in Beijing with the central government that he's become his intermediary for petitions and pleas and all the rest of that wink-and-handshake crap. But I hope you're not getting any naughty ideas – I ought to be more than enough for you. And trust me, he's not your type.'

'Don't be an idiot. His face rings a bell, that's all. I didn't know you had a business partner.'

'You don't think I just sit round here all day, do you? No, no, I'm a businessman, darling! I guess you might call it Venture Capitalism and Speculation. It won't be long before I'm way more important than my father. After all, Hong Youchen says —'

'Hong Youchen? That potbellied greaseball up there is Hong Youchen?'

'So you do know him? How funny. I mean, really, what are the odds?'

'Li Yang, listen,' I said, my mind whirring so fast I thought it might overheat and send smoke billowing out of my ears. 'Please tell me your business interests don't include a mine down in Jawbone Hills.'

'Now you're looking for business tips, are you? I hope you're not thinking of setting up in competition with me. I don't think I'd like that at all.'

'This isn't a joke. That landslide on the news last week. That was because of explosives used in an illicit mining operation. I've spent the last five days trying to piece it all together. People were fucking killed!'

Li Yang shrugged. 'It was an accident. No one knew that would happen. But it's all been sorted out now. And anyway, how do you know so much about it?'

'My friend was there at the time. Investigating. I've been going mad trying to find out what happened to him. I've seen bodies, Li Yang. For fuck's sake. Cold, dirty corpses dragged out of the ground. I've even been down the mine myself, looking for something that might explain any of it. What the hell were you thinking?'

He looked at me as if I'd gone mad.

'If you're that worked up about it, I'll tell you. I certainly don't want you having a heart attack right here in my living room. Do sit down, though, I can't bear it when you pace around like that.'

'What could you possibly have hoped to find out there? I know for a fact there's no gold or diamonds or oil anywhere round there. Just mud and clay. And why on earth was a history professor involved?'

'The history professor? He was the one that got Hong Youchen fired up in the first place. They'd met at some fancy dinner and got talking about an antique map Youchen had recently acquired. Got him really worked up with all these stories about crows.'

'Crows? Are you winding me up?'

I felt sick. This wasn't happening. I thought of Jing Ren's body, laid out in the cold room. The little black tattoo on his arm. The picture on that scrap of paper. The way I'd been torturing myself the whole week when the answers were all here. I felt sick. This wasn't happening. Li Yang sat down on the sofa, curling his legs up, and patted a spot beside him. I couldn't believe he was still smiling, as if it was all just a silly mistake. Reluctantly, I sat.

'Really, it's pretty interesting stuff. As soon as Youchen pitched it to me I knew I had to be a part of it. Let me tell you what he told me. You must know that shamans used to divine the future from listening to the calls of crows, right? Now, one of the early emperors was preparing for a war with the horsemen tribes across the border. On the eve of the battle, the emperor was overcome with last-minute nerves, so he asked his chief shaman to do his thing. The shaman retreated to the hillside and listened to the crow tongue. And as always it told him of death, of widows tearing at their dresses, of children crying for their fathers —'

'Li Yang, cut the bullshit. We're a bit old for bedtime stories! What does any of this have to do with the mine?'

'I'm getting to that, ok? Just listen. The shaman went back to the emperor and told him he had nothing to worry about: the crows had foretold that he would inflict death and destruction on his enemy. The emperor was so delighted with the news that he sent his sons out in the front line so that they could experience the glory of victory. The next morning rolled on, and they rode out into battle. The emperor watched his army get butchered, his sons slaughtered and their heads carried away by the enemy tribes as spoils.'

Li Yang was getting carried away again. Once he got started there was little you could do to stop him. I wanted to punch him in the face, to shake him and tell him how serious this whole mess was. But if I did that I might never find out what any of this crap had to do with Wei Shan. I tried to keep a lid on my anger. 'So let me guess, he took it out on the shaman.'

'Exactly. The emperor ordered his men to pluck out the shaman's eyes and leave him in the centre of the desert to wander blind and lost in the scorching heat until it killed him. And so the blinded shaman found himself alone in the sand dunes of the great plains, the burning sun peeling the skin from his body. He fed on sand, walking for days in the direction of the wind. Death came close enough that he could feel its clammy breath. Then he heard that raspy caw; the call of the crows.

'He followed the sound, crawling through the desert until the birds led him to the corpse of a wild dog. They shared their meal with him, and to survive he ate the raw, bloody flesh. The taste of death made him strong, and he began to follow the crows away from the wilderness. Finally, he came to a town. By then he'd been living with the crows for months, sharing their carrion, and immersing himself in their calls. So as soon as he got to the town, he asked a young boy to take him straight to the house of the local scribe. There he asked for a brush and ink and, despite his blindness, he began to write. He sat there scribbling for four whole days and four nights without moving and, when he got to the end, he collapsed to the floor, never to wake again.'

I couldn't contain myself any longer. 'What the fuck?' I could hear my voice pitching upwards as I rose to my feet. 'Is that it? Is this stupid story somehow supposed to explain all the shit that I've been going through this week?'

'Don't be silly, that's just the beginning. Calm down, will you? You wanted to know about the mining operation, so I'm telling you. Now, the shaman had been writing down what he'd learnt from the desert crows about the future, desperate to set it all down so that it wouldn't be forgotten. He wrote a book that contained everything.'

Li Yang was almost beaming now. There was nothing he loved more than a captive audience. Was he getting off on this? It took a colossal effort to stop my hands clenching into fists. 'What do you mean, everything?'

'I mean, every single thing about the earth. Everything that had happened, everything that was happening, and everything that would happen from then until the world ended, from Qin Shi Huang to Mao Zedong right down to you and me snuggling up together on my brand new bed. Once he fed on death, he saw everything, past and future, just as the crows see. Now, why do you think the shaman wrote all of this down?'

'I'm not playing some ridiculous guessing game with you, Li Yang. Just get to the point, will you?' I couldn't take any more. I pushed past him to the kitchen and poured myself a large glass of *baiju*. Then another. Half of me wanted to run straight out the door and never come back. But the other half had to know where this was all going. For Wei Shan, I told myself. I took a deep breath and walked slowly back to the living room.

'Li Yang, please, enough of this lunacy. Can't you just tell me what the hell you were doing?'

'Don't be a spoilsport. I said I'd tell you. So go on, why do you think he wrote it all down?'

'I don't know.' I sat down again at the end of the sofa. I felt defeated. I felt drunk. Li Yang was still smirking away, and I still wanted to hit him, but there was also something about his enthusiasm that was strangely compelling.

'Go on, have a go.'

'Ok, ok. Hmm, to prove he really could divine the future, I suppose,' I said. 'To make the emperor see the error of his ways? No? All right. Was it some noble bullshit to enlighten mankind, to make people understand their place in the world?'

He clapped his hands together. 'Not even close. The shaman did it because the emperor's punishment had left him bitter and consumed with hatred. He did it to torment mankind. The shaman knew that seeing the future, knowing how you would die and what your life would amount to would be enough to drive most people mad. And he was right. The book destroyed every one of its readers' lives, and those who hadn't read it fought each other to get their hands on it. And it took a few centuries – maybe more – but people finally realised that the book was a curse, and so one man took it and buried it where it would never bother anyone again.'

'Come on then, let's have it, then. What's this old myth got to do with your dodgy business dealings and my dead friend?'

Li Yang's eyes lit up. I couldn't believe it. He was enjoying himself. I'd seen that look before. On the most zealous Red Guards just before they started an interrogation. A look of fire and fervour. He was starting to scare me.

'Look around you. Ten years ago, everyone was still wearing the old blue jackets and caps. Not any more. People are turning back to the old ways. They're moving their beds according to feng shui again, they're going to temples and putting little offerings before the Buddha or Lao Tzu, they're putting the altar to the Kitchen God in pride of place next to the hearth once more. People are asking monks for horoscopes, they're casting hexagrams to predict the future with the help of the I Ching. The Cultural Revolution failed, so now people are looking back to the old ways to give them hope, to give them purpose. They're beginning to believe again. And just as there are always people who believe that eating a potion ground from tiger bones will make you more virile and potent, there will always be people who go looking for this book of prophecy. After talking to that professor, Hong Youchen and I thought that we'd better get in on the act before someone beat us too it. Youchen just needed a little capital to get the venture started. I was happy to help him out. It's exciting – a little adventure, a little mystery. Don't tell me you don't like the idea of finding out what tomorrow might bring.'

'I don't understand – you actually believe this stupid book exists? It's a story, Li Yang! A fucking story. All this money and all this mess for a little adventure? You must have invested millions. Not just digging the mine itself, but on bribes and deals to make sure no one looked too closely at what you were up to. And that history professor – I saw him myself, Li Yang, and he's fucking dead! And my friend. And the others! They're dead! People died and you don't seem to understand or give a shit about any of this!'

My head was spinning and I felt a wave of nausea rush through me. I pushed myself to my feet again. I had to get out of this place. I stumbled towards the bedroom to get my clothes, smashing my foot against a chair.

'Sit down, please. Just calm down … look, you're going to hurt yourself. Listen to me, I didn't know what would happen. It was an accident. And you've no idea how much we paid out to make it up to the bereaved – more than you make in a decade! None of those peasants whose houses collapsed are complaining – they've all got nice little flats in the city now. What else am I supposed to do? Feel guilty? Come on, you're being ridiculous and I'm not in the mood for this.'

I made it to the bedroom and began pulling on my clothes. I'd known it all along but I hadn't admitted it to myself. Now it was blindingly obvious: Li Yang was a fucking child, a spoilt, arrogant little child, completely oblivious to the effects of his actions on the people around him.

'And now you going to run back to your wife, right?' he asked, following me into the bedroom. 'Though of course you won't bother telling her where you've been, or what you've been doing all this time, will you? I guess it's all right for you to have secrets, but when I do something without telling you first you have a hissy fit! Talk about hypocritical.'

'Fuck you.'

'I think you'll find you've already done that, darling.' His mouth was wrung into a sneer, his hair still misty with sweat.

I found my jacket on the sofa and quickly downed my drink. There were a hundred ways I'd hoped the evening would turn out, there were a hundred things I'd wanted to say to Li Yang, to confide in him. But not like this. He obviously didn't understand anything at all.

'You're actually going?'

He had followed me back into the living room. He stood there naked with his hands pressed to his hips.

'You're actually going to walk out of that door and leave me like this? What's your problem? Do you know how much crap I put up with for you? You're a shitty drunk and a bad lover and you're going bald. I get offers from better men most nights of the week.'

'Why don't you invite them round instead, then?'

'Ugh!'

For a moment I could see his eyes growing moist, his face beginning to crumple, then he stormed away, leaving me to slam the door on an empty room.

Back in the lift, I checked my jacket and hair, trying to make sure I looked the same as when I had arrived, but the doorman was still engrossed in his paper and barely looked up as I left.

This whole thing was obviously Li Yang's fault. This wasn't only about the mine. He just didn't know when to stop, when to just let things go. I found my car and began the long drive out of this part of town I so clearly didn't belong in. I realised my whole body was shaking, and I gripped the steering wheel tighter and tighter. The more I thought about it, the angrier I got. Every time, no matter how much I thought of leaving him, of never visiting him again, I always went back. But not this time.

It started to rain. Fuck Li Yang. Fuck the rain. I passed office workers getting soaked in their best suits. Umbrellas being tugged inside out by the wind. People holding smudged newspapers over their heads. The beams of the streetlamps sliced through the rain. Headlights blinked and dipped through puddles. Clouds were sweeping further down to obscure the hills I'd been driving to and from over the past week.

The hills, the city, the province, its crooked Party man and his bastard son, the whole damn country – had anything really changed at all? For all the talk of revolution and class struggle, was it really that different from hundreds of years ago? We'd stopped foot-binding only for baby girls to be left outside to die in weather like this. We'd got rid of the emperor and the power-crazed eunuchs around him only for Party men to hoard power and influence in exactly the same way. We'd freed the proletariat to rise up and control the means of production only so that men like Hong Youchen and Li Yang could buy their whole lives for a bit of loose change.

I swerved away from a mangy dog limping across the road. Fuck. This was Li Yang's fault. He'd even got me questioning my country, questioning the Party. This was getting ridiculous. I needed to get both Li Yang and Hong Youchen out of my head. I needed another drink.

I realised I had no idea where I was going. I sure as hell didn't want to go home and hear about the school's anniversary celebrations. And there was no way I was going back to Li Yang. He'd blown it.

What do you do when everyone you know wants you to be someone you're not? Fishlips wanted me to forget about Wei Shan and get on with my work, and I couldn't. My wife wanted me to be the same man I'd been fifteen years ago, back when we first met and I could happily spend whole evenings just sitting beside her, listening to our brand new radio. Li Yang wanted me to forget the fact one of his idiot schemes had turned my whole life upside down. I just wanted to turn off my brain and get some rest from the whole fucking lot of them.

I was driving in circles, slowing through street after street, trying my best to get lost in a city I knew as intimately as the contours of Li Yang's body. I felt in my pocket. One last Double Happiness. I took the scrap of paper from the mine out of my pocket and cranked down the window. Then I tossed it out. What use was it now anyway? I watched it in the rear-view mirror for a while as it fluttered behind the car, the wind battling to keep it afloat as the rain battered down on it. Good riddance.

I couldn't go home now, and I didn't have anyone to call on except Xiang, but I couldn't face having to explain everything to him right now. There was nowhere left for me but the Golden Dragon Seafood Palace. I drove past my office and continued past the train station, where even now, marching out into the downpour, was a new swarm of migrants carrying their possessions tied up in old sheets. I pulled up next to the bridge. From there I could see the rain wash the colour from the city, leaving only the fuzzy brightness of the blinking streetlamps and the blurred reflection of my shitty hometown drifting out across the murky water.

I parked at the back of the restaurant and made my way inside. As always, it was nearly deserted. I sat down at the usual table, though I'd given up hope of Wei Shan striding through the door and joining me. The manager came to my table and asked my name. Against my better judgement, I told him. He nodded and handed me a letter.

'This came for you this morning. I guess you must be our most important customer – no one's ever got their post delivered here before!'

'Very funny. Just get me a bowl of pork noodles and a bottle of the cheap stuff, will you?'

He chuckled as he walked away. I looked at the little brown envelope. Who the hell was writing to me here? I waited for the bottle to arrive and took a deep swig before I ripped the letter open. It was empty. Very fucking funny. An envelope with no letter. I shook it a couple of times to check whether there was anything small hidden inside. Nothing. This day couldn't get any stranger. I scrunched it up and pushed it across the table.

I felt like shit. So I'd found out why Wei Shan, Jing Ren, Fatty, Spotty and Horseface had died. Did that give their death meaning? Nope. Did it make me feel any better? Not even a little bit. Would the same thing happen again? Yes, in a hundred different cities dotted like scabs across the country, where a million different rich brats do whatever the hell they want as the authorities look away, their pockets that little bit plumper. For every worker crushed, mangled, drowned, burnt, electrocuted, dismembered, asphyxiated, blinded, blown up or buried alive another hundred rush forward, eager to take their place. I took a few more large gulps and closed my eyes.

What the hell was I going to do now? I wasn't sure. I could drink until all these thoughts evaporated and then drive back home in time to hear about the performances at the school celebration before I collapsed on the sofa. I could forget about the mine and the book and the crows and the corpses and do the same thing everyone else does: just close my eyes to the outside world and worry about myself. I could try to be a better father. I could push on with the cases on my desk and try to get back into Fishlip's good books. I could even try to make things up with my wife, though that might be pushing things a bit. I could forget Li Yang. Perhaps I could even learn to stay at home a little more. I could slowly teach myself to become someone else.

Or I could be a hero. I could ignore every order, every word of advice, every instinct and every urge towards self-preservation and get Hong Youchen arrested. Would that be justice for Wei Shan and all the others? No. But it would be a start. Then I could bask in the smug moral glory of it for a few hours before my life got flushed down the shitter. I imagined they wouldn't even bother with rumours and smears. No, the police would probably just turn up and take me away. The papers would be tipped off, of course. My face might make the front page, along with some spiel about my secret deviant encounters. My wife would die of shame at having been married to a degenerate. My daughter would get mercilessly teased and bullied, and her chances of going to a half-decent college would disappear overnight. I probably wouldn't even get a trial. I'd just be locked in some damp cellar for the next decade. Or get sent to a labour camp, maybe even set to work in one of the last state-owned mines – nothing fate loves more than a bit of irony.

And what would I have achieved? Pretty much fuck all. Even if I arrested Hong Youchen, he would never go to trial. He'd be out within an hour. Within a few years he'd take over his father's position, and there'd be a lot of backslapping all round. I couldn't change any of that, whatever I did. But at least I'd feel good about myself. Perhaps.

Or else I could take the bottle and head back out onto the bridge. In this weather the surge would be unstoppable. Let my secrets scatter out towards the sea. It wouldn't matter what people said about me then. My daughter would get pity and condolences, and in time her mind might gloss over the bad memories and remake me into a good man, a well-missed father.

So those were the choices. The slow drift of daily life, the frantic tug against the currents of history, or something more final. I took a deep swig of *baiju*. For a moment I let myself believe in all the crap about the book – that whatever I ended up doing was already written down, somewhere, that the decision was beyond me. It was out of my hands. A sudden gust of wind whipped the restaurant door open and slapped it back upon its hinges.

Then something caught my eye. The postmark on the letter. No, it couldn't be. I pulled it closer and held the scrunched envelope up to the light. It had been posted in Mizhi County, Yulin. I slumped back in my chair.

I topped up my glass. The sly bastard. This was worth a drink. How the hell had he pulled it off? I took a long swig, and slowly it all became clear.

Maybe he'd stopped off on the way to Jawbone Hills to get a packet of Double Happiness or to fill up the car. And when he got there the landslide had already started – he must have thanked his lucky stars he hadn't arrived ten minutes earlier and been buried alive in the mud and rubble tumbling down the hillside. Then he'd probably thought about phoning home or contacting the office to let everyone know he was all right. After all, the call had been logged in the records book and everyone at work knew where he was going – people would start to worry if they heard about the landslide on the news. Then it must have hit him. Everyone would think he was dead.

The sneaky devil. I thought about the Buddhist temple I'd smashed up when I was a Red Guard, and about the old monks who believed that once you died you'd be reborn as someone else and get to start all over again. Somehow Wei Shan had pulled it off. Sure, he'd prattled on about escaping to the countryside often enough, but it was hard to take him seriously. I raised my glass to him. It's not often you get the chance to rewrite history. To catch a glimpse of a possible future, then swap it for another. That took balls.

I could picture him turning up in Mizhi County. After he abandoned his car at Jawbone Hills he must have hitched a lift along the highway, or else used up the rest of the cash in his wallet on a series of bus trips. The journey alone must have taken him days. But it would have been worth it. To start a new life on the farm, to shrug off the intervening years like a snake slithers free from its dead skin. To marry the woman he'd been dreaming about – so what if she was a little wrinkled round the eyes now, a little heavier around the hips? I stuffed the envelope into my pocket. At least one of us had worked out how to get out of this shitty town.

But then another thought entered my head, and I could see Wei Shan once more at the end of his journey. By the time he found his way to the old village his suit would have been creased and crumpled and splattered with mud. He'd probably have done the last part of the journey on foot, trusting his memory to lead him back to a place he'd last visited more than fifteen years before. A smile started tugging at my lips. I could see him as clearly as if he was in front of me. There he was, wearing a dirty suit and trudging through mud and grass towards his dream, his heart beginning to beat faster. And right in front of him, where the farm used to be – where he had spent all those blissful days with the peasant family, working beside them in the field from dawn till dusk, laughing and joking with the farmer's eldest daughter, swapping stories with her brothers, sharing their house and their food, and feeling by the end as though he was one of them – he sees a line of shops, or a block of flats, or a cluster of bright orange cranes and bulldozers working on a new highway. Still, he carries on unfazed – after all, he's come this far. But after asking around, he finds the farmer's daughter is married, with children of her own, and she and her family have long since moved south, to some sunnier province like Yunnan or Guangdong. And then he's stuck – because our future is never what we think it will be. And he can't go back home now, can he?

Then I began to laugh. For the first time in weeks, a giddy snigger burst from my lips. I couldn't stop myself – thinking of him standing ankle-deep in mud and manure in the middle of nowhere, trying to chase a dream. Even though the manager turned around to stare at me and the other customers tutted under their breath, I couldn't control myself. I leaned back in my chair and laughed, a stomach-shaking, hiccup-inducing, eye-watering laugh – a laugh that spilled out from somewhere deep inside of me and rattled my whole body with its erratic rhythm – and I laughed so hard I thought I'd never, ever be able to stop.

# On the Principles of Nature

This is a country with too much of everything. Too much sun between Prime and Vespers and too bitter a wind after the hour of Compline. Too many dangers and diseases waiting to ensnare us. The men have too much haste and recklessness, and their womenfolk too little shame. There are too many deserts and yet, at the same time, I have crossed larger and more fearsome rivers than I have ever seen before. And each one alive with ducks and fish and frogs. Many men spend their whole lives upon these waters, and I have been most intrigued by those Cathaian fishermen who sail out with a number of birds perched upon the prow of their narrow boats. These birds have their necks bound with a knot of rope, so that they may not swallow. The fishermen draw a light over the waters to attract the fish, and then their birds dive. When they return to the surface, the fishermen squeeze the fish from their mouths, and so have their dinner, with none of the long trawl of nets and bait that our own fishermen spend hours upon.

It is amazing how man might harness nature for his own purpose. The world brings us bounteous possibilities – this is why the Lord entreated us to make ourselves the masters of the fish and the fowl, of all the beasts and all the waters of this world.

The sun is now sinking further and further into the west, so I call a servant to find out whether Lovari is yet woken. When I receive a reply to the affirmative, I make my way across the camp to his tent.

He is still shivering despite the late afternoon heat, though his skin is now a sickly white and his cracked lips bloody. I kneel beside him and push a few damp strands of hair back from his brow, so that he might know I continue to care for the state of his undying soul.

'Do not trouble yourself to speak, brother. I can give absolution, and we may sit in silent vigil together.'

'No.' His voice is cracked, harsh. 'If my sickness progresses at the same speed as D'Antonio's and Nazario's, then I still have a little time left. I shall finish before night falls. The rest has done me much good, Rosso, and now we must proceed to the last sin. We may gloss over my years in Ancona, for you know only too well the routine of a monk's life. Understand only this, that whatever my brethren thought of me, there was another man lurking underneath my skin. I never gave up on my quest, and if I studied harder than the other monks, if I read more widely, travelled farther, argued more vehemently, it was only because my goal was more immediate, more important than theirs. Yes, I hid myself in the habit of a hypocrite, espousing poverty and separation for monks, whilst, like my brethren, turning my eyes away from the real poverty and suffering endured by the common people in the villages and towns around us. Monasteries, after all, are designed for hiding in.

'I kept up coded correspondence with the Carthusian – though I never learnt his real name, and that was perhaps the secret of his survival in a time when so many others in our Order were rounded up and purged by various Papal Inquisitions or infiltrated by traitorous spies like that old turncoat, my erstwhile friend Alessio. In each of the journeys I undertook for our patron Montecorvino, and for a number of others, I learnt a little more. Everything pointed to the lands that lie to the east of the country in which our Lord was born to Mary and Joseph. Thus when this chance to go to Cathay arose, I made sure I would be chosen.

'Perhaps it would surprise you to learn how many of the merchants and cartographers that travelled with us at some point or guided us through those perilous mountains and plains were members of the Order, though to my sadness none was able to remain with us for this return journey. And there were many too in the Khan's capital, explorers and traders and merchants who visited me while you were praying or studying, for what better location for secret meetings than that street of iniquity?

'Now, do you remember the day we were finally admitted to the Khan's palace?'

I nod, not telling him that I had myself revisited those days only hours before.

'Indeed. The cherry blossoms had begun to bloom, and I fear both of us were overawed by the magnificence of the gardens through which we were led. We had been waiting to be seen for what, two, three weeks? And all that time we had been told by everyone we met about the great wisdom of the Khan, his remarkable benevolence, and his unparalleled knowledge of every corner of his vast kingdom – we were both easy prey to nerves, I think, and rightly so.'

Lovari manages a tight smile, the dry skin of his lips crackling as they purse.

'Yes, we were well fooled. It did not take long after our many prostrations to realise that the great Khan barely noticed us. It is his eyes – more than his long dark beard, his long knots of black hair, his small curled hands or stubbed nose – that I remember most clearly. They were the night without a moon; great black lakes in which I suspect many a man has drowned. He lounged back upon that fierce dragon throne, gazing at something above our heads. The mass of attendants, servants, guards, advisors and dignitaries, however, would not stop staring at us.'

'They seemed distinctly unimpressed, I recall, by our grey cloth habits,' I say. 'Perhaps they had never seen anything so plain and godly. The thing that most sticks in my memory is the disproportionate amount of words we devoted to our entreaties compared to the number the court interpreter used in his translation to the Khan.'

Lovari coughs up a laugh like a coin jangling in a clay jug then clears his throat.

'Yes, he was a wily creature. As you know, I never judge a man by his appearance, yet there was something reptilian about that interpreter. His great bald dome of a head, his pinprick eyes, his high-turned nose. I too got the feeling that he was not translating everything we said. I spent close to five minutes making a most formal greeting, praising the Khan and his achievements, pledging our support and allegiance and giving the most high regards of our master, and when I had finally finished speaking, the interpreter uttered only three words to the Khan.

'The Khan, if you remember, nodded his head benignly, making it clear that he had to sit through a thousand such speeches daily, then spoke slowly, in a low drawl that, even though I could not understand even a little of that lilting, melodious language, make my bones shiver.

'The interpreter then turned to us to give an explanation, and though his formal Latin was grammatically correct in every way, did you not think there was something odd about the way in which he spoke, as though to part his teeth would have been too much of an effort? His words thus had the timbre of a hiss.

'"His most noble Excellency Kublai Khan, celestial ruler of the kingdom in the centre of the universe, most benevolent of emperors, bids you tell your masters that they may come and build their temple. We welcome trade with any other nation who will bow before us, and indeed already have many believers such as yourselves."

'I know, Rosso, that you were as surprised as I at this last statement, for it is well known that there is no church, no mission and no altar to Christ throughout the entire kingdom.

'"I beg your pardon, sir, but we know of no other Christians here," I believe I replied, as politely as I could.

'The interpreter did not need to turn to his ruler to answer me. "Yes, we have many. Like you they cover their heads and will not wear good clothes."

'I was embarrassed to have to tell him he was confused. "These are Mohammedans, kind sir, not Christians. The distinction is of great importance, for the heathen idol they worship is malice and ignorance, while we strive in the light and truth of Jesus Christ. I know you have many mosques and even the Jews have a fraternity here, yet —"

'The interpreter did not let me finish my sentence, for he held up one of his bony hands, clearly uninterested in my explanation.

'"It matters not. His most royal highness has received tributes from men who pray to shadows, men who worship clouds and men who kneel before the graves of their fathers. The immortal Khan looks benevolently upon you all – if you act as faithful, respectful children, then he will reward you as a tolerant father should. He welcomes men of all faiths, of all creeds, of all ideas. His Excellency well knows that there are as many kinds of truth as there are men."

'I do not know whether you noticed, Rosso, but I was then struck dumb. For as the interpreter bowed his head at the end of his speech, I caught a glimpse of the large scar that could be seen poking out from his robe at the very back of his neck. You must have noted it, for it looked akin to those marks you see on criminals who have been branded by hot irons. Yet do you remember the shape? It resembled a great dark crow, its wings spread in flight. I was amazed, for I had been searching for days for a clue within the great city and had found nothing, yet suddenly the subtlest of hints, which only an adept such as myself might read, was presented before my very eyes. Truly, as the most Holy Bible reminds us, if you seek, then you shall find.

'I barely heard what you were saying, Rosso, as you picked up the thread of the conversation and thanked the Khan for his audience and ensured the necessary red seal was stamped upon our papers, but my ears pricked up again when the interpreter bid us farewell – again, upon his own initiative, for the Khan had clearly lost interest in us by then.

'"Farewell, men of the periphery. His Excellency, the most noble Kublai Khan, exhorts you to enjoy your stay in his kingdom. We ask only that when you return to your own lands you bring word to your fledgling princes that we shall always welcome men who come to us in peace."

'We bowed again – imitating their manner of touching our very heads to the floor in front of the dragon throne – then left.'

Lovari shifts in his blankets, clearly wracked by pains though trying his best to shelter me from the worst of his suffering. Yet it seems apparent that there is something he wants to tell me about the day we spent in the presence of the Khan, so I make an effort to pick up where he left off.

'Yes, brother, it was indeed a strange conclusion to our brief meeting. We had both expected long negotiations, many questions about our motives and purpose, or at least the formal process of swearing allegiances and promises, yet in truth we were in that great hall less than an hour. The Khan and his followers seemed to regard us as little different from fruit-sellers asking to set up a stall on one of the small street corners in the city, and they gave the palpable impression that talking to us for too long would be a waste of their time. I remember I had to do my utmost to stop feeling slighted and offended. I recall also that you felt suddenly sick, my friend, as we were walking back past the cherry blossoms in the courtyard. You were so overcome that you could not walk, and had to be set down upon one of the ornate benches.'

Lovari sighs, and reaches a feeble, shaking hand from his blankets, searching for mine. I let him take it, albeit reluctantly, and feel the clammy damp of his sickness as he squeezes weakly.

'I am truly sorry, Rosso, that I had to deceive you. It was never my intention to bring you into my plans, but I realised that it was perhaps the only opportunity I would get to stay within the palace grounds a little longer. In truth, I felt in rude health, but you were evidently taken in by my charade and, thankfully, you agreed to let me sit and recuperate for a few minutes while you carried the Khan's seals to safekeeping back at our lodgings.

'For a while I waited, feigning stomach cramps and nausea, while the rest of the palace passed me by. It was surprisingly easy to fade into the background, and I am not sure I received more than a couple of glances the whole time as haughty officials strolled past, bearing piles of bound scrolls to the taller buildings beyond the carp pond. It was perhaps close to an hour before I saw the interpreter emerge from the great hall with another advisor and begin to stroll towards the gate. No doubt the Khan was to retire to a great feast, some rich and sumptuous banquet where, I know from personal experience, invitations are rarely extended to functionaries and lowly men of letters.

'As soon as I saw the interpreter I covered my face in an imitation of a fit of coughing lest he should catch sight of me and then, after he had passed, I rose and followed on as casually as I could.

'It was not difficult to pursue that dome-shaped head through the crowds that milled outside the palace gate, though at times I had to push past men bearing petitions and pleas for their ruler in order to catch up with him, for he was a lithe man and carried a good ten years less than me. Men in fine robes were stepping out of the nearby courts and government offices, and it was a hard job keeping pace as they too blocked my path. Yet the interpreter slipped through the busy throngs with ease, and I nearly lost him when he turned abruptly into a tight lane between two rows of tall, stately buildings. I followed him down as quietly as I could, my back pressed against the damp brick as I sidled slowly in his wake, dodging a clutter of stray hens that pecked viciously at my sandals.

'I emerged into a wide, almost deserted street, and thus found it easy to spot the interpreter. Just as in Palermo, the houses of officials and noblemen are nearest the palace, and any common loiterers are soon dealt with by the servants and attendants who wait upon these grand buildings. If I had not been so focused upon my mission, I would have had a mind to stop and admire the fine curved architecture of those great stone houses, their wooden gates topped with brass baubles, and signs covered with strange symbols announcing the status of the families within. The smell of herbs and fragrant flowers drifted from the high walls of the palace behind me, and I felt a sudden pang of nerves when the great gong from the drum tower rang out the hour.

'Do you know, Rosso, that it is the most confident and assured men who are the easiest to pursue? They are so certain of their place in the world, so sure that they are untouchable, so aloof from the lowly world of servants and beggars, that they rarely bother to pay attention to the world around them. I trailed the interpreter all the way to his home, a small house just outside the affluent district undoubtedly reserved for men of titles and ancient honours.

'His abode was of old brick, the red paint faded upon the sloping eaves. I stalked the perimeters, and was a little surprised at how modest the whole place was. Isn't it always thus, that men of intelligence often rise to the top through sacrifice and perseverance, only to stand as mute witnesses to ignorance and indolence? It appeared, from my cursory glance through a low window, that he had only three servants and, in place of wife or children, lived with a handful of elderly relatives. The walls were covered with ink paintings of peonies, bamboo and feather grass, and I saw the old men of the house hold aloft curious vessels of curled wood, which they would occasionally press to their lips before breathing out spiralling plumes of grey vapour. I felt an affinity with the interpreter, for it seemed he too had turned away from women and family that he might remain utterly focused upon his studies.

After an hour, I forced myself to turn back and return to our lodgings in the southern precincts of the city, for I knew that you would be worrying for my health. Yet that was not the last time I visited the interpreter's home. Though I admit the evidence was paltry, I could not give up the idea that the crow scar had been a sign.'

Lovari begins to cough, and I take the opportunity to wipe the sweat accumulating upon his brow. When he finally clears his throat once more, I see his lips are broken and bloodier than ever.

'Over the next few days, I returned whenever I could. Yes, Rosso, those things I said – about having to work on our report for Father Montecorvino, or meet with some of the local merchants or begin

assembling new recruits for our return journey – all were fabrica-
tions. Whenever you and the rest of our retinue left our rooms to
visit the Dragon Observatory or the Source of Law Temple, I crept
out and retraced my steps back towards the lanes that lay in the
vast-reaching shadow of the Khan's palace.

'Something within me was awakened by this stealth, silently
skulking through the city streets as though I was young again, and
I thought of Father Teodoro. Suddenly my tired limbs ached a little less. Whenever the interpreter was at home, he could be seen
sitting at his desk; a bulbous red lamp hung beside him for when
the light grew dim. He seemed to work tirelessly, either hunched
over old books, or else composing himself, making casual swipes
with a fine brush in an ink that he seemed to miraculously conjure
by dabbing a black stick in water. We fellow linguists know, however – do we not, brother? – that though the grammar and guiding
principles of a language may be gleaned from a long study of the
appropriate texts, the accents and stresses of its speech require frequent practice. He must therefore have often met and spoken with
others from our own continent, and this knowledge fuelled my
conviction that he was somehow of vital importance to my search.

'On the second day of the second week that I kept watch, he left
the house shortly after noon. This was not unusual, and I kept a
leisurely pace as he wandered up towards the well-guarded mansions, for it seemed clear that he was simply making his way to the
palace where his services were required. Yet when he ignored the
thin alley leading to the courts and kept walking westwards, my
curiosity was piqued once more. I was confident now that his scar
was no coincidence; I was certain that he knew something of the
Book of Crows, as Father Emiliano had called it, and that he would
lead me to it.

'He was moving away from the centre of the city, away from the
homes of princes and governors, away from the Altar of Land and
Grain, where it is said that countless crops are stored lest there
should be a bad harvest in the future and the populace grow hungry,
and away from the Royal Ancestral Temple, where the Khan and
his family are said to offer sacrifice to the ghosts of their fathers.
However, when he left the more populated streets, navigating the
great curved lake and then passing by the lines of workers digging
ditches which, I heard it said, would one day divert the grand canal

to bring it to the capital, it became increasingly difficult to find spots to hide in. I resigned myself to walking freely in the open, yet, as before, the interpreter did not once look about him. He was a man of a very singular purpose.

'I was quite out of breath when, over an hour later, we arrived at our destination. I was not overly surprised to find that he had led me to a temple, for where else does the learned man turn for answers but to the solace of the eternal? Yet this was no ordinary Cathaian temple, such as those we had seen dotted across the centre of the city. There were no red walls nor high-lipped green eaves, no wooden idols, no dog-faced lions nor ornamental arches; instead, as we passed through the successive courtyards, all I saw were piles of rubble, half-smashed walls and broken bricks, blackened pillars and clumps of ash. Even the oriental cypress trees, which I hid myself behind as I kept a safe distance away from my target, were burnt and shrivelled, the bark a crumbling black, still holding the sweet, cloying smell of bonfires. The whole place must have been destroyed with the rest of the old city when the Mongols invaded, and, while the rest of the capital rose up anew, this place was forgotten. I looked down and saw that my sandals were already caked in a muzzle of dust.

'"Whrar tunge nee poong yowe."

'A deep, throaty voice suddenly emerged from somewhere in front of me. It did not belong to the interpreter. I crouched down and managed to make my way carefully to a hiding place behind a collapsed wall. Once settled behind the smoke-stained bricks, I was able to peer through a crack to see the final, largest courtyard, where the interpreter was talking to a man who had evidently been awaiting him. Yet where the interpreter was lithe, his companion had a quite remarkable girth, as well as a long, pointed beard.

'The interpreter seemed to respond in the same haughty manner we had witnessed in the palace and, though I could not understand a word the two men were saying, it was clear that he spoke always with the same refined hiss. I shall not again try to imitate the prattle of their conversation, Rosso, for that would be tiresome for the both of us. However, one does not need to understand a language to work out what is being said.

'The fat man seemed belligerent, anxious. His breath was so laboured that I could hear it from my hiding place, and he kept a hand to his chest at all times while his dark eyes were restless and agitated. He spoke in long, serpentine sentences that seemed to rise into questions before faltering back into mumbles.

'In contrast, the interpreter stood calm and still throughout the exchange and, when he deigned to reply to his companion's nervous queries, it was only with the most perfunctory of retorts. They had conversed for only a few minutes before the interpreter seemed to grow tired, and raised his voice. The fat man fidgeted, and finally produced a scroll from the folds of his robe, which the interpreter snatched from him. The fat man seemed about to protest, but evidently thought better of it, and so merely bowed his head in resignation. He gave what I presume was a brief farewell before walking away, leaving me to cower and hide once more, lest he see me on his way out.

'When I raised my head again I saw that the interpreter had settled himself upon an old gnarled stump and was examining the scroll, which he had untied and opened and held at arm's length in front of him. I had to see it, so I began to crawl along behind the broken wall, until I felt I could risk raising my head above it. The interpreter did not stir; so involved was he in his study that I doubt he would have noticed had a whole army appeared at the gates of the temple. I was so close that, if I squinted, I could make out the pattern on the waxy red seal that adorned the scroll. It depicted a lone crow, its wings stretched out in flight.

'My heart began to beat a little faster. I had to see more. And here, I must shamefully admit, my curiosity took precedence over my sense of caution. An irrational fear swept over me: that if I did not get that scroll right then, I would not get another chance. We were scheduled to begin our return journey in just under a week, and I knew that if I missed this opportunity – even if it was to come to nothing, like so many of the avenues I have explored – it would be tantamount not only to wasting the whole journey, but also to spitting upon the work of Father Teodoro and all the other brethren who had given their lives in this most sacred search.

'The beauty of our habit is that the loose flow of the cloth enables the concealment of a number of pouches and, if necessary, a dagger. I had one such blade knotted to my calf, for from a young age I had resolved to always be prepared for the darker edge of human behaviour. Yet the constricting silks and tight robes worn by officials and notaries in Dadu meant it was unlikely that the interpreter had any such means to protect himself.

'I could have crept up on him, delivered a blow to the head to render him unconscious and stolen the scroll for myself. I could have pressed the dagger to his throat until he had revealed its secrets to me. Perhaps in my youth I would have done such things, but experience is hard won, and I have always believed that more can be discovered through dialogue and debate than through threats and violence. Thus I stepped forward and revealed myself.

'"Good sir, I believe you have something that may be of interest to me," I said in my most formal Latin.

'His eyes flickered up, though at first they seemed uncomprehending. It must have seemed strange to hear this mellifluous language in such circumstances, perhaps akin to you or me hearing the high Greek of the Old Testament in a tavern. Yet recognition came quickly and I noted that he betrayed little astonishment at seeing me there.

'"No. You come to this nation as a guest, I believe, not as a thief. The dungeons of the Khan will be able to enlighten you as to the distinction between those two categories if you cannot fathom them for yourself," he hissed, before returning to his reading.

'"You do not seem surprised to see me. Perhaps you already know why I have come."

'He raised an eyebrow, then set the scroll down upon his lap.

'"I understand enough of the greed of foreigners to know that they will take whatever they can from the people they purport to help. You do not even know how to read the writing on this paper, let alone of what it speaks, and yet you desire it nonetheless."

'He sighed wearily, in a manner that implied the mild disappointment a father might have for an unruly child.

'"Let us stop pretending. I know what you have there, and it is of vital importance, not only to myself, but to the whole world. It is some kind of map, am I correct? It will lead you to the Last Gospel. You must give it to me," I implored.

'Suddenly his face changed, his narrow eyes creasing into venomous fissures, and he rose to his feet, his bony hands clenched tightly about the scroll.

'"You are a fool. So you recognised the crow, the sign of my brotherhood? No doubt you think you know all about us. You are not the first, and as long as the legend survives there will be more like you. The ignorant, the foolish and the vain."

'He laughed and gestured around him.

'"It is fitting that you have followed me here. There is a lesson for you in this ruined temple."

'I looked around at the crumbling bricks, the swirls of dust and ash, the black tatters of dipped branches. "From dust are all things roused, and to dust they will return. Perhaps you seek to remind me of the futility of my quest by showing me what can happen to a religion if its truths are tugged at, frayed, untangled," I answered.

'His lips twitched, as if caught upon a hook – neither smile nor sneer but something grotesque between the two.

'"The seekers are always men of the most fervent faith, or men of no faith at all. Those in betwixt live content with what they can see and what they can grasp in their hands. No, I come again and again to this old temple because it is secret, it is forgotten, and that is how it should stay. The same is true of the book you seek. It brings only misery, pain, suffering."

'There, I had him – he had admitted he knew of the book. It meant the end of my thirty-year search was in sight. I could not believe how easy it had been, how much turned upon a symbol, a single phrase, a word. I could not help but think that somehow the book exerts such power that it draws those who know of it together, that it tugs us into its circumference, that we are like sun or moon responding to the pull of the earth as we circle it, moving ever closer. I rejoiced that the Lord had chosen me to find his work and bring about a new age at last.

'"Then by the Grace of our Lord Jesus Christ,' I exclaimed, "you do know of the Last Gospel! You must lead me to it, my friend, that together we might lead our brothers – of all nations – out of darkness. I understand that you must test my faith, my motives, yet you must believe that I only seek to bring the truth to light. I have spent my life working for this, that we might save the souls of our brothers who toil in poverty, in ignorance and in shadow."

'The interpreter's features seemed to soften as I spoke and, when I had finished, he sighed and bid me sit beside him on what re-mained of a burnt ledge. This I did – making sure, however, that the dagger strapped to my ankle remained in reach.

'"I too wasted much of my life in search of answers. As you can see, I am a Han, which means I cannot become a high official, a judge, a governor. My grandfather came from a long line of noblemen, and yet I must bow daily before the Mongols and give thanks that the Khan has deigned to allow a Han inside his court. If I were not the best translator in his empire, I would not even have that luxury. Our mansion and farmland was, my grandfather told me, burned in the invasion. History turned, and we were left behind. As the furious army of horseman darkened the horizon, all that was saved – or so our family legend has it – were my great-great-grandfather's books.

'"While other children helped their parents with work or played games in the mud, I read. We lived thirteen of us in a two-room shack beside a marshy plot that grew little but mould, and every winter, to my eternal sorrow, we would set yet more of the books upon the fire to keep our bones from turning to ice. And so I sought to remember every word of every page, that they might somehow survive the years of storm and snow. It was in my fourteenth year that I found a reference to the Book of Crows, and by the beginning of my sixteenth I had moved to Dadu and joined a fraternity of other Han looking for the most important work of our ancestors. If we could find that mythical book and learn from it the events of the future, then we would be able to find the weaknesses of the Mongols and so ensure that we were on the right side when history turned again.

'"I met great men ruined by unforeseen turns of history; mandarins fallen suddenly from favour; landowners and farmers ruined by unexpected storms; governors and generals who had seen their careers cut to nothing by unheralded changes of allegiance. I met monks and philosophers, merchants and mercenaries, and even a number of foreigners like yourself, each consumed by the quest for the book, so that they might ride upon tomorrow's wave. And consume them it did, for each of them was broken by the search, and each was left finding they had thrown away their chances to live in the present day for the chance of a future that never arrived."

'He sighed again most deeply, and for a second I felt a little sorry for him. The sin of doubt is a most oppressive thing. I had never considered that there might have been others besides the Order that sought the book, but the lure of forbidden knowledge is a dangerous thing, as Adam learnt to all of our peril in Eden, and I could only give thanks that the sacred book had not been found by one of these unscrupulous fellows who might have used it purely for his own vainglory.

'"I hope you do not think by this story that you will dissuade me from my crusade. I too have known many men who have given their lives that one of us might find it. And you yourself obviously still long to discover its location – for why else would have you taken possession of that map?"

'He looked up into my eyes, his sallow cheeks puffed out into an inscrutable mask. For a second I suspected that he might laugh at me, but instead he simply shook his head.

'"You still do not understand. If you will hear me out, I will tell you something of our history, for the more I learnt about the Book of Crows, the more I realised what sorrow it had wrought.

'"The Tang Dynasty was perhaps the pinnacle of the achievements of our great Han nation. Thousands of people daily passed through the incomparable capital of Changan in the south, bringing rich goods from distant lands. Music, opera, dance, art, philosophy, poetry; for all of these it was truly a golden age. And when you have all of this – peace, prosperity and harmony – it must seem even more terrible to watch it slipping from your grasp. Emperor Xianzong made a deal with the Devil, as you might say: he gave the eunuchs power so that they would help him overcome the border rebellions that were plaguing his kingdom. He won those battles, but at a great cost. The eunuchs became unstoppable, and when the emperor himself began to challenge them, they smiled demurely and filled his wine glass with poison.

'"His son, the crown prince, was distraught. As soon as he ascended to become Emperor Muzong, he set about trying to find the Book of Crows, believing it could help him find a way to defeat the eunuchs. Popular history records him as a drunk, a pleasure-seeker, a fool. Yet those are lies that the eunuchs propagated – the lesser-known documents I saw all depict him as driven, calculated, noble, fair. As a young man, he was even briefly taught by the great poet Bai Juyi. However, he spent the taxes of an entire year on excavations that might uncover the book, on employing a secret force of men to hunt it down. While he was thus preoccupied, it was easy for the eunuchs to paint him as a negligent, uncaring ruler, and so, only four years into his reign, he too died in highly suspicious circumstances.

'"Emperor Muzong had three sons. To these he left nothing but a dying dynasty and the secret knowledge of the book. They took up the quest, each one committed to restoring the kingdom to its former glories. Yet all this time the eunuchs themselves also knew of the book. So what do you think they did?"

'"No doubt they tried to find the book themselves," I replied, "that they might harness its powers for their own wicked gains."

'"On the contrary, they never had any interest in finding it. Perhaps it is due to their unique physiology, but they are no gamblers. What need did they have of a book that would tell them only what they had already learnt – that men are foolish, gullible, greedy and, more than anything, predictable? They were much too wise to waste their time grabbing at ghosts. Instead, through intermediaries and double agents, they fed false information about it to each emperor in turn. Imaginary leads, wild goose-chases, carefully forged maps, dropped hints and fraudulent documents. And while, one after another, emperors spent their time following the false trails of these precious clues, the eunuchs were able to consolidate their grip upon the country.

'"As I said, Emperor Muzong had three sons. His eldest became emperor at the age of fifteen, and was murdered inside the palace at the age of eighteen. His brother then ruled for more than ten years, but almost half his reign was spent under house arrest after his plot to round up and slaughter the corrupt eunuchs was uncovered. Naturally, the eunuchs found out what was planned well in advance. He died a broken man. The youngest brother inherited a corrupt kingdom beset by military difficulties; as an emperor, he slipped into a paranoia so deep that he ended up purging all religions, from Buddhism and Taoism to Manichaeism, since he had become convinced that there was only one truth, that of the Book of Crows, and all the other faiths had been created simply to try to confuse him. The country fell into famine, war and poverty – it became broken and divided, and it is only now, enslaved to Mongol masters, that we are united again.

'"The book teaches us one lesson. Do not give up today for tomorrow. Prize the moments you have, keep them safe, make them last. The crows sent us a warning. The book is a curse."

'I stared hard at his dark eyes. There was a danger there, some leviathan lurking beneath the calm surface.

'"All you have said of corrupt officials, of wicked men and poor rulers, all of this could be changed if we were to find the book. If we knew what would happen, if we could anticipate each move, we would be able to stop them. And it is clear to me that you still seek the book, so your entreaties to dissuade me from doing the same make you nothing but a hypocrite," I said.

'He leapt to his feet and thrust the scroll beneath the loop of his sash.

'"You idiot! Do you not understand?" he shouted. "I do not mean to read the book. I will make sure that no one ever gets ensnared in its traps. I shall find it and destroy it, and then I will make sure the whole world knows that it is gone forever!"

'I rose to face him, my hand reaching towards my dagger. Yet I vowed to keep myself composed.

'"I cannot allow that most heinous blasphemy. You speak, my friend, of the Last Gospel of Our Lord Jesus of Nazareth, who died that you might live. The whole of Christendom shall not be threatened because of you. Give me the map."

'He laughed in my face, spittle flying from his lips.

'"You are even more deluded than I thought. The Book of Crows was written by my ancestors, the first Han people, who wrote it with brushes made from the feathers of those dark birds. You are an ass to think it has anything to do with your worship of a man who was executed along with other petty thieves and criminals."

'As he spoke I sidled slowly to my left, biding time, so that I might be able to block off the only clear exit from the courtyard. It was imperative that I keep him distracted.

'"I am afraid it is you who are mistaken. I can assure you that this book is no vainglorious history of the Han! Let me tell you the real story behind the Last Gospel. Your blasphemous comments suggest you know a little of the Gospels of Matthew, Mark, Luke and John, which record the details of Christ's ministry on earth. Yet the Church uses these Gospels not as it should, to bring Grace to all, but instead to hold mastery over the common man, to keep him labouring in darkness and poverty. That is why we need the Last Gospel! It shall set us free! And that is why the Church has done its best to deny all knowledge of the great book, for it fears there will no longer be any need of priests and bishops when the whole world can see the complete truth revealed before their own eyes.

'"It was born from the Transfiguration – that miraculous day when our Lord Jesus Christ led Peter, James and John to the top of Mount Tabor, and there Moses and Elijah appeared to Him. A great cloud enveloped our Lord as the Father spoke to Him and He was transfigured. It was there that the Father, from whom all history flows, revealed the future of mankind to His only Son. Coming down from the mountaintop, Christ told those three blessed apostles who had accompanied Him what He had learnt, though He swore them to say nothing until the first of these prophecies – His betrayal and resurrection – had come true. And so it was that some time later, Saint James the Greater set down all he could recall and spirited the book away so that one day the truth might be known. I have no doubt that the book will tell us about the Second Coming, as documented in the Revelation of Saint John – who no doubt learnt about it while upon that very same mountaintop. Mark my words, once I find the book, the whole world will change."

'I kept going, telling the interpreter everything I had learnt over the past thirty years, every single secret of the Order of the Eternal Light, keeping him engrossed so that he might not notice that I was gradually moving to cut off his only chance for escape. I talked of how the apostles had kept the book secret, fearing that new converts would be frightened away by the accounts it provided of the persecutions the first Christians would suffer; of how Saint James carried it east, away from the Roman authorities, so that it might be kept safe until the world was ready for its revelations; of how the early Church decided it could not risk letting its followers know that such a work existed, and so censored all accounts of it from the Synod of Hippo in the fourth century, when the council of bishops agreed upon the canon of Sacred Scripture; of how it lived on in myth and rumour and how the first Crusaders searched for it in the Holy City after the siege of Jerusalem; and of the clandestine work of my companions in searching for the hiding place of this most sacred work.

'"The Western Church has grown corrupt, just like those eunuchs you spoke of. It speaks of charity while amassing money for churches and monasteries as the poor die of famine and plague; it speaks of justice while sending the Papal Inquisitions out to rack and burn the faithful. The Eastern Church, meanwhile, is riddled with heresy, and the barbarous Moors still clamour at our gates.

The Last Gospel shall tell us of the future, and then there will be no need of the Church at all. Think upon it.

'"Today man is stuck thinking only of the present. He thinks of the hunger in his stomach, the pain in his back, the lust in his loins. The Gospel shall teach man to think of the future. It shall free all from doubt, for everyone will be able to watch with their own eyes as prophecy after prophecy comes true, and thus they shall come into the arms of the Lord. All shall see the truth of Jesus Christ for themselves, and shall be bound in a brotherhood of belief. There will be no need for kings, for popes, for money, for countries, for we shall all be united in our Christian mission to fulfil the will of the Lord. Sicilian and Genoan, Han and Mongol, all shall work together to build a new Christian world. Everyone shall see that the Second Coming and the resurrection of the dead are unstoppable, and we will work together in peace. Everyone shall see that all is predestined.

'"The Church fears this brotherhood of men. It fears that when the truth is made available to all then the church shall become obsolete, for who shall need the guidance of a hypocrite priest when they can read of the Lord's plan for themselves? Man is a weak creature, but with the guidance of the Last Gospel he may at last transcend his fallen nature."

'I smiled, triumphant, for I now stood between the lithe man and the only path back out through the ruins.

'"I care little for religions that worship men,' he sneered. 'We too have temples devoted to figures from the past, from the Taoists who study the wisdom of Lao Tzu to the great schools based upon the teachings of Confucius. Some men bow down before their ancestors, and even now we are standing in what is left of a shrine that remembers Siddhartha Gautama, who is said to have escaped this bitter cycle of suffering and rebirth. Yet I spit upon those who would worship another man. For, as you so rightly say, man is a weak creature. He is lazy, greedy, corrupt, and cares only for himself. You do not truly believe that all men shall one day work together, do you? Even if all mankind knew the future, there would be those who would buck against it, those who would challenge it, those who would seek to control it. If you were ever to read the book, you would see that it talks not of peace and fraternity, but of war, carnage, slaughter, revenge. Nothing more."

'His teeth were gritted tight as he pulled the scroll from his sash. He held it aloft with shaking hands and began to tear. The ripping sound let loose something terrible within me, and I bent down and tore the dagger from the knot around my ankle. I was overcome with a most righteous rage, and with a cry I threw myself towards him.

'By the time he had seen me it was too late; though he stumbled back, crying out some fearful oath, his foothold was uncertain and his path blocked. As I raised the dagger, he threw his long, bony hands over his face, unwittingly allowing me to plunge the blade deep into his gut. His scream was shrill, an animal squeal, and I pulled down through the torn flesh much as I had seen butchers do to a bound lamb. His shaking hands flew to my neck, but his lifesource was seeping from him. With one more heavy thrust I split the seams of his stomach and, dragging the dagger back, let the great gaping flaps of skin belch open and spill forth the bloody slop of his entrails.

'He staggered back before sprawling to the ground. I pushed at his body with the stub of my sandal, and managed to turn him onto his back. He was still conscious, blinking up at me, his breaths fast and urgent and his hands clutching frantically at the dark mess that was staining the front of his silk robe.

'"You will not find it," he spluttered from between clenched teeth, his accent slipping and his words half slurred.

'"My friend, if you have strength left, I implore you to commend yourself to the Lord Jesus Christ and seek absolution for your sins before it is too late. I fear that you are one of the damned, but nonetheless I shall say a prayer for the passage of your soul."

'He let out a howling laugh, blood and spittle spraying from his pale lips. He seemed as if he wished to speak, no doubt to curse or mock me, but his words were swallowed by wheezes.

'I knelt down beside his head so that I might whisper into his ear.

'"Know that you have made a most noble sacrifice. Once the Gospel is found, there shall be no murder, no vice, no sin, for everyone shall learn that their own righteous path is written for all to see, and they need only follow the Lord. Our Saviour may yet forgive you, just as he forgives me for doing what needs be done that the whole of mankind be delivered to the light. And so I show you mercy, that you may suffer no more. Give yourself to the Lord, my child."

'And thus I raised the dagger high above my head, then drove it down into the centre of the interpreter's chest, and pierced his heart. He gasped, then his head slumped back, and I waited a few moments in the shade of the blackened trees before touching the points of the cross upon his outstretched body.

'It took me an hour to dig a hole deep enough that his corpse might be safe from beasts, for he was deserving of a Christian burial, whatever his mistaken beliefs.

'I then returned through the streets in which the artisans have their workshops, and managed to considerably lighten my purse by employing the services of a craftsman to mend the scroll by fixing the torn pieces upon a fresh base. This I communicated through a tiresome labour of mimes and gestures, though I was thankful that the craftsman was shrewd enough not to draw attention to the flecks of blood upon the corners.

'Finding someone to translate it proved much more difficult, but my contacts among the merchants in Dadu proved most propitious, and just before we left on this return journey across the deserts I was supplied with a rough translation. It took me many more weeks, working every night in this very tent, to fit the pieces together, until finally, only a few days ago, the secrets of the crow map were revealed to me. No doubt you have glimpsed the old scroll I have been constantly working on, though of course its meaning must have been unclear to you. Suffice to say that when I deciphered it I was elated, for the patterns round which my studies had stalked these many years suddenly became clear, just as when a gentle wind disperses all fog and mist and the mountains beyond are suddenly revealed.'

✥✥✥

Lovari's eyes are closed once more, and he takes a slow, gargled breath. I am unsure how to respond. His recollection of the murder of the interpreter did not invite absolution. He does not even seem to regret it. How, I wonder, does one attempt to ease the passage of such a barbaric man? I try to remember that we are told to love our brothers, though I cannot stop a shiver from trembling through my body as I tuck the blanket up around his damp neck. He is a heretic, a thief, a murderer, and there is not even the slightest part of me that doubts that he will writhe and howl in the torturous fires of hell for all eternity. I do not, however, say this to him.

'Go to my chest – yes, that small one there in the corner – and open it for me.'

Reluctantly I do as he asks. His voice is frail now, a wisp, the sound of moths flitting their wings. Though his sins are repulsive, sickening, most wretched, I shall remain with him. It is up to the Lord to punish him now.

The chest is no bigger than my arm and contains a single scroll. I sit back down and then untie the loop to roll the parchment out across my lap. Lovari is right, I have observed the strange symbols before, for he has not been as scrupulous about hiding it as he might have been, but I do not mention this to him.

'This is what you killed a man for?' I ask, though I already know the answer.

'It is the crow map.'

It is a pitiful thing, dog-eared and stained, with the rips and tears peeling up from where they have been crudely fixed. The depiction of mountains, deserts and rivers is clear enough, and I have no great trouble deciphering its secrets.

'It will lead you to the Last Gospel,' Lovari rasps.

'You are not serious, brother. Now is the time to make your peace, to ask forgiveness for your sins and give yourself over to the Lord's mercy.'

'This is my life's work, brother. I have told you of my most terrible sins that you might understand how important this is. The fate of every Christian soul now rests with you.'

He groans, his eyes bunching up into wrinkled creases.

'You would have me understand that you have broken almost all of the Lord's commandments for a book that tells you what will happen in the future? A book you claim was written by Saint James about what he was told by Christ himself?'

'It is no idle claim!' he coughs, his pale face reddening. 'The Transfiguration showed Christ the magnitude of His task, and He trusted the great burden of this knowledge to his disciples. Saint James set it down because he knew that in the future the book would be found and all men would thus be freed from the tyranny of doubt. But even then the early Church authorities feared its power. Now, after many centuries of searching, it will finally be reclaimed by Men of God, and it shall help us deliver mankind from darkness.'

This desert sickness is clearly overcoming his senses – D'Antonio, Salvitici and Nazario were also delirious towards the end.

'Brother, this is all myth, legend, supposition. The Gospels are the only word of God, and you must put your faith in these or else be damned.'

'It does not matter if you do not believe me. Follow the map, go to the hiding place and see for yourself. You are a master linguist, my friend, and I do not doubt that with your mastery of Greek, Hebrew and Aramaic you are the perfect person to translate this most Holy of texts. You know as well as I how corrupt the Church has become, how evil kings can be. Why else do men like us become monks if not to escape the sin and corruption that has overtaken the world outside our cloisters? Let us have a just world, where all of us might live together as brothers. Let us have the City of God here upon the earth. The Last Gospel can give us that, and so much more. It will tell us the exact date that Christ shall return, that we might prepare for his coming. We will be free from doubt, forever.'

I feel a most bitter anger rising up within my blood.

'Listen to me,' I say. 'Even if all this is true, then this is a book for scholars and bishops, not for laymen. Knowing the future would be a terrible thing for man. We need doubt. Without it, faith is impossible. Knowledge and belief are two different things. Faith is a choice, a daily struggle that we fight to keep on the right side of. Absolute certainty – of what will happen to us tomorrow, of when we will die, of Heaven and Hell – would destroy all need for faith, for that inner struggle that brings us closer to God, and so we would neglect our Holy duties. Without faith we would become like these Tartar barbarians, with no morals and no sense of right or wrong, and we would thus condemn ourselves to hellfire.'

Lovari struggles to rise during my speech, but I try to comfort him and keep him lying back in his blankets. His lips are like pewter.

'You are wrong. It is doubt which is man's greatest weakness. It is that terrible fog of doubt that drives him to steal, to murder, to war. It is doubt that leads to sin, doubt that leads to hatred, doubt that leads to sorrow and pain. Without doubt, all men would be good, for they would be sure that they would be rewarded in heaven. Everything is predetermined, everything is known. If the true words of Christ exist somewhere, then they must be given to the world, Rosso.'

'Think what you are saying, brother. Moses was visited by God in the form of a burning bush, and when the prophet Ezekiel was visited by the Lord he saw fiery clouds and an obscure storm of strange and haunting images which left him bedridden and distressed for days. As you just mentioned, even Christ himself, His most Holy Son, saw only a bright cloud enfolding Him when He met His Holy Father and was transfigured upon the mountaintop. No man, however Holy and just, might look upon the Holy Father and live. No man can understand the mind of God. Tell me, if such a book does exist, then how has it remained hidden for a thousand years? The whole idea seems to be a test of our faith. We must not give in to our temptation, like Adam, and risk the wrath of the Lord by seeking knowledge that was not made for mortal minds.'

'No, Rosso. You ... you do not —'

Again he begins to wheeze and cough, sending blood spluttering out onto his chin and hands. I put my palm upon his brow. It is ice-cold.

'Do not say any more. You are vexing yourself too much: you must rest.'

'Mogao.'

'Brother, I must be firm with you —'

'Mogao. In the caves of the Thousand Buddhas you will find the one true Gospel. Within the many, you will find the one. Among the crowd of false gods and graven images there, find the idol with eyes set in the palms of her hands, burning as though they were nails. Dig beneath her feet, and find the chest that holds the book. Some of my contacts from Dadu promised to send regular scouts to monitor the progress of our caravan – when you make the detour to Mogao, they are sure to realise that I have worked out the map's secret and follow. They will help you bear the book back to Christendom. Promise me, promise me, you will free mankind from the fetters of kings and churches, from the shackles of ignorance and doubt, from the chains of sin. Let us have a new future, a better future, brother.'

He retches, once, twice, but brings up nothing but a little more blood. His breaths are little sodden gasps, those of a drowning man struggling against great waves.

'Promise me, promise me.'

I place my hand upon his own, and try to calm him.

'I promise I shall do what needs be done,' I whisper.

Lovari lets his head fall back upon the cushions and seems to smile, though his face is quickly twisted into a grimace. I retrieve the oils from beside me and anoint his damp head, thus beginning the Last Rites that might sew the seeds of eternal life. I bring my hands together and begin the final prayer, asking for mercy to be shown upon him despite everything, asking that he might suffer only a few centuries in Purgatory before being welcomed back into the Lord's ever-loving embrace.

I say the Lord's Prayer aloud, in as firm and steadfast a voice as I can muster, and when he does not rejoin with a hardy 'Amen' at the end, I know that his time on earth is over. Yet, for a second, my eyes remain closed, for I fear – ridiculously, heedlessly – that his death mask will be hardened into a look of reproach, of disappointment at the cheap trick I used to assail his fears. When I finally venture to look I see that his chest is still, his lips pursed as though on the verge of speech, his dark eyes mercifully hidden beneath the blistered lids.

There are preparations to be made. He shall be buried in a manner befitting a most distinguished prior and scholar, and then we may leave this accursed place and hurry on upon our journey.

✛✛✛

While he was in the desert, the Devil tested the Lord with heresies, fallacies, paradoxes, hypotheses and false cosmologies, and between the skin-shrivelling sun spurring the sand and the buzzing in his ear, Our Saviour must have been driven to the brink of madness. This is how I feel, returning to my tent in the dim light of dusk as some of our men tend to Lovari's corpse. My thoughts are so a-whirl that I barely notice Paul approaching. Fortunately, I am able to cut him off by raising my hand as he begins to speak.

'Tell your men they have no reason to fear any longer, for we shall leave this place tomorrow morning, as soon as our noble brother is buried.'

He bows curtly. 'I shall make arrangements.'

He seems nervous, his eyes flittering left, then right. He is no doubt troubled by the occurrence of yet another death in our camp, and may even harbour some pagan superstition about where the spirit travels after death. I try to put him at ease.

'Do not worry. No one else is ill, at least at present. I pray that we have seen the last of this desert sickness. And you must trust that Prior Lovari's soul is far from here now. He is in the hands of the Lord, who will judge him as He sees fit.'

He does not look at my face. Instead he shuffles upon his feet like some indolent mule. I am growing tired of this; I must retire, get some rest, give some space to my grief.

'I wish to be left alone now. Ask one of the servants to bring some bread and pottage to my tent, for I shall take a little food before I retire. I must pray for our souls, that we will be ready to leave tomorrow morning.'

Paul bows once again. 'I will ask. First you rest, then we go. You need more insects?'

'No, as I told you this morning, I shall not be needing more of those beasts. They have served their purpose.'

Paul's mouth opens but he does not speak, and I wonder for a moment whether he knows. However, I brush such concerns aside, for it is clear that Tartars have neither an understanding of morality nor the sense to grapple with such notions as sacrifice and the greater good, and so I leave him standing most befuddled in the sand and make my way back towards my tent. He calls to me just as I am grappling with the thick netting that keeps the insects out.

'We leave with the light?'

'Yes, we'll go with the first rays of dawn. Make sure everything is ready for the next stage of the journey. Tell the scouts we'll head north towards the outpost at Nami where we can replenish our supplies and where the men might have a day of leisure in reward for their hard work. Be sure to tell them that, so they might know I have been most grateful for their labour and their loyalty.'

'Then we don't go to the caves of Mogao?'

'As I told you earlier this very day, we shall not set foot in that place. We have wasted quite enough time already, and the godly among us would be much offended by such idols as they have there. Remember, the cartographers in our retinue are carefully mapping our path for future travellers, and I could not bear to think that our actions would lead any Christian man to that heathen place and thereby put the very safety of his immortal soul in peril. No, the risk is too great. We head to Nami.'

I slip inside the tent before he has the chance to raise another objection. Now that the party is under my charge, I shall make it a priority to teach the natives some respect for their betters, for it is clear that the common man would be lost to his baser instincts were it not for the firm and guiding hand of his superiors.

I take the frayed map and set it at the bottom of my chest, then sit down upon my makeshift bed. The sound of raised voices and hushed argument soon reaches me from outside. I take some comfort that Giovanni da Montecorvino may soon safely begin his mission and bring the light of true faith to this most desperate land – one does not need to be able to see the future to know that all shall one day bow low before the Lord. Even these barbarians might be saved, and guided along the righteous path. All shall have meat that their souls might feast upon the Word, and the Lord's own emissary on earth, the most Holy Pope, shall be as a beacon to them, for it is the Church alone that may baptise man and so save him from the eternal fires of Hell.

For all his tales of predestination, it is a queer thing that Lovari never stopped to think that his own future was written long ago. Some are damned, and some are saved. Once he found the map, the final steps were unavoidable. Everyone could see how his foolish quest would end but him.

I must prepare myself to give the funeral mass this evening; I shall assuage the fears of our men by speaking of the strength and fortitude of unwavering faith, since it is well known that the common man may be made mad by the truth if it is not carefully administered by a wise and loving pastor. Then I shall to bed, and at dawn we shall away, that soon I might return to the monastery in Assisi and go once again to the infirmary to sit beside my dearest friend and mentor, the elderly burnt monk, Brother Alessio, and tell him that all is safe once more, for the Lord's will hath been done, on earth as it is in Heaven, for ever and ever, Amen.

# Rain at Night

PART 3 · NOVEMBER 815 CE

Yuan Chen,

My dearest friend, please accept my most profound apologies. The horseman brought your recent letters, one by one, and many of them have given me the greatest comfort. To the first – how many moons ago now? – I drafted a reply, complete with a copy of a poem I had been working on, but that was before my life was tipped upside down.

Everything has changed, and it cannot now go back to how it was before. There have been nights when the rain on the rooftop sounds louder than war drums and I cannot sleep, wondering how those poor and cold hundreds – huddled under a few bent stems of bamboo and weathered blankets – survive in the slums and tents near the city walls. There have been days when the shrill call to prayer from the Muslim quarter echoes out like the call of some exotic bird, and I feel suddenly scared by the sheer extent of the ideas in this world that I do not understand. There are even times when I catch myself wandering from room to room, and at those moments it seems as though I am trailing her – each time I enter a room it is as if she has just left, and I must therefore continue my search.

Over the last few days, as a respite from all the packing, I have managed to find a little time to take out my writing brushes. Yet where can I begin? My thoughts fly from me. Sometimes I think it is I myself who have become a ghost, out of time in this great city and dressed in ideas now either outdated or condemned to be forgotten. This thought – which should, by rights, further the depths to which my melancholy often tests me – in truth brings me a little comfort. For if I remain, though the world would forget me, then perhaps she too – somewhere, somehow – is still among us.

Yesterday evening my wife suggested I venture out, to take in the city for one last time, and without thinking I found myself in the officials' gardens on the other side of the Big Goose Pagoda. Do you remember when we first sat there together, watching middle-aged men gather with their songbirds and listening to the trills and warbles of the fringilline orchestra? When I returned I was one of those older men, quite adrift from the world, while young couples and the new crop of mandarins fresh to the capital wandered past me, in thrall to the myriad delights of the gardens. Yet the evergreens, the rising rocks, the lotus ponds, all seemed dull to me now.

You will say I am dwelling too much in my melancholy, that I threaten to let it take hold again. Perhaps that is true. To dwell of course means to live in, to inhabit, and maybe I have lived too long in the shadows of my thoughts. It was a listless hour I spent in those gardens, looking for something I could not put my finger on. However, when I returned to the house I felt something stirring within me, and so, for the first time in many months, I sat with my scrolls and began to write by the light of a single candle. This is the poem that emerged from those sleepless hours:

> *The bloom is not a bloom, the mist not mist —*
> *she is here, then gone.*
> *Midnight comes, then dawn. Dreams linger, disappear.*
> *Morning clouds wipe the night sky clear.*

I shall not venture to explain it, for I trust you will understand it better if I leave it as it is, unadorned by excuses or expositions.

Yet this is not the letter I meant to write – my friend, you will by now have noticed that my thoughts are somewhat scattered. There is a reason for this: I have been sent away. There, I have written it (with shaking hand). After only two meetings with the crown prince, my time has been stolen from me. It was a few days ago that I was summoned to the Central Palace. That alone was enough to set my stomach on fire, and I was barely able to eat in the few days between receiving the fine scroll bearing the message and the date specified therein, even though I knew exactly what would happen once I arrived there.

The Central Palace. I had been in the presence of Emperor Xianzong twice before. Do you remember the first of those occasions? It was shortly after we first met. Though I was nowhere near as young and fresh-faced as you, my friend, I fear I was just as naïve and eager.

I had arrived in the capital only a few days before the imperial examination, and was sleeping on the dirty floor of a tiny house belonging to a man who had known my father. I spent all day and all night buried in books of history and poetry, preparing for the most important day of my life. By the time the morning of the exam arrived, I was overcome with a giddy sense of excitement and responsibility. I recall looking around on the way to the palace and wanting to shout out in glee as I spotted men of every conceivable tribe and nation, as I passed the towering outposts and bright pagodas, the soldiers and the merchants and the mandarins all marked out by their different-coloured livery, and I was beside myself with pride. What other country, I wondered, could boast such noble traditions as a government examination open to all men, regardless of wealth, geography or social standing? (Oh, my friend, see what the city has since done to that earnest young man.)

I recollect little of the exam – the hours passed in seconds. The wait for the results, however, was longer and much more excruciating. Each morning I hurried from the cold and splintered floor of the house in which I resided to the palace gates, hoping beyond hope that the results would be posted. I believe – though correct me if I my memory is mistaken – that it was on the day before the results appeared that we first met at those gates. You were carrying – the image is as clear as if it were branded into my brain – a few loose slips of bamboo on which you had copied a number of poems written by the great Du Fu. I remember you pinned them under your arm as you stood to catch your breath (like me, you had run to the palace gates as fast as you could), and they fluttered mischievously in the spring breeze, as if they might escape at any second. Who spoke first? Can you remember? Was it I quoting from memory some of the poems you could not be parted from (for I was more than a little precocious in those days, was I not?) Or was it you enquiring whether I had composed pastoral or didactic verses for the last part of the examination? I cannot recall. Yet I know that by that same evening – after we had shared our life stories, our favourite poems, our dreams – we both knew we had found that most elusive of things: a true friend.

This reminiscing is perhaps getting in the way of my point; nostalgia, more than aching joints and flutters in the chest, is the true curse of aging. I meant only to remind you of the following day, after which we found we had both received exemplary results, when we assembled with all the other new mandarins in the main courtyard of the Central Palace. Though we were by no means near the front of the nervous group, I was afraid that my heart was beating so loudly the emperor might hear it when he passed by fleetingly to oversee us.

The second occasion on which I saw him was after I had been promoted in the Imperial Library and was cataloguing the collection of officially sanctioned histories of the previous dynasty to be printed using the new system of wood blocks – a labour which required no little amount of delicacy and tact. Once again, it was for a mere few seconds, and as I bowed down I caught sight only of the hem of the long-flowing yellow dragon robe as it swished majestically across the floor. The whole feeling of the room changed, as it might were someone to run in shouting 'Fire!' The great emperor stopped and spoke to one of the chief mandarins – some question about the life of a long-dead general loyal to one of his noble ancestors – and his thunderous vowels, though muted, echoed like temple bells. Then I heard the scuttling of the attendant eunuchs' hurried steps, and the door hauled shut behind the departing group. When I dared look up again, I was sweating and my limbs were shaking.

The recent summons thus heralded the first time I might see more of the emperor than just the glittering fringe of his silken robes. Of course, I have spent many years passing various portraits of our heavenly guide, and though these undoubtedly eschew realistic depiction in favour of exaggeration and flattery, most of the pictures that line the hallways of the Eastern Palace possess a certain radiance and coldness that somehow correspond to the feeling one becomes aware of when the emperor is near. In short, I was afraid. No, that is not quite right. I had been summoned to the presence of the great celestial dragon, the son of heaven, the central force of the entire planet, and there was not a small chance that his wrath would fall upon me like thunder and storm. I was terrified.

By the time I had been led through the echoing antechamber, where the ancestor altar was aflame with pungent offerings, and kept waiting outside the vast meeting hall for a couple of hours, I was dizzy and nauseous. When I was finally admitted, I was almost overcome by the sight of the dazzling banners hanging down around me. As I sunk down to the cold stone floor to kowtow, I could not help but notice how some areas had been rubbed shiny where a thousand heads had dipped down in reverence. For a terrible moment I thought that my back might give in and that I would not be able to rise up to my knees again. It would not be an exaggeration, my friend, to say that it took all my strength to push up from my palms until I rose in front of Emperor Xianzong.

Although for most of my brief time in his presence I kept my head down, I could not help but steal a couple of glimpses at the most important man on earth. Up close, the yellow robe – across which a golden dragon skittered in search of its finely stitched phoenix bride – was dull, a little faded even, while the looseness of the cloth seemed designed to accommodate a man of more than average girth. His face was heavy-set, his pale jowls shaking as he spoke. Beneath a small nose his long moustache was flecked with grey, and it was this that struck me more than anything else; to know that the celestial ruler was at the mercy of time, just as I was at the mercy of his benevolence, somehow had a calming effect on me.

'Bai Juyi, poet of no little renown throughout the capital, former diligent officer of the Imperial Library, and lately counsellor to the crown prince, welcome.'

His voice was timorous and deep, though there was something subdued about the way he spoke, as if his mind was on other things. Hearing my achievements and titles listed, however, did little to arrest my fears.

'My son has only words of the highest praise for you, and I am grateful for the attention you have shown him.'

'Your majesty, it is I who am honoured to have been allowed to spend time with a young man of such remarkable foresight and intellect,' I stuttered in reply.

'Quite.'

There was a short silence, and I wondered whether I had committed an unforgivable breach of etiquette by speaking directly to the emperor. Had he invited reply, or had I trespassed upon his speech? I could feel my leg shaking beneath my robe, and I could do nothing to still it.

'Yet I feel your immense talents are wasted here. You must know that when I first took the throne, our illustrious nation was plagued with the worst kind of treachery: regional governors amassing power for themselves and, in some cases, even turning away from the word of heaven. I have waged war against these rebellious governors and their traitorous armies for more than ten years now, and I will not stop until each one of them bows down before the heavenly rule of the almighty Tang. I have worked hard to subdue these pernicious forces so that I may secure peace and fortune for all of my children throughout the provinces. This has not been easy, and many sacrifices have been made.'

It was not difficult to tell that this was a speech he had given many times, an analysis of his reign that he implicitly expected my agreement with.

'I know you are a loyal servant of the nation. That is why I ask you, Bai Juyi, to help me keep the provinces secure, to help ensure that the people are not threatened by war and rebellion. I am entrusting to you the position of deputy-governor of Jiujiang. I know you will not let me down. My advisors inform me that the people there are a peaceful lot, and bind their lives to the bounty of the great river. I trust you and your family will be happy in your new home. I believe relief from the pressures of life in the city will allow you to spend more time on your compositions. Nature rewards our poets more than citadels and towers ever could.'

He paused, and the room was still. I did not move. Then I realised it was not a pause. This was the end of the meeting.

'Thank you, great majesty. I will serve to the best of my abilities.'

Once again I kowtowed and then retreated from the room, careful neither to turn my back on, nor look directly at, the heavenly ruler. I was ushered from the antechamber before I had time to catch my breath, and it was only on my slow walk back across the city that I had time to process what I had been told. I took the long way home, avoiding the web of alleys that surround the Muslim quarter and making my way instead through the midweek market. I passed huge shivering slabs of crystal white *doufu* set up on wheeled stalls, ornate daggers laid out across makeshift tables, monks shaking pots and waving ink brushes ready to set out horoscopes, and a hundred other common sights that I might never see again. It seemed that everything I looked at threatened to reduce me to tears.

Despite the way the emperor had talked of the new position, it was an obvious demotion. No, it was more than that. It was exile, dressed up in the thinnest of praise. I was being sent thousands of *li* from the palace, to the backwaters of the country, to be forgotten. And when the emperor had said that I would have more time for my poetry, what he had meant was that my new position was largely symbolic, and that I would therefore have few official powers or responsibilities. In short, there would be no one to hear my complaints about corruption, no one to listen to my ideas about reform, no one to influence or inspire. I was not to be allowed to speak to the crown prince again.

I have spent the last few days packing and saying my farewells. Perhaps because of this, I have found myself returning again and again to the memory of how I felt when I first arrived in the capital. I can remember swelling with pride when I sent news back to my family that I had passed the imperial examination. There is nothing greater in the world than fulfilling your family's expectations. Yet I fear I have now let everyone down – especially you, my dear friend, whom I ask to accept my apologies for destroying any chance of achieving the things we once hoped for.

My uncle laying down a fried fish at the base of our ancestral altar – that is the memory that returns each night, as I toss and turn to the tune of the tower bells marking the changes of the guard. I can still see each grey scale gleaming in the candlelight as he set the plate down. It was a giant fish, a mighty river carp, all plump lips and inky eyes. We bowed our heads as he offered it to thank the spirits of our forefathers for watching over me and ensuring my success, and I remember there was a warmth in his voice as he spoke of how proud my own father would have been had he still been with us. My uncle's words – and the dark, unseeing eyes of the pan-fried fish – stays with me until dawn rises over the city walls and the calls for work begin. That day when I brought the banner home, when I told my family I was to be a mandarin, my whole life seemed pure potential. I was in flight on the wings of my dreams. How strange to think that dreams also grow old.

But once again I am letting my memories distract me! How, you must be asking yourself, did all of this come about? Why was I being commanded to swap the ear of the crown prince for an endless expanse of murky fields and fetid marshes? What was it that had marked me out as dangerous? It is simple.

You will recall that in my last letter I told you of my meeting with the crown prince, and that he confided in me that he was searching for the sacred book of his ancestors, which is alleged to record the history of all future dynasties. Now, upon my travels I have met many men entranced by the mysteries of the I Ching, men who have spent their lives trying to divine the future. But for some, the vague auguries brought forth by that mysterious text are not enough. I have met men made half mad by their desire to know what tomorrow might hold. Patriarchs wanting to be sure that the family line will continue to flourish, generals longing to know the outcome of a battle, or emperors wishing to see which of their closest allies might turn traitor – all have attempted to see beyond the sunset.

It is common knowledge, however, that only the dead know the future. To this day, emperors offer sacrifice to their ancestors that they might help guide them forward, and though the practice of consulting oracle bones has now disappeared, necromancers and shamans are much in demand at the imperial court. Therefore it should not have surprised me that the crown prince wished to go one step further and so sought to find this mythical book of prophecy. Yet what he had said troubled me deeply.

Indeed, I wandered from the palace after the meeting I described in my last letter with my head burning with worries. The crown prince's recent predecessors had ceded too much power to the eunuchs, and the disastrous effects of this decision were visible everywhere, from the competent officials frequently being sent into exile to the rows of beggars lining the streets, victims of the mismanagement and corruption that had spread throughout the palace. Yet I barely noticed the beggars crowding round me, nor the noodle-vendors pushing their rickety carts through the streets, nor the novices returning to the temple, for I was thinking about how much worse the country would become if the next emperor wasted the opportunities and resources offered to him in the foolish pursuit of an imaginary book, instead of devoting himself to good government.

However, the prince had asked me for my considered opinion, and thus he deserved a more considered answer. (Perhaps, I thought at first, it might even be some kind of test, designed to help him ascertain whether or not I would make a worthy advisor.) Did it matter that I did not believe in the book, that I found the very concept of it unspeakably ridiculous? Not even a little, for the only thing that mattered was that the prince believed. I therefore decided that before daring to give any kind of answer to the Son of Heaven, I would need to find out more about the book itself.

For once, I had no need to scour the Imperial Library or turn to my more learned friends for advice, for almost instantly I thought of Master Zhong, the shaman I had met on my journey back to the capital. If anyone could tell me something about a legendary book of prophecy, I reasoned, then it would be him. Taking a few days' leave from my duties, I rose one morning before dawn, mounted my horse, and set forth upon my journey.

I travelled alone and, accompanied neither by my wife nor servants bearing provisions, I found I made great speed. After only two nights I had returned to those familiar fields and, soon enough, had found the dwelling I was looking for. As had been the case the last time I had visited, a long line of peasants waited outside the door to Master Zhong's hut, and I found myself smiling at the thought of seeing the kind old shaman again.

While I waited for my turn under the shade of an old tree thick with cicadas, I spoke with a thin, middle-aged woman in front of me. Her face was etched with wrinkles and frown lines, and her faded white robe announced her status as a widow. It did not take much encouragement for her to confide to me that she had come to see the famous Master Zhong to ask him to contact her late husband, who had been killed by the sleeping sickness four moons ago.

'I wish to ask his permission that I might marry again,' she told me in a shrill, plaintive whisper. 'I have had nothing but evil looks and bitter words from the families in the village, but my boys need a father and a home. If my husband's spirit allows it, we could begin again.'

I wished her success, though I could not help reflecting that it is a peculiarly human curse that we so often place our lives in the hands of ghosts. When her turn finally came, she can have stayed in the dwelling no more than a few minutes before she came out smiling, her eyes dancing light with tears. As she made her way down the hillside, I moved to the door to ask permission to enter. A call came back and I made my way back inside that cramped hovel.

There was the old shaman, fat and bald as ever, sitting cross-legged in the centre of the room, and for a moment it was possible to believe that he had not moved from that position since the last time I visited him.

'My friend, you have returned!' he grinned. 'Come, sit down, please. It is so pleasant to see a familiar face. Indeed, this calls for a celebration. Tell me, will you take some tea? Or perhaps a little rice wine?'

'Thank you, but I do not intend to impose upon your hospitality for long,' I replied as I sat down before him. 'Though tell me, how is it you have a supply of rice wine when you live so far from the city? Surely you do not have the equipment here to ferment your own liquor?'

'No, you are quite right. I own nothing more than what you see before you. It is really very simple, my friend. Those who visit me bring gifts. As a kind of payment, you understand, for the services I offer. Some bring a little rice, some bring a handful of eggs, some a bottle of liquor. Whatever they can manage.'

He opened his hands expansively, the ripples of a grin racing across his face.

'And you give them your expertise in return.'

'In a manner of speaking. I do my best to make their dreams come true. It is not so different to what you officials do in the capital with your handshakes and mediations, though I would warrant that most officials demand a lot more in recompense when lending a helping hand to the common man.'

I sighed. 'I am the first to admit that things are not as they should be in the capital. There is corruption, yes, but there are also honest men pushing for reform.'

'Then they ought to beware, for everyone knows what befalls honest officials! My father used to work at court, and I spent the first twelve years of my life in Changan. I would not return for all the silver in the emperor's caskets.'

'Your father was an official?'

'Ha!' he laughed. 'Do you really think the locals would walk for hours to visit the son of a petty bureaucrat? No, he was a shaman, just like his father before him, and his father before him. For a time, he was the emperor's favourite. But I am sure you have not come here to talk about my family.'

'No, please go on. I am intrigued. I am eager to know more about your father,' I said.

'Well, then I shall not disappoint you. Every time the emperor wanted to know which enemy was plotting against him, or what the outcome might be in the latest frontier war, he would turn to my father and ask him to consult the spirits, to tell him what to do. My father was given riches, titles, servants – anything he wanted. All of his dreams had come true. That is, until one day when he was called upon to divine whether the generals on the northern front could be trusted.

'He dutifully climbed the hill outside the city where he knew the crows to reside, and waited to hear them call. He was used to waiting, to spending hour upon hour in prayer and submission to the spirits. Yet night fell, and still he had not seen a single bird. He sat up all night, doubling his efforts. He burnt incense, chanted incantations, danced and sang until his feet were blistered and his tongue was ragged. Dawn crawled up the hill, but no crow accompanied it. My father did not give up. He turned instead to the I Ching, he cast lots, he studied the stars, he summoned his own dead father and grandfather, he drank cup after cup of tea just to witness the patterns the dregs might form, he sacrificed a dove to try to read the future in its entrails, but nothing gave him a clear answer. In the end, he realised the most terrible truth. His powers had deserted him. He would have to guess.'

I found myself nodding along, drawn into his story, for something in it was oddly familiar. 'I thought that it was possible to finds signs in almost anything. Surely it is impossible to look and find nothing,' I said.

Master Zhong smiled again. 'You are a knowledgeable man, my friend. That is the point of augury and divination, is it not? The principle that the whole world is a book that can be read if only we can understand the code in which it is written. The idea that every crack of thunder might be an omen, that every sunset contains within it clues to the outcome of the day it precedes. The world is a metaphor that refers only to itself. A sceptic might say that any fool can try his hand at deciphering signs, and it is true that many fools have tried. What my father found, however, was that the world no longer made sense to him. It no longer seemed explicable. And yet still he had to do what was expected of him.'

'I suspect I know where this story is going. Your father made the wrong prediction, and after the emperor found out he was harshly punished.'

Master Zhong shook his head. 'Perhaps if that had been the case it would have been easier on everyone. No, although he had been forced to resort to making wild guesses, he was shocked to find that events turned out exactly as he had told the emperor they would. Of course, only my father knew that it was just luck. But still he could not bring himself to give up his position of power and all the trappings that went with it, despite knowing that he was no longer able to do anything more than disguise his guesses as prophecies. I think you can imagine the pressure this placed on him. I was only a boy then, and yet I recognised the terrible change in my father. He began drinking, and would fly into terrible rages without provocation. And it was around this time that he began raving about a Book of Crows.'

I drew in my breath. This same book was the reason I had travelled all that way to visit him. Could he have known that?

'I see that you have heard of it. I am not surprised. My father was not the only person who became convinced that there existed a book that foretells the future. Some say that it was written by Lao Tzu after crows brought him messages from the dead. You look doubtful, but you must remember that there are books that the Muslims and the Romans swear have been dictated by gods. Others argued that this book was the work of the Buddha, who told his followers to write down the whole history of the earth that they might see that suffering is repeated again and again, that mankind never learns from his mistakes, in the hope that this knowledge would lead them to renounce this cycle of suffering and embrace nirvana. They are said to have written this black book using ink made from the fallen feathers of crows.'

'Always crows,' I said.

'Naturally. Few other birds feed so wilfully on death. They are perhaps our mirror image, for we humans do the same – picking over the question of death again and again. But in any case, the origin of the book is unimportant. All that mattered to my father was finding it. That was the only way he could think of to relieve the pressure upon him, to set him free from the terrible fear that afflicted him every time he was forced to lie in front of the emperor. He made excuses to go on trips that lasted months, he attended clandestine meetings, he bribed corrupt officials, all in search of this mythical book. After more than a year of looking, he seemed suddenly to give up. He looked defeated. Then one day, on the eve of a battle in which he had predicted success for the imperial forces, he left the house to head to the hills where he had once read the auguries of the crows. We never saw him again. The emperor's army lost the battle, and my family was subsequently driven from the city. That is why you find me here, my friend, living alone in the country. I saw what damage the desire for power, for knowledge, can do to people, and I long ago renounced that world.'

He smiled once more, and raised his hands to gesture to the room around him, as though it was proof of all he had told me.

'But if your father brought about such sorrow from his divination, then why do you continue dabbling in such arts every day?'

'Because it is expected of me. Is there ever any other reason for people to act as they do? I fully intended to live alone, seeing no one and spending my days in uninterrupted meditation. But you know how rumours spread. One man sought me out and asked if I was indeed the son of the shaman who had disappeared with the crows. Once I admitted it, he would not leave me alone. I finally consented to divine his future simply to get rid of him. From that day on I have been fairly besieged with visitors. I find, though, that it gives me a sense of satisfaction, and of course a few comforts that aid my survival.'

'And it does not bother you that the same thing may happen to you as happened to your father?'

Master Zhong began to laugh.

'I can see why you became an official, my friend, for you cannot stop asking questions. But I will answer, as I see you have not understood me at all. I am nothing like my father. Though the locals put about gossip that I can converse with crows, I do nothing of the sort. I know little of divination, and to be honest I am not particularly interested in it.'

I smiled then, beginning to understand. 'You do not tell people's fortunes, do you? I'll warrant you've never even consulted the I Ching.'

'You are right, I have not and nor do I plan to. What a waste of time! I thought you already knew that I am no shaman. I would not know how to draw up a fortune if my life depended on it! I simply tell people what they want to hear. Yes, you may call me a liar and a fraud if you so wish, but do not think I do it for my own gain. I am helping people. Take the woman who entered before you. She was a lonely woman of poor means, treated harshly by her in-laws. All she wanted was the chance to marry again and secure a better life for her children. Of course I did not really communicate with her dead husband to ask his permission for her to remarry. Do you really think I can? But I did tell her that her dead husband granted her permission. I pretended, as I always do. And my words set her free.'

'But how can you be sure you will not cause even more trouble by your meddling?'

'Nothing is certain. If I cannot be sure of the consequences of my words, I tell my visitor that I can be of no help to them. But most people's questions are simple enough. What they really want is someone who will listen to their worries. Let me give you an example. If a man asks me whether he should set about building a house although it might take him years of work, or if he ought to attempt to go into business with his in-laws despite the risks involved, I will always tell him yes, do it now, the omens are good. Because if a person comes to believe that something is possible, that it is within his grasp, then he will work hard to achieve it. It is as simple as that.'

For a while we sat together in silence as I pondered his words. I could not help recalling what he had told me the first time I visited him, when I was still deep in mourning for my daughter. He had urged me to move forward without giving up hope, and for that I had been very grateful. Finally, I spoke.

'I have travelled far from my home and my job to find you again, for I had hoped you would tell me something of the Book of Crows. Yet from what you say, searching for the book brings only pain and misery. But still I must ask, do you believe that such a book exists?'

Master Zhong ran a hand over his great round belly as he mulled over my question.

'No, I do not. It is just a myth, though a powerful one at that. All of us at some point have intimations that life must be more than a random series of events without meaning or coherence, and many yearn to believe that there is some grand purpose that sets the beat to which time marches. Yet there is no safety-net in life, no certainty. For myself, the book is a symbol of everything I seek to renounce – the desire for power that begets only the desire for even more power, the desire to know what we cannot know, to tame the whole world so that it is under our command, to control the things that remain beyond us. The world is to me as it was to my father in the end: ineffable. Yet unlike him I rejoice in that. I have no wish to tame it.

'But there is no doubt that many people do believe that such a book exists, and spend their whole lives searching for it. I should think there are enough works of prophecy around to keep them sated, and I have no doubt that as long as man lives there will be people predicting the future. Perhaps the myth is part of some cosmic joke, a trick the gods or the crows play on us, knowing that we shall never find out its truth, no matter how hard we search. Or perhaps it is simply a way of reminding us that no action, however small, is without its consequences, and any of these might change the world irrefutably. Though to be honest, I prefer not to think of that silly myth at all, for those who live happily in the present should never have need of it.'

I thanked him profusely for meeting with me once again, though in truth his words had done little to dispel my worries. For the entire journey back, as I rode past field upon barren field, I went over my dilemma again and again. Should I tell the prince that there was no such book – that the quest had destroyed each man who searched for it – and risk his wrath? After all, men have been gaoled or exiled for less. Or should I hold silent, and try to exert influence more subtly, gaining the prince's trust and so guiding him slowly away from such foolish notions and back towards the more pressing issue of restoring our great country to its former glory? I arrived home exhausted.

The question, it seemed to me, was this: what is more important to a man, the truth or his dreams? Though all our ideals tell us resoundingly that the former must always take precedence, for the good of the country and the common man, this last year I have come to believe it is the latter that provide kindling for the fire of the heart. If I were to leave the prince to his maddening quest, would I be abandoning my duty to the country? Yet if I were to destroy his hopes of finding the book, would I also risk destroying his ambition of remaking this nation as a grand and noble empire? I felt myself tugged this way and then that, my worries only made worse by my suspicion that if you take away a man's dreams you steal something of his soul – you leave him with a hole inside him, and who can tell what might emerge to fill such a hole?

My sleep soon suffered under the weight of these questions. I found myself retreating back into my grief and melancholy, and I have not been able to escape the strange certainty that she is here. For the idea, however ludicrous, that there might be some book in which every life is written out only made me think of my daughter more and more.

Prompted by the sight of the Big Goose Pagoda rising above the southern market, I tried to take comfort in the Buddhist scriptures. You see, if – as they assure us – our lifetimes are but studs on the great wheel and our souls live many lives, then she might yet be here. And so I find I see her everywhere – perhaps she is one of the birds that alights on the window ledge as the bells from the palace announce the beginning of the day, say, or perhaps the tawny fox that slips past the guards to scavenge in the courtyards of the larger houses after the curfew. It sounds ridiculous, I know. And yet, the bright, blissful song of those birds, the glinting eyes of that fox …

Yet there were many moments during those days leading up to my meeting with the crown prince when I could not bear to even look in the direction of the Big Goose Pagoda, and I had to turn my head away from the great tower of wood and brick, since not only did it prompt thoughts of reincarnation and memories of the fervent debates you and I had once had in its shadows, but it seemed also to taunt me with my own shortcomings. For it was built (as I am sure you well know) a century ago to provide sanctuary for the Buddhist scriptures that the great monk Xuan Zang carried back from the west. The journey took seventeen years, during which time the monk faced snowstorms, dust-storms, sandstorms and thunderstorms, getting lost in the burning desert and near-buried under avalanches on mountains whose snowy tips pierced through cloud, meeting nefarious bandits and vicious border guards and sentries, his sandals baked by the sun and his fingers twisted rigid by the frost – yet still he persisted.

One man – neither emperor, nor king, nor even official – wading out into the slipstream of history and diverting the flow. If he had not brought back those scriptures, who knows the number of truths that would still elude us? One stubborn man holding out – despite innumerable hardships – for the single thing that mattered to him. He defied imperial bans on travel, faced death countless times, and remained away from the comforts of home for all those long years, driven onward only by a singular purpose. If this one man could change history, the pagoda seems to whisper, then why can't I? I sometimes wonder whether I have capitulated too easily, whether I have failed our promises. What is it that makes one man stand firm while another gives in? There must be some untamed drum of the soul whose throbbing beat can only be heard by those who cast aside all else to listen. Or is it that although our convictions sometimes get in the way of life, more often than not life gets in the way of our convictions?

Enough. Let me put a stop to these fruitless meanderings. I do not wish to bore you with the longwinded hypotheses of my dotage, and besides, I have not yet finished telling you about the circumstances surrounding my exile. You see how my thoughts continually slip away from me these days? I am at their mercy now. It was not always thus. You and I used to spend whole evenings debating the finer terms of the fiscal policy of the Central Palace, but now I have barely begun giving voice to one thought when another rushes in and joins the clamour to be heard. But I must restrain myself and return to the story. I came back from my meeting with Master Zhong feeling more confused than ever. I was scheduled to meet with the crown prince three days later, and I had little doubt that he would press me for my opinion. I ate little, and slept even less, spending my nights fidgeting and turning, trying to work out what to tell the crown prince about the Book of Crows.

I became distracted at work, yet would not allow myself to stay at home. Three days became two. Two days became one. The only time I felt at ease was in the early hours around dawn, on the journey between my house and the palace, caught not quite between two worlds. Have you noticed how frost bathes stone pathways in a light sheen that seems to shift when the first fuzzy light hits? It seems as if the ice is slowly moving, rippling out across the city – and though you feel it crunch and crackle beneath your feet, you cannot shake off the perception that the narrow streets and squares have been transformed into a billowing ocean. For those few minutes each morning, as I held the furs tight about my robe and tried not to slip, I was almost able to pretend that I was once again at home in the capital, that it needed me as much as I needed it, that this was where I would remain. Despite the hour, there were always men already hunched over street fires, farmers unfolding sheets of grubby vegetables, servants making the breakfast errands for the mansions, a few coaches rattling down the wider streets and teahouse owners preparing for the day's trade.

The yawning palace guards were never surprised to see me so early – in the current climate of nepotism and sycophancy, it is common to see officials arrive as early as they can in attempts to appear more dedicated than their colleagues. In the gingko garden surrounding the lotus pond, I usually spotted groups of men in official robes bowed together in heated discussion, forming bonds and contacts. There were always eunuchs about, of course (perhaps their unusual constitution allows them to forgo sleep entirely, since it has often been remarked that they cannot be entirely human), yet they are renowned for their ability to move without making a sound, born – I suspect – from the amount of creeping and spying they do.

It was during an early morning walk around the palace gardens on the day before my audience, as I contemplated my dilemma of what to say to the prince the next afternoon, that I happened to meet an old acquaintance of ours. Indeed, my thoughts were suddenly interrupted by a voice booming behind me.

'Ah. The great poet Bai Juyi caught daydreaming within the palace. What has the world come to!'

I turned from my trance to see a strange man before me.

'I – wait. Hua Jinbo? Is that you?'

The man in front of me was short and fat, and must have been close to my own age. He began to laugh.

'I'm sorry, I couldn't resist it! Still, it's a bit of a shock to see you wandering about here when we haven't bumped into each other for, what, five years?'

It was indeed Hua Jinbo. You must remember him. He was the small fellow who used to join us occasionally to listen to those ancient operas about the earliest dynasties. I recall he used to screw up his eyes as we sat in some teahouse or snack-theatre and would sing along to every single performance we watched. I am afraid to say I have memories of us making cruel jokes about such behaviour behind his back, though I think secretly each of us envied his ability to fully immerse himself in those wondrous stories of love and death, of hope and sacrifice. It had taken me a few moments to remember that high voice of his, yet as soon as I did I too began to smile, and bowed down before him.

'Can it have been that long?' I asked.

'I fear it must. If my memory serves me, we last met shortly before I left to take up that post in Fuli. Do you remember we all went to see a performance of The Lotus Bride in Bo's teahouse? What a tremulous voice that young man playing the bride had! Sometimes I wake at night and can still hear his tear-stoked notes trembling in my ears. Oh, that really was one of my favourites.'

'I am sorry to have lost touch with you.'

'And I with you. I had no idea you had also returned to the capital. In the time since we were last together I have devoured your poems ravenously, and I have been wanting to discuss a few of them with you for some time.'

'Perhaps we could share some cups of rice wine by the lake this evening?'

'That would be delightful. Shall we meet at the gate to the sweet bread street at the muezzin's last call?'

And so it was agreed. You may be wondering why I labour so to tell you each word that passed between us, yet let me assure you that there is a reason, for it was Hua Jinbo who helped me make my decision.

Barely had I ensured all the affairs of the day were in order when the sun began glinting on the western towers and the youngest of the apprentices made for the door. I soon left and hurried towards the Muslim quarter.

It was not difficult to spot Hua Jinbo's squat, pale form amid the traders and lean labourers. He beckoned me over, and I reached the alcove where he was standing just in time to avoid the throng of people that set off once that melodious call to prayer rang out from the two-storey tower. We watched the tide of unshaven men in their white cloth hats as they hurried past us, heeding the lingering summons of their faith. It amazed me that even in the midst of the most important work they would set down their tools, and even then I found myself wishing that I could turn from my daily worries to the comfort of the eternal as quickly and as easily.

On the days the cattle market is held in the city, or when the first merchants return from foreign expeditions in the spring, a man risks getting trampled to death by the crowd of Han rushing frantically to be the first to view the wares. Indeed, you are likely to be elbowed and kicked and shoved mercilessly if you impede their progress by accidentally getting in their way. But there was patience and composure in the way the men in the Muslim quarter joined the slow wave building towards their brick-walled temple. I must admit, I know little of their philosophy, yet I wonder whether this calmness comes from having only the single deity to submit to. It must bring a little peace of mind – we Han must choose among the powerful spirits of our ancestors, the Jade Emperor, the former Celestial Emperors who have ascended to heaven, the Dragon of the Wind and the Dragon of the River, the noble Lao Tzu, the Buddha and all the hundred Bodhisattvas, the Money God, the Luck God, the Kitchen God, the demon-catcher Zhong Kui ... no wonder our heads are cluttered as we rush to our destinations, often causing us to forget where it is that we intend to go.

Hua Jinbo led me to a dilapidated wooden restaurant standing near the northern corner of the city walls, and he was quite surprised when I told him I had never visited it before. He seemed somewhat subdued by the muezzin's call, for he said that it reminded him of a song whose title and lyrics always remained, regrettably, just on the tip of his tongue. He professed a weary astonishment that the Muslim men should voluntarily deny themselves the delights of wine, for he found that the sweet, languorous warmth and light-ness of head induced by a few cups were quite conducive to a con-templation of the infinite.

For the most part, we spoke of the old times – isn't this why we hold our oldest friends close, that they might anchor us to the people we used to be? Jinbo could still recall each of the operas we had seen some ten years or more before – he could name the actors, replay perfectly the most haunting scenes, catalogue the hiccups and mistakes, and even hum the themes to aid my ailing memory. Yet as he recounted those long nights in sweaty, overcrowded tea-houses – or described some of the blushing women we often beck-oned to sit beside us, or the way we used to shout each other down, to interrupt and insult as we debated anything that came into our heads – as he drank and spoke and tried to engage me, I could not help but think of all the people who were not there. Not only your-self, my dear friend, but Liu, Wang, Xu and Bao, and the others who sometimes joined our table. It is a curse of age that everywhere you go the past trails behind you, and sometimes it seems that nothing else quite measures up. The world feels more and more like those marked city walls, which, even after they are lavishly redecorated, still reveal – if one examines them closely – the scrawled curses of different years languishing just beneath the new coat of paint.

Our talk soon turned to poetry. Jinbo lavished praise – indeed, perhaps a little too much – upon my Poems of A New Music, telling me how much he enjoyed the folk song rhythms I had employed in order to mimic the voice of the ordinary man (though he seemed careful not to mention the criticisms of the official corruption and excessive taxation that are implicit in many of those verses). He even quoted some of the shorter poems back to me, half singing and half chanting in a high, mournful voice, and by the time he had finished his face was quite red. It was thus only after we had ordered a second bottle of rice wine that the conversation turned to the subject that had been bothering me.

'Can I ask you a question, my friend? Do you still feel the fire burning within you? The fire we once all felt – the passion, the zealous fury at the world and the burning desire to change it, to remake it?'

Jinbo sighed, and let his hand curl around the knot that bound his thinning hair.

'Fires cool, or else they consume everything in sight. There is no other way. Do not misunderstand me: I still yearn for change, but I have learnt the value of pragmatism. Besides, it is impossible to work so long within the palace and not become caught up in its machinations, in the slow and arduous balancing act of politics, the delicate compromises and the careful diplomacy. Change comes slowly. It takes patience and reserve, not youthful bluster and idealism.'

I nodded in agreement, and my friend raised a toast to the un-dimmed dreams of our youth, and to the peculiar sorrows only experience can teach.

It was only then that I saw the sadness etched upon his face. How old he looked, how tired. That passionate young man who used to weep and rage at every tragedy or instance of injustice in those teahouse operas – all those years of toiling within the palace bureaucracy seemed to have worn him down, made him wistful and lachrymose. It was then that I decided to confide in him, for I knew he would understand. Thus I told him of the prince's words, of the Book of Crows, and of everything Master Zhong had told me – all the doubts and questions that had been spinning like a fierce gale within my mind those past weeks.

Hua Jinbo's answer was simple: he advised me not to tell the prince what I had learnt, not to risk everything because of some useless vestige of idealism. The truth, he told me, was a luxury not everyone could afford. 'Why waste this opportunity to guide that impressionable young man?' he asked me. 'Gain his trust, and work from the inside to make the country a better place. You would only make an enemy of him if you were to tell him the book did not exist, for no one can bear to see their hopes torn away.'

The careworn look in his eyes told me that he was speaking from experience. I raised a toast and thanked him. He had helped me make my decision. I knew what I had to do.

The following day I met with the prince. The following week I was summoned by the emperor. You know the rest.

Yes, against all my better judgement, against all the sage advice of our old friend, I told the prince the truth. I said what I had to say – that the book was nothing but a myth, a foolish dream, and that the longer he spent chasing such airy fantasies the more the eunuchs would consolidate their power and the faster the country would fall into ruin. There is no need to repeat all the arguments that passed between us. It is enough to say that I condemned myself to exile by sticking stubbornly to some old ideal, and therefore I have no one to blame but myself.

And so my strange story is finished, another ink stick has been rubbed down to a stub, and I must return to my packing. In just three days, we leave for Jiujiang. I am resolved to begin again, and perhaps I will take to this new life better than I have taken to the city. On reflection, I think it is always best to move to something new instead of trying to reclaim something that is gone forever. The city has too much past for me, and I for it. A ship that has lost its anchor must drift endlessly at sea, never returning to land, and that is how I have felt since my daughter's untimely death – as if there is nothing tying me to the world. Yet I have been wrong. I still have hopes, I still have dreams, and I will not give up on them. I still have my poetry, and perhaps a new province might inspire me to pick up the brush more often.

I must leave this house, where I will always feel the call of the past. And wherever I go, I shall have my wife beside me. Perhaps I may, in time, talk with her as I used to talk with you. Perhaps some good may come from this journey after all.

It is now late, and everyone sleeps but me. Mercifully, there is no rain tonight, though the city is as noisy as ever. I shall miss it. Often these days I find myself wondering what my own life might have been like if I had known what would happen – if, say, I had access to my own Book of Crows. Would I have done things differently, or would I have lived my life exactly as it has been? Yet whenever my thoughts stray towards these melancholy hypotheses, I recall that old proverb you told me during one of those long teahouse evenings. Can you guess the one of which I speak? I will refresh your memory: 'If one man walks through the wilderness we call him lost. Yet if ten men walk the same way, we call their steps a path, and we call their route a journey.' It seems to me that most paths are invisible until you are upon them.

Please accept my apologies for bothering you with my foolish ramblings. Send my best wishes to your children, and keep them close to you, for nothing brings as much happiness as the happiness of those we love. Keep them at the centre of your world, and spoil them as much as you can, for one day they must leave for other homes. I say a sutra that your worries will be stolen by the wind, and that your children long outlive you.

Bai Juyi